A STEPBROTHER

NYT AND USA TODAY BESTSELLING AUTHOR

TIJAN

Edited by Jessica Royer Ocken
Proofread by Kara Hildebrand and Chris O'Neil Parece
Formatting by Elaine York
Allusion Graphics, LLC/Publishing & Book Formatting
www.allusiongraphics.com

DEDICATION

For Jason.

CHAPTER ONE

Kevin was kissing another girl. And he wasn't just kissing her—he was inhaling her. He pressed against her, her dark hair twisted in his hands, his lips moving down her throat and lingering between her breasts.

It was a trainwreck.

I saw it coming. The lights were bright and impending, and I could have gotten off the tracks. But nope, I was the idiot blinded in place. I couldn't look away, though I should have.

This was Kevin—my Kevin! Okay, not my boyfriend Kevin, but my stepbrother Kevin. The same Kevin I'd been in love with for two years—since my junior year of high school, since my mom died and my dad decided he was in love with the most popular guy in school's mother.

Sheila Matthews, aka Kevin's mom, was the nurse who took care of *my* mom during her stay in hospice. It had been such a scandal. How dare Mr. Stoltz fall in love even before his wife passed? It didn't matter that my mom had been dying of cancer for years. My dad's timing sucked, but it happened. The night after my mom was buried, he was at the Matthews' house.

One positive, even though my dad and Sheila hadn't kept their relationship a secret, was that I didn't have to meet her until later. Actually, I met her at the dinner where I also found out she was going to be my stepmother, and so the summer between my sophomore and junior year, I got a stepbrother, too. Of course, I already knew who Kevin Matthews was.

Everyone knew who Kevin Matthews was.

A year older than me. Football captain. Basketball captain. Track captain. He was on the Student Council—and I'm ashamed to admit I never paid attention to what he did for them. I didn't really care. He was so much more. He was the guy all the guys respected and all the girls wanted, including me and his rotation of six-month girlfriends. He'd date a girl for six months. Then they'd break up because he'd fallen in love with another girl, and she'd last the next six months.

Despite all my knowledge of him, before he joined my family, Kevin didn't know who I was. I wasn't anyone special. I mean, I wasn't unpopular. I was just...average, I guess. I'd been told I was beautiful, but that was by all the people who were supposed to tell me that. My mom told me every day, then my dad every month or so, and finally Sheila did once we moved in. She said it every two weeks. It was nice to hear, but come on. That's what parents are supposed to do. All three of my parent-like figures did their job well, and so did my two best friends, May and Clarissa.

May was a feisty little Asian who got asked out on a weekly basis, even when she had a boyfriend. And Clarissa was a few inches taller than me with a body like Britney Spears circa "Oops!...I Did It Again." I had long, dark brown hair and a slim-enough body. I'd never thought I was anything great, but both May and Clarissa had made enough comments about how they'd kill to look like me that I began to feel more confident.

My mom always told me I had perfect lips and almond eyes with long eyelashes that I'd inherited from my father's side. My grandmother had been gorgeous. I never met her, but in photographs she had dark eyes, dark hair, a heart-shaped face, and an alluring air to her. May and Clarissa saw a picture of her once and fell back on the bed, groaning at how much I took after her—something I hadn't realized until then.

So yeah, none of us were hurting, but we never really made it into the popular and exclusive high school social circles. Maybe it was because the three of us had our own exclusive clique, or maybe it was because none of us passed out at parties, slept around, or joined the cheerleaders. Nothing against anyone who did that. It just wasn't us.

We were almost boring.

We got good grades. We went to a few parties, but not every weekend. Bowling, slumber parties, shopping trips, and regular old going out for dinner were our social activities. I could've lived at the local bookstore too, so I think that's why we weren't at the top of the food chain where Kevin and most his girlfriends were. And not that we wanted to be. Well, May might've wanted it, but Clarissa and I were content.

Every now and then, Kevin would date someone at the social level below. Once he dated a girl who was two levels below, and pandemonium hit the hallways. Girls wore skimpier clothes. The hallways smelled like a professional salon, and I heard that the makeup aisle at the local department store sold out.

"Kevin," the girl moaned now, drawing me back to the trainwreck. She lifted one of her toned legs to wrap around him, pulling him more tightly against her.

I wrinkled my nose. Good God. I needed to look away, but I couldn't, not while his hand traced down her side. He lifted her leg higher to press against her, and they both moaned from the friction.

They were still dressed. That was one blessing, but they were *barely* dressed. Kevin's jeans looked loosened, like they were already unzipped, and the girl's skirt had been pushed high. Lacy pink underwear peeked out, and the way it moved…like something was going on in there…and yeah, that was his hand.

Time to reverse it.

They'd found their spot in the back room of the basement, which was close to Kevin's room at his fraternity. They just hadn't gotten all the way in there. I should've realized what was happening when I saw the basement door had a rubber band on the handle.

I slipped back out the door, and I was petty enough to grab that rubber band. I stuffed it in my pocket as I went.

Okay. Yes, I had loved Kevin for years. Yes, I had lived with him. Yes, he was sort of my brother, but no brotherly/sisterly love had formed between us. We were *compadres*, friends, buddies. And I'd thought there had been flirting. Yes, yes, there *had* been flirting.

We only lived one year together, and yeah, he was quiet most of the time. He was barely at the house, and when he was, he had a girlfriend with him. But there had been times! When I loaded the dishes in the dishwasher after dinner, he hung around a few times. He even wiped down the table some of those times. There were grins. I got a wink once. A couple hugs. It seemed like something at the time, but thinking about it now, I realized how non-more-than-friends it had been. Until the summer. It changed after that.

Kevin came home from college for my high school graduation, and there'd been drinking. There'd been debauchery—between the two of us. Kissing. Groping. Touching. Remembering it now, I could feel it all over again. His hand on my breast, then inside my jeans. I'd pulled his shirt up and over. Ooh, that glorious chest of his. He'd hovered above me. I'd felt his back, running my hands up and down, and he had done the same. He'd done *more* than the same.

I slept with him.

Well—I still cringed thinking about it. No. I hadn't actually slept with him. We had sex, and he was gone when I woke in the morning. Like, *gone* gone. He'd gone all the way back to his fraternity house that was four hours away.

It wasn't weird, though. Nope. I hadn't thought so. He called to apologize that night, saying he forgot about a commitment, but he didn't want me to think there was any weirdness between us. See? No weirdness. Then there'd been other calls over the next couple months—like, four of them. (That was four more than normal.)

Of course, he usually called to talk to his mom, but there was chit-chat with me as well. *How are you? How's your summer?* He'd tease me about whether I had a boyfriend or not. I teased him back about girls while my stomach did flip-flops, hoping there'd be no one serious. Based on what he'd told me, there hadn't been anyone.

Face it, Stoltz. You thought you were that girl.

I did. I really did, and I realized now how stupid I'd been.

And I was stupid for coming to this party. That was it. I needed to go.

There were people everywhere once I got back upstairs, and as I swung around I heard, "Whoa. Settle, girl."

My elbow had made contact with someone, and as I looked to see who my victim was, my eyes first landed on a very muscled and defined arm. And the tattoos. Holy crap, the tattoos! They covered the entire arm.

I kept staring. I shouldn't have, but I couldn't help it. The bicep bulged a bit, and as it did, a snake tattoo moved with it, giving the illusion that there was actually a real snake on the arm.

"Something wrong with you?"

My gaze jerked up, away from the snake and right into a pair of startlingly dark (and gorgeous) eyes. They were fixed on me, bearing a mix of irritation and confusion.

"What?" *He asked what was wrong with you.* I shook my head. "No, sorry." I'd hit him. "I didn't see you there, and I was trying to leave."

The irritation faded, and his eyes crinkled up, along with the right corner of his mouth. "I figured with the whole hitting thing." He paused a moment. "You're leaving?"

I nodded. "I don't know anyone here."

He looked behind me. "Didn't you come up from the basement? You don't know anyone down there?"

"I got lost," I said quickly. A blush was working its way up my neck. "Are you in this fraternity?"

His mouth pressed together. "Unfortunately. Why?"

Kevin loved being an Alpha Mu brother. He'd been so proud when he announced his pledge was accepted. His father was an

Alpha Mu, too. Why this guy didn't seem happy about it was lost on me. Kevin had only talked about how supportive the Alpha Mu family was of its brothers and the strength of their national network.

"I was wondering if you knew where the door was."

He seemed to relax. His shoulders lowered a bit and that snake moved again as his bicep bulged out, then flattened. He gestured behind me.

"Take the first right and follow it through. It'll take you out the side door. You'll want to avoid the living room. The guys are trying to get girls to play naked beer pong, and—" His eyes moved down and back. "—no offense, but you're an easy target."

I was what? I drew to my full height and prepared a scathing remark…and he turned to leave. He took two steps and the group behind him had swallowed him up. He was gone.

Asshole!

I slipped out the side door, begrudgingly grateful to the asshole because no one was there. As I walked past the living room from the outside, a loud cheer spilled out, just as he'd warned me.

"We got some boobies!" That was met with more cheering, more laughter.

I was on the sidewalk when I heard another shout. "She's in there! She's with Matthews."

I picked up my pace and stepped away from the house. I could see a guy being pushed back from the front door when I rounded the corner. Two guys held his arms as they moved him down the steps, toward the sidewalk.

I stopped underneath a tree where they couldn't see me. Matthews? Was he talking about Kevin?

The door behind them opened, and one yelled over his shoulder, "Get Caden. This is his brother."

Whoever was coming out turned around and went back in without shutting the door.

"And shut that damn door!"

The door closed with a bang.

"No." The guy they were pushing away from the house put on the brakes and twisted to evade their holds. "I'm going in there to get my girlfriend! I don't care what my brother says."

"Don't, Marcus." The first guy got in front of him.

Marcus puffed up. His nostrils flared. "Don't tell me *don't*. She's my girl, and Matthews is a piece of shit."

I shifted closer to the tree so I could hear better.

"Yeah. Maybe."

"No maybe. Look, let me go in the side door. No one will see me. My brother doesn't have to know. I'll go in, find Maggie, and we'll leave. I promise. No fighting. I swear."

The first guy snorted, folding his massive arms over his equally massive chest. His legs stood apart in a bouncer's stance, like he was ready to go against an angry crowd. He shook his head slowly. "We can't do that, and you know it."

"Your brother is probably coming out here anyways," Silent Muscle added, speaking for the first time.

Marcus gave a frustrated growl, and his hands clenched into fists for a moment. The fraternity guys held their ground. I had a feeling this wasn't their first time keeping an angry boyfriend outside.

The door opened, and a familiar voice said, "What is going on out here?"

The two fraternity brothers moved aside, letting the newcomer step forward. As he came into the light I could see it was the *asshole*, snake tattoo guy who "helped" me inside.

"Caden." Marcus stepped toward him. "Let me go in and get Maggie. That's all I want."

"Right." Caden/Asshole grunted. "Because you're not going to beat the shit out of him at all."

"Kevin's a piece of shit, but I wouldn't."

So it *was* Kevin they were talking about. That girl had a boyfriend.

"I want to rearrange his face, but I won't. I know the tough spot that'd put you in." Marcus added, "I swear."

The door opened again behind them. A new guy stepped out. "Kevin's coming."

A girl's voice carried from inside the house. "Something's going on outside. What's going on out there?"

Caden stepped around the new guy and pulled the door shut. "When Matthews comes out, close that fucking door."

"Yes, sir, Caden. I will."

"Business like this doesn't spill to outsiders."

"I know. I'm sorry. I'll keep guard better. I promise."

To prove his point, when the door opened once more, Kevin appeared and the guy shut the door behind him almost as savagely as Caden had. He looked at Caden with a slight smile and nod as if to say, *I got it. See?*

Caden shook his head and turned to my stepbrother. "What's going on?"

Kevin regarded Marcus, who had his hands back into fists. He was barely holding himself back.

"Matthews is here now," Caden said to his brother. "You can state your problem."

Marcus snorted. "Are you kidding me? Maggie's snuck out by now, probably the same way I would've snuck in."

A thought entered my mind, and I turned. There, just coming out the side door I had come from, was the girl Kevin had been kissing in the basement. She stopped when she saw me. Panic flooded her face, but then she took off, heading the opposite direction down the sidewalk, and she wasn't quiet about it.

"Maggie?"

Oh no. I knew what was going to happen, and I braced myself.

Marcus flew around the side of the house, stopping at the sight of me. He frowned, then focused behind me. I looked too, but she was gone.

"Who are you?" Marcus asked.

I prepared for the question that would follow. *Have you seen my girlfriend?* But when I looked back, the rest of the guys were standing behind him.

Kevin stepped toward me, his eyebrows bunched together. "Summer?"

I gulped and found myself looking beyond his shoulder to Caden, who was glaring at me, pinning me to the spot.

I gave a half-hearted wave. "Hey…everyone."

CHAPTER TWO

"Summer?" Kevin said.

Caden frowned as he stepped up beside him. He turned to look between us. "You two know each other?"

I opened my mouth, but Kevin said hastily, "She's my sister."

"Stepsister," I clarified.

"Stepsister." Kevin turned so he was closer to me than Caden.

The two were almost squaring off, their sides to me, and for one really weird and tense moment, no one said a word. I glanced between them. Caden was taller by a few inches. Both were gorgeous, but in different ways. While Kevin had the dashing good looks, blonde locks and pretty eyelashes, Caden just looked badass. He had a pretty face too with chiseled cheekbones, but his dark hair, tattooed arms and no-nonsense demeanor gave him an air of authority. He was more muscled than Kevin, who was lean, but something had me guessing that Caden could out-fight *and* out-run my stepbrother.

I'd always had Kevin on a pedestal, and for the first time, he looked less than. He now stood against a guy who seemed more male in almost every way—except being a smooth-talker with the ladies. *But no.* I shook those thoughts away. They didn't make sense. Kevin was… I frowned, guilt flaring up inside of me. No matter my hurt at seeing Kevin kissing another girl, he was family, right?

Raising my chin, I moved next to him. I stared back at Caden, showing my support for my stepbrother. "I actually came to surprise him, but changed my mind. He was on the phone downstairs. That's why I left."

Marcus exhaled a loud breath, stepping back from the group.

I ignored that, and I tried to ignore the sudden shift in the suspicion Caden had been sending Kevin's way. It landed right on me, and I gulped, feeling the full force of it. The guy was smart. He knew exactly what I'd just done.

So did Kevin. I sensed his sideways glance, and then the back of his hand brushed against mine. I figured that was his way of thanking me.

"Really?" Caden raised an eyebrow.

"Really." I raised my head in challenge, despite how I felt inside. I was covering for Kevin, the guy I was in love with, and it was wrong. I blinked a few times. Whatever. It would work out in the end. It had to.

"Yeah." Kevin coughed. "I was on the phone with her dad. He called because he couldn't get ahold of her." He said to me, "You're supposed to call your dad."

"Uh, thanks." *Was I really?*

He shrugged, trying to look casual and cool at the same time. "No problem."

Caden didn't say a word, only observing the exchange between us, but Marcus snorted and rolled his eyes.

He flung his hand out, pointing to me. "Come on, you guys. You can't be believing this chick. She's Matthews' sister. Of course she's going to lie for him."

"Let it go, Marcus." Caden's tone was weary, and I had a feeling this showdown had happened before.

I studied the other brothers' faces, and they were all the same: tired. Kevin shrugged his shoulders again and cocked his head to the side, but he didn't say anything. His gaze fell away from Caden's, and he looked at the other two fraternity brothers.

The bravado he'd adopted when I covered for him fell away, just slightly, but he still cleared his throat and forced a happy note in his tone. "I'm thinking it's time to get down and get a drink. You guys game?"

They regarded him, and Silent Muscle grunted. "I'm always down for a drink. Fuck this drama shit."

Kevin stepped between the two, clapping their shoulders. "Let's do shots. It's that kind of night now."

The three headed inside, leaving Marcus, Caden, and me behind. Before they disappeared, Kevin glanced back over his shoulder and nodded, giving me a half-grin. Then they were gone.

Kevin had left me. Again. Déjà vu hit me. I felt like I had three months ago when I'd woken up the morning after and he was gone. I'd just covered for him, and he went off to take shots with his fraternity brothers. I frowned, not liking how that sat with me. The fucker.

"Why?" Marcus spat the word at me, his jaw clenched. "Just, why? I know you saw her. You must've."

Guilt spread in me, but I didn't say anything. What *could* I say? He was right.

Caden sighed. "Leave her alone. He's her family."

He reached a hand out to rest on Marcus' shoulder, but Marcus dodged and turned on him, his eyes flashing.

"I get it. He's your fraternity brother, but I'm your *real* brother. One of these days, you're going to have to pick a side, Caden. Fuck Dad. Fuck him and his stupid fucking fraternity." He seared us both with an accusing look. "I don't give a shit who covers for Matthews. It's going to be an all-out war."

Now Caden was pissed.

I didn't know the guy, but I knew that much. He didn't strike me as the type who let someone talk to him like that and walk away. I stepped back, expecting a punch, but none came. There was just silence. Brother glared at brother, both with clenched jaws.

Then Caden glanced in my direction, and it dawned on me: They weren't saying anything because of me.

"Oh." I flashed a grin and a wave. "I, uh, I should probably go call my dad. Because, you know, that's what Kevin said to do."

Marcus snorted. "Right."

Caden just observed me, his stare unrelenting. I backed up a few feet, and he still watched me. It shouldn't have bothered me, but a little fluttering feeling bloomed low in my stomach. I started to turn around, then paused halfway with my head bent. I could still feel him. I didn't like that sensation, not at all. It was…unnerving, just like him. I glanced up one last time, and my shoulders immediately sagged in relief. They were gone.

I pressed a hand to my stomach to calm the unwelcome fluttering going on in there.

I went in search of Kevin. This time, the plan to avoid Caden/Asshole was in full effect. Kevin was probably fast on his way to getting drunk, or sneaking back out to find that girl again. I wouldn't put either past him, but I really did want to see him. Only the reason had changed. Instead of wanting to see him because of *us*, I needed to find out if I really did have to call my dad.

…Or that's what I told myself.

I snuck back in the way Caden had told me to sneak out and darted for the basement when the coast was clear. I didn't expect Kevin to be there. I planned to get into his bedroom, then text him that that's where I was. He'd have to come down to talk to me. He wouldn't want me around in case the Asshole found me and took another shot at interrogating me.

I was wrong.

Kevin's door was open just a crack, and I could see him sitting on his bed, his phone pressed to his ear. I paused just outside.

"You got home okay?" he asked. A pause. "Good…yeah, he was pissed. No. No, he didn't hurt me. I know." Another pause, longer this time. "Yeah. I know. We'll figure it out. I promise. What?" He groaned. "Uh, that girl was my stepsister, actually." I could hear a feminine laugh from the phone, and he chuckled with her. "I know. I know. No, she won't narc. She covered. Yeah. She's good like that."

I reached for the doorframe. My fingers curled tight around it.

"Don't worry. I mean it, Maggie. She won't say anything. She loves me. We're family. She's not like that." His voice dropped, growing husky. "I love you, too, and I mean it. Everything will be fine. I got your back. I promise."

My nails dug into the wood.

"Okay. Okay. Yeah. I should get back up. I'll check on Summer—that's her name. I'll text her right now. Love you. Bye."

I heard the beep when he ended that call and had just a moment before I felt my phone buzzing. It was in my pocket on silent, as was my habit, and before I pulled it out, I took a moment to collect myself.

He was an asshole, and this time I didn't mean Caden. Kevin slept with me a little over three months ago, and he'd led me to believe he'd been involved with no one else seriously since then. I thought this would be our time, now that we'd be in school at the same place, but he was in love with another girl—one who had another guy fighting for her.

My throat burned, and I blinked back the tears.

I wouldn't cry, not for Kevin.

I had the answer I came for.

I pulled away from the door, leaving my phone in my pocket. I wouldn't even look at it. I made my way back up the stairs. I was turning down the hallway for that side door when I heard a familiar voice behind me.

"Your stepbrother is a dick."

I turned around, my throat still burning. Caden stood there, not looking surprised. His hard eyes were locked on me, despite the girl plastered against his side. She had her arm around his waist.

He was waiting for a response, and maybe he expected a denial. I didn't know, but all I said was, "I couldn't agree with you more."

His eyes widened, and surprise flashed in them, but I was done.

I slipped out the door and left.

I'd been so stupid.

CHAPTER THREE

I'd driven up to North River University ahead of Sheila and my dad last night.

Today was move-in day for me since I was coming up earlier than others, so I'd told them I had a friend to stay with. They never questioned me. That "friend" was supposed to be Kevin, and because that didn't work out, I'd checked into a hotel room.

Now here I was, bright and cheery—not so much—waiting in my dorm's lounge for their SUV to arrive. Sheila and my dad were planning on seeing Kevin too, but I was hoping they'd go find him after my stuff was moved in.

"Summer."

No such luck.

I looked up from the couch, and my heart sank at the same time the old butterflies lurched up into my throat. Kevin looked so damn good. Freshly showered—his hair was still wet—and wearing a snug shirt over jeans, he kept his shades covering his eyes. My heart did a little flip-flop.

I hated him.

No. I only wished I did.

He flashed me a grin, showing his perfect, white teeth, and he came forward, holding two coffees. He offered one to me. "Got you your favorite. Sugar free, right?"

I took it, my hands closing around the warm cup, and I let out a silent sigh. I could already feel a traitorous grin tugging at the corner of my mouth. It was like I lost control over myself when he was around. I hoped it wasn't always going to be like this.

"Yeah." I held the cup in front of me like it was a shield and made a point of looking around. "Uh, where's our mom and dad? Did they call you already?"

He didn't move. I felt like he was studying me, but I couldn't see through his shades. He nodded, slowly. "Yeah. They called when they were a half-hour away." He glanced around.

A few girls lingered by the front desk, stealing glances in his direction, but no one else was in the lounge. I purposely sat across the room, in the farthest corner, but he moved close, even though he didn't need to. He cleared his throat, and I got ready.

"Um...so...about last night—"

I waved him off. "No worries."

He frowned, his forehead wrinkling. "But—"

I looked away. "No. I mean it. I came early and stopped to say hi. That was all. You looked busy, so yeah, I left." *Please leave it alone. Please leave it alone.* I prayed silently.

After another beat, he coughed and shifted back in his seat. "Okay. Well, thanks."

I nodded. My neck was stiff. "Yeah. No problem."

"Summer, are you sure?"

"Oh, yeah." I bobbed my head up and down, clenching the coffee cup like it was going to slip away. Then, as if in answer to my prayer, they pulled up to the door. "Look. They're here." I couldn't keep the relief out of my voice.

As I started forward to meet our parents, I caught how Kevin had looked out the window, then jackknifed back to face me. But I was ahead of him and hoping to leave the awkwardness in the dust behind me.

"Mom. Dad." I waved as they got out of their SUV and started our way.

I set the coffee on a bench as I knew this one-day-apart reunion would consist of hugs. Sheila liked hugs, and I was soon engulfed in her arms.

"Summer." Sheila held me to her, murmuring into my hair. "You dear girl. I'm not letting you go, you know. Nope. Not going to happen. You're firmly glued in my arms. I'll hug you to death."

"Mom." I could hear the smile in Kevin's voice as he stood next to us. "You gotta let her go. She's going to need oxygen at some point."

"Nope." She shook her head, rocking from side to side with me. "I lost you to this hell called *college*. I'm not ready to lose this girl too."

I laughed. It felt good to hear the words. Sheila had never pushed to replace my real mother, but in some ways, she'd stepped into her shoes seamlessly. There hadn't been any problems when the two families merged. There should've been, but there just weren't. It might've helped that I knew my mom would've wanted my dad to be happy, and he was. I couldn't deny that. Sheila had let me set the pace, and when I'd started doing my homework out on the dining room table instead of holed in my room, I knew she'd rejoiced. Food had begun to pile up around me. Then drinks. Then her own work.

A part of me had felt sorry for her. Kevin was rarely home.

The nights he did come home alone, it wasn't until nine or ten. I'd heard him stop to talk to Sheila and my dad only a few of those times before going to his room. A few times I'd gone downstairs and sat in the kitchen, hoping maybe he'd want a late night snack or glass of water, but that rarely happened. Once he was in his room, it was for the night. Or maybe he saw me and came back later when I wasn't sitting there.

There were the occasional family dinners, but those were congenial. Thinking back on it now, I realized everything had always been polite. That didn't seem normal. I wondered—watching as Sheila released me and hugged her son—if Kevin really *had* been okay with getting a new dad. It had always seemed like it to me.

My dad came over to give me a hug now, and then he and Kevin shook hands.

That was it.

It was like a mask fell from my face, and I could see things differently. I saw a lot of stiffness and distance between Kevin and my father, but then my dad caught my gaze, and all of that went away. Warmth shone from his eyes, and my concern slipped away.

"You okay, pumpkin?" He rested his arm around my shoulder and pulled me close.

I nodded, my head brushing against the top of his arm. "I'm good."

"Ready to start college?"

Sheila harrumphed. "Hell. That's what it is," she mumbled, but she was trying to hold back her grin at the same time.

"Yeah." I nodded. "I'm ready."

Kevin was watching me, and my body tingled. That was my normal reaction around him, but it felt different, like so much else this day. I snuck a peek. He looked at me like I was a stranger, or like he saw something new in me. Whatever it was, well—I didn't know how I felt about it, but right now I had a dorm to move into.

"You got here ahead of time and checked in already?" Sheila turned to me, her arm now around Kevin's back. He didn't seem to mind and leaned into her.

I nodded. "Yeah. I'm all checked in. I met my resident advisor and everything too." She'd been fine with me moving in ahead of time.

"What's her name?"

"Avery. I'll introduce you when we go up there."

"And your new roommate? Is she here already? When do you meet her?"

"She's not." Classes would start on Thursday, and final registration was Wednesday. Today was Saturday. "I have a few days yet."

"Oh." Her eyebrows knitted together. "What are you going to do? Maybe you should come back for those days."

"No." I shook my head. "I'll take my time, look for a job on campus or something." I glanced at Kevin. I'd come up early to spend time with him, and as if sensing my thoughts, he looked away, his Adam's apple moving up and down.

He stepped out of his mom's hold. "I actually need to get going." He gestured toward the campus behind him. "I have to meet my academic advisor about declaring my major this year."

"Yeah?"

He nodded to his mom. "Going pre-law, Mom. You proud?"

She smiled, but it look stilted, like she wasn't sure how to feel. "Pre-law, huh?" She nudged him with her hip. "My son's following in his father's footsteps."

He continued to hold her gaze. This had been the only topic not talked about since we'd moved into their house: Kevin's dad, Sheila's ex-husband.

Glancing at my father, I saw the same tight-lipped expression and knew that Mr. Matthews was still not going to be talked about.

An unspoken look passed between Kevin and his mother before he sighed, cracking a side grin. "Hoping to, anyways."

"Well." She lifted her chin. "I'm proud of you, Kevin."

He pressed his lips together, showing a slight grimace. "Thank you, Mom." He looked to my dad. "It was nice seeing you again, Daniel."

My dad held out his hand. "You too, Kevin. We don't see you enough at the house."

The two shook hands, and I felt I'd stepped into the Twilight Zone. Things were so stiff and...just awkward with them. I was mystified. I'd really thought everything was fine over the last year, that the two of them were close like Sheila and me.

Kevin swung his beautiful eyes my way, and his voice softened. "See you later, Summer?"

"Uh, yeah. See you later."

"You two will have such a great time. You're both at the same college. My son going pre-law. My new daughter already deciding on sports medicine. You'll have to have weekly dinners." Sheila pulled Kevin in for a last hug. "You take care of your stepsister, okay?"

"I will. I promise." Another last farewell and he headed across the sidewalk, stuffing his hands in his pockets.

"Your room is on the sixth floor?" my dad asked.

I nodded. He had a friend come with them to help take the heavier stuff up and he was standing behind us, already holding a box.

"Room 614." I pointed to the side of the building. "My room's at the end of the hallway. You could probably use the back stairs to get to it. It'll be easier."

"Okay." He went to the SUV to move it closer to the door while his friend headed inside with the box. "We'll get everything up there within an hour, I'm sure."

"Well." Sheila clapped her hands together, beaming at us. "We should get you unpacked, and then you're stuck with us for one more day." She bumped me with her hip. "Start thinking now, Summer. We'll go anywhere you want to eat tonight. Kevin will probably be busy with some girl, but he's got no choice. I'm pulling the mom card tonight. We're going to have one last family dinner. Your choice."

That sounded fine with me. I'd have all day to prepare to see Kevin once more. I hoped he wouldn't bring the current girlfriend.

But later at the restaurant I'd chosen, I looked up and sighed as he came in.

Not so much.

He walked in holding Maggie's hand.

CHAPTER FOUR

The dinner sucked. Like, seriously sucked.

But I wasn't surprised. Kevin had the habit of bringing his girlfriend to family dinners, so why would he suddenly change now? And this also told me something had changed between last night and tonight. Kevin no longer seemed to care about getting caught.

I snorted, thinking about that. No, no. Last night had been about him not getting his ass kicked. Tonight was about not giving a damn. I eyed the two of them—holding hands, giggling, blushing. They kept giving each other those stupid looks only people who've had sex share, like the rest of us are idiots and don't know what those long, lingering sighs mean. Right. Kevin + Maggie = me throwing up.

And yes, I knew it was my problem because of my stupid feelings. But dammit, when Kevin showers you with attention, combined with how he looks, and there's always this softness to his words—there's a reason he can get so many girls.

The only upside to the dinner was that Kevin and Maggie's glorious coupledom overshadowed the reserved politeness between him and my dad. I caught a few moments, though. When Kevin kissed the back of Maggie's hand and my dad coughed, tugging his collar from his neck, or while Sheila gushed about the family weekend when they came up last year. Neither Kevin nor my dad said a word. They just sat there, lips pressed together, no facial expression on either of them.

I suddenly wondered what the hell else had I missed all year.

When the two lovebirds left and Sheila asked if I wanted to stay in my dorm for the night or bunk with them in the hotel room, I was feeling a bit more raw than normal. The hotel it was. And I spent the next day with them, too, doing some more school shopping before they dropped me off for my first night in my place. Alone.

I spent my first official college night on the internet. How sad was that?

So of course, trying to convince myself how unsad I was, I decided to go to bed early. Because I was being responsible. Not sad. Responsible. I'd get up early. I might go for a run? Register for classes...by being the first in line. See? Responsible. I'd be the most prepared freshman there was, and I had actually convinced myself this would be great when my resident advisor breezed into the bathroom.

Avery literally did breeze in.

A burst of wind opened the bathroom door, and she stepped forward, her hand pushing the door the rest of the way. She was going so fast that I felt that same wind as she hurried past and slammed the stall door behind her. A second later, she asked through the door, "Are you going to bed already?"

I glanced around. No one else was in here.

"Summer?" she called.

"Huh?"

"You're in 614? You got here yesterday. You're the sports medicine girl, right? Am I remembering that correctly?"

She meant me. "Yeah. That's me."

The toilet flushed. The door opened a moment later and she eyed me, coming to wash her hands. "You're Summer, right?" A confused look appeared. "Wait. Are you Autumn? It's a season, I thought."

"No. Summer. I'm Summer."

"Yeah." She finished washing and grabbed for the paper towels. "Your brother is Kevin Matthews?"

I gritted my teeth. "*Step*brother. Yes."

"You're not related by blood?"

"No."

She snorted after drying her hands, then crumpled the paper towel up in a ball. "Wonder if Maggie knows that."

I stilled. "You know Maggie?"

She tossed the crumpled ball in the garbage, opening the door and holding it with her foot. "Yeah."

I grabbed my bathroom utility bucket. She kicked the door wide for me and stepped out into the hallway. We fell in line together, heading to our rooms.

"The 'great love' of Kevin Matthews." Her fingers formed quotation marks, and she grinned. "I love Maggie. We roomed together last year, and there's a whole group of us that are friends from high school. However, no offense to your stepbrother, but she's delusional."

"What do you mean?"

Avery opened her mouth, then paused mid-step and mid-speech. Her head cocked to the side and she seemed to realize what she'd been about to say. She grinned ruefully at me.

"Sorry. I probably shouldn't say anything. I'm not being a good friend." She waved her hand. "Forget I said anything."

I clipped my head in a quick up-and-down motion. "Said what?"

She laughed. "Thank you."

Her room was closer so we paused outside her door. I could hear techno music blaring inside, and she gazed at the door for a moment, her forehead wrinkling. "You know," she chewed on her bottom lip. "Do you want to come with us?"

I widened my eyes. "You and Maggie?"

"What?" Understanding dawned. "No." She laughed again. "Sorry. No, no. Maggie's probably off with your stepbrother or—" She caught herself again. "Some friends and I are going to a house party. This is a totally different group. Maggie won't be there."

"Oh." Now I chewed the bottom of my lip. What to do? Be pathetic, or...party? "I'm in."

"Great." She straightened up, her shoulders rolling back. "Okay." She pulled her phone from the back of her jeans and scrolled through it. "Okay, yeah. We're meeting at my friend's room in twenty, so want to come back here in ten? My friend's room is all the way across campus and..." She paused for another beat, her chest lifting and holding. "Uh, we're going to be drinking. I shouldn't invite you with, but you're here, and you seem cool, and we're in college."

I nodded. "Not another word. Kevin's a big partier. I have no problems with it."

"Okay." She gave me a relieved grin, her shoulders loosening up. "Okay. Yeah. Go make yourself more gorgeous, and let's head out in ten."

"On it. Be back."

I didn't know what kind of party I should dress for, but I decided to assume this would be the normal deal: Kegs. Making out. And more kegs. Right. So that meant jeans, black tank top, and sandals.

When I got to Avery's room, I could see I'd dressed right. The only difference between her outfit and mine was a black bra underneath her almost translucent tank top. It was white, but so thin that I could see her belly button clearly. She'd pulled her hair up into two high side braids. With hoop earrings and her tight, faded jeans, she looked edgy and ready to party.

When I met her yesterday morning, I never would've suspected she'd go out partying, with me, dressed like this. In her official role as RA, she wore khaki shorts and a red, collared shirt, her bleached blond hair combed and loose, resting beyond her shoulder blades. Seeing her blue eye shadow and red lipstick, I realized she must've been wearing natural-tone makeup when I met her, or none at all. I remembered how she'd stood, holding a clipboard, when she met my parents. Her head had been lowered, her shoulders slumped a little. She'd looked demure, and really sweet.

Now she flashed me a grin with blinding white teeth. "Two minutes!"

Typing on her laptop, she paused a moment, then shut it off. She pulled her purse strap over her head and across her body as she came out, keys in hand.

I stepped back as she came into the hallway, and she locked her door. Then she scanned me up and down. She nodded, a look of approval on her face. "Looking good, little Matthews."

I frowned. "It's Stoltz."

"Oh." She nodded. "Sorry. I gotcha."

Avery would've fit in with the popular girls at my high school, so I wasn't surprised to find out she knew Kevin. She was beautiful, but it wasn't just how she looked. She was confident, and sexy too. May would've been jealous of her, and that meant we all would've hated her because one of us did. This was different now, though. Avery seemed easygoing, and that made me feel comfortable with her. I wasn't being judged as Kevin's stepsister. In fact, it seemed the opposite. I almost felt like Avery didn't care for Kevin, and for some reason, I liked her even more.

As we trekked across campus, Avery had a way of asking me questions, but also talking so I never felt put on the spot. I could see why she was a resident advisor, except that I was pretty sure RAs weren't supposed to party or drink with students on their floor. Still, Avery was good with people. We ran across different groups along the way, and almost everywhere someone knew Avery—not only knew her, but liked her. They waved, said hello, or threw out a joke to her.

She returned it every time. If it was a quick, teasing insult, she gave a grin and sent one right back. If it was as simple as a hand wave, she did the same. She was very even keel.

That made me relax even more, and when we got to her friend's room, I wasn't worried. I would've expected to have my stomach tied up in knots, but not with Avery. Whatever happened, I knew it'd be fine. I wouldn't be left out, or left behind, or made to stand out like a social outcast. In the past, being around girls like Avery and her friends had always made me feel those things.

As she introduced me, her friends seemed to be a lot like her. There were six of them, and I didn't get all their names during the introductions. We had to wait for one more girl, and as we did, they prepared their drinks. Wine, rum, soda, vodka—all of it was poured into water bottles. Each girl had a backpack, and they stuffed the containers inside, sometimes two of them. They offered me one, I took it.

I'd had drinks before. The act of drinking or getting drunk wasn't a big deal to me—it was who I drank with. In a group of strangers, I wouldn't have taken one, but I trusted Avery. She asked if I wanted to stash a back-up in her bag, and I nodded.

We'd just finished when the last of the group arrived, and the whole alcohol-prepping process started again. The last girl took three bottles.

"When we go to a big party, we bring our own booze," Avery told me. "We might know the guys who live in the house, but we don't always know everyone. We've heard too many stories, and none of us feels like getting drugged or raped. That's why we look like full-on alcoholics."

I nodded. That made sense. These girls were smart.

Another girl chimed in. "And we move in a buddy system. It's not obvious at the parties, but none of us is ever alone unless we explicitly tell the others we're doing a one-nighter."

"One-nighter?" I echoed.

"One-night stand." A different girl shrugged. "It happens. There's no judgment here."

"Unless someone has a boyfriend." A third girl nudged the one who'd explained. "Right, Shell?"

Shell rolled her eyes. "I still wouldn't regret a night with Caden Banks."

I paused. "Wait. What?"

The girl who'd nudged Shell laughed and looked back over her shoulder at me. Her eyes twinkled. "Caden Banks. He's one of the bigwigs in a fraternity around here. If you meet him, trust me, you'll know it."

I was pretty sure I had.

Avery glanced sideways at me. "She might already have met him. Kevin Matthews is her stepbrother."

I wasn't prepared for the effect those words had.

Everyone stopped and turned around. I suddenly found myself the center of attention as seven girls each gave me a different look—surprise, caution, intrigue, nervousness. Everyone was silent for a moment until Avery laughed out loud, forcing the sound a little bit.

Her hand perched on her hip, and she lifted her chin. "What? Don't hate her because of what her stepbrother's done."

Wait. What? I fixed Avery with a look and raised an eyebrow. "What haven't you told me?"

One of the girls stepped forward. "Your brother's an asshole."

"Claudia," Avery reprimanded.

I held my tongue on that one. I couldn't really argue with her, but I did say, "*Step*brother."

Shell let out a sigh. "He dated me last year and slept with two of my best friends." She paused before adding, "In the same weekend."

"We're an against-Kevin Matthews group. Neither of those girls is friends with us anymore." Claudia looked at Avery. "Well, the rest of us. They're not friends with *us*."

Avery shifted back on her feet, letting out a small sigh. She crossed her arms over her chest. "One of those they're talking about is Maggie." She said to them, "And I went to high school with Maggie. There's a whole group of us who are still friends. I can't just leave them."

Shell said, "We know. We've talked about it, but you know how we feel about him and Maggie." Claudia raked me up and down.

"And if you think bringing his stepsister around us is going to make us soften, think again, Av."

"I'm not," she protested. "I didn't bring her because of that. I'm no fan of Kevin either, but she's cool. That's why I brought her."

I felt a full-body flush coming on. Avery had taken pity on me. I knew it, and she knew it, but she didn't tell them that. I'd been alone in that bathroom and looking pathetic. She'd invited me out because she was nice.

"Look." I gave them a tight grin. "I'm under no illusions about Kevin." *Liar.* "He's my stepbrother, so he's family, but trust me, I'm well aware of his history with women."

And you need to remind yourself of it. Over and over again. And again, I chided myself as I waited for the hostility to cool to a simmer. When it did, I knew I'd said the right things.

Now I just needed to listen to them myself.

CHAPTER FIVE

The party was huge, and we had to walk three long blocks from campus to get there. As we went up the driveway, a guy held open the front door. I ducked under his arm and voila—I was inside my first party of college. With the hip-hop music blaring and girls in bikinis running around, I felt like I'd stepped into a music video. I could practically see the champagne spilling in slow motion and girls washing each other, bending over a Lamborghini. But no wads of cash were waiting for me inside; Avery and her friends were instead.

A deep chuckle sounded behind my ear, and an arm appeared, extending a tray of red plastic cups. "Only the finest beer for my ladies."

Avery had said they didn't trust the booze offered at these parties, and I stiffened, looking at her first.

She rolled her eyes. "Take it away. You know we bring our own."

As if they had rehearsed it, the girls all raised the bottles they'd been sipping on the walk over. The tray was lifted back over my shoulder, and I stepped to the side. That arm was seriously big. I needed to see who this guy was.

My eyes met his chest…then trailed upward. If I was ever going to meet a bodybuilder in person, I knew this was the guy. He had muscles in his throat, wrists, everywhere—including places I didn't want to think about.

He smiled as he rubbed his jaw. "Oh, come on. You know this house is different. We're rape-drug free."

Avery snorted. "No offense, Dave, but you know how *we* are."

"Yeah, yeah." He waved her off. "Got it." He pointed over his shoulder. "Can I offer up a wet T-shirt contest? We've got one about to start in the back. Ten minutes." He wolf-whistled, assessing us. "I do think you all have a chance at winning."

"You say that to every girl." Claudia rolled her eyes.

Dave winked at her. "You can't hold that night against me forever."

She turned away. "You bet your ass I can." Then she disappeared, heading into the party. A second girl went off with her, and I remembered the buddy system they had. Did I have a buddy?

Avery must've read my mind because she said, "You're with me."

One of the other girls added, "She brought you in. She's in charge of you."

I slid a look to Avery. "Sorry." A feeling of being hazed as a freshman washed over me. Awkward.

"Just don't tell anyone who your brother is."

"Stepbrother."

"Stepbrother." Avery corrected. "Does it really matter that much?"

Dave had moved so he was standing behind us, and he leaned forward, sticking his head between us. "Who's your stepbrother?" He looked from her to me and back again.

Avery placed a hand on his forehead and pushed him back. "No one to you, and where's Marcus?"

I stiffened at the name. Not the Marcus I met...

Dave frowned. "Why do you want to know where he is? He's with Maggie."

I didn't think he was referring to the guy's physical location.

"You mean Maggie is here?" Avery held a warning in her tone.

"Uh." Dave grew still. "I mean, they're dating. I think he said something about her studying with friends tonight."

Avery's eyebrows snapped together, and she turned to face him directly. I was scared to move. I glanced from the corner of my eye and saw the other girls had had the same response.

All eyes were glued on Avery.

Her eyebrow lifted.

Dave seemed to realize he'd said something stupid. His eyes widened, and his mouth formed a small O, as in *Oh, shit*. He edged back a step. Then he scratched behind his ear, making it look casual, "Uh…I mean…" He expelled a breath of air. "Fuck."

Avery spoke, stiffly, "I'm aware he's with Maggie. This is his house. I'm assuming he's here, but I want to avoid him. That's why I'm asking."

Dave bobbed his head up and down. "Got it. You're right. And he's out back."

"*Is* Maggie here?"

He closed his mouth and shook his head.

"That's all I need to know." Avery gave him a grin.

"Okay. I hope you all have a great evening, and…" He edged back another step, clutching his tray of drinks. "See ya!" He was swallowed by a crowd of people.

"What was that about?" I asked.

Avery shrugged, her shoulder jerking up. "He must've thought I gave two more shits than I do." She grabbed my hand in a tight grip, then released it and shook out her hand so it was softer. "Come on. We need to find the dancing and get back to drinking."

That's exactly what we did.

Avery led the way, weaving in and around so many people. Just like on campus, the ones who recognized her yelled a hello. Some wrapped their arms around her, giving her big drunken hugs, and like before, she returned whatever they sent her way. It took us an extra twenty minutes to find the dancing in the basement.

We settled in a back corner, and right away a guy pulled Avery out to the dance floor. Watching her go, I leaned closer to one of the others and yelled over the music, "Is it always like that?"

She nodded. "That's the deal if you're friends with Av. She's liked by everyone." Her eyes shifted upward and she added, "Well, almost everybody."

I wanted to ask more questions. I wanted to know everything, but when she turned and began talking to her buddy, I didn't get the sense that either of them wanted to give me the rundown. The genogram would have to wait.

I pulled out my water bottle filled with rum and orange juice and leaned back to enjoy the rest of the night, which was filled with lots of laughing, lots of booze, and lots of dancing. Avery eventually pulled the rest of us out on the floor with her. Shell and Claudia joined us again, and a couple of the girls cozied up with guys. The ones who didn't were turning offers down.

Avery leaned close when we were at a table later. "They've got boyfriends!" she announced over the music.

"That makes sense," I yelled back.

She frowned slightly. "You have a boyfriend? I didn't ask before."

I shook my head. "Nope. No boyfriend."

"*What?*" Her head bent closer to hear me better.

I shook mine again. "Nothing. No! I don't."

"Oh." She gave me a thumbs-up sign. "Me neither. It's the best! Being single is a lot more fun."

Yes, it was, it's just that I thought I'd have a boyfriend by now. She didn't know I'd been hoping for one. But it wasn't that simple. It wasn't just wanting a boyfriend. I wasn't that type of girl. I'd dated a couple other guys, but I hadn't felt for them what I felt for Kevin, or thought I felt. Things were getting cloudy about that, but this was supposed to have been our time.

"Okay." Avery stood up from the table. "I'm hot and sweaty, and the slow song is killing my buzz."

Shell leaned forward, resting her elbow on the table, and gazed up at Avery with drunken, tired eyelids. "Where's Marcus?"

Claudia came off the dance floor and plopped into the chair beside Shell. She grimaced, picking off strands of hair that had been plastered to her cheek and neck with sweat. "What's going on?" She had a glazed-over look similar to her buddy's, but she seemed a bit more alert.

Avery answered, "I'm ready to go outside."

"Marcus is out there."

No outside. No Marcus. I silently willed the girls to come up with another plan. I should've left as soon as I found out whose house this was. This was Marcus' territory. If he remembered me from the other night, I was pretty sure he wouldn't want me here.

I stood up. "You know, I've got more dancing in me. They'll change the song soon, I'm sure."

Shell snorted. "Not likely. Once the slow stuff starts, they keep it up. It's how they get people to leave. The kegs must be empty."

"I don't care what we do except for Marcus," Avery announced. "Wherever he is, we should not be."

I agreed, pumping my head up and down. I *so* agreed.

Avery rolled her eyes as her hands found her hips. "But I still want to go outside." She sent a puff of air out, blowing a strand of hair off her forehead. "Come on, guys. We can do this. I can do this."

Shell said, "You're drunk. It's not a good look."

Avery's eyebrows shot up, and her head cocked to the side. "Excuse me?"

"Marcus is still in the backyard. You're drunk. It's not going to look good for you. We all know that you speak first and think later when you're like this."

"I can handle Marcus."

"No, you can't." Claudia joined in. "Not when you've been drinking."

The more they talked, the more intrigued I became. The more anxious I felt, too. Avery and Marcus? He'd been proclaiming his love for Maggie two nights ago.

"I told you guys, I can handle this, and I will." With that, Avery whipped around and shoved through the crowd, heading for the stairs.

"Fuck."

I wasn't sure who said that, but Shell and Claudia scrambled to their feet and ran after her. Another girl that had been dancing caught the exchange. She tore out of her partner's arms and grabbed her buddy, pulling her behind. I was the last to go, because I was a little bit more drunk than I realized. I stood, but the dance floor spun with me. I had to wait until the couples righted themselves, and once they did, I headed off too. The girls were long gone by the time I got upstairs.

I grabbed a guy passing by. "Backyard?" I asked.

He pointed farther ahead.

I came to the rear of the house to find Avery and the girls huddled together in a corner outside, their backs to the rest of the yard. They kept glancing over their shoulders toward a bonfire on the other side. A group of people lingered there, but I could tell the two everyone was focused on: Marcus and Asshole. Both sat in lawn chairs, their legs sprawled out and beers in hand. At first they looked like they were just relaxing, chilling, not paying attention to anything, but Caden was watching the girls. So was Marcus. He looked a little tense, but Caden… I frowned, studying him a bit more. I didn't see the annoyance and anger from two nights ago. He actually seemed to be enjoying himself, and when his eyes darted from Avery to his brother, I got the feeling he was enjoying watching his brother squirm.

That pissed me off for some reason.

I pushed open the door a little harder than necessary. The thought of Asshole having fun at the expense of his brother didn't sit right with me. I stepped outside and down the stairs. Joining Avery's group, I turned squarely to face Caden and his brother. I thought they both saw me, but neither showed a reaction. I mean, I wasn't sure if they did. It was dark. I was clear across the yard and a bit drunk. I didn't think so, though, and I was going with that.

"What are you doing?" Avery hissed at me.

I stood next to her, but faced the guys while she faced her friends.

I crossed my arms over my chest. "I'm not pretending, that's what I'm doing." I was almost glaring.

"What?" She sent me a horrified look. "Why are you acting like this?"

I didn't know, but there had to be a reason... *I think.*

Marcus leaned forward. Caden's amusement was evident, and now he zeroed in on me. Completely. I raised my chin, challenging him.

He grinned, lifting his beer for a drag from the bottle.

"Stop, Summer. I don't want Marcus to come over here."

I frowned, breaking whatever kind of stare I had going with Asshole, and looked at her. "What? I thought you did."

"No." But it was too late. Marcus had left his chair.

Avery groaned, turning around. "Oh, no. He's coming over here."

The other girls drew closer. "What'd you do?" someone asked.

They weren't talking to Avery. All were now glaring at me.

"Oh." *Oops.*

"You here to come clean?"

The question came from behind us, and I turned to face forward again, but I already knew who it was. Marcus. He was right there, holding his beer in front of him, an almost lazy smirk adorning his face. His eyes kept skirting from me to Avery, but when she stood facing him too, I realized his question had been directed at me.

I jerked upright. "What?"

Marcus narrowed his eyes. He skimmed me up and down before lifting his beer again. "My girlfriend. Your brother. I assumed you came here to 'fess up about what you really saw."

Sooo uncomfortable. I wanted to squirm. I could feel the attention from Avery and her friends. "Uh, I mean, why would I?"

He arched an eyebrow. "This is my house. My party. And here you are." He took another drink. "That is why you're here, isn't it?"

Avery cleared her throat, her arms folding to mirror my stance. "She came with me."

Marcus just stared, but his amusement was now evident, just like his brother's.

"She lives on my floor," she added, shifting her feet.

"The floor where you're an advisor?"

"Yes."

His eyes fell on her water bottle. "Setting a good example already, huh, Av?"

She flushed. "Like you have any place to say anything."

He indicated me with his beer. "You know who her brother is, don't you?"

I corrected, "Stepbrother," but it didn't matter.

Avery rolled her eyes. "Again, like you have any place to say anything."

That got a reaction. Marcus had been all easygoing, slightly cocky, but now any trace of humor vanished. A flash of anger sparked in his eyes. "We used to be friends, Av."

She snorted. "Right. Because friends screw each other over."

His eyes darkened. Smoke could've come out of his eye sockets. I was getting heated just watching the two.

"Okay." Shell stepped up, a disapproving glint in her eyes. "We're separating the two of you before a full fight ensues." She took hold of Avery's arm. "Marcus, it's been a lovely party. Thank you for letting us come here, dance our asses off, and get drunk, but it's time to head out."

Marcus said something, but I began to tune them out. Avery was going willingly with Shell. There wouldn't be a fight.

My eyes followed Marcus. I didn't intend to look for Caden. I didn't even like him. I'd named him Asshole for a reason. But somehow, I'd been aware of him the entire time. He was like a bug, always buzzing at the periphery, nagging at my concentration. I'd half expected him to step in, take over the situation, and pull his brother back like he had at the fraternity house. He'd done none of that. He wasn't even still sitting in his lawn chair. He now stood with another group of people, like he was part of their conversation, but he wasn't. The beer bottle was gone, and his arms were crossed over his chest. A girl even put her hand on his arm, but he wasn't paying attention.

He was watching me.

Our eyes caught and held, and I frowned.

There was no hostility, not like the other night, just a slight flicker of amusement—like he was finding me funny, or the situation funny. I glanced behind me, but there was nothing comical there. Wait—I started to look back at him, but whipped around again.

There was nothing behind me *at all*. The girls were gone.

Shit.

I had no idea how to get back to the dorm. I started back to the front of the house. The girls weren't there. They weren't in the living room, kitchen, or bathrooms. They weren't upstairs or downstairs. I went back to the backyard for one last futile attempt, and again, nothing.

Then I felt him.

He came to stand next to me, his hands in his pockets, and looked over with those eyes that could see through me. "They took off while you were glaring at me."

"I wasn't glaring." I didn't think I was, anyway. A headache formed behind my temples. I lifted a hand to rub at my head.

One side of his mouth curved up. "You were, but that's fine." His eyebrow raised. "You need a ride back?"

I sighed. "We had a buddy system."

The other side of his mouth lifted, and the distinct feeling that he was laughing at me washed over me again.

"Come on." He gestured toward the street. "I've had one beer. I can drive, and I'm heading out anyway. Trust me enough for a ride?"

I held my breath. He'd been laughing at me earlier, now he was outright making fun of me? I weighed my options. I could call a cab and hope the driver knew where my dorm was, or walk and try to find it myself. A third option was calling Kevin. A part of me wanted to do that, and I reached for my phone. What if he didn't answer? I let go of my phone. I didn't want to test that theory.

My last option stood in front of me.

I nodded. "After you."

CHAPTER SIX

Caden/Asshole drove a Land Rover.

I don't know what I expected, but it wasn't that.

And it was clean. I paused after I opened the door and could only stand there. It was impeccably clean.

He'd already gotten inside. "Please don't tell me the leather offends you."

"It's so clean."

"Yeah?"

I had no clue what came over me, but I broke out in a "Ta-daa!" and my arms lifted like heaven's gate had been thrown open. A full choir and orchestra played out in my voice. "Behold the gloriousness!" Then I dropped my arms and was met with silence.

He tilted his head. "How much did you drink?"

Yeah, maybe it was the booze. Shrugging, I got inside. "Sorry. I'm just surprised," I explained as he pulled away from the curb. "Kevin's car is always a mess. The floor of the front seat where my feet are supposed to go is his personal garbage can. He throws everything there. I always have to move a bunch of junk aside so I can get in."

"He doesn't clean it for you?"

I shrugged again. "He cleans it for his dates."

"Not even for his mom?"

"If they go anywhere together, they take her car. Nope. Just his dates." I was rambling. I sat on my hands.

He noticed. "What are you doing?"

"I do this when I feel like I'm saying stuff I shouldn't, and I'm only doing that because I'm nervous." I blinked a few times at him. "You make me nervous. Though that's better than being enraged."

"I *enrage* you?"

I nodded, then thought about it, and my head bobbed down as my shoulder jerked up. "You did earlier, but I don't know why. I think it's just you. I call you Asshole in my head."

"You what?" We stopped at a stoplight, and he looked fully at me. "I didn't do anything to you."

I bristled, remembering the first time we met. I echoed his words from my memory, "'Something wrong with you?' That's not the nicest thing to say to a girl. Especially one that just got her hear—" I clammed up.

Oh dear God. I'd almost spilled the beans to him.

"I mean..." I had nothing to cover that up. It really was the booze speaking. I couldn't even attempt a redirect, so I just sat in humiliating defeat.

The light turned green, and we started forward again. He threw a sideways glance my way. "You mean that wasn't a nice thing to say to a girl whose heart was just broken? Did I get that right?"

"No." *Yes.* So much yes.

He grunted, taking another turn, and I saw the top of my dorm approaching.

"That's what I thought," he said.

He knew I was lying. He knew a whole lot more than what I'd just lied about. And I couldn't do anything. Panic rose in me as I imagined how upset Kevin would be. I'd covered for him. He was counting on me, and I just blabbed to the guy who seemed to be one of his enemies, or rivals, or something. Or the brother to one of his rivals/enemies/whatever. Kevin always had those.

Although, the guys who'd wanted to pummel my stepbrother in the past were usually boyfriends from other schools. Kevin must've had some sense of self-preservation because he'd steered clear of the girls with the big boyfriends at our high school. And now that I was thinking about it, he'd always made sure he had friends bigger than he was. There'd been a few close calls, but once his friends had showed up, the fight suddenly dwindled. The guy had backed down, or Kevin got away.

"Huh."

"Huh what?" the asshole asked.

"What?" I glanced over and saw that he was watching me again.

Then I saw the rest. We were at my dorm. He'd parked right in front of the main entrance.

"Never mind. Thank you for the ride." I grabbed for the seatbelt, but he caught my hand, stalling me.

"Wait a minute."

Good Lord. I gulped. The touch of his hand sent tingles through me. That snake tattoo was right there, so close to me. I pulled away hastily. *What was that?* But then he was talking, so I tried to focus. All the other sensations and emotions that he'd unleashed should be shoved down. Way down. *Way*, way down.

"What?" I asked.

He shook his head, exasperation showing across his face. He held his hands up, like he was surrendering, and he leaned back in an exaggerated manner. "I'm not going to hurt you. I just want to talk about your stepbrother."

I flushed. He'd given me a ride back, and he knew I was lying about Kevin. So hearing him out was the least I could do. I sat back, releasing the door handle. "Okay."

"Okay?"

I nodded. "Okay." My eyes cut to the side as I said, "I know you weren't going to hurt me."

He waited, studying me. I almost flushed again. I wasn't looking at him anymore, but I could feel his scrutiny. He was acting like I was a feral animal, just waiting for the right opening to scurry away. I wasn't. I had some decency, even though I was acting like an idiot.

But that was him. *He* made me act like a nervous, rabid bat. I wasn't like this with other people. I was normal, sane. Fuck, I was almost boring.

Not with Asshole Caden, who I was starting to think maybe wasn't that much of an asshole. He wasn't acting like one anymore, and maybe he hadn't been when I'd first labeled him as such. I *had* been acting weird, and he'd really only just asked me if something was wrong.

If a girl asked me that question, I wouldn't have thought anything of it. But it had been him, and that question coming from a male someone who was obviously strong, muscular, gorgeous, and self-assured—holy shit, Asshole Caden was confident with an extra layer of authority too. It rolled off him in waves, very sexy and alluring waves, and I couldn't believe I was having these thoughts.

My gaze jerked to his. "What were you going to say?" A traitorous blush warmed its way up my neck. I prayed it didn't spread over my face.

He gentled his tone. "Why are you covering for your stepbrother?"

"You mean for your fraternity brother?"

He didn't reply, only clenched his jaw.

"I can't say anything." *I can't say what you want me to say.* "Call it family loyalty?"

"So you *are* covering for him?"

I held my breath. "What?"

He leaned forward a tiny bit. "Was he with Maggie?"

He was testing me. He didn't know for sure. Realizing that, I kept my mouth shut. I would not incriminate myself.

I started to open the door again. "Uh, thanks for the ride. That was nice of you."

"Wait."

I opened the door enough to clamber down. I shut it and had to walk around the front to go into my dorm.

He opened his window and called out, "He's not worth it."

I was close to ten feet away from him, but I stopped and looked back.

His eyes bore into mine. "Whatever reasons you have for being loyal to him, he doesn't share the sentiment." There were no doubts. No questions. Nothing in Caden's statement besides dead-set resolve.

The wind picked up, sending shivers through me. "What are you talking about?"

He put the Land Rover into drive. "He wouldn't have your back. Guys like him never do."

Claudia was coming out of Avery's room when I got upstairs.

Her eyes skimmed over me. "You're back."

She didn't smile. I took note of that. I didn't smile either. "Yeah."

"Listen," she said as she started toward me, sliding her hands into her back pockets. "Avery was your buddy, and, well, she was upset. She and Marcus dated last year. They broke up, and two months later he was with Maggie." Her disdain came through loud and clear when she added, "I don't understand why Avery won't stop saying she's Maggie's friend. The girl's a bitch."

I frowned. What was I supposed to do with that? "I feel bad for Avery, but I was told you guys don't leave your friends behind. You left me behind."

She stared at me.

I stared back.

She should've had some reaction, but there was none. I guess that told me everything. She wasn't going to apologize, and I wasn't her friend. I nodded to myself.

"Okay then."

She shrugged. "It wasn't personal."

We were at an impasse, and I had two options. I could ignore her and pretend it was fine, or not.

I sighed. "But it was, you see." I was going with option B. "What?"

"It was personal." My hand touched my chest. "To me. You left *me*."

"Look, Avery will apologize to you tomorrow. We got her back, and she's sleeping now, but if you're the type to need that sort of thing, you'll get it tomorrow."

Her eyes moved past me. She straightened up like she was going to leave, but I had a bee up my ass.

I stepped to the side, as if to block her. Her eyes found mine again, and her pathetic half-grin fell flat. "What?"

I was about to start a confrontation with an upperclassmen. I didn't really know her. I didn't really know my RA, but something was going on with me. I suddenly wasn't willing to let anyone roll over me. I braced myself for whatever was going to happen and forged ahead.

"Look," I said. "Avery might apologize to me tomorrow, but you're the first one I'm seeing from the group. I have a hard time imagining that you guys completely forgot me. I don't think it was a mistake leaving me behind."

Her eyes narrowed.

I kept going. "So yes, I'll probably get an apology from Avery tomorrow, but you don't seem sorry. That makes me wonder if you have a problem with me."

What had gotten into me? I was more wallflower than confrontational, or at least I used to be.

She folded her arms. "How did you get back?"

That was it? Nothing? I cocked my head to the side. "I got a ride."

Her left eyebrow lifted. "Someone gave you a ride home?"

I nodded. "Not everyone forgot me."

She snorted, rolling her eyes. "Who gave you a ride?"

"Marcus' brother."

Her eyes widened. "Caden?"

He might've been an asshole to me, or maybe not—my head was all muddled about that now—but I enjoyed seeing the surprise from Claudia. "Yeah."

"Are you sure?" She gave me a dismissing look. "I'm not trying to be mean, but Caden's a big guy around here. He's not known for dealing with girls like you."

I hated asking, but the question burned in the back of my mouth. "Girls like me?"

"Yeah." She smirked. "Nobodies like you. Freshman and forgettable."

My lips were stiff. "Is he a senior?"

"Junior, but it doesn't matter. He's known, if you know what I mean. I have a hard time believing he just *gave* you a ride here. What'd you do? Blow him?"

"Why? Is that what you do to get rides?" I stepped closer. "Is that what you're implying?"

"Maybe I was implying that that's the only way someone like Caden would pay any attention to someone like you."

God. She really was a bitch. "I thought you guys were nice." I shook my head. "That's the joke here. Not me." I patted myself on the chest again. "Me looking up to you, thinking how cool you guys were, that's the joke. I liked Avery."

Claudia wasn't the only one who could be cold. I iced my tone, letting her hear my disdain too. "Too bad about that. Too bad about you."

She'd looked bored while I was talking, but now she perked up. "Wait a minute. Kevin is Caden's fraternity brother."

So now it was because of my stepbrother.

I reached for the wall. I needed it to ground me because I was about to launch at her, consequences be damned. "What does Kevin have to do with it?"

"Caden was being nice to you because of Kevin. That's why you got a ride home, not because he's interested in you or anything." She looked me up and down again. "Can you really question why I was confused?" She laughed, moving past me down the hall. "Give Avery hell tomorrow. She'll be groveling, because unlike me, she likes you for some stupid reason. Have fun!"

She left me alone in an empty hallway, with an empty feeling inside me.

I was back to square one of no friends. Lovely.

CHAPTER SEVEN

Claudia was right about one thing. Avery *did* apologize the next morning. She did it with bags under her eyes, oversized sweats on her body, messy hair, and a slight green tinge to her skin. She had a water bottle in her hand.

She was hungover.

I didn't say anything about my encounter with Claudia. It wasn't Avery's fault her friend was a bitch, but when she invited me to dinner the next night with the same group of friends, I declined. She asked me to lunch the day after, and I had the same response. She wore a puzzled frown after that, but I didn't think she was going to invite me anywhere else. I hoped it wouldn't matter. My roommate would move in soon.

The next day was finally the official move-in day for freshmen, but even while the hallway was busy with people bringing in stuff and unpacking in their rooms, I sat alone in mine. That night I found out the reason.

Avery knocked on my door to let me know she was holding a floor meeting in a few minutes, and that I wasn't getting a roommate.

"Why? What happened?"

She held a clipboard to her chest. "I got a phone call this morning, but I haven't had the time to let you know. There was a death in the family, so she's coming next semester. She's starting late."

"Oh." I glanced over my shoulder to my room. It was all cozy, but just with my stuff. There was still an empty bed, an empty desk, an empty dresser, and an empty closet.

"Don't get comfortable. They might move someone else in, or you'll get lucky and have your own room for the semester."

"When will I know?"

She lifted a shoulder. "People transfer in late all the time, or someone could ask for a room transfer. If you move your stuff around, just be prepared that you might have to move it back."

"Okay."

She smiled now, resuming the professional advisor demeanor she'd worn when she'd first met me and my parents. The Avery that had invited me to the party faded.

"I'll see you at the meeting then?" She checked her phone. "You have two hours. The campus ice cream shop is open tonight just for incoming freshman, so I was going to invite everyone over there. It'll be a great way to meet new people."

During the meeting, Avery told me and my freshman floormates the rules as we shared similar nervous looks with each other. When she finished, she gave us a half hour to change or freshen up, or whatever we needed, before we were supposed to meet back in the hallway to go for ice cream.

I went back to my room, still alone, and puttered around for a few minutes. I was heading back out the door when my phone buzzed. I glanced down and saw a text from Kevin.

It was only three words. **Can we talk?** But those three words had my heart racing. My hand closed around the phone, and I couldn't move for a second.

I knew my feelings weren't going to magically disappear, but this was ridiculous.

A rush of memories flooded me. How he'd leaned in close, a hand on my shoulder as his lips grazed mine. Heat had spread through my body. I could feel his lips again now. His hand on my shoulder, pressing lightly there before sliding down my arm and curving around my waist. My chest had pressed to his as his mouth opened over mine, demanding more. I gave it to him. Lifting my arms to twine around his neck, my heart had stampeded against my chest. I would've given him anything.

I did give him anything. I gave him me that night.

My phone buzzed again, breaking through the spell. A cold dose of reality poured over me as I read the next words: **We should talk about Maggie.**

Yes. We should. I groaned internally. That was the last thing I wanted to do, but I typed back, already knowing I'd push off the ice cream social thing because I was a weak dumbass when it came to Kevin. **When and where?**

I didn't have to wait long. His text buzzed right back: **Now? We can meet at Brown Building. Front steps.**

This was all sorts of wrong. Why didn't he just come to my dorm? He could see my room, maybe help me meet anyone who didn't go to get ice cream? I could have pressed the issue, but I didn't. Instead of joining the crowd gathering outside Avery's room, I bypassed them and went down the stairs.

Outside I walked toward the area where I thought Brown Building was located. I'd registered for classes the day before and gotten my books at the bookstore, but I'd only wandered around campus a few times. I knew it was broken up into three large quad sections with the student center/cafeteria in the middle of it all. One of my classes was in Brown Building, so I needed to find where it was anyway. After cutting through the student center—and walking right past the ice cream shop—I pushed open the doors leading to the last quad area. I hadn't explored that section yet, so I was surprised to find that it was quiet. And dark. There were more lights posted in the other parts of campus. I felt like I'd stepped into a closed sanctuary.

Two sidewalks led from the student center, breaking into separate directions. Trees blocked my view, but based on where I remembered seeing Brown on the map, I headed right. Brown was the third building down, and the sidewalk circled around the building, taking me past a side door.

Kevin wasn't at the side door.

I stayed on the sidewalk and continued around the building, finding a large set of stone steps leading up to another door. They overlooked a small pond, and I went to sit down. I could see why Kevin chose this spot. It was private, and with the pond and its fountain, it was almost tranquil. I didn't even feel like I was on a college campus, or that a bunch of freshmen were a few buildings away.

"Hey."

I looked up. A dark silhouette came around from the opposite way. Kevin had his hands in his pockets and his shoulders hunched forward.

"Hey," I said back.

He moved closer, stepping into the single light positioned above me. A dagger sliced my heart. I could see the apology on his face, and I gritted my teeth. I didn't want to hear it. He'd hurt me, yes, but I didn't need him to pour salt on the wound.

I had a feeling I had no say over that.

"Look," he started. He didn't come any closer. He cleared his throat. "Uh...so this is weird."

Maybe it was because I saw him with Maggie, or because I found out minutes later she had a boyfriend, or because he never checked on me after I lied for him. Or maybe it was because I hadn't seen him at all since our ridiculous family dinner, but whatever the reason, as I waited for him to continue, the image I had of him in high school was stripped away.

That made me feel cold and vulnerable, like he was a stranger.

I could remember every time we'd talked during that year we lived together, but I couldn't remember a joke, a hug, or anything affectionate. It was always me gazing at him, and feeling close, feeling warm because of my own daydreams.

That'd been it. He'd been present, but he'd been quiet unless with a girlfriend. He would laugh then, and I'd always heard that as a sound of relief—like he could only relax if a girl was with him.

Why had I cared so much then? What was I missing? I didn't think I was completely delusional…or was I?

Kevin started to say something, but I interrupted. "Was I a mistake?"

"What?" He'd lifted a hand to scratch behind his ear. A dumbstruck look came over him, and his hand moved slowly back to his side. "What?"

"Me. That night we were together. I was a mistake." My chest burned. "Wasn't I?"

He blinked rapidly, then coughed to clear his throat. "Well… um…"

That was my answer. Those two stupid words were my answer.

The burning intensified, and I jerked, scooting away until my back hit the step behind me.

A week ago, I would still have been waiting for him to give me an answer. Things were different now. The unspoken told the truth, and I could hear that. I'd just been not listening for two entire years. Two fucking years.

I hung my head. "I'm so stupid."

"What?"

"I'm so stupid."

"Wait." He started forward, his hand outstretched, but he paused.

I could see the thoughts crossing his face. What could he say? Nothing. That was the thing. If I was a mistake, he couldn't tell me. I might tell his secret then, and if I wasn't a mistake, it was too late. He was with someone else now. Right? It was one of those two choices.

Why was I trying to rationalize this for him?

After a moment he sighed and slid his hands into his front pockets. "I really love Maggie."

There it was. That was his reason for everything. I'd just go with it, for now. "Okay."

He stepped toward me. His voice grew clearer. "I know you've been here all week, and you've been alone. I would've called earlier or come to see you, but I needed to make sure Maggie was okay. You know what I mean?"

I didn't, but my head bobbed up and down anyway.

"You understand?"

Not in the slightest, but again, I was nodding. Apparently I still had some wallflower in me.

"Good." He sounded so relieved. "I was kinda worried. Your floor advisor has history with Maggie. I didn't know—"

"Avery told me she's friends with Maggie."

He went still. "Oh. So you've talked about me and Maggie with Avery?"

"She knows our parents are married."

"Oh." He sounded surprised now. "You told her about me."

"She knew, but—" My mouth was suddenly dry, and my palms were sweaty. I rubbed them together. "Why wouldn't I?" *What is going on here?* "Am I not supposed to tell people?"

"About you and me?" he asked.

I leaned forward. Did he mean…

He continued, pointing between us, "That we're stepsiblings, right? Everyone has to know my goddamn business. I don't really know why you're talking about me at all." His hands went back into his pockets. He rocked back on his heels. "Besides, we were more housemates, really. That was it."

I knew this, but still felt slapped in the face. "Housemates."

"Yeah. I mean, yeah." He frowned, acting like he was so confused. "I didn't even know you before our parents got married. And that one year we lived together, I was barely around, and you were always in your bedroom. We never got close. Then last year I was hardly home. Like, ever."

Except for that one night, I added silently. *When you went out to a graduation party with my friends and me. When you got drunk with me. When we went home and kissed, and did more than I want to think about right now. You were hardly home, except for that one night.*

I looked down. "I see."

He coughed again, his feet shuffling on the sidewalk. "And I really love Maggie. I really do, but you see, she's with that Marcus guy for now, and Marcus comes from a big-name family around here. His dad is a legacy legend in the fraternity, and even though Marcus isn't a member, his brother Caden is one of my brothers. It's just sticky. If they ever find out what you really saw that night—"

I started laughing. Maybe I shouldn't have. Maybe it was wrong, but it began to bubble up inside me, and I couldn't stop. The joke was on me, but it was on him, too. He didn't think people knew. Everyone knew!

"What?"

I shook my head, still laughing. My shoulders started to shake. "Nothing. It's—" More laughter. "Nothing. I'm sorry."

But I couldn't stop, and he glared at me, anger evident in his eyes.

After a few more beats, I was able to calm myself. "Is this what you did in high school? Do you really think you're not going to get caught? You don't realize everyone already knows?"

"What do you mean?"

"You date a girl, then at the five-month mark, you get bored. You start looking around for a new girl. Then you date both girls, thinking the girlfriend won't know, but she always does. It's *always* a nasty break-up. Everyone knew about it at school—"

"They did?"

"Yeah. And I'm sure you thought you were in love with them too, just like Maggie now. But Kevin, are you serious? People know. You brought her to the restaurant."

"I don't have another girlfriend now. And this town is big enough. I didn't think it'd matter if she came to dinner or not."

"Whatever. But she's got a boyfriend. He went to your frat house the other night, looking for her. He knew she would be with you. Your fraternity brothers and I are the only reasons you didn't get caught. How much longer do you think this will last? I mean, be realistic."

He scratched his head again and shrugged. "I don't know. We're going to be more careful."

I thought I'd take a stab at this. "You're going to be together in her room and not yours?"

I thought he'd laugh and give me a more detailed plan of action. I thought he'd say, *Oh, no*, and proceed from there. He didn't.

There was silence instead, and I had a second realization for this evening. The stepbrother I had loved, or thought I'd loved, for so long was a moron. There was no other way to explain his stupidity.

"Are you serious?" I asked. "That's your plan? Instead of hanging out in your room, where Marcus actually wouldn't have a reason to drop by, you're going to hang out in her room, where he does have a reason to go. Because, you know, it's his *girlfriend's* room."

"No." Kevin shook his head, taking another step backward. "I mean, of course that's not our plan. But Caden's at my place. He lives there too."

I snored. "You think Caden's going to hang out in your room?"

Kevin didn't reply right away. He seemed to mull things over before he asked, "What do you mean by that?"

I wanted to smack myself in the forehead. "He covered for you that night. He didn't let Marcus inside."

"He didn't know—"

I cut in. "He knew. Trust me, he knew."

"What do you mean?"

"I—"

No. I wasn't doing this. I wasn't going to explain that Caden had caught me, or questioned me, or given me a ride home from Marcus' party. That was none of Kevin's business, and even though it stung to admit it, he and Maggie weren't my business either—except for the fact that I had COVERED FOR HIM! *Okay. Breathe, Summer. Breathe. Calm down.*

I counted down from ten to one, then tuned him out. If he said something during my calming time, it fell on deaf ears.

He was driving me nuts.

My feelings were still there, buried deep in my chest, but my God, I was learning how exasperating he could be at the same time. I couldn't wait until those feelings were gone. I had a feeling I'd be looking at life in a new way.

Deep breath. Calming thoughts. Think Zen. Buddha. Boring-ass music. Yoga. Anything to lower your heart rate.

"You okay?"

"What?" I refocused and saw he was watching my hands. I looked down. I'd been fanning myself. "Oh. Yeah. I'm fine."

He glanced behind him. "You know, it's weird talking to you about this."

"You don't say." No sarcasm there. Not one bit.

He nodded. "Listen, in case you run into Maggie or Marcus again, he's not a bad guy. I don't want you to think that, because he and his brother are popular on campus." He lifted a shoulder. "Not that I'm not, but I'm not in their league. You don't have to hate the guy or anything. I know you're in my camp."

I stifled a groan.

He continued as if he hadn't heard me. "You know what I mean." He peered at me, blinking a few times. "You're going into sports medicine?"

My head moved back an inch. "You know my major?" Or my soon-to-be/I was hoping to declare major.

I lifted a hand to my chest. I'd talked to him about that graduation night. I hadn't realized he'd actually been listening. He'd seemed focused on removing my shirt.

"My mom told me."

"Oh."

There was that then.

"Marcus is sports medicine too. You're probably going to see him."

That clicked.

He smiled for the first time tonight. "I don't want to make things awkward for you."

Awkward. For me. "How thoughtful of you."

His smile grew, and he finally crossed to where I sat on the steps.

"Come on." He motioned for me to stand. "Let's hug it out."

He held me to his chest, murmuring in my ear, "You know, it is nice to have you here."

My throat burned again. He said that like it had *just* occurred to him.

"Thank you."

He gave me one more squeeze before he stepped back, offering a crooked grin as he raked a hand through his hair. "I'm glad we had this talk. We should meet up for dinner every now and then. That might be fun."

Dinner. Every now and then. That *might* be fun.

I'd come to college thinking I'd be with him, and turned out his plan was that we "should meet up for dinner every now and then."

This entire talk felt like one giant punch to my face.

CHAPTER EIGHT

"I owe you an apology. Again."

I heard this as two feet stopped next to me. A large textbook and notebook dropped onto the grass with a muted thud, and I glanced up in time to see a pair of bare legs bend.

I was attempting to study on the east quad's lawn between two of my classes. It had been a week since school started, and everything was going great. Well, almost everything. My classes were easy so far, but I hadn't really clicked with anyone I'd met yet. A few of my floormates had ordered pizza and binge-watched *Dirty Dancing*, *The Breakfast Club*, and *Pitch Perfect* the other night. I went. I'd enjoyed a slice of cheese pizza, and I'd been humming "Cups" nonstop ever since, but mostly it had all been…dull.

I was dull.

I didn't know what my problem with that was. Clarissa and I had been dull in high school. May hadn't been, but we were, and we were okay with it. But now… The girls on my floor were nice. They were steady, tame. Okay, they were boring. And I should've loved hanging out with them. *I should've* the two operative words.

Instead I almost loathed it.

I'd been leaving during the Barden Bellas' grand finale when I'd heard laughter coming from the bathroom. Avery had come out, and she wasn't alone. Shell, Claudia, and two others whose names I still didn't remember had trailed behind. They all saw me. Avery had waved, giving me a friendly smile, and Shell and one of the other girls did as well. Claudia didn't. She hadn't flipped me off or anything; she just didn't care. Her face had been a mask, and I'd stared a bit longer at her than necessary. Avery noticed, and she'd looked between us as they all headed out. I recognized the backpacks and pre-loaded water bottles, and I guessed they were going to another party. Maybe even another one Caden's brother was throwing.

They'd left, and I'd turned to go to my room. I'd been planning on going to bed, but I couldn't deny the feeling inside of me.

I'd wanted to go with them.

I didn't want to watch *The Breakfast Club* or *Sixteen Candles* on my weekends like my floormates and a lot of my freshman classmates seemed to. I didn't want to order pizza—at least not on a Friday or Saturday night. Maybe during Satur*day*, when I was hungover after I'd been living it up. That's what I wanted, but Claudia had stopped me from reaching out.

I couldn't say anything, I couldn't do anything because of her. Bitch. I'd be stupid to try to enter her world of friends again, not when I was a lowly freshman. So I'd watched them go.

Avery settled in next to me in the grass now, her books ignored at her side. She had a determined look in her eye.

"Claudia," she said.

"What about her?"

"She has this disorder."

"Really?"

"It's called Bitchitis." Avery's shoulder lifted up and down in a breath. "She was a bitch to you after we went out that time, wasn't she?"

She didn't wait for my response.

"I saw how you looked at her in the hallway this weekend, and I cornered her later. I made her tell me what happened. She didn't explain everything. I'm sure of that, but it was enough. I can read between the lines. I'm really sorry, Summer."

"Oh." I had no clue what to say now.

"I'm not making excuses for her, and she *will* apologize to you too, but some of her attitude was to protect Shell. She thinks if you're around, Kevin will be around. She doesn't want that."

I sat back. "Well, after that ringing endorsement..." I laughed, looking away. The sound was hollow. "I mean, wow."

"You should know something else, but you can't tell because the other girls don't know."

I regarded her again. "What?"

"She dated your stepbrother. She was two girls before Maggie."

"Wait. Shell dated him too, right?"

She nodded. "She doesn't know about Claudia. And Claudia didn't know about Shell until the summer. She felt horrible when she found out. I'm the only one who knows, and now you too. Please don't say anything. Kevin dated a ton of girls last year, and he had everyone keep quiet, saying some bullshit line about how he's private about things."

I grunted, tugging on the bottom of my shirt. "Yeah. People are idiots sometimes."

"That's why you haven't come with us the other times I've invited you, isn't it? Because of Claudia."

I nodded.

I could feel another invitation coming my way, and I wasn't sure what to do. I shifted, wrapping my arms around my knees, and I held tight to my jeans.

"You don't have to, but the girls and I are part of this program called Community Core Services, and a couple other groups on campus teamed up with us for this big flamingo fundraiser. I was just going to one of the meetings. We'll all be driving around, handing out flyers." She bit her lip. "You want to come?"

There it was.

I didn't know what a flamingo fundraiser was, and I had no intention of finding out, but at that moment, two freshman girls from our floor passed us on the sidewalk. They waved, their bags slung over their backs, and I recognized the look in their eyes. Fear.

They were feeling the freshman fear—fear of getting to class, fear about finding friends, fear of being rejected, being alone, having no one else.

I changed my mind.

"I'm in," I told Avery.

I wouldn't be afraid. I *was* going to have friends. I wasn't going to be alone.

An entire parking lot was filled with vehicles, guys and girls milling around. Some taped banners that said *Community Core Services* in big bold letters to the sides of trucks, with the phrase *Flock Your Neighbors* underneath. Pictures of flamingos were everywhere, and large flamingo lawn ornaments had been taped to the tops of the trucks. One truck had a pool in the bed, filled with the same flamingo ornaments and a group of guys wearing swimming trunks. Some had pink flamingo inner tubes around their waists and drinks in hand.

Avery waved to someone, heading across the parking lot. I paused. I had to take in all the pink glory.

"Hey."

I turned to find Kevin coming toward me.

"What are you doing here?"

I gestured around the lot. "What? And miss this flamingo haven? The real question is why didn't you invite me first?"

He stared at me, then let out a laugh. "I'll steal one for you at the end of this."

"Speaking of, what is this?"

Avery stopped talking to her friends and glanced back over to find me. Seeing Kevin, the corners of her mouth turned down, but she waved. I waved back as she turned to her group again.

"It's a fundraiser," Kevin said. "A bunch of us are members

of CSC. We're raising money for the Brain Injury Association of America." He grunted. "Banks suggested it, of all people."

I pointed at the nearest flamingo banner. "What's up with the pink birds?"

"Oh." He laughed again. "I don't even see them, I'm so used to them by now. People pay us to 'flock' their friends' front lawns. It's three dollars a bird. We put 'em in overnight and leave a sign that says they've been flocked. Then we take 'em out the next day. It's all in fun and for charity. We're just driving around today to hand out fliers and raise awareness that the next opportunity is coming up."

He folded his arms over his chest, yawning, as he nodded at me. "How'd you get pulled into it?"

I pointed to Avery. "She asked if I wanted to come. I had no idea what I was signing up for."

He leaned back against the nearest truck. "It's all good, but I think we're taking off pretty soon."

"PEOPLE!" A girl shouted, clapping her hands and waving her arms near the truck where Avery was standing.

When people didn't stop talking right away, she put her fingers in her mouth and let out the loudest wolf whistle I'd ever heard.

"People! Fellow CSCers and friends!" People were still talking, so she yelled, "ASSHATS!"

A few girls gasped, but a couple guys laughed. One hollered, his deep baritone booming over the group, "SHUT UP, FUCKERS!"

"Flockers," the girl corrected him.

"Flockers. That's what I said."

"Yeah, right!" came from the back.

Kevin leaned in close and murmured, "That's Jill. She's the CSC president and the fucker next to her is her boyfriend, Niall."

He was being nice, but I wasn't going to remember their names. Still, trying to be polite, I glanced over my shoulder. I searched for the fucker, but my gaze collided with a pair of hostile eyes I wasn't expecting.

Maggie stood two trucks down with her arms crossed over her chest, glaring at me. I stiffened and narrowed my eyes, cutting to the rest of her group. I didn't have to look far. Marcus Banks stood beside her, his arm holding on to the truck over her head as he spoke to someone behind him. His shoulders shook with laughter.

"Kevin."

My one word was enough. He twisted around and saw what I was seeing. He cursed under his breath, and his hand came to rest on my shoulder. "She doesn't believe we're just siblings. Forget about her, though. She'll see we're really like brother and sister."

Except we weren't. I gritted my teeth. We'd been lovers.

His hand burned into my shoulder. It was like I wasn't wearing a shirt, like he was touching my naked skin. Maggie saw his touch, and her eyes narrowed even more. She started forward, but when Marcus turned around, she jerked back in place.

I pressed my lips together, almost daring her to say or do something. *Bring it.* I wanted to open my arms and bob my head at her. I *wanted* her to do something. *Say something. Come over here and stake your claim. Forget you have a boyfriend at your side. Bring it.*

But she didn't. She forced a smile when Marcus said something to her, pulling her to his chest. But as soon as he looked at someone else, her glare returned to me.

No matter what Kevin said to her, she could see my feelings.

"Okay!" The leader shouted, pulling my attention back to her. She paused, then circled her hands in the air. "Let's get on it. We're out of here in FIVE MINUTES!"

As soon as she finished, a frenzied rush came over the group. People ran across the lot. Guys climbed on top of trucks and stood in the beds. Car doors slammed shut and everyone began hollering and whistling.

Shit.

Everyone was leaving. I'd completely missed whatever the leader had been saying. I turned to Kevin, but he was gone. I saw him climbing into an SUV down the row. Wait. Avery? I began searching for her as vehicles pulled out of their spots and passed me.

I hurried forward, still looking for Avery. I couldn't find her. Then I stopped as I saw the last of the trucks pull out. I twisted around, and there was one left—the heavily decorated one with the pool. A group of guys and a few girls were in the back, and the leader prepared to join them.

"Hey, uh…" I called to her, but paused. I didn't know her name.

She looked up. "Yeah?" Her eyes darted around. "Your friends left you?"

I nodded. "I was with my stepbrother. My friend must've thought I'd go with him, but…" I gestured to the empty lot now.

"Gotcha." She looked over her truck, a frown forming. "Listen, we're full. You're a volunteer? I don't remember your name. You must not be a part of CSC. I'm Jill."

"Summer. I came with Avery. You know, it's fine. I can head back to the dorms."

"Okay. Sorry about your friend and brother."

I waved it off. It was fine, just the small burn of humiliation, but then I heard the sound of another vehicle pulling into the lot. I turned around, expecting to see Avery or even Kevin, but nope. Caden pulled up, and my welcoming smile faded.

His window rolled down. "Is my brother still here?"

Jill stepped up next to me. "Hey, Caden! Are you joining the cause?"

He shook his head, looking between us, then at me as he answered her. "No, just need to find my brother. His phone is off. I knew he was doing this with you guys."

She glanced down at her clipboard. "Uh…his group is supposed to cover the Rose Creek neighborhood. No surprise there. You could head up there to find him."

"Okay. I'll do that. Thank you."

"Is something wrong?"

Caden shook his head. "No. That's fine. I'll track him down." He glanced at me again, lingering one more time.

Jill noticed. "Oh, hey—" She jerked her head toward me. "Do you mind a stowaway? She got left behind by her buddies. She can hop in with the others if you find them."

I closed my eyes a moment. The burn of humiliation went up a notch.

Caden grinned. His cold look lifted, just a bit, and he pointed to the passenger door. "That's fine. Hop in, little Matthews. This is starting to become our thing."

Jill regarded me, her attention suddenly more focused when she realized Caden knew me.

I felt my face getting red, and I shook my head, backing away. "Nah. That's okay." I pointed over my shoulder. "I should get some studying done."

"Summer."

Caden's voice stopped me. I wanted to make my escape. The thought of being in his vehicle again, in such close proximity with him, had sent a whole host of sensations through me. I had knots in my stomach, and stupid butterflies doing somersaults around them, but as much as I tried to make my legs leave, they didn't move.

"Get in."

It was a softly worded command, but those two words had more power over me than my own brain did. I found myself going around the Land Rover and getting in. As I shut the door, I saw Jill get in her truck, still watching me.

I'd come to this event a nobody, but suddenly, with the acknowledgement that Caden Banks knew me, I knew I wouldn't be a nobody for long. I wasn't sure if I was ready for that or not. Girls who were somebody were also targets. Maybe I still wanted to be a nobody?

CHAPTER NINE

"Why'd you do that?" I asked Caden as he pulled away. "And it's Stoltz. I'm not a Matthews."

I couldn't keep that question in. A touch of panic settled at the bottom of my stomach, lining my insides, and I couldn't get rid of it. I knew I was overreacting, but I couldn't shake the look that Jill and everyone else in her truck had given me.

Maybe I liked being boring after all. I could be invisible.

Caden threw me a frown, turning at an intersection. "Say what?"

I twisted in my seat, facing him, and ignored all the other emotions going on in me. It was him. He made me crazy. I only acted like this in his presence. "They were all looking at me. Why did you do that?"

He gave me a crazy look, like I'd grown two heads. "What the fuck's your problem?"

A new, more-alarming sensation dipped low in me, all the way down between my legs. I was attracted to him. I slammed back into my seat. I couldn't be attracted to him. He was Asshole Caden. Granted, he was *my* asshole, and that was the wrong thought too. I took a breath. I had to calm down.

I had to be reasonable.

"Now people know that I know you."

"Is there something wrong with knowing me?"

"Yes."

"What? What was I supposed to do? Pretend you weren't there?"

"Yes."

"You might not like me, but I'm not a complete dick."

"You're an asshole."

He grunted, turning onto the interstate. "Don't hold back, Stoltz. Tell me what you really think."

"I—" was being the dick. Not him. "I'm sorry." I sighed. "I'm not used to this."

He glanced over at me. "What are you used to?"

Being invisible. "Kevin was the popular one in high school. I..."

"Wasn't?"

I nodded. "I wasn't an outcast or anything, but I wasn't what he is, or was back then. I just was."

He gave me a half-grin. "If it makes you feel better, the only people Kevin's popular with here are girls who want to cheat on their boyfriends."

I raised an eyebrow. "Touché."

He chuckled, and I closed my eyes. His laugh slid over me like a warm caress, and a tingle shot through me, giving me an excited buzz low in my stomach. I pressed a hand there, trying to calm my nerves.

"You shouldn't do things like that," I told him.

"What?"

"Laugh like that."

"First you didn't want me to acknowledge you, and now I'm not supposed to laugh?" He shook his head, rubbing a hand over his jaw. "You have issues."

I sat back, dumbstruck for a moment. It was true. Kevin was my issue. "I meant that when you laugh like that—" I stopped. I was about to confess all the tingles and warm feelings. He was right. What the hell was going on with me? I'd never been like this before. I frowned to myself as I thought back.

I'd been nice.

I'd been quiet.

I'd been boring.

That was all in high school. I snuck a glance at Caden. I was saying things I normally wouldn't. I was feeling things I normally wouldn't. This guy was an asshole at first. I hadn't liked him, but now he was different. It had been Kevin for so long, and now suddenly someone else was getting inside of me.

"I'm sorry."

He took an exit and turned into a ritzy neighborhood. "Sorry for what?"

"For being crazy."

A small laugh left him. "You're a bit much. I have no idea what's going to come out of your mouth, and I'm usually prepared when it comes to chicks."

My lip twisted as I held back a grin. "Chicks?"

"Yeah." He took a right, slowing down, but he looked at me for a second. "Why? Was that wrong to say?"

"No. I don't know why that's funny to me."

He didn't reply, but nodded toward the street. "This is the neighborhood Jill said Marcus is in. Keep an eye out. I don't know if your people are with them or not."

The houses were extravagant. Some had gated driveways. Some had fountains on their front lawns. Some were completely hidden behind a wall. My dad was the general manager at a large company in the town where we lived, and Kevin's mom was a nurse. I knew both were well-off, and we'd moved into Sheila's home because it was the bigger one. More space. We'd had our own pool and an extra floor of guest rooms, but it wasn't anything like these houses. These weren't houses. They were mansions.

I regarded Caden. "Are you from here?"

"What?"

I pointed to the houses. "The girl back there implied you'd know this area. Is your house one of these?"

He started to laugh, but stopped himself. "You're serious?"

"Yeah."

He straightened in his seat and shook his head. "I live with your stepbrother. And you were at Marcus' house. We don't live up here."

"Why'd she imply you would know this neighborhood?"

"My brother knows this neighborhood. His girlfriend lives up here."

"Maggie?"

He nodded. "She's from North River. She still lives with her parents."

"Oh."

"You mentioned a friend before. Was that the same girl you were at Marcus' party with? Avery?"

I nodded. "She said she went to high school with Maggie. She must be from North River too."

He took another right, turning into a cul-de-sac, and slowed to point out a large white-bricked house. "That's Maggie's. I thought they might come here to hang out for a bit."

There was no gate or wall, so we were able to see the house. The only car parked in the driveway was a silver Prius. "That's not hers?"

"I don't think so, but it doesn't matter. Marcus' truck isn't here." He leaned forward to get a better look, then sat back and maneuvered his Land Rover in a circle, heading back out. "I'll keep looking."

"Maggie's with him, right?"

"Yeah."

"His phone is off, but is hers? You could call her."

He raised an eyebrow. "You have her phone number?"

"You don't have your brother's girlfriend's phone number?"

The corner of his mouth lifted up in a half smirk. "Do you?"

Well. I squared my shoulders. Fuck. He got me with that one.

"Stepbrother," I mumbled, but I shut up after that. We drove for a few more blocks in silence, but we weren't finding them. The few blocks stretched into a few miles, and it wasn't long before we had searched the entire neighborhood. Caden paused at a stoplight.

There was one more street to check, but he hit the turn signal. He was going to go left, which led back to school.

"Is it important?"

"What?" He didn't spare me a glance as he waited for the light to turn green.

"Whatever you need to find your brother about. Is it important?"

He grunted. "Fuck yeah, or I wouldn't be driving around searching for his ass." He eyed me. "Why? Don't tell me you actually do have Maggie's phone number?"

I flushed, shooting him a dark look. "No, and I'm sticking with my story." I'd been holding my phone in my hands the entire time, and it had grown heavier and heavier the longer we looked. "But I could call Avery and ask for Maggie's number."

"Fuck, girl. Why wasn't that option A?"

There was no heat to his words, and I smiled as I dialed the number Avery had made me program into my phone the night we went to Marcus' party. Caden turned off the blinker and when the light turned green, he went straight, pulling into a gas station. The phone was still ringing when he got out to fill up with gas.

"Hey." Avery answered. Loud music and laughter almost drowned her out, but she yelled, "What happened to you? We just ran into your stepbrother, and you're not with him. I thought I saw you get into his truck. Where are you?"

"Yeah, no. That didn't happen."

She let out a groan. "He ditched you, didn't he?"

"What?"

"He did, right? You can tell me if he did. Again. I know full well how shady he can be. Ditching a girl, even if she's his stepsister, is something I can totally see Kevin doing. I'm so sorry. You must've felt like I ditched you too. I really thought I saw you get into his truck. Wait, where are you? Did you go back to the dorm?"

"That's why I'm calling."

The gas stopped, and I felt Caden take the nozzle out of the truck to put it away. I glanced over my shoulder, but he wasn't paying attention to me. He bypassed his door, heading inside as he pulled out his wallet. I held back a sigh, watching him from behind. He was gorgeous. His tattoos were a little too enticing. Even a loose-fitting shirt couldn't hide the athleticism beneath, and as my gaze fell from his broad shoulders to his trim waist, lingering on where his jeans rested over his ass, I must've let out some sound.

Avery piped up in my ear, "What? What's going on?"

"Huh?" I couldn't tear my eyes away. His ass was one I'd cup in a drunken stupor and smile from satisfaction at the memory when I was sober.

"You totally sighed, like a dreamy type of sigh. What's happening? Where are you?"

Caden stepped inside the gas station. He'd be back in just a minute.

"That's why I'm calling," I said again. "I didn't go back to the dorm. Caden Banks showed up, looking for his brother. Jill asked if he'd give me a ride to find you."

"She did? Wait. *He* did?"

"What? I'm confused."

"Caden Banks gave you a ride?"

"Yeah. Why?" I frowned. *Did she have to say it like that?*

"Are you with him now?"

"We stopped for gas. I was hoping to get Maggie's number from you, so he could call Maggie to talk to his brother. And I was hoping I could talk him into meeting up with you guys. I can switch to your car then."

I waited for her response, but none came.

She was silent on the other end until I said, "Hello? Are you there?"

"I'm here." I could hear the confusion in her voice. "This is the second time Caden Banks has helped you out. That's not normal."

My eyebrows bunched together. "Claudia said something similar."

"She was right with what she said, not about you, but about Caden."

Her hesitation pissed me off.

"He's big time. Are you guys hooking up or something?"

"What? No! Why would you even think that?" However, the image of his ass appeared in my head again.

"Calm down. I didn't mean it as an insult. The opposite. Caden doesn't go out of his way to be nice to girls. He's not *not* nice. He's just—"

I gripped the phone tighter. "Yeah, yeah. He's on another level. I'm getting it. Believe me."

"No!" She laughed into the phone. "Again, it's not an insult to you. Caden's just not known for messing around with freshman, even sophomores. And he doesn't sleep around. He's got girls he can call to have sex with, but they're girls like you've not even met yet. Maggie told some of us that he was sleeping with Ashley Fontaine from that show *Hit Club*. I've no idea how they know each other, but yeah, he's usually with girls like that."

Now I felt one with the dirt on his Land Rover's floor. I leaned over to inspect where my shoes sat. Yep. I could see myself down there, trying to make friends and failing like I had for the last two weeks.

"I'm not into him like that, so don't worry," I told her. "Besides, he's fraternity brothers with Kevin, remember?"

"Yeah. I'd buy that if I didn't know better. Summer, Caden hates your stepbrother. I'm friends with Maggie, remember? She's told me stories. So no, if you think he's being nice to you because of Kevin, it's not true. If anything, Caden would try to *hurt* you because of Kevin, but he's not that type of guy. If he's being nice, then there's something about you he likes."

I straightened up. "Really?"

"You should sleep with him."

"What?!"

"I mean it. I don't usually encourage casual sex, but if it's with Caden Banks, then hell yes. Get some if you can. You'll look back when you're old and thank me."

I started laughing, then realized she was serious. "You're not joking, are you?"

"I mean it. Forget being your RA, I'm being a friend. Fuck Caden Banks if you get the chance, then tell me all about it afterward. I'll live vicariously through you."

Just then Caden walked out of the gas station with two cups in hand. "I have to go. He's coming back."

"Okay," she said quickly, her voice sounding hushed suddenly. "I mean it. Screw his brains out."

"Wait!" She was about to hang up. "I need Maggie's phone number."

"Oh yeah. Not needed," she said.

Caden opened his door and got in, observing me. "Still on the phone?"

I held up a finger. "What do you mean 'not needed'?"

"They just got here."

"Where?" I covered the phone and said to Caden, "Maggie and Marcus are wherever Avery is. They just got there."

"We're at the country club," she said. "It's almost five o'clock. We figured all the rich folks would be drinking here, and I guess they thought the same thing. Tell Caden we're at the Rose Creek Country Club. He'll know where it is."

"Okay."

I hung up, and when I told him, he rolled his eyes. "Fuck's sakes. Of course they're there."

"I take it you know the place?"

"I used to work there. I hate that place."

CHAPTER TEN

After pulling into the country club's parking lot and parking between a Ferrari and a Porsche, Caden grunted. "Yep. I still hate this place."

"You worked here?"

"My freshman year. My dad's friend owns it."

"What happened?"

He took his keys out and reached for the door handle, but paused to look at me. "I hate fake people. Guess what kind of people hang out in country clubs?" Then he was out the door and heading inside.

I didn't have time to sit back and laugh because I agreed. He was halfway across the lot by the time I got out and hurried behind him. I caught up to him on the sidewalk, but instead of going through the main entrance, he circled around the building to a wooden patio. It was full of people eating, drinking, or just sitting and talking. Caden cut through the tables and went down a flight of stairs. I paused behind him, in the middle of the stairs, to get a look at where he was going.

Three different pools spread out at the base of the hill, a lazy river connecting them. Caden headed to the middle pool, and I recognized Marcus, Avery, and others from the CSC lot. I kept scanning for Kevin.

I found him.

He was by the third pool, which was relatively empty, with only a few women swimming. One guy was doing laps, and my stepbrother stood underneath a palm tree near a bunch of other shrubbery. I could see the walking path behind him, and I knew he was trying to hide. He wasn't succeeding. A hand appeared, cupping the side of his face.

My chest tightened, and I looked over to where Caden was approaching Marcus' table.

I didn't know who it was under that tree with Kevin, but I had one guess. It started with M and rhymed with saggy.

I'd started toward them when Avery blocked my path. "Hey." She held her hands out, gesturing to where Caden and Marcus were talking. "What's up with that? He looks pissed."

Caden was the least of my problems at the moment. "I don't know. I, uh, I have to go to the bathroom." I looked around. "Where is the bathroom?"

Her eyebrows shot up and she moved back a step. "If you had to go to the bathroom, you would've gone inside, where the bathrooms are." She studied me intently. "What's going on with you?"

I sucked at being an actress. I rolled my eyes. "Fuck it. Look." I nodded in Kevin's direction.

She looked and then gasped, stepping in beside me. She shook her head. "Caden and Marcus are *right* there. They're so stupid. I don't get what Marcus even sees in her. Does she have a magical vagina or something?" She sighed. "I mean, she can be really fun, but still I don't get it. I honestly don't."

I started forward again. "I'm going to put a stop to it."

"Wait." She grabbed my arm, holding me back. "Why?"

"What do you mean why?"

"Why?" She pointed to Kevin and Maggie, who were now kissing. Or I thought they were kissing. His head was moving a little. I felt a twinge of hurt in my chest—the way he had with me that one night.

"Think about it," Avery said. "They're going to get caught. I mean, they're stupid enough to get together at the same place Marcus and his brother are, and it's during the day. It's inevitable." Her voice lowered. "So, let it happen."

"Let Kevin get pummeled, you mean?"

"No, let fate happen. Don't protect him. Don't protect any of them." She snorted, raking a hand through her hair. "They don't deserve it. Trust me."

I was tempted. I could feel his lips on mine, his hands touching me, how he'd pressed down on me. A whole host of sensations coursed through me, but they didn't matter. I gritted my teeth, and I had to actually shove down the longing I'd been experiencing since that night, but I did it.

I wanted those feelings to go away, but when I tried to actually shove them out of me, something else took their place—a different pain, a different longing. A feeling I didn't want to feel. It was ten times worse than the lingering daydream of Kevin, so every time I felt it, I ended up giving in to my old thoughts. Besides, he was family. That should count for something. His mother loved me like I was her daughter. That meant something to me, so even if Kevin was a lame asshole, I still had to keep him from getting killed.

"He won't know." Avery touched my arm again, lightly.

I moved my arm away and stepped forward. "But I'll know." And that was really all that mattered. I would know.

In just a few moments I was almost to them, but I had nothing planned. I was going to grab Kevin and drag him out. I figured he'd see reason once I pointed out Caden and Marcus, who were within eyesight. I was just a few steps away when I heard yelling behind me.

I twisted around, and my heart leaped to my throat.

Caden had Marcus pinned against the wall, leaning close. A group of guys ran for them, and without thinking, I changed course. Kevin became an afterthought as I pushed through the small crowd that had formed. Two men held Caden back now, though he wasn't fighting or trying to get to his brother. He stood there glaring at Marcus.

"I can do what I want," Marcus spat, his nostrils flared. Several guys held his arms too. "I'm sorry, Caden, but I'm not doing it."

Caden grew still, eerily still.

I moved forward, almost close enough to touch him. One of the guys holding him moved to the side and cut me off, so I edged to the left until I was front and center.

Caden saw me then, and I could see the wheels turning in his mind.

Something not-good was coming. I chewed the inside of my cheek as I locked gazes with him. What was he going to do?

A cold and almost feral smirk adorned his face as he turned back toward his brother.

Oh no...

"Well, fuck," he said, his voice so cold it sent shivers down my spine. "If you're not going to help Colt out, you might as well take care of your own shit."

Marcus went still. "What are you talking about?"

"Your girlfriend." Caden's smirk grew into a smile, but it didn't reach his eyes. They were dead. "Last I saw, she was making out with Matthews back there."

"Where?"

Caden laughed, cold and empty, and pushed past the two guys holding him. "You might want to examine your surroundings, Mark. Or maybe just check behind the palm tree between the last two pools." He started to leave. He added over his shoulder, "Or not. I'm sure once she's satisfied, she'll find your side again."

Then he was gone. The crowd swallowed him.

No one said a word, and I waited a beat, then pushed forward. Screw Kevin. Screw Maggie. Screw whatever happened to them now. I went after Caden.

He didn't have to push his way through the crowd. It automatically opened for him. Not so much for me. I was at a disadvantage, and when I ran to the parking lot, he was already in the car and peeling past me.

"HEY!" I yelled, raising my hands in the air.

He braked, a little too close for comfort, right next to me. The passenger window rolled down. "What?"

I reached for the door. "Let me in."

His eyebrows pinched together. "Why?"

"Let me in."

He unlocked the door.

I opened it and climbed in. "Okay. I'm with you." I had no idea what I was doing.

"Excuse me?"

"I'm with you." I clapped the dashboard, pointing ahead. "Whatever you're going to do, I'm in. You seem to need a friend. You're in luck. I could use one myself. So I'm in."

"I'm going to get drunk and have sex."

"Oh."

He cocked an eyebrow. "You still in?"

He was laughing now. He was still mad, but he was laughing.

For whatever reason—maybe I did want to go with him, or maybe I heard my own voice calling me boring and pathetic again—I sat back and folded my hands in my lap. "I'm in."

He shook his head. "You have no idea what you're getting yourself into." He shifted his Land Rover into drive and started forward. "But that's your problem, not mine."

He careened out of the parking lot, and I fell against the door. I grabbed the *oh shit* handle above my head, and I had a feeling that was going to be the theme for the rest of the night: Oh, shit.

CHAPTER ELEVEN

North River had close to 250,000 people, so when Caden drove to the opposite end of town, I started to worry whether he knew where he was going. I was concerned right up until he pulled into a Mexican bar and grill. Just like at the country club, he bypassed the front door and went around to the back. He clearly knew where he was going.

Rounding the building, he hopped over a small iron fence that surrounded a copper-bricked veranda. Yes, it looked so easy as he merely touched the top of the side wall and leaped over like a damned gazelle.

I, on the other hand, was a tortoise. I eyed the bottom of the fence, trying to find a place where I could crawl under, but there was nothing.

Suddenly two hands found my waist and picked me up. Caden had that look in his eyes again, the one where he was half laughing at me and half exasperated. I grabbed his arms as he lifted me over the fence and set me down in front of him. And his hands didn't move. He held me in front of him, looking down, and my pulse sped up.

"You sure you want to do this?"

"Do what?" I tried to appear confident, so I could ignore the stampeding herd in my chest. "Get drunk? I can drink with the best of them."

He closed his eyes a moment, shaking his head as he stepped back. His hands left my sides. I tried to pretend I didn't miss them:

the warmth of them, the slight weight of them, or how they'd made me feel safe for a split second.

Nope. None of that was going on.

"You're going to meet people I really care about."

"I'm down with caring people."

His eyes narrowed. "Don't fuck anything up."

"What?" I touched my chest. "Me? What have I fucked up? It's like you don't know me." I laced my fingers and pretended to crack my knuckles. "I'm ready for this. Let's get the sexing and drinking started."

He grabbed the back of his neck and continued to stare at me. "You can't handle this."

"I can too."

I swung around. Eight tables were spread out across the veranda. Some matched the bronze-colored metal fence, while others were white picnic tables. A couple girls sat at the table at the far end, smoking, and one of the picnic tables was filled with large, muscular guys in sleeveless shirts, covered with dirt and grime, and also smoking. No one looked particularly friendly, and all were watching us. I stepped back instinctively, finding Caden.

His hands came to my waist again, and for a moment, I rested there. I was against his chest, and I felt safe again. I didn't even mind the snake tattoo so close to me. I was starting to like that snake. I should name him.

A twinge of pain sliced through me.

I'd have to pull away from Caden, and the sooner the better, but I didn't want to. I liked standing here as he held me. A lump formed in my throat. I liked it maybe too much, and because of that, I swallowed that damn lump and moved to the side.

I could do this.

He moved around me, his hands falling from my waist, but he took my hand and tugged me behind him to an empty table tucked into the corner. I tried not to grasp his hand too tightly. These people looked seriously tough.

A pergola hung above us, partially shading us with the vines and foliage wrapped around it. The sun peeked through a few of the squares, but as I sat down, I adjusted my seat so my face wasn't in the light.

Caden didn't sit with me. "Be back in a second," he said, pinning me down with a fierce look over his shoulder. "Don't let anyone buy you a drink. Okay?"

I nodded, and he went inside.

A server came over in the next second, her hair pulled up in a braid. Her gaze lingered on the empty seat next to me. "Someone's coming back?"

I patted Caden's chair. "I hope so."

Her gaze moved to mine. "You're not sure?"

"I'm not sure about a lot of things these days."

Her eyebrows arched. "Are you sure about what you'd like to drink?"

I opened my mouth, but Caden dropped into his chair and answered for me. "She'll have water or soda."

"And you?"

A guy dropped into the other empty chair, beer in hand. He was older, in his forties, with his black hair combed back. There were laugh lines around his eyes and mouth. He had a sharp nose and pointed chin. His face didn't seem like it should be handsome, but it was. He wore a black shirt, and I glimpsed tight jeans before he sat. He stared at me as he spoke to the server. "This motherfucker to my right will have tequila." He held his hand out to me. "And who is this delicious drink of water on a hot day?"

Caden leaned forward, grabbed the guy's hand, and placed it back in front of him. "She's no one, and I'll have a Corona. No tequila for me." He paused, glancing at me, and amended, "At least not yet."

"Diego?" the server asked.

The guy grinned from ear to ear, still gazing at me. "What?"

"You want something else to drink?"

"Just her." He nodded at me, his grin molding into a smooth smirk. "How about it, *mi hermosa?*"

The waitress rolled her eyes and left. Caden groaned. "You're laying it on a little thick, D."

Just like that, Diego dropped the Casanova mask and leaned back, his shoulders shaking with laughter. "Sorry. But I had to come over and hit on your girl. You know, returning the favor from last weekend."

"To be fair, your girl hit on me. I didn't hit back."

"I know." A look of genuine fondness came over Diego's face, and he leaned over to clap Caden on the shoulder. His hand stayed there, squeezing for a bit. "That's why I love you."

Caden nodded toward me. "And she's not my girl. I suppose you can lay it on as thick as you want since you're newly single."

"I am." He swung his head back to me and smiled. "Please tell me you are too?"

I snorted. "Sadly, yes."

The old me would've blushed and said something boring—like I was interested in a guy or I didn't have enough time for a boyfriend. My honesty surprised me, and apparently them as well. Both were quiet for a second. Then Diego threw his head back and started laughing. Caden grinned, and suddenly I was too.

Or I was trying to grin so I didn't look like an idiot. Sometimes that wasn't possible.

Diego tipped his beer. "A salute to you. I'm right there with you." He nodded in Caden's direction. "This too-good-looking son of a bitch came in last weekend, not looking for anything except a drink with a friend, and my girl couldn't help herself. He doesn't even try. He just sits there, and girls throw themselves at him. After the fifth pick-up line, I had to kick my girl to the curb. She was no longer my girl."

"I'm so sorr—"

Caden burst out laughing. "Like you didn't still take her home and bang the fuck out of her."

Diego's smirk turned prideful, and he puffed up his chest. "Well, I mean, she was sexually frustrated after getting the boot from you. What could I do? Send her home unsatisfied?" Diego shrugged. "I do what I can. I banged the fuck out of her, and it felt so good. Then I banged her sister the next night, and that felt even better."

Caden turned toward me. "He didn't explain that before his girl hit on me, her sister was hitting on him."

"What can you do? The ladies love me." Diego pounded his fist on the table, sitting upright. "But those girls weren't worth it." He softened his tone, his eyes finding me again. "But you, *mi bonita*, you would be so worth it."

"Nope." I shook my head. This was an easy decision. "If that means being laughed about later and not hanging out with you again, I'll stay single. Thank you, but no."

"What?" His hand touched his chest, over his heart. "I'm hurt."

"I don't want to make things awkward with Asshole here either. I'll still have to go to his fraternity house sometimes."

Diego burst out laughing. "Asshole. That's what she calls you?"

The server returned, setting our drinks in front of us. I hadn't ordered, but she placed a soda in front of me.

Caden waited 'till she left and grabbed his beer, watching me the whole time. "Apparently."

Diego was loving this. "To her credit, you can be."

Caden frowned. "Yeah, and you like when I'm an asshole, especially when I back you up after you get yourself in some stupid fight."

"I never do that."

"Last night."

Diego quieted, then bobbed his head up and down. "You're right. I could've not punched that guy. That one was on me." He saluted Caden with his drink. "Thank you for having my back."

Caden shook his head, drinking his beer.

Diego didn't seem to care that he wasn't saluted back. He took a long drag from the bottle and set it down. He wiped the back of his arm over his mouth and turned to me. "Now we've gotten through the obligatory chit chat and small talk that's really a facade for how much I care for this big oaf." He winked at me, "Or asshole, as you call him. I want to know more about you. Caden's not brought a girl here with him before." He leaned closer. "Are you two doing?" His hands lifted and began to form a crude gesture—until Caden slapped them down.

"Diego."

Caden was ignored. Diego lowered his voice. "I mean it. Are you guys? Because if not, I'm serious about my invitation. You can sleep in my bed any day or night of the week. I'm here for you." He raked me up and down, his smirk showing again. "All of you."

"Fuck this." Caden stood, holding his beer. "I'm headed inside. I thought I saw someone I knew in there."

I tried to gauge how furious he was, but to my surprise, he didn't seem angry at all. I knew he'd been mad leaving the country club, but since arriving here the tension had quickly fled. He held my gaze for a split second before turning to go, but even then, he didn't have his usual look.

"How does he look at you, then?"

"What?"

Diego gestured over his shoulder, where Caden had gone. "You said he looked different."

"Oh." I hadn't realized I'd spoken out loud. I shrugged. "He usually looks like he wants to either snap my neck or throw an arm around my shoulder because I amuse him. It's those two things mixed together." I frowned, thinking about it. "It's odd. I've never been looked at like that before." Then again, I hadn't acted like this before either.

Diego pursed his lips, studying me. He hummed under his

breath, holding his drink in his hands. When his head started moving up and down in rhythm with the music, I rolled my eyes.

"What?" I asked him.

"What?"

"Stop. You were thinking something. What was it?"

His eyes narrowed slightly before he leaned back and lifted a shoulder. "Nothing. Maybe something." He grinned crookedly. "But whatever it was, I'm not telling."

"That's annoying."

"I can be annoying. Annoying works for me." He winked as he lifted his drink. "Annoying makes me charming, and girls like charming. I can charm almost anyone's pants off, if I really want to." He shook his head, taking another long drag before setting his drink on the table. "Not you, though. I'm going to pass you up, though it'll pain me. I think I have to."

"Why?"

He leaned back, throwing his arm across the back of Caden's empty chair and kicking out his leg. He had a twinkle in his eye, one that I already recognized as troublesome.

"When it comes to my friends, my true friends, my lips are sealed. And regarding you, and why I'm not going to charm your pants off, my lips have to be sealed. Though it really does pain me. I'm hurting in my heart right now."

I rolled my eyes. "Please." The table of girls had been watching us, and two of them were eyeing Diego openly now. "I've got a feeling that pain won't last long."

He barked out another burst of laughter, shaking his head. "I like you. A lot. If anything goes wrong, you can come here with or without Caden. You hear that? You're welcome here." He gestured around the veranda. "I'm part owner of this place, and what I say goes. And you go. Know that. You're always welcome."

I was touched. "Really?"

He nodded. "Yep. Always welcome. No matter what."

"Thank you, Diego."

"Oh." He laughed again, waving his hand in a dismissing motion. "My name's not really Diego. I'm David. Everyone calls me Diego, though. You can call me whatever you'd like. And now that we're bosom buddies, tell me all about Caden. He's been coming here for the last couple years, but he doesn't talk much. I want to hear it all." He leaned close, waiting for me to spill some Caden beans.

CHAPTER TWELVE

I didn't tell Diego anything, but I didn't know anything to tell. Caden was a big deal. That's all I knew. And Marcus. And how Caden had sicced Marcus on Kevin before we came here.

I must've been grinning, because Caden asked, "Do I want to ask what you're thinking?"

I would've flushed, but my face had been on perpetual hot flash since we'd gotten to Diego's. I hadn't moved from our table, except to visit the bathroom. And those trips had been a quick dash with my head down as I veered right back to my seat. Only there could I relax. We were in the corner, and even though I knew people were watching, or could be watching, it hadn't bothered me. I'd felt protected having both Caden and Diego there.

Between laughing at Diego's stories, and then laughing at Diego's stories *about* Caden, I'd started sipping Caden's drink. The sipping turned into having my own beer, and soon Caden wasn't getting any at all. It was just me.

When Diego went to the bathroom, I asked Caden if he could get in trouble since I was underage.

"Nah." He didn't seem too worried. "If the cops show up, we'll run out the back. Diego's is a family-owned bar and restaurant. Cops like him. They like his family too. They donate a shit ton for their softball team. They won't be checking. Just don't pass out in the bathroom or something." At the thought of it, he eyed me up and down. "You're not that bad, are you? You've only had two of my beers."

Two beers, and I'd sipped one more before that, but my stomach still did a backwards flip at that moment. I pressed my hand over it. "I didn't eat all day. I don't think those nachos were a Tinder match with all the beer."

He leaned forward. "You need to go?" His expression grew serious.

"Can you drive?"

He nodded. "I'm good. I stopped drinking a while ago. It's been only water for me."

Diego returned to the table as we were standing up. He had another two drinks in hand. "No. Are you leaving?"

"We are. I need to check on Colt before it's too late. I'll miss my chance."

Colt? That was the second time Caden had mentioned the name, and I sensed he was involved somehow with his need to get drunk and laid earlier—which hadn't happened. Only I was drunk, and there'd been no sexing. I should probably apologize for that, but I was distracted. *Who was Colt?*

Diego nodded. "Ah, yes. I can see that. Tell him hello from me. You need to bring him here too." His eyes fell on me and lit up. "And this beautiful one. Please bring her again."

Placing the drinks on a table, he wrapped his arms around me, lifting me in the air for a tight squeeze. He set me back on my feet, but his hands rested on my shoulders.

"I've enjoyed her. If all your friends from the university are like her, bring more friends."

A quick scowl formed on Caden's face. "They're not."

That killed the mood. Or it would've if Diego hadn't been Diego.

His smile flickered, but he still beamed at me. "Well, then keep her close, and I insist she comes again." His eyes lit up and he snapped his fingers. "For the family picnic night. I know Felicia asked you to come." He shifted, wrapping his arm around my shoulders and pulling me to his side. "Now you have a built-in date."

Caden's scowl lifted a bit, and he gave a grudging, "Maybe," before jerking his head toward the fence. "We're going to go. I paid our tab."

Diego stiffened. "You didn't—"

Caden waved him off. "I did. You know I pay my way. Come on, Stoltz. Let's go."

I followed behind, feeling attention from everyone on the veranda again. Diego obviously knew a lot of people here, and Caden had told me he cared about the people here, but I was still surprised to see how many called out to him as he passed their tables. More than a few had come over earlier to say hello.

I followed Caden to the fence, feeling all those eyes on my back. A little tingle warmed and spread all through me. I couldn't hold back a smile, and I didn't want to. I felt special.

But this wasn't real. I wasn't really *with* Caden. I'd forced my way into his vehicle, and he'd let me come with him. Still, I'd had a taste of what it would be like as his girlfriend, and it had been magical. Whoever he dated, I envied her.

Then he was over the fence. I waited, anticipating. Like last time, he merely reached for me. His hands found my waist, and lifted me up and over—like a girl in any fairy tale.

He placed me in front of him, and I closed my eyes for just a second, and savored the feeling. It wouldn't last. I didn't know if it would ever happen again, but I was buzzed enough to admit something to myself.

I wouldn't have minded being his girlfriend.

"Ready?" He stepped around me, and just like that, the moment was done.

"Mmm-hmmm." I walked beside him the short distance to the Land Rover, but it wasn't until we pulled up in front of my dorm that I thought about asking the obvious question.

"Why did you let me go with you tonight?"

His forehead wrinkled, but he didn't pretend about what I was really asking. He shrugged, relaxing back in his seat with the engine still running. "I thought you were another Matthews groupie."

My gaze fell to the floor.

"Then I thought you were another one of him—a pain in the ass—but you weren't."

I looked back up, but Caden wasn't looking at me. He peered out the window, almost lost in his own thoughts.

"I don't know Avery very well, but I know she dated my brother, and I know he wasn't as much of an ass when he was with her. And that girl seems to like you. I figured out you weren't much like your stepbrother at Marcus' party." A twinge of humor lined his voice. "You made me laugh when you stood next to those girls and stared right at us. Marcus was on edge because Avery was there, and they'd all been pretending he wasn't there, but then you came out." He turned to look at me and grinned.

My heart fluttered.

"I liked that you didn't pretend," he said. "I'm surrounded by too many people who do."

I stamped down the fluttering. That was a bad idea. Very bad. I coughed. "So, what you see is what you get with me."

"I guess so. You're a little awkward in some social situations, but you're not fake. You're honest. And you're funny."

I am?

"I like that about you."

I was warm all over. "Thank you for letting me come."

I reached for the handle and was about to open the door when he stopped me. "I didn't *let* you, Stoltz. You kept me company. That's different."

My throat swelled. "Thank you for that, and I'm sorry you didn't get drunk or have sex tonight."

He smirked. "The night's still young."

"Oh."

He laughed. "I'll see you tomorrow, I'm sure. Have a good one."

I got out and headed inside, this time not caring about the girls who noticed I'd gotten out of Caden Banks' vehicle. I was funny, honest, and awkward. He liked me.

The flutters started again, and I didn't try to stop them.

I was on cloud nine all day the next day, and my classes sailed by. The girl I was partnered with for a project in my last class had kept giving me weird looks, but I didn't care. I kept on doing me, and I only felt better as I headed back to the dorm at the end of the day. I hummed under my breath as I passed Avery's room on the way to mine. She was just leaving.

"Hey," she called.

"Hey back." I smiled on the way to my room.

"Have you talked to Caden today?" Her gaze shifted away. "Or anyone else?"

My smile faded, and I stopped. I looked over my shoulder. "What are you talking about?"

"Caden. You took off with him last night, right?"

I nodded. "Yeah." She'd mentioned anyone else. Why'd she say that?

My euphoria was leaving. Avery was about to pull the rug out from under my feet. I waited for it. "Why?"

"Was he pissed when he dropped you off?"

She should've asked what we did last night, where we went. She wasn't saying anything about that. She didn't ask if I got laid. There was no excitement. She was all business. The rug started to move.

I swallowed tightly. "He was fine."

"Was he drunk? Everyone's saying he was drunk."

"No. He had a couple at first, but he was sober. He drove home."

"Oh." I heard the worry in her voice.

"Did something happen last night?" I slowly pulled my bag around to hug it to my chest. "Is Caden okay?"

She snorted. "Caden's just fine." She began backing away. "I wasn't there, and I have to get a meeting, but you might want to call him. I know you guys have some type of friendship going on."

"What happened?" I started after her.

"Call him, Summer."

"Why? What'd he do?"

She was at the door to the stairs now. She paused and let out a sigh. "He beat the shit out of someone last night."

"Who?"

"Your stepbrother."

One quick yank and the rug was gone. I was on my ass.

CHAPTER THIRTEEN

I didn't have Caden's phone number so I tried Kevin. No answer, so pulling on my big-girl panties, I marched the eight blocks to their frat house.

Okay, I didn't march. I started out marching. I was dragging myself when I finally got to their block. My calves were tight and burning.

Note to self: I needed to work out more—or *at all*. This was embarrassing for a sports medicine major.

I walked up their front sidewalk and rang the bell.

I wasn't sure who to ask for, Caden or Kevin. For some reason, the sympathy card wasn't there for my stepbrother. With the shit he'd been doing, he probably had it coming. I knew Caden wouldn't kick me out this time, but as I waited for someone to answer, I still felt some nerves in my gut.

…and I kept waiting.

And waiting…

I frowned, knocking again, this time harder.

"It's a frat." A girl spoke up behind me, reaching around me to open the door. She held a box in her hand and stepped inside. "Just go in. No one's going to answer the door unless there's a cop on the other side."

That made complete sense.

I followed her in, and sure enough, the living room was full of guys playing a video game. Across the hall two other guys stood around the pool table. The girl yelled out a greeting. The guys gave her distracted hellos before she disappeared down the hallway and up the stairs.

I stood in the foyer.

And no one cared.

The pool game finished, and both guys walked past me, into the kitchen. The video game ended, so the guys rotated. One of the players who'd finished sat down on the couch to watch, and the other started to walk past me.

"Hey!" I stood in front of him.

"Hey." He looked me up and down. A second, and much warmer, "Hey" came out, and he stepped closer to me. "Who are you here for?"

I scratched my chin. *Kevin or Caden?* "Is Kevin Matthews here?"

"Oh." He sounded disappointed, and he pointed to the basement. "If he's not in his room down there, who knows. He got his ass kicked last night. You're the new chick already?"

"New chick?"

"He and the old one split yesterday, in a nasty way. He got his ass handed to him last night, so if you're going down for a quick poke, expect to be on top."

"I'm not here for that." I frowned. "And not with him."

"Oh?" Interest bloomed in his eyes.

"Not with you either." Then, screw it. "Is Caden here?"

His shoulders dropped completely. "Him too?"

"No." Everyone just assumed sex all the time. Was that normal? "We're kind of friends, I think."

"I don't know if Matthews is here, but I know Caden isn't."

"Do you know when he'll be back?"

He headed down the hallway, shaking his head. "Caden doesn't really answer to anyone."

Kevin's door was slightly ajar, and I pushed it open to see him putting clothes into a box. With his back to me, he was flinging shirts, pants, socks, and shoes across the room. I wasn't sure what to say. I could tell he was upset, but this wasn't a situation where he would want my opinion. *Support.* That was my purpose here. I was here in the family capacity, because that's where our relationship needed to go.

"Hey."

He whipped around, instantly tense, but when he saw me his shoulders dropped back down, loosening. "Oh. It's you. Hey." He turned back and grabbed a pair of shoes, tossing them into the box on the floor. "What are you doing here?"

I circled around him. "Stop."

He had two massive black eyes, half his face was swollen and bruised, and he had a cracked lip. I checked his knuckles. They were split open as well, dried blood covering them. "When did you clean these last?"

He snorted, tucking them back by his side. "Right. It'd be nice if someone helped me with that."

"No one did?" I sat on his bed as he went back to his closet, pulling out more clothes. "What are you doing?"

"What do you think? I'm moving out. This fucking fraternity isn't a brotherhood. Loyalty, my ass. They all chose him."

"They kicked you out?"

"No." He whipped a sandal at the box, but it hit the side and fell to the floor. "I'm leaving. I'm not staying here, not when they take his side over mine."

"Okay." Pressure built behind my temples. I felt a headache forming. "What happened? Avery told me Caden beat you up last night?"

"Avery?" He shifted back to me, going still.

I gulped. "Yeah."

"She hates Maggie. You know that, right?"

I was confused. "No, they're friends. But wait—are you still with Maggie?"

"Why wouldn't I be? She's my girlfriend now."

My mind whirled. "Didn't you get in a fight because of Maggie?"

"What?"

"Wait. Back up. What happened yesterday? I saw you in the parking lot. Then you took off, and the next time I saw you, you were kissing Maggie behind a palm tree at the country club."

"You were there?"

I nodded. *No thanks to you.* "Caden and Marcus were talking, and I was on my way to tell you to stop, you were going to get caught, but then—" I caught myself. I'd been about to tell him Avery stopped me. "I got distracted. I had to find the bathroom."

"What then?"

He remained uncharacteristically still.

Alarms were going off in my head. I had to tread lightly, but I didn't know why. "I, uh, ended up just getting a ride home."

"That was it?"

"Uh-huh." I blinked a few times. "Why? Did something happen at the country club?"

He regarded me for another beat, then he tossed a pair of socks into the box. "You could say that again. Caden ratted us out. My own fraternity brother. Can you believe that? What a piece of shit."

"Yeah," I remarked. "Your fraternity brother told his *real* brother...that sucks."

Kevin collapsed in his desk chair. He bent forward to rest his elbows on his knees and cradled his head. "I know, but whatever. It happened. Yes, Maggie and I were making out, and yes, we should've been more discreet, but Caden Banks is a huge asshole."

I almost couldn't take it. I had to actually sit on my hands. Kevin was a dipshit. My sarcasm went over his head. *Support, Summer. Support. You're here to support him, whether you agree with what he's doing or not. S-u-p-p-o-r-t.*

I had to clamp down on my tongue to keep from saying something snotty. I was not in a supportive mood.

I was trying, though. "Well, I mean, now you don't have to hide anymore. Right?"

"Yeah." He looked up, and his face relaxed into a grin. "You're right. That is one good thing. And after tonight, I won't have to live with these dickwads anymore."

I eyed the box. "Where are you going to live?"

"Maggie's parents. She said I could move in there. She's been alternating between the house and her dorm room, but since I'll be there, she'll move back full time." He perked up. "It's a pretty big place, too. I've been there a few times. It'll be nice, you know? A break from school political bullshit."

"Yeah." I had no other words. I couldn't wrap my head around what was going on.

He had been sleeping with someone else's girlfriend. Her boyfriend was the real brother to one of his fraternity brothers, and Kevin was acting like the victim. My bullshit meter was off the charts, probably along with my blood pressure.

So all I said was, "Yeah."

He frowned, a line forming in the middle of his forehead. "Thank you."

"For what?"

He motioned around his room. "For coming here. For checking on me." His eyes softened, matching his smile and tone. "For caring."

My heart flip-flopped. There he was. There was the Kevin I'd crushed on for years and fallen in love with, the one I'd slept with three and a half months ago. I instantly scowled. Brother. He was my stepbrother. Enough with the annoying feelings, and whatever was underneath them.

"Oh, no problem." My voice was raspy. I could feel the big black hole my feelings for him were covering up. Why was I so scared to feel whatever that was? "I wanted to be sure you were okay after I heard about the fight."

"That was bullshit too. Marcus caught us yesterday, and there was a whole huge scene, but no fighting. Maggie went home with him. I didn't hear anything about it again until late last night. I was in my room, minding my own business, when Marcus burst into the house. Maggie dumped him, and he couldn't take it that I got his girl out from underneath him."

"Did he hit you?"

"No. He just shoved me into the wall and was yelling. That was it. Everything was fine and calming down when Caden showed up. As soon as he stepped inside, I don't know what happened, but Marcus went crazy. He was yelling things about a horse or something, and those two looked ready to battle it out. I was just in the wrong place at the wrong time. Those two were duking it out—"

"Hitting each other?"

"—yelling, and then suddenly Caden turned and popped me in the mouth. I didn't do anything. I was just standing here, watching. That was it."

Kevin began talking faster, louder. "I fought back. I got him right in the face. I'm sure that dick had to go to the hospital. I mean, I would've, if I'd been hit as hard as I got him."

I was pretty sure his bruises turned another shade while he was talking.

"And these bastards, guys who are supposed to be my brothers, took his side." He shoved the chair back, surging to his feet and pointing to his chest. "They told me to get out of the room. Me. *Me!* He coldcocked me, and I was supposed to leave the room."

Feeling some unease, I shifted on the bed, sliding my hands out from under my legs. I rested them next to me, pressing them into the cover.

"What happened after that?" My mouth was dry.

He flung a hand up, his middle finger extended, to point at the door. "I came in here and called Maggie. She picked me up, and I stayed with her last night. This is the first time I've been back. I don't even know if the guys know I'm down here." He looked me up and down. "Did they tell you I was down here?"

"The guy I asked didn't know."

He rolled his eyes, cursing under his breath. "Figures. They're always going to take Caden's side. It's like he walks on water around these parts. I'm sick of it. Hey!" An idea came to him. His eyes suddenly focused right on me. "Are you busy this weekend?"

I glanced away before answering. "Why?"

"The guys are going to the football game. I'm going to grab the rest of my stuff when they're gone. I could use all the help I can get."

I was at a loss for words.

"Really?" That was it. That was all I could manage.

No. Wait. I added, "Huh."

"Maggie said she'd ask some of her friends, and I'll call our parents. I'm sure your dad would come up and help." He inspected the box and then opened his second closet door. More boxes were stacked in there. "I don't have that much. Desk, bed, and dresser all stay here." He kicked at one of the boxes. "I'll need more of these. Maybe I won't need your dad after all, but then again, you're all girls. You won't be able to lift these. You think you could call your dad for me?"

My eyebrows arched, and I had to swallow a ball of disbelief. "You want me to call and have him come four hours to carry some boxes?"

"It'd give you two time to bond. I'm sure he'd want to take you out to dinner."

My mouth fell open. I couldn't even.

"He could stay over," Kevin continued. "He'd have to get a hotel room. I wouldn't feel comfortable asking Maggie if he could stay at her parents' house. That wouldn't be right."

He was—I didn't know what he was. Considerate, sensitive, rational—those were all things he was *not*. My anger grew more and more as he kept talking. I had to get out of here. If I didn't, I was going to blow up, and I didn't want to say something I'd regret later.

I stood and gestured to the door. "I'm going to head out. I just wanted to check on you. I see you're still alive."

I meant to leave after that, but he caught me. He touched my arm, pulled me in for a hug. I stiffened, but he didn't seem to mind. He buried his head in the crook of my neck.

"Thank you. I mean it. Thank you for coming. It means a lot." He let go, leaning back but still holding me in his arms.

My heart would've soared not long ago.

He smiled down at me. "I've taken you for granted. I'm sorry, Summer. I really am."

Standing there, in his arms again, and with those words carrying a note of sincerity—my heart still did another somersault, and I hated myself.

I stepped back until his hands fell to his side. "I'll see you later, Kevin."

He waved. "See you. Don't forget to call your dad. Thanks!"

He shouted the last word at me as I hurried down the hall. Once through the basement door, I leaned back against it.

I closed my eyes and cursed. *Fucking hell.*

"So you *do* have feelings for him?"

I recognized Caden's voice, and my heart froze.

CHAPTER FOURTEEN

Caden looked delicious.

That was my first thought as I stood there, unsure what to say. Jerking away from the basement door, I tried to speak, but my jaw had ceased working for some reason.

He had a beer in hand, his jeans riding low on his hips. His tattoos peeked out from under his shirt. It was nothing except a simple white T-shirt, but holy goodness—it was a sight, hugging his body. I could see every stomach muscle he had. They bulged, stretched, and shifted as he lifted that beer to his lips.

I licked my lips, and I even knew I'd licked my lips. *Goddamn.*

Then I clued in to one simple fact: the annoying Kevin flutters were gone.

Caden laughed bitterly, moving around me. "I thought you would at least lie, but no. Gotta hand it to you, Stoltz. You're honest to a fault." He moved past me and glanced down with a half-smirk. "Thanks for that."

"Wait." I turned with him, following him down the hallway and out a back door. "What do you mean?"

We crossed the backyard, and I followed Caden inside the shed. It was like a mini apartment. A coat rack hung to my left with a bathroom right in front of me. The first part of the room was a living room, with a sectional couch in front of a large projector screen. The kitchen was against the back of the shed, and as I stood there, taking everything in, Caden set his beer down on a counter and ducked behind the bathroom into a bedroom. He left the door open as he reached up to pull his shirt off.

My heart jolted.

Holy mother of—desire like I'd never felt before rushed over me. It started low and exploded. I should've looked away, but all restraint was gone. I found myself tracing every part of him, even the muscles leading down into his jeans, which, as he finished tugging a shirt down, dipped even lower.

Primal lust rippled in me, taking a dizzying hold, and when Caden lifted his head, his eyes finding me, he saw it. I knew he did. He paused, his eyes darkening in response. Then that damned smirk was back, and he came toward me.

My heart leaped to my throat.

He was going to touch me...nope. He didn't. He went right past me, his arm grazing mine as he asked, his breath teasing my ear, "Want a beer?"

Then he was gone, moving a safe distance away.

The refrigerator opened behind me. I didn't move. For a second, I stood with my back to him and tried to get control of myself. I raked my hands through my hair and silently cursed. My hands were trembling.

I'd always been in control around Kevin. Always. I might've been delusional, seeing things that weren't there and convincing myself he was half in love with me too, but the entire time, I'd had total and complete control.

I saw Caden with his shirt off, and I damn near wet my pants. Literally.

I drew in a ragged breath.

"I know I'm hot, but don't get ahead of yourself."

This was so embarrassing, but I forced myself to turn around. He held a beer out for me, his smirk too suggestive and cocky for his own good.

He added, "It's called the rebound. It's a knee-jerk response."

I took the beer. It was cold. I wrapped both my hands around it and was half tempted to rub it over my face. "What are you talking about?"

"I don't know what Matthews did to you, but it's obvious he broke your heart."

The lust was fading…kind of…it was on a low simmer now. "On a scale from one to ten, where ten is being blatantly billboard kind of obvious, where do you place me?"

He studied me for a beat. "An eight."

I sucked in my breath. "Are you serious?"

He sat at one end of his couch and kicked his feet up on the coffee table. I took the other end, sitting sideways so I faced him.

"Just because of the first night. If I hadn't seen you that night, I'd never know."

"Really?" I could breathe easier.

"You're attracted to me because I hurt the person who hurt you."

I gave him a dubious look.

"Or not?" His eyes narrowed, thoughtfully.

"Have you seen yourself?" I blurted.

He'd been lifting his beer for a drink. His hand froze in mid-air and his eyes widened a fraction before he shook his head. The smirk morphed into a smile. "Why are you wasting yourself on your stepbrother?"

"What?"

He put his beer down and leaned forward, moving his feet to the floor. "No bullshit. I took you to Diego's last night. You made me laugh when I normally would've stayed angry and screwed some girl I didn't give a shit about. So no bullshit between us now. Got it?"

I bobbed my head. "Got it." I grabbed the top of the couch and held on, unsure what was coming at me.

"Your stepbrother is a dick. Why do you have feelings for him?"

I had no answer for him. I just knew I was really afraid of letting those feelings go, though at the same time I desperately wanted to. I couldn't explain any of it. But there was a different something else going on with Caden and me, something underneath the layer of words and moments of honesty between us. I didn't know what that was either, but it held me suspended. I didn't breathe. I didn't formulate a word or a thought. I was just feeling, and I felt myself pulled toward him.

His eyes darkened again, almost smoldering, but he didn't close the distance. His head remained tilted toward mine as he waited for my answer.

"Um…" I tried to remember the question.

His voice softened. "Why do you have feelings for him?"

Because you can't control who you love. And I have to, or — I stopped myself. I couldn't finish that thought. I lifted a shoulder, holding it against my cheek for some reason, like it was keeping me grounded.

"Sometimes you can't choose." I was too lost to even try talking about whatever else was happening.

Caden's gaze left me, and so did whatever storm had been going on. I felt released somehow.

He murmured, almost to himself, "I suppose."

My teeth sunk into my lip, and then I remembered my reason for coming in the first place. Scanning his face and hands again, I noted, "You don't have any bruises on you."

"Like your stepbrother could touch me."

"He said you probably had to go to the hospital."

His lip curled into a slow smile. "That's funny."

"So you didn't? You're okay, I mean?"

He glanced to me, his eyes warming. "I'm okay."

"What happened?"

"Kevin walked into a fight that wasn't his, and he made it his. He started mouthing off."

"You hit him?"

He nodded, looking down. "He walked into my fist. A few times." He sighed. "And I'd been wanting to hit him for a really long time, since last year when he hurt a friend of mine."

My ears perked up. "A friend of yours?"

"I think she was the second girlfriend? He had quite a few last year."

My mind was going, trying to remember what Avery had said about Claudia. Was she girlfriend number three or two? Did that mean Claudia and Caden were friends?

"Is her name Claudia?"

"No. And I'm not telling you her name."

"But it wasn't Claudia?" Claudia who was gorgeous, tough, and a bitch because she trying to be strong for her friends. When he shook his head, I explained, "She's the first one who made a big deal about you. It would've made sense then."

"A big deal out of me?"

The knots, whether formed from desire or something else, were beginning to loosen now, and I sank back into the couch. My chest felt looser too.

"When you gave me a ride home after that party, Claudia couldn't believe it. She told me something about how you weren't known for dealing with underclassmen, and certainly not freshmen. She said you weren't mean, but not that nice either."

"She told you that?" He leaned forward. Slowly.

My neck stiffened, but I nodded. "Yeah."

"Then she's a bitch, and she doesn't know me." The corner of his mouth curved up again. "I have nothing against giving freshman girls rides."

I would've rolled my eyes, knowing it was a joke, but Claudia's assessment of me still stung. I couldn't hide it. Caden watched me. I knew he'd figure it out, and a moment later, the couch shifted. He reached over—my stomach twisted—and tugged me next to him. He pulled me into his side, his arm draped over my shoulder.

I sagged into him. I couldn't help myself. He was warm, strong, and fast becoming an addiction.

"I don't know why she said that to you, but I've had people around me all my life who judge and misperceive things. I have a reputation. I know that, and some of it is true, but most of it isn't. One of the truths is that I am picky about my friends."

"Yeah?" I looked up.

He tapped the cleft in my chin. "And for whatever reason, you've become one of them."

"Yeah?"

"Yeah."

We sat like that. It felt nice. It felt right. We watched television, and every time Caden got up for a beer, he brought one back for me and resumed our position. Eventually he laid down on the couch. I shifted so I was half sprawled on top. I was three beers in by then, and with the feel of his arm over my back, holding me in place, and my cheek resting against his chest, hearing his steady heartbeat, I fell asleep.

I woke once when he carried me to a bed and pulled the covers over me. He asked when I had to get up the next morning, and then the light streaming from the door darkened.

The sun shone into the room, and it took me a few moments to realize where I was. I didn't recognize the king-size bed, or the black sheets, but then Caden walked past the open door and all the memories flooded into place.

I slept at his place.

I glanced around the bed... I slept in his bed!

"Your alarm's about to go off in ten minutes," Caden called from the doorway. He had a cup of coffee in hand and wore only jeans.

I tried to keep my eyes front and center, but I lost. The tattoos were a nice little zig-zag pattern, pulling my gaze down, all the way down. Caden's slow, smooth chuckle told me he knew what I'd just done. My cheeks only warmed a little.

I shot him a look, falling back to the pillow. "I feel like this should be the first skip day of my school career."

"You've never skipped before?"

I shook my head, rolling it side to side on the pillow. "Am I missing out? Should I embrace my inner deviant?"

He smirked. "You can skip a class for any reason in the world. It's your life."

I sat up, eyeing that coffee. "You were supposed to be the bad influence."

His eyebrow lifted. "I'm not selling it enough?" He lifted his cup. "You want some coffee?"

"I'm wondering if today is the day I try coffee too."

"You've never had coffee?"

"I'm beginning to think I'm lame." I thought about it. "Really lame."

"You slept at some guy's house last night. Think of it that way." His smirk was back. "Not so lame now."

I could do one better. "I slept at a *fraternity* house."

"*And* you drank beer."

"It was the second night in a row that I drank beer."

"See? Not so lame after all."

"You're right." I sat up. "I'm halfway to total badass."

He grinned. "We cuddled last night, and you could think of it as dry humping. You almost got some last night."

Except I hadn't, and we were in the friend zone. Why were my hands curling around the covers into tight balls? I glanced down and forced them to loosen, then shrugged, trying to be the nonchalant badass I was.

"You carried me to bed. Almost the same thing."

Suddenly, the joking was gone, and his eyes burned. I could feel his heat from across the room, and my body reacted, instantly warming even before he said a word.

"Nothing's the same as sliding inside," he murmured after a moment. "The feel of being in there, feeling that clench around you, knowing you can push as deep as you want, as hard or gently as you want. Nope. I've gotta step off the joke train for a moment here. Nothing is remotely the same as that feeling."

Fuck. My pulse spiked.

He tossed me a look. "Maybe I'll cop a feel the next time."

I pretended to groan. "One more notch on my badass peg. You better cop a feel next time."

"Is that all I am to you? A notch on the bedpost? I feel so used, Stoltz."

Okay. My last name. We were back on familiar ground here. But my grin was still a little shaky.

"Get used to it, Banks. I'm only disguised as this plain Jane. Inside there's a wild woman just waiting to be let loose."

He didn't reply.

He stared at me for a few more seconds, then straightened from the doorway. "There's nothing plain about you, Summer. Don't let some dickhead like your stepbrother make you think like that." He saluted me with his coffee. "I'll make you something special. There'll be no turning back for you after this morning. You'll be a coffee lover."

He left, and I felt a tiny bit faint. "Only a coffee lover?"

CHAPTER FIFTEEN

Caden gave me a ride back to my dorm, and there was nothing awkward about it.

Nope. Not at all. Just friends here. Here was me, getting a ride back from a pal…who was gorgeous and I was currently fantasizing about. Yep, just platonic. Nothing more.

I was lying to myself, but I still enjoyed the looks I got when I exited his Land Rover and headed inside. More than a handful of girls did double-takes when they saw Caden.

I had a couple classes that day, and one I made it to was Intro to Physiology. I picked my seat and sat back, then shot upright as Marcus came down the aisle with two friends. It was a big class, but I know I would have noticed him in here. What was he doing?

He saw me and glared as he passed my seat.

Whatever. I wasn't his enemy. I wasn't Kevin. I looked away, slumping forward on the desk. I could feel his hot gaze on the back of my neck the entire class. If he could've given me a sunburn, I had no doubt he would've. The girl next to me tried talking to me. I must've responded because she didn't seem to think I was rude, but if someone had asked me what we talked about, I would've had no idea. *Where had Marcus been the first two weeks?*

The girl must've noticed that I kept sneaking glances back at him. "You got a thing for Marcus Banks?"

"No." I frowned. "How do you know him?"

She gave me a wry look. "Everyone knows him, and his brother."

"I didn't know he was in this class."

"He wasn't. A friend of mine has a mad crush on him. Don't ask me how, but she knows his schedule. He switched hours for some reason, so he's in here with us now."

"Oh." Joy.

When class was done, she stood with me. "Hey, uh. Would you like to study together sometime?"

I was going to say yes, but Marcus' gaze found mine and I forgot everything else. His jaw set in a determined look, and I gulped.

"I gotta go," I told the bewildered girl. I hot-footed out of there and didn't slow until I was a few buildings away. Looking back, I didn't think Marcus had followed me, so I calmed a little.

I needed to catch up on some studying, but Avery stopped by my room later that night. I thought maybe she'd ask about Caden, but she didn't. She wanted to gossip about Kevin.

I had to remind myself that was a good thing. If she only came to talk about Caden, it would be weird. I told her what I knew about the Kevin situation. He was still with Maggie, and he was moving in with her parents. I'd agreed to be a lame ass and help him move this weekend.

I never called my dad, though. The line was drawn there.

I was surprised when Avery said she'd help too, and when she showed up that Saturday morning, she'd gotten a few others to help, including a couple guys. Kevin and Maggie were shocked, but Maggie and Avery hugged at the end of the sweaty day.

I wondered then if Avery came more because of their friendship, rather than just to help me. Over the next few weeks, I was right. Maggie started coming over to the dorm to see Avery, a lot. At the same time, I settled into a pattern of going to classes and eating dinner or lunch with Avery and the girls. I began to study with my physiology classmate, and sometimes some of our floormates sat with Avery and me at lunch. Of course, her friends weren't ecstatic about that, but it was Avery. Everyone loved her, and to their credit, I'm sure my floormates were confused when they saw me with her. I don't think they realized we were friends outside of the dorm.

One night, I was heading out to see Caden as Maggie was coming into the dorm. I asked Avery later if she'd told Maggie about Caden and me. She shook her head, and I was relieved.

My friendship with Caden wasn't a secret, but it wasn't something I broadcasted. I knew other girls would misinterpret how much time I spent at his place. I hung out there most nights. Sometimes I studied. Sometimes I watched movies, but I mostly watched sports and drank beer with his fraternity brothers. They never hit on me, and they never acted weird when they saw me. I was accepted.

Avery asked me one time if I was heading to Caden's, and I stopped short. I felt like I'd been caught cheating, but then she laughed and waved me on.

"Go have fun. Don't feel bad about being friends with Caden Banks. I can tell you do. People might not understand it, but they don't need to."

"What do you mean?"

"Nothing." She gave me reassuring smile. "I mean it. People just don't know you, so there's buzz about who you are. People have noticed that you walk there, and he drops you off later. His fraternity brothers always say hi to you on campus too."

I knew all that, but hearing it made it more real.

"Has Kevin said anything about it?" Avery asked.

My panic bloomed, and I shook my head. "I think he's still in MaggieLand." I wasn't looking forward to him checking on me, though. I was friends with someone he considered an enemy. #betrayal

She snorted. "I think Maggie's getting sick of him."

"What do you mean?"

"She's been here a lot. She said something the other night how her parents asked Kevin if he was going to find his own apartment or move back to campus. He got all upset about that, and Maggie came here, saying she was fed up with him."

That wasn't his normal method. "Kevin usually cheats first, and then gets dumped. The girl doesn't get tired of him."

"Until now. A girl is finally going to get fed up with him. It's inevitable."

"Yeah. Maybe."

"And because I really suck at transitioning, I'm just going to drop the bomb on you."

"What?"

She glanced down, picking at her nails. "Um. Okay..." Her throat worked up and down. "I have a weird favor to ask you."

Why was she suddenly nervous? This was not like Avery at all.

She took a breath and let it out. "Marcus and I might be... maybe...I don't know what we're doing really, but I think we might be getting back together."

"What?!" I started to smile.

She waved that off. "No. Don't get all excited. I don't know what's going on or even if something is happening again. He's been calling, and we've eaten lunch together a few times at the cafe on campus. I mean, there's more. We've been fooling around a little, but only a little. Please don't judge." She drew in a ragged breath. "I'm almost pissing my pants just thinking about it, but *ugh*. Anyway, I was thinking that since you're friends with me and Caden, maybe the four of us could go bowling together."

I furrowed my eyebrows together. "Bowling? I thought Marcus hated me?"

"He doesn't hate you."

I was pretty sure he did. Class was always awkward. I always felt him glaring at me, but she sounded excited. "You sure Marcus is okay with that?"

"Oh, yes. It'll be great." She brushed my concern away. "You. Caden. Me. Marcus."

"That sounds like a double date."

"No. Yes. I mean, kinda? It's not really. Unless you and Caden are dating. Are you guys dating?"

"What?"

"Dating. Is that what you're doing?"

"No." I shook my head, maybe a bit too quickly. "No way. We're friends. That's it, but wouldn't that be awkward for you and Marcus? Unless that's the intention? You really would be dating again then?"

She groaned, pressing her fingers to her temples. "I don't know if I can handle dating Marcus again." She dropped her hands and true agony shone back at me.

My heart clenched.

"He broke me last time. He says he didn't start seeing Maggie until a couple months later, but I've always felt like he dropped me for her. Obviously it's not something she and I talk about."

I surged forward, grabbing her hands. I squeezed them. "Then it's a friend thing. I'll mention it to Caden, but I'm sure he'll be fine with it. And just friends." I raised her hands between us. "I mean it. Just friends. Just focus on that. Don't get ahead of yourself with Marcus, not unless you really want to go there."

"Okay." She nodded to herself, closing her eyes. "Okay. You're right. I'll just focus on being friends with Marcus first. First friends, my new motto."

I nodded with her. "Thatta girl."

Her grin became crooked. "Well, the benefits are there too, but nothing more. I won't focus on anything more."

"What?" My head went the other way, left to right. "No, no, no. First friends, only friends. Say it with me."

She laughed and repeated with me, but it was bullshit. We both knew it.

I had assumed Avery and I would drive together to the bowling alley, but she had other plans. She said she was coming with Marcus because they were doing something else before they met us. She'd launched into a long explanation, but it was too complicated. The truth was that she wanted to spend more time with him, have an opportunity to be alone.

The bowling alley wasn't too far away, so I walked from campus.

I was crossing the street as Caden pulled into the parking lot. He slowed and leaned forward to see me better as he turned in. I waited for him. He was shaking his head as he pocketed his keys, coming toward me.

I tried to ignore the little heart flip I always felt at the sight of him. He wore a black leather jacket over a white T-shirt and jeans. I almost missed seeing the snake. He looked like a mean, sexual being, but with muscles, and a jawline that made me want to melt. I sighed. I kept waiting for this attraction to go away, but it'd been almost a month and a half of friendship, and it was still going strong.

In fact…

No. I wasn't going there. I wasn't *more* attracted to him. Not possible. One of these days, something would happen and he'd settle into the brother zone, wouldn't he? All the more reason to enjoy him now.

When he stopped in front of me, smiling down, a delicious thrill zinged me. I cracked a grin, feeling the breath knocked out of me for a second. "What's up?"

"When are you going to stop walking places and just call me for a ride?"

"Never. I'm badass like that."

He rolled his eyes and reached for the door. Holding it open with a hand above my head, he tapped my chin with the other. "I'm just going to start coming to give you a ride everywhere from now on."

"That'd be awkward." I moved ahead of him, enjoying his presence as he let the door go and stepped close behind me. I could feel his heat. It added to that thrill, making me feel buzzed. "That's something you'd do for a girlfriend. I'm not your girlfriend."

"That's something you'd do for a friend, and you are my friend."

"Yeah." A secretive smile tugged at my lips. "How'd that ever happen again?"

He chuckled, stepping up to the desk first. He motioned to me. "One lane."

The attendant asked, "How many games?"

"Reserve three, but my brother sucks. He'll probably quit after two."

"I heard that."

Marcus and Avery came up behind us, and Marcus removed his hand from her back and pretended to pound his brother in the shoulder.

"You're already starting the shit-talking, huh?"

Caden gave his shoe size to the clerk, then said to his brother, "It's not shit-talking when it's the truth."

The two did the man thing where they hit each other's biceps while Avery and I stood and grinned at each other. I'd seen her a few hours earlier, so I didn't feel a hug was necessary, and I eyed Marcus, not sure what to do there. I remained convinced he wasn't a big fan of me. And sure enough, his grin fell away when he saw me. "You, huh?"

I could get behind that. I bobbed my head. "You too, huh?"

Avery's laugh squeaked a bit. "Look at us, already off to a great start."

Caden picked up his bowling shoes. "And there's my brother, showing off his moody-asshole side once again." He shook his head as he passed him. "She's my friend, dipshit. Be nice."

Caden led the way to our assigned lane and sat down to put his bowling shoes on. The rest of us followed, and Avery went with me to pick out a bowling ball.

I tried a hot pink one, but my thumb would've been crushed. I set it back and picked up a yellow one. The finger holes made a smiling face.

"It's weird, isn't it?" Avery said.

"What?" The smiley face ball felt like it was frowning at me. I picked up a purple one and named him Barney.

She reached for the smiling ball. "How Marcus still hates you. It shouldn't bother me, right?" The smiling ball didn't work for her either.

I handed her the Barney one. I wasn't feeling his love. "It would bother me."

She sighed, sinking her fingers into the ball. "I think he still has feelings for Maggie."

There was a rainbow-colored one. I had a feeling it might work. "Or do you think it's just because it still stings? I'm a reminder that he was cheated on. That's gotta suck."

Barney didn't love her either. She waited for my rainbow ball. "If that's the case, he better get over it. He did the same to me."

My feeling was right. Rainbow worked for me. "Get your own ball, woman." I hugged it to my chest.

She laughed. "Are you being a ball hog?"

"When I've found my bowling ball soulmate, hell yes." I turned a nose up at the others. "I had to try many balls before the perfect one came."

She reached for a white ball with a single pink streak, and my heart did little somersaults. I had a feeling I'd be a ball-cheater. The single pink streak was speaking to me. She fitted her fingers in it and lifted it up. "It's perfect." She sighed.

We turned as one, Rainbow and Pink Streak held against our chests, and started back to the guys. They were already warming up.

"Caden's kinda…" She hesitated. "Overwhelming, isn't he?"

"What do you mean?" He was a big teddy bear to me now. Well, a hot and delicious teddy bear that wasn't a teddy bear. He was more of a grizzly bear. No, not even that. What was I thinking? He was a damned panther, but I could hope one day he'd turn into a teddy bear. Much safer.

We stopped a few lanes down from them and watched. Neither seemed to notice us, but I knew that wasn't true. Caden knew we were staring; he just didn't care. He did what he wanted, no matter the audience. He didn't give a damn.

He was raw power, the kind that was primal, rippling over everyone in a room, overtaking them. Avery loved Marcus, I could tell, but she wasn't immune to the effect Caden had on people. It just seeped into your pores, lining your lungs as you breathed. It wasn't a conscious manipulation. He wasn't purposely affecting everyone with his presence, he just did.

"Picture him wearing only underwear," I suggested. "It offsets him a little bit."

Her eyes widened.

"Grandpa underwear," I added.

Her eyes went back to normal, and she shook her head. "It doesn't work. He's Marcus' brother too. That adds to the intimidation factor."

I tried to look at him from her perspective—someone getting back together with his brother—and she was right. Caden was downright scary.

I flashed her an apologetic look. "I'm sorry."

"It'll be fine." She switched Pink Streak to her side. "Besides, it might not work out with Marcus. It didn't before."

"Because of *him*." *I'm not even sure he's good enough for you, Av.* I didn't say those words. She already loved him.

There was no reaction on her face, but she aged in front of me, looking tired and worn for a moment. I noticed a glimmer of sadness in her eyes.

She was scared. He could hurt her again.

I nudged her shoulder with mine, gently. "Let's not think of the hurts right now." I patted Rainbow in front of me. "It's only about Rainbow and Pink Streak tonight. *Mano a mano.*"

"Our bowling balls are male?"

"*Chica a chica.*"

Avery laughed.

Marcus called, "Is the girl talk portion of this evening done with? Avery, we got a game to win."

"My rainbow ball laughs in the face of your arrogance," I told him.

"There's nothing wrong with feeling sure of yourself," Marcus countered.

"Said the lone camper when he didn't realize a hungry lion was behind him."

"What?"

I placed my ball with theirs. Avery did the same, snickering under her breath.

Marcus looked at his brother. 'What the hell?"

Caden shrugged, sitting down behind the score sheet. "Just nod and smile. That's what I do."

I plopped down into the seat beside Caden. "And let the games begin!"

CHAPTER SIXTEEN

Caden won. Marcus was second, but I got the best prize: Most Gutter Balls. Apparently Rainbow and Pink Streak both liked to curve to the left—all the way left. Avery tried to take my win from me, but alas, I had three more gutter balls than her. I was a little miffed there were no trophies. Marcus informed me that I had to join a league for those, but the type of trophy I wanted wasn't handed out.

I sniffed as we headed for the doors. "It's their loss really."

Marcus glanced back with a question in his eyes, but he didn't say anything.

I didn't expect him to. He'd been giving me those looks all evening. Since settling in at college and becoming friends with Caden, I'd embraced my tendency toward random statements. Even I didn't know when they were coming, but they always meant something.

Caden and Avery were used to me. Marcus wasn't. His loss too.

"Dude." Caden placed his hand on his brother's back and urged him forward. "Just keep going. Her comments will hit you as being funny a couple hours later."

"Yeah?" He didn't look convinced.

"Trust me." Caden eyed me. "Once she grows on you, you can't get rid of her."

I perked up. "Like mold."

And again, no reaction from Caden and Avery, but Marcus' eyebrows arched.

Bowling had been fun. It had soon become more fun to watch Marcus' reactions to me than the actual bowling itself. Avery was reserved at first, but she relaxed once she realized Caden didn't care about her. He wasn't mean, he just focused on talking to me or his brother. Then Marcus began teasing her, and the flirting commenced. After that they flirted all night long.

The only bad part had been earlier in the evening when I'd returned from the bathroom.

I'd come back to find Caden's seat empty. Marcus was up on the lane to bowl, and Avery had scooted into Caden's seat.

She'd poked my arm. "How was the bathroom?"

I poked her back. "An adventure to check off my bucket list. I sailed the golden seas and cleansed myself in the Greek sinks. I'm quite proud."

A line marred her forehead. "You keep getting a little bit weirder the longer school goes on, you know?"

I shrugged. "It's like crack cocaine."

"Wha—never mind." She shook her head and gestured over her shoulder. "Who's the girl?"

This had been the bad part.

Caden had been in the bar of the bowling alley, leaning against the counter with his arms crossed over his chest. A girl stood in front of him. She was close, so close I'd felt a growl building in the back of my throat. She was stunning—long blond hair that fell almost to her ass, and it was a cute, tight little ass.

I knew how guys thought. Plus, a table of guys across from them had been checking it out. She wore a short white skirt. If she'd bent over, I was sure her underwear would show, and that was if she was even wearing underwear. She turned to give us a side view of a cropped white shirt that was skin-tight and dipped low. She had long, dark eyelashes and a mole just above her lip, seemingly placed there to give her a Cindy Crawford look. Her lips were a pale pink, and Caden had been watching them intently.

"Dickhead."

I could feel Avery's pity as I spoke. I didn't want to look any more. I slumped in my chair.

I was doomed.

Avery's voice had dropped low. "His arms are crossed over his chest. That means he's closed to her."

I looked again, and as if he'd heard her—even though they were clear across the bowling alley and I knew he couldn't have—his arms dropped to his sides.

I groaned. "He's open to her now."

They'd continued to talk, with smiles, batting eyes, and pouting little lips—that was the girl, not Caden—and then she'd reached out and touched his chest. He didn't bat her hand away, or shift to the side so it would drop. He continued watching her, but his smile seemed more welcoming. She inched closer so her hand and half her arm lay against his chest, then her hand trailed down, all the way to his stomach.

Avery had sucked in her breath.

In the back of my mind, I knew Marcus had probably finished his turn. We needed to turn around, pretend we weren't spying on his brother, but I couldn't bring myself to look away. It was like watching a car accident. People were going to die. Hearts were going to be shattered. And it was my heart getting stomped on.

Caden had wanted to sleep with her. I could tell. Being around him for the last few weeks, I'd started to know when he was interested. There wasn't really a look in his eye, but I felt it in my gut every time, and I'd felt it as I watched him with that girl.

He would've said he wanted to plow her. Judging by how she kept flicking her hair back and touching her face, her other hand still lingering on his stomach, I wouldn't have been surprised if he'd taken her to the bathroom.

I didn't know what would be worse, if he took her now, or if he took me home and called her for an actual date later.

My throat had burned when I got my answer.

The bartender brought over Caden's drink. The girl had leaned forward, brushing her breasts against his chest as she reached behind him for a pen. Grabbing it and holding Caden's arm, she wrote something on him.

"She's giving him her number," Avery had hissed.

"Duh." Marcus had sat in one of the side chairs. "She's hot. I'd get her number too."

Avery had twisted around. "Really?"

"If you didn't exist," he'd quickly added.

"Better." Her tone had been cool, but I'd heard the smile. "Quick thinking, Banks."

Marcus had chuckled, and the fondness in it had me gritting my teeth. I'd torn my gaze away. Finally. Pain smoldered in my stomach.

"Hey." Caden had come walking back. "Who's up?"

"You."

I loved my friend at that moment, so much. Avery's voice had just the right amount of scathing mixed with niceness. I knew Caden had noticed, but he couldn't say anything. I glanced over and saw that she'd covered it up with a fake smile.

"Okay." He'd set his drink in front of me and touched my shoulder. "I got that for you, if you want it."

Fuck him, I'd thought. *Fuck his niceness. Fuck his thoughtfulness, and fuck how he didn't notice when I didn't respond.* I could see her phone number scrawled over his arm like a cute tattoo.

Yes. *Fuck him.*

I'd taken the drink and gulped down half of it.

"Summer, you drink?" Avery asked.

Caden had his ball in hand, poised to take his shot, but he looked back. "She drinks all the time."

Avery gave me an incredulous look.

I shrugged. "I drank at Marcus' party."

"You did?"

Marcus laughed, stretching out his legs and resting an arm across the back of the seats next to him. Avery moved into one of them and relaxed as Marcus began drawing circles on her shoulder.

"If I'm remembering right, you were wasted that night," he told her. "Doubt you'd have the best memory."

"Oh, yeah."

She'd given him a dreamy smile, and I'd wanted to gut punch anyone happy at that moment.

"You okay?" Caden had dropped into his chair again.

I'd given him two thumbs up, stuffing everything down inside. "I'm gut punchy and happy."

His eyes had fallen to my drink. "Maybe you shouldn't have the rest of that."

"Too late." I'd opened my throat and thrown the rest back, letting the booze burn all the way to my liver.

"She's fine," Avery spoke up for me. "She's just tired."

"We can go," Caden had said. "We don't have to play the last game."

Oh, yes, I'd thought. *So you can get home and still have time to call the stunningly beautiful hussy up for a night plow.*

I'd forced a smile. "Sure."

Avery had been watching me when we handed our shoes back, but Marcus pinched her butt. She'd swatted him back, and the flirting distracted her again.

Marcus reached forward now to open the first set of doors on the way out of the bowling alley, but then he paused. He stood there, holding the door open. I'd been waiting for Avery to go ahead, but she didn't. Her shoulders went rigid, and she didn't move.

Two people stepped inside. I could see the top of the guy's head and held my breath. I recognized that hair.

Caden moved forward, his hand sweeping me behind him. He stood between Avery and Marcus, facing the two new people with me tucked in the back. Normally, I'd be all, *Screw that. I want to see the action,* but in this particular moment, I was content to burrow into Caden's backside.

"You guys are back together?"

I felt the growl coming back from earlier. I could hear the disdain in Maggie's voice. Why was Avery friends with her again?

"We're hanging out. Yeah."

"Don't even go there, Maggie." Marcus' voice was a warning. "You've got no say in who I see."

She laughed.

I winced at the sourness.

"You're right," she said. "I have no say, but Avery's boring. You told me so yourself. You think taking her out with your brother and whatever floozy is with him is going to make her fun? Think again, hotshot."

Avery wasn't boring.

I waited, expecting Marcus to say something. He didn't. I waited some more, expecting Avery to say something. She didn't.

My hands balled into fists, pressing into Caden's back. Fuck it. I was going to say something. I pushed forward, but he held firm. He knew I was pissed. One of his hands swept back, touching my side, as if to calm me down. I didn't need calming down. I needed to back my friend up, and I tried again to get through.

He held me back. Again.

So I yelled from behind him, "Avery's not boring!"

"What?"

That came from Kevin, in a sharp strident tone.

"Summer?"

The crowds parted for me. Or, well, Avery and Marcus stepped aside. Caden didn't. He was a big boulder that I couldn't move an inch—not that I minded trying—so I stepped around his side.

Kevin's eyes were narrowed as he took in the way Caden tried to block me with an arm in front. I pressed into it, ignoring the guys and glaring at Maggie. "You're stupid."

She started laughing. "Really?"

"You say stupid things. You sound stupid." It wasn't the best argument, but hey, it was true. She *was* stupid.

"What are you? Five?"

Maybe, but I wasn't done. I gave her a savage smile. When she saw it, she started laughing again. Obviously, she was not taking me seriously. All the better.

I softened my voice. "I don't know who you dated before Marcus, but you messed up. Big time. You should've stuck with that guy."

I cut to Kevin, ignoring how angry he seemed. "You're stupid too. You picked a girl who's just like you. Congratulations. Are you going to cheat first or is she? Or are you both already cheating?"

Maggie's laughter dried up.

Satisfaction bloomed in me. I threw all caution to the wind. "Kevin, what are you thinking? You're like the bitch in this relationship. You were hiding in your room from Caden and Marcus. Then when you got caught, you threw a temper tantrum. You didn't even man up when you moved. You had to sneak behind everyone's backs, like a sulking little kid, and now where are you? You're still hiding, but at your girlfriend's house. Do you really love her that much? She's going to get sick of you. It's obvious she wants Marcus back. What do you think when she leaves the house and you're not with her? Do you remember all the times you've left a girlfriend behind to go see the next one? Are you thinking about all the excuses you've used? Has she used any of the same ones on you?"

"You're such a bitch."

I turned back to Maggie. "I can graduate fast from being a five year old." I lifted an eyebrow, throwing my head back in a defiant challenge. "But can you? Because that's what cheating is. It's immature, and selfish, and narrow-minded thinking. Anyone who dates you after knowing what you're like is a goddamn idiot."

I could feel Kevin's anger rising. I'd handed him his ass on a platter and served it up hot. I was done supporting him, or at least done being his wallflower. I felt a stirring inside of me. The hole that my feelings for him had helped cover up was opening. I gulped. I didn't want to feel that hole, so I tore my thoughts away. I had a few more moments before he'd explode, and when that happened, I didn't trust what Caden would do.

Maggie jerked toward me, "I don't think—"

Marcus and Caden both moved forward, but Avery stepped in front of them, her hands on her hips. "I don't think you have anything more to say here, do you?"

There was a warning in those words, and everyone felt it. Avery threw down the friendship gauntlet. She'd been hurt by Maggie, but she got over it and remained friends with her. Now Maggie was throwing it all away. Correction—Maggie was stomping all over their friendship tonight. There was no going back, for any of us.

I felt Kevin's gaze and snuck a peek.

He was simmering, his eyes locked on me, and I could almost see the steam rising out of his ears. We'd have words. I had no doubt about that. His eyes slid to Caden's hand, which was on my stomach as he was still half holding me in place.

Maggie said something. Avery responded. Then Marcus joined in. The three of them were having an exchange, but Kevin, Caden, and I were involved in a different sort of exchange. Okay. Maybe it was really just Kevin and me, but even though it was silent, I felt it was the loudest.

I didn't want to stay there. I ducked around Caden's hand, but Kevin stopped me.

He snarled down at me. "How long have you been sleeping with him?"

I went still. Could he—no. Kevin couldn't see how I felt about Caden...could he?

Kevin wasn't done. "Was I just the warm-up, or did I give you the taste for screwing? Everyone's been talking about Banks' new friend, but I didn't know it was you. Or maybe you think of me when he's inside you—"

He went too far.

Caden grabbed Kevin's throat and lifted him up, holding him against the wall.

Avery gasped. Marcus swore, launching forward and trying to pull his brother off. Maggie, for once, had no words. Her eyes got big, and she fell back, standing next to Avery. Her hand reached for Avery's, as if she would comfort her. I snorted at that, feeling white-hot panic at the same time. I didn't know what Caden was going to do.

I hurried forward, right alongside Marcus, and while he was trying to pull Caden's hand away from Kevin, I yelled, "Stop!"

Caden ignored both of us. He was that damn boulder again, and he leaned close to say something in Kevin's ear. I paused, my heart slamming against my chest, and watched as Kevin went completely still, his eyes sliding to me before he nodded.

Caden pulled back. "Got it?"

"Yeah." Kevin's head bounced up and down. "Yeah. Got it."

Then Caden's hand relaxed, and Kevin slid out, landing on the floor. He went to Maggie's side, grabbing her hand.

Two security guys appeared, rushing toward us.

"We gotta go." Marcus pushed his brother out the door, yelling over his shoulder. "Avery! Come on."

Avery and Maggie shared a last look, and I felt a pang in my stomach. Tonight's words couldn't be unsaid. Avery had officially lost a friendship this evening. She knew it. So did Maggie.

Kevin was coughing, massaging his throat.

One of the security guards asked, "Are you okay?"

Kevin looked up at me. He could call off the guards, have them let Caden go, or he could have them call the police. I was sure there were cameras in the building. The evidence was plain as day, but I narrowed my eyes. If he did, we really were done.

Kevin gave me a small nod as he spoke to the guards. "Yeah, I'm good. I smarted off when I shouldn't have."

The guard didn't look convinced. "Are you sure?"

"Yeah. Yeah." Kevin waved at the door, dismissing the situation. "Leave him be." He stared right at me when he added, "It's not worth it."

I took his meaning loud and clear: I wasn't worth it.

CHAPTER SEVENTEEN

The cat was out of the bag.

I felt like a trap door had opened underneath me, and I'd fallen through. No one had known I slept with Kevin, but they did now. Everything was going to change. I knew it.

I wanted to talk to Caden, plead my case, explain Kevin away, but his jaw was set and he wasn't looking my way. I knew not to push him, so I stuffed down all my questions and begging, and slid out of the Land Rover when he dropped me off.

I felt like I was kicking my heart ahead of me as I walked away from him. It was there on the sidewalk and—one kick, two kicks—I just kept going until I was in my room. Avery texted me that she was staying with Marcus and would check in with me the next day.

I stayed huddled up in my room all day long.

"I didn't know about you and Kevin," Avery said right away as she came in to sit on the floor the next afternoon. "When did it happen?"

I went back to my bed and tried not to cry. "My graduation night." My throat swelled up. "It was a mistake."

"But you have feelings for him?"

I wrapped my arms around myself. "No. I mean, I did then. I do now, but I don't at the same time." That hole. I felt it gnawing at me, wanting to be revealed. It wanted to wreak havoc over my life. I closed it back up. "None of that matters anymore, anyways."

"Because of Caden?"

I looked at her. She could see through me. She could see my pain, and she understood.

"I guess. I don't know. We're just friends. There's nothing more."

"But you'd like there to be more?"

I didn't know why she was asking. "It doesn't matter. He doesn't see me like that."

"You don't know that."

"I do. He barely talked to me last night after we saw them. He couldn't wait to get rid of me when he dropped me off."

"Marcus offered to drive us both home."

"When?"

"When we went to the parking lot. You were there, but you must not have been listening. Caden said no. He wanted to drive you home."

I shook my head. "Because he wanted to give you and Marcus time together."

"Marcus could've come to my room last night, if that was the case. He's been staying here sometimes. I sneak him in and out." She gave me an impish smile, ducking her head slightly. "Don't tell anyone."

"Oh yeah," I joked. "Like that's the first thing I'm going to turn you in about."

She laughed, her eyes brightening. "You never know."

"I'm sorry about Maggie."

Her smile dimmed, and she lifted a shoulder to shrug it off, but it didn't work. "She's not a good person. I knew that, but it still sucks." Avery let out a deep breath, grabbing hold of her knees and locking her arms in place. "It's not really about Maggie. It's more about the rest of our high school friends. They'll take her side. That's how it was in high school too."

So she hadn't lost just one friend. She'd lost more than a few. "I'm sorry."

"It is what it is." She tried again to shake it off, rolling her eyes. "People usually fade from high school anyway, right?"

"Sometimes." I thought about my own two high school best friends, May and Clarissa. I hadn't heard from them since starting college, and I suddenly missed them so much. I hadn't realized how much. We'd emailed, then called, but lately it had been nothing. I hadn't thought about them even.

"Do you think you're going to hear from Kevin?"

"I have no idea." I was okay with that too. The confrontation would come, but I had no burning desire to meet it head-on. "I think I'm going to go see Caden today."

"What are you going to say to him?"

There wasn't anything to say really. "Well, I might apologize for beating him in the Most Gutter Balls competition."

She laughed, shaking her head. "Only you thought that was an actual competition."

I scoffed at her. "Says the runner-up by only three gutter balls. If you'd won Most Gutter Balls, you'd be demanding a trophy too. Admit it."

"Okay." She kept laughing. "Maybe. I'll get you a sash to wear."

My eyes lit up. "And a tiara too."

I was nervous going to Caden's.

What did he think of me now? Did he look down on me because of Kevin? Was he disgusted? Did he hate me because I'd lied to him? I hadn't felt nervous around him in so long, but it slammed back to me now, like a two by four across the chest.

I'd grown used to our evenings. Studying. Sometimes movies. Most of the time beer. I watched the games with him. He liked sports. He watched them more than I think others realized, and he knew information even the commentators didn't. I never cared; whatever was on television I was happy to watch, and he returned the favor. If I didn't want to miss an episode of *The Walking Dead*, he flipped the channel for me, no matter what game he was watching.

When he'd started recording *Gilmore Girls* for me, everything melted.

I had feelings for Caden. They'd been there, under the surface, constantly being stirred up, but now they were on top—ripe for everyone to see and me to feel. I couldn't deny them anymore. I wasn't about to lose his friendship. I couldn't. I wasn't going to let that happen, and I couldn't even summon a joke. That's how serious I was.

My hand shook as I knocked on the door. *Please don't let Bowling Bar Girl be in there.* I prayed internally, and when Caden answered the door, I blurted, "Is that girl here?"

"What?"

I gestured to his arm. "Arm tattoo girl."

He glanced down. "I didn't call her."

Instantly I could breathe easier, and I walked inside. "Why not?"

He shut the door behind me, following me to the living room as I plopped down on one of his couches. "Why didn't I call that girl?"

"She was gorgeous. She wanted sex. Seemed like a sure thing to me."

He shook his head. "You completely confuse me sometimes."

"I'm used to that reaction." I sat up when he went on to the kitchen, and pulled a pillow onto my lap. "But why didn't you? Call her, I mean."

"You want something to drink?"

"A diet soda?"

He reached inside his fridge and pulled out a can. "Because she hit on me in a bowling alley bar. That's why." He handed it over, sitting on the chair next to me.

I popped it open and sunk back into the cushions behind me. "But she was beautiful."

"She's not my type."

Good grief. What was his type? "She was beautiful."

He raked a hand through his hair. The snake bulged, winking at me. "Why are you stuck on that? Looks aren't everything."

I snorted. "That's not what I've been told."

"By who?"

"By society. Guys like boobs and ass, and lips, and a body, and a face. Guys like gorgeous girls. Don't act like what I'm saying isn't true."

"It is, but sometimes the hotter the girl, the crazier she is. Trust me. That girl is not my type. I don't go for the crazies." He thought about it and added, "Unless I just want a screw, but even then." He cringed. "Bad idea." He nodded at me. "What are you doing here? I thought you'd be making up with your stepbrother lover?"

Stepbrother lover. I sighed. Two words I hated to hear now.

My hands began to shake again, so I put the can down and tucked them around the pillow. "About that…"

"You don't have to."

I looked at him. He'd been joking before, but his last words were soft. I gulped. Soft and gentle, and I could feel them wrapping their hold around my heart. When had he woven this magic over me? I hadn't realized, or maybe I hadn't wanted to admit it.

"What do you mean?" I asked.

"I'd already guessed, remember?"

"When you found out I had feelings for him?"

I suddenly felt warm, holding his gaze. He leaned forward, resting his elbows on his knees. "I figured something happened to make you fall for him. I doubted it was because of his personality."

My lips twitched at that. "You're not mad?"

"I was furious last night. It was all I could do not to go back and beat the shit out of him. Again."

"Is that why you were so quiet going home?"

He nodded. "I'm sorry for that."

"For being quiet?"

"For attacking your family."

He sounded so sincere. I looked down at the pillow on my lap, my hands wrapped so tightly around it, and let out a deep breath. "He's not family. He never was."

"But you wanted him to be?"

I wanted him to be something else for me. "His mom loved me when mine died. I think no matter what happens between him and me, I'll always feel something for him, just because of his mom. Sheila's a good person."

"Then what happened with him?"

I shrugged. "Ha. I don't know. His parents got divorced before we moved in, obviously, but no one never talked about it. Ever. Kevin was always with a girlfriend the one year we lived together." I remembered when they helped me move into my dorm. "Kevin showed up to help me move in, but he didn't really help. He took off. Things were chilly between him and my dad. I don't think my dad likes him much."

"Your dad's smart."

"What do you mean?"

Caden clapped his hands together and rubbed them back and forth. "Your stepson always has a girlfriend around. He's obviously sexually active. You've got a gorgeous daughter, and you're bringing her into the same house with that guy. That's like bringing your most beloved creation into a lion's den. I'd be worried too. Hell, I would've put cameras in that kid's room. If he touches my daughter, all bets are off. Someone's losing a dick."

...gorgeous daughter... He called me gorgeous. I couldn't...

"You think I'm gorgeous?"

Caden frowned. "Do you not look in a mirror?"

Caden thought I was beautiful. "You think I'm hot stuff?" I must've been glowing.

"Summer, you shouldn't need me to tell you you're beautiful."

"Says who?"

He laughed again. "Guys must've told you. Right?"

I shook my head. "I dated a few guys in high school. One was president of the debate team. The other was b-string on the junior varsity baseball team. The last was a summer fling when I joined

4-H. I did a lot of baking that summer." None of them had told me I was pretty. "One said I was cute, but that was it."

"Then they're all idiots."

Tingles spread through me, warming me all the way to my toes. An excited buzz started low in my stomach. "Thank you."

His eyebrows pinched together. "For what?"

"For making me feel good."

An emotion I didn't know, one I hadn't seen in someone other than maybe my father, passed in his eyes. "Well, it's the truth. I'm not blowing smoke up your ass."

"I'm hot stuff, remember?"

He sighed, standing. "You're going to make me call you that all the time now, aren't you?"

"I'd settle for Hot Tits." I glanced down at mine. "Maybe the positive reinforcement will help them grow."

"Okay, Hot Tits." He held his hand out to me. "Come on."

"Where are we going?" I put my hand in his, and he pulled me to my feet.

"I got roped into saying I'd help put those flamingos in people's yards. You can keep me company."

I glanced out the window, my hand still in his. "It's getting dark out."

"That's the point." He looked me up and down. "You're going to have to change."

"What's wrong with what I'm wearing?" I had on jeans and a grey sweater. I thought I was fashion forward today. Then I noticed him. He wore black, all black. "I have to dress like you?"

"That's the idea."

I had no idea what was going on, but Caden gave me a ride back to my dorm, holding my hand the entire time. I tried not to think about it, but friends didn't hold hands. I was pretty sure that was a rule...or was it? I couldn't imagine holding Avery's hand, but then again, I couldn't imagine Caden holding anyone except a girlfriend's hand.

He let go when I started to get out of the Land Rover. "Hold on." He put it in park and turned the engine off.

"What are you doing?"

He gestured up to my room. "I'm going up with you."

"Why?" All the girls would want him. He was mine.

"I have to go to the bathroom. We have to pick up the flamingos at Jill's house, and I've been there before. She has seven roommates, and they always have friends over. I'll take my chances in a girl's dorm." He followed me out, shutting his door. "You must have a guy's bathroom in there, right?"

"I guess." I had no idea. My life was spent between my room, Avery's room, classes, the lunch area, and Caden's. The possibility of sneaking a guy into my room had eluded me, but it was still technically day hours, so Caden was allowed on my floor. As he followed me, I ignored how the clerk's eyes got big, and how she watched us go past with hawk-like precision. I also ignored all the girls in the stairwell who got quiet, and how the reception was the same when we got to my floor. Some of the girls had their doors open, and when we walked past, the conversations stopped.

I went to Avery's room and knocked.

She opened her door. "How'd it go with—Caden!" Her eyes got big too, just like the clerk's. "What are you doing here?"

"I know you sneak my brother up here. Where's the bathroom for him?"

"Shut up!" She looked up and down the hallway, then seemed to relax when she didn't see anyone. I didn't have the heart to tell her they were all listening, probably standing as close as they could to their open doors without being seen. She gestured all the way down the hallway to the back door by my room. "Take the stairs all the way to the basement. There's a bathroom to your immediate left. Guys can be down there all the time, just not up here."

He started off, shooting her a look. "I know the rules. I dated someone in here my freshman year."

"You're old. I didn't know if the dementia would have kicked in yet."

He flipped her off, and then disappeared past my room and through the exit door to the back stairs.

Once he was gone, Avery clamped onto my arm. "Holy shit. What's Caden doing here?"

She yanked me into her room, slamming the door.

I held up my hands before she could pounce any further. "It's nothing. We're fine."

"Fine?" An eager grin started to show. "Like *fine* fine? Like we just screwed fine? Or—"

"Like, we're friends fine. He's doing that flamingo thing tonight. I'm helping him."

"Really?" Her shoulders dropped, dejected.

"I know. I thought you guys did the flamingo thing a long time ago."

"No." She scratched behind her ear and laughed softly under her breath. "I didn't mean the flamingo thing, and we did, but it was so popular that a second round is going tonight. A bunch of guys are supposed to flock the lawns. He must be helping Marcus. It's his crew that's in charge of it." She paused, a glimmer of regret appearing. "I got excited. I'm sorry, Summer. I thought maybe him being here meant something else."

"Well, it doesn't. He's a friend." *A friend who held my hand and told me I was beautiful.* I kept that to myself.

She studied me, and a determined gleam appeared in her eyes. "Maybe he just needs more convincing?"

She reached for my hair, but I backed toward the door. "I'm good. I don't want a change my appearance."

"Come on. Just let me experiment."

"No. My hair is shiny. I don't need to lose weight. I know my skin is clean and smooth. Other than having bigger boobs, I don't want any other changes."

"I know. Your hair is gorgeous, long and thick. Those doe eyes don't hurt either. Maybe he wants you to show more skin." She began to reach for my shirt.

I slapped her hands away, yanking the door open. "Hands to yourself, woman. I gotta change clothes anyway. I'll be back."

"Summer!"

"Can't hear you," I yelled over my shoulder, hurrying to my room. The once empty hallway was not empty anymore. My floormates had taken point, sitting down with textbooks, laptops, notebooks, and whatever else they needed for studying.

I snorted as I opened my door.

Studying, my ass.

CHAPTER EIGHTEEN

As I swapped my clothes, Caden texted that he was downstairs in the lobby waiting for me. I found him leaning against the front desk, talking to a girl and a guy. His back was to me when I came around the door, so his friends saw me first. The guy looked me up and down, and the girl gave me a side-eye. I didn't care. I took that as a compliment.

Maybe I was only going to be riding around in Caden's Land Rover, maybe I was only helping him run an errand to help his brother out, and maybe I was just wearing black so what did it matter how I dressed? All those thoughts swirled in my head while I was changing, making me feel a little foolish. But Avery's voice had been even louder, and the result was an outfit that got me some attention. Score.

Their eyes really opened wide when I stepped forward, and Caden turned to me.

I wasn't wearing anything sexy or skimpy, but the combination looked killer. Even I had to admit it myself. Skin-tight black jeans, a black tank top, and a black leather jacket—Caden had never said what kind of black clothing was needed, so I improvised.

His eyes darkened, and his hand jerked. Then he lingered on the leather jacket. "Really?"

"Why not? You think you're the only cool one around these parts?" I pulled it tight, knowing it'd emphasize my boobs a little more. "I've recently been told I've got hot tits."

Caden laughed, his hand coming to the small of my back.

The girl noticed that too. Her mouth turned down in a pout.

"Come on. Marcus just called. He's getting worked up that we're not there already." Caden nodded to the other two. "I'll see you guys later."

The guy fist bumped him saying, "What are you doing later tonight?" He indicated the girl with him. "Felicia and I were thinking of checking out a Mexican place in town. It's not new, but it's new to us."

"Yeah." The girl moved in. "My sister told me about it. It's one of those hidden gems. She goes there all the time now. Diego's—that's what it's called." She touched Caden's arm. "You should come."

You. Not *you guys.*

I had visions of yanking her hand off of him and stuffing it down her throat, but Caden stiffened and pulled away, saving me the trouble. His tone was noticeably chilly. "No, thank you." His hand pulled me tighter against him. "We've got plans anyway."

I waited until we got in the Land Rover. "That's your spot."

"I know." His jaw clenched. "I get territorial over things I love."

A tingle went down my back.

I reacted to the possessiveness in his voice, the knowledge that he'd protect a place or person no matter what. He was a damned live fairy tale, someone who'd love and care for you, who was capable of protecting you—that's why my stomach was doing flips again.

Not for any other reason. That's what I told myself.

I sighed, pressing my hands together. I sucked at lying, even to me.

He glanced over with a smile. "You do have hot tits, by the way."

I preened. "Damn straight."

"Okay." The leader stood on the bed of his truck and clapped his hands over his head. "Listen up, everyone."

No one was really listening, though they had dressed right. Everyone was all in black. A few guys wore ski masks, and others had black marks on their cheeks like football players. Personally, I didn't understand the need for the black camouflage. Caden had explained that the cops had already been looped in on the operation. A few of the lawns getting flocked tonight actually belonged to cops, and anyway the whole blending-with-the-night effect didn't work when you were carrying a bright neon-pink flamingo.

Still, I couldn't deny the little spark of excitement building in my stomach.

We were all standing in some guy's driveway, and as I looked around, I seemed to be the only girl. These guys meant business. I was in the middle of a real life *Call of Duty* operation.

The leader began speaking, his voice booming. "This is going to happen with precision and professionalism. No lingering, loitering, acting like stupid shits, and definitely no joking around. We're not ladies. This isn't going to be run like a bunch of pansy-shopping, pink-nail-polish pussies. You got that?!"

I frowned, tucking my nails inside my jacket.

"Every vehicle's been filled with birds. The driver should have a text with all the locations, and the number of birds for each target. Pull up, find the group of birds labeled for that house, and work together. Take one bird a trip, two if you can manage, and ram those suckers down in the grass. Hurry back to the truck and keep going until all the birds for that location are in the ground. Shotgun Sally is in charge of hanging the sign on the bird closest to the street. Once the sign is hung, get back in the truck, and move to the next target. NO TALKING! This mission is all radio silent. Communicate with signals, and if you don't know the appropriate signals, just SHUT THE HELL UP! Okay? Now, go flock some fuckers!"

Caden laughed under his breath.

I tensed.

The leader's gaze snapped to us, but he lifted his head in greeting when he saw it was Caden. "All right, guys," he said. "Get going." He jumped off his truck.

Caden tugged on my sleeve. "Let's roll out."

I tried to hop out and help with the flamingos at the first house, but the guys moved too fast. A second vehicle had come with us to make things go as fast as possible. By the time I got one flamingo in the ground, Caden was at my side asking where the sign was.

Apparently I was Shotgun Sally.

I found a folder in the Land Rover, and I hurried to hang one of the signs: "You have been flocked by your friendly neighbors. Please don't disturb. All birds will be removed within 24 hours and moved to their next nesting home." A phone number was attached for further information, and the bottom noted that all proceeds would go to the Brain Injury Awareness Association.

I was impressed with everyone's efficiency, and we were at the fourth house within an hour. Once the Land Rover was emptied of birds, we followed the second truck and helped them, but I wasn't in charge of the signs anymore. Now I was able to help stuff the birds into the lawns, which gave me a perverse thrill. It was quite satisfying to wind up and slam a flamingo rod into the ground, leaving the grass thoroughly flocked.

We were at the eighth house when I saw someone walking toward us, his hands in his pockets and shoulders hunched forward. I would've recognized him anywhere, and I paused. The guys were a well-oiled machine by now, so I knew the house would be done within seconds.

Caden stood next to me as Kevin approached. "You want me to stay close?"

"He's got the perp-walk look to him. I don't think he's here to be a dipshit." I hoped not.

"I'll be waiting back here."

The guys finished when Kevin stopped in front of me, his baseball cap pulled low. My heart twisted. I always liked how he looked when he wore that hat. Somehow it made him seem angsty, more mysterious. Now I couldn't help but wonder how Caden would look in a baseball cap.

Kevin assessed me with tired eyes before taking in the guys behind me. They were heading to the second truck. Caden waved them on, gesturing to me and Kevin at the same time. I had no doubt he was explaining that the Land Rover might be a while.

"Hey."

I was right. He didn't sound like a dipshit tonight.

"Are you here to apologize or attack?" I asked.

He gripped the back of his neck, letting his arm hang there a moment. "Neither. I was hoping just to talk." He gestured to the truck that was now pulling away, moving past us. "I was told the fraternity was helping out with the flamingos tonight. I was coming to lend a hand. I see some of Marcus' crew is here too. I didn't know you'd be here, actually, but I'm glad you are." His hand slid into his jeans pocket. "I wanted to come see you."

"I thought you were pissed at your fraternity." He wanted back in. I could see it on his face, in his envious look when the truck left.

"I am. I'm not. I don't know. I've had time to think stuff over, and I was an idiot."

I snorted. "Just this one time?"

"Summer, come on."

We stood on the passenger side of Caden's Land Rover. I knew he was on the other side, listening. I folded my arms over my chest. "You need to apologize to me. You attacked me at the bowling alley, and you had no right."

He grew quiet, shuffling his feet around, but staying in one place. My chest tightened. Was he not going to say anything? At all?

Then he did, half-mumbling. "Why'd you lie to me?"

"About what?"

"You couldn't stand Banks. Then the next time I see you, he's protecting you. From me."

"He's my friend, and the first time you saw me, he wasn't. It's as simple as that."

"You could be a little nicer about it."

"Why? What do I owe you?"

"You know he's my enemy."

I shook my head. "You were dating his brother's girlfriend. That makes you Marcus' enemy. Caden is your fraternity brother."

"Come on. Seriously? You could've told me you were friends."

It wasn't his business, but he was right. I hadn't told him on purpose. I sighed, leaning back against the Land Rover.

"I knew you wouldn't like it. I guess that's why I didn't tell you. And he is, you know. He's a good friend to me."

"Caden Banks doesn't have female friends, Sum. You should think about that."

"Well, now he does." My tone cooled. He needed to back off. That was also none of his business. "And stop, Kevin. You don't have a right to use a nickname for me. We were housemates, remember?"

He looked up, eyes blazing. "Don't start with that."

"With what?"

"Summer, I…" He kicked at the gravel on the road. "Listen, what we had—"

I didn't want to listen. "Our one-night mistake, you mean?"

"Stop."

I pushed off the Land Rover, but wrapped my arms around myself. "What do you want, Kevin?"

"Stop. I haven't said anything."

"I can see it. I don't even want to talk about this. What we did was a mistake. I see that now, but I'm doing my own thing. I don't care if you don't like it. It's none of your business." My lungs were stinging. "What, are you jealous that I might be interested in someone else?"

He was such an asshole. I'd had enough. I reached for the door.

"Yeah. Maybe I am."

I turned back. He had no right, no right at all. I felt punched in the chest. "Oh my God."

Kevin stepped in front of the door so I couldn't close it after I got inside. "I'm sorry, Summer. I am."

"Just stop it." I tried to move him out of the way, but he pressed even farther inside, resting his hand on my leg.

I shoved his hand off. I wanted to tell him not to touch me, but Caden would've been there in a flash. I bit back the words, for now.

I couldn't talk. I couldn't look at him either.

"I should've stayed and faced that night head-on, together, but I didn't. I'm a coward, Summer, and I'm used to my old ways. Being a coward is easy for me. I've been that all my life, just like my father. He's a coward. He ran out on my mom and me." He paused for a moment. "I always have to have a girl. I loved that you came to see me in the beginning of school, but what could I say? I was with Maggie. I am with Maggie. I...I can't say anything to make that situation right, but I'm trying to change. Coming here is a first step for me. I want to change."

I didn't know what he was talking about, but it didn't matter. I was over it. I was over him. I reached for his hand, squeezed it, and then pushed him back so I could close the door.

He didn't fight me, instead he rapped on the window so I'd roll it down. "Our parents are coming up for family weekend."

"I know." Why was he telling me this?

"You know they'll want to do a family dinner. Don't bring Caden."

"What?"

"I won't bring Maggie, if you won't bring Caden."

"You have no right to ask that of me. If you don't bring your girlfriend, that's on you. If I don't bring a friend, that's my decision. It has nothing to do with you."

"Please?" His hand curled over the window. "Can we have it really just be family? You, me, my mom, your dad? The four of us."

The driver's door opened, and Caden climbed inside. I didn't look, but I felt the tension in the air. Kevin looked past my shoulder, and a wall came over him. He let go of the window and without a word, he backed away. Caden started the vehicle and we drove off.

I watched Kevin the whole time, until he blended in with the night.

CHAPTER NINETEEN

Marcus drilled holes in the back of my head during Intro to Physiology again. He hated me. I was okay. Now he hated me again. He must have seen me talking with Kevin the night before.

Even Shayla, my study partner noticed. "I can't figure out if Marcus Banks hates you or wants to screw you."

"Hates me." The horror of the other option. "I'm friends with his brother."

And that was the wrong thing to say. She suddenly wanted to be more than study partners. She wanted to be lunch buddies, hanging-out-on-weekends buddies, and before she babbled out any other idea she could think of, I said my goodbye and slipped away at the end of class.

Avery came to my room when I got back, and I filled her in on everything that had happened last night.

"So Kevin just showed up and dropped all that bullshit on you, and then Caden drove you away?" Her nose wrinkled. "I'm so sorry, Summer. What an asshole."

"Pretty much."

"Guys like that piss me off." Her hand formed a fist, and she hit her leg. "If he's going to be in a relationship with you, he should say something." Hit. "If he's not, he should say that too." A second hit. "You know he's a douche. And you know you shouldn't be with him, or wait for him, but until he actually says the words, you can't. Asshole! He should actually say the words." Three. Four. Five hits.

I frowned, watching the way her other hand tugged on the side of her jeans. She'd wrapped a string there tightly around her finger, cutting off the blood supply.

"Okay." Grabbing the scissors, I bent forward and snipped her string. "Let's not lose a finger over this. And wild guess, I'm betting we're no longer talking about Kevin?"

She let out a breath, her shoulders sagging forward. "Ugh. You're right. Marcus won't come out and say what he wants. It's driving me crazy. *Men* drive me crazy. Why can't they just be transparent? Tell us their thoughts, and then we'll know."

I shrugged. "Being transparent sounds scary."

"What do you mean?"

"Think about it. If you told everyone your thoughts and feelings…I don't know." Another shrug. "I'd feel exposed. Someone could come and hurt me."

A light turned on in her eyes. "You think that's what it is? Marcus doesn't want to get hurt by me?"

"What?"

She perked up. "I never thought about it that way."

What had just happened? "No." I touched her arm. "I was talking about myself. I didn't mean Marcus. If *you* were totally transparent about your thoughts and feelings, he could hurt you."

"No." She shook her head, eyebrows knitted together.

An uh-oh feeling dropped in my gut. I could see the wheels turning in her head, and this wasn't a good idea. "Wait. What? I didn't mean—"

She scrambled to her feet. "You're totally right. I'll do it. I'm the one bitching about not knowing what he wants, so I'll make the first move."

"You will?" The uh-oh feeling had formed a ball, and it was lodged in my throat. "Can we talk about this before you do something?"

"Like what?"

"I don't know. Like, what are you going to say? You looked more than friends-with-benefits at the bowling alley."

She slumped, her bottom lip sticking out. "No, that's it, I think. I want to either get together for real again or nothing. I can't do the benefits stuff any more. I thought I could, but I can't. It's eating me up inside." Her hand grabbed her shirt where her heart was and formed a fist.

I felt a pang in my chest. "I'm sorry, Avery."

"It's my fault. I was stupid and thought I could handle it. I can't. I'm realizing that now." She eyed me intently. "Are you and Caden FWB too?"

"FWB?"

"Friends with benefits?"

My eyes went wide. "No. No!" I couldn't shake my head enough to emphasize that point. "We're just friends. You know, the whole p-l-a-t don't know why I'm spelling it. Platonic friends. That's me and Caden."

A platonic friend who cuddled, who carried me to bed and tucked me in so gently…who held my hand for an entire ride. Yeah. We were that type of friends.

"I don't know how you do it," Avery said.

"Do what?"

The ball fell from my throat, but it was in my chest now. I felt it pressing against my sternum, like it was trying to burrow its way out of me.

"Be friends with Caden and not develop feelings."

Really? I cringed, hearing my own thought like a high-pitched squeal. I almost laughed out loud and said "*You don't say.*" But I held it together and only responded with a casual-sounding, "Mmm-hmmm. Yeah."

"Claudia was talking about you guys at lunch the other day. She doesn't get it either. She'd be all over him within a day of trying to be a friend." Avery laughed. "But then again, Claudia's always had a thing for Caden too. The others had crushes on him too when we were freshmen last year. They've moved on. Caden's picky about who he dates, but Claudia's still hung up there."

"She dated Kevin too?"

"Yeah. That turned out horribly."

"And she still hasn't told Shell?"

Avery frowned at me. "She doesn't want to make it awkward. That's the only reason."

I'd spent enough time with that group of Avery's friends to know that was bullshit. I'd heard their stories. Claudia knew Shell had dated Kevin early in the year, and she dated him later that year. She'd kept her mouth shut not because she didn't want to make things awkward, but because she'd violated girl code. You aren't supposed to date a friend's ex.

I pressed my lips together now. "That's…" I tried to control my voice so no cynicism slipped out. "…nice of her."

"I thought so too."

I didn't understand Avery. I wasn't super socially savvy, obviously, but May and Clarissa never went after guys I said I liked. Shit, if they had, we wouldn't have remained friends all through junior high and high school. A sudden longing washed over me. I missed my friends. A lot.

"Is something wrong?"

"What?"

Avery was studying me. "You just sighed. Is something wrong?"

"No." I waved that off. "Just stupid thoughts."

"Like what?"

"What?"

She leaned forward, matching my grin. "What were you thinking? Tell me."

"I was just missing two of my best friends from high school."

"Have you kept in touch with them?"

I shrugged, feeling that stupid ball moving back into my throat. "I've called a few times." And emailed, and texted, and left a lot of voice messages. Spending time with Caden had consumed me. I wondered if something similar was happening with them.

"Where'd they go to college?"

May went to New York, and Clarissa was a few hours away. "One's not far. The other's across the country."

"Do you want to go visit her?"

I'd been picking at the carpet, but I lifted my head. "What?"

"We could go see your friend, the one that's close. I mean, as long as it works for her schedule. I know some of the girls would totally be up for a road trip."

"You mean you and Shell? That group?"

"Maybe even Marcus."

Lovely. He could drill holes in the back of my head close up.

"Caden might go, since it's you," she added.

My head was swimming. "You guys would go on a trip for me?"

"Of course. Road trips are fun." She laughed, leaning forward and pressing her hand over mine. She squeezed. "It'll be fun. Where's she at? Let's plan something."

A road trip was a new concept to me, especially with such a large group, but that's what ended up happening. Once I got a hold of Clarissa and May, we picked a weekend. May would fly in from New York. Soon all the details were ironed out.

We were going in a few weeks—the second weekend after Family Weekend. Avery had been right about Caden too. He'd said he'd come, but he'd drive, and only I could ride with him. The girls were unfazed by that request.

Claudia even said, "We figured he'd say something like that."

And since Caden was coming, Marcus was in too, as well as some of the other guys from Caden's fraternity. In fact, most of the guys from the fraternity were coming. They had a chapter at Clarissa's college, which was smaller than North River. We had fourteen thousand students, and Dubrois College had about six thousand.

Caden's chapter reached out, so the chapter there was taking care of finding a rental house for everyone to stay in. The list of travelers kept getting longer and longer, but I figured if there wasn't room at the house, I could crash on a couch in Clarissa's dorm.

"Like fuck you are."

That was Caden's response when I told him my plans. We were at his place, and two other guys were sitting in the living room with us. They'd been talking about a football game, but quieted after Caden's statement.

I sat up on the couch, squaring my shoulders. He was at the other end, a beer in hand. He'd been half watching the game with his brothers, and half listening to me talk about the road trip.

"What are you talking about?" I asked.

"You're not going off and sleeping at your friend's place. We're all going with you." He gestured to the others with his beer. "Almost the entire house is coming. You gotta stay where we are."

"But there's so many people coming now."

Avery was adding one or two more people every day, or so it seemed. I half expected her to reveal she was friends with Maggie again, and Maggie wanted to come. That hadn't happened, so far.

But Avery didn't say much about her ex-friend, and I knew her well enough to know that wasn't good. She was probably talking to her again. Which reminded me that I wanted to ask Claudia about it. Despite my issues with Claudia, she was a pit bull when it came to Maggie. She hated her more than anyone.

"It'll be fine," Caden assured me. "A third of the people will be sleeping together. People can bring sleeping bags."

"The guys will crash wherever," one of the guys added. "Don't be surprised if you find people sleeping on top of tables."

"Or below them," the second one grunted. "Shit, I woke up outside last weekend. Best sleep I ever got."

The first one laughed. "That warm bed of grass and sprinklers?"

"It was nothing. Cold water on my face. It was a nice alarm clock."

They snickered, turning back to the game.

Caden was watching me and suddenly, he pointed to the door. "You two, get out. I need some privacy."

"What?"

The first started to protest, but the second slapped him in the chest and gave me a meaningful look. Whatever the message was, he got it. They stood and headed out.

Caden continued to focus on me, a deep frown on his face.

I sighed internally. God, he looked beautiful. He'd been working out more so he'd trimmed down a few inches, giving him a leaner look, but his muscles hadn't gotten smaller. They seemed bigger, sculpting his body so he looked more and more like a Greek god or something. When he wore tight-fitting shirts, like he had today, I was having a harder and harder time remembering what kind of friends we were. We hadn't held hands again, but even thinking about it, my hand itched to touch a different part of him. I wanted to trace some of his tattoos, find out where they ended.

I tucked it behind me. "Why are you mad at me?"

"I'm not."

He was. I could hear it in his voice.

"Fucking hell." He gripped the back of his neck. "I am."

"Because I said I'd stay at my friend's place if the house gets too full?"

"Yeah." He shot me a dark look. "I don't want you staying somewhere else. We're all coming because of you. You should be where we are."

"Well." I lifted a finger in the air. "I don't really think I'm the reason everyone's coming. I think I'm the excuse for a road trip."

"Exactly." His jaw clenched.

I waited for him to elaborate, but he didn't. I leaned forward. "Exactly...what?"

"Why are all these stupid fucks coming? I thought this was going to be small. You. Me. Avery. Marcus, maybe a few of his friends. Now it's thirty plus idiots joining in."

"Most of those idiots are your fraternity brothers."

He bit out a curse, adjusting his hold on the back of his neck.

"And how the hell did they even get invited? I didn't say anything to them."

"Wait." I sat back. "You don't want your fraternity brothers to come? I thought you invited them."

"I didn't."

"What?" My mouth was on the floor. I remembered the first night I met Caden. He'd sounded irritated that he was in a fraternity, but since then I'd realized he did everything they asked. He was present when the fraternity had events, and if they had a party, he went, but he called me later. We'd watch movies in his shed while music blared from the house.

I was stunned to hear he didn't want his brothers on the road trip.

"I didn't invite them," I said. "So who did?"

"Fuck if I know." He grabbed another beer from the fridge, sinking back down on the couch.

I pulled a pillow into my lap and hugged it to my chest. He stretched his legs out, placing them on the coffee table right next to mine. I gulped, feeling his leg graze against mine. My fingers sank further into the pillow, and I struggled to keep from moving my legs on top of his, nestled between them.

I could've. Caden wouldn't have cared, but I held back. I'd want more. That small touch wouldn't be enough.

I felt my body warming so I spoke hurriedly. "Can I ask you something?"

"Since when do you ask to ask something?" He grinned at me over the top of his beer.

I ignored that. "Do you like being in a fraternity?"

I held my breath, expecting him to show some sort of surprise at the question. I got none.

"No. I don't, but not because of them. They're okay. This just wasn't my first choice. I don't like belonging to anyone."

"Then why are you here?"

He hesitated, studying me intently before his gaze slipped away. "Because my dad is a big deal with this fraternity, and someone had to join to make him happy."

I wasn't expecting that. "You joined because of your dad?"

"And for someone else."

He didn't say any more, and this was one of those moments when I should have read the signals. I should've held my tongue.

"Who?" My curiosity was killing me. "We can pretend we're in a trust tree. I love those things. Go ahead. Ask me anything, and I'll give you an honest answer. But I have to know. Who are you doing this for?"

Please don't say a girl you loved from high school.

"My brother."

"Marcus?"

"No." He laughed softly at my disbelief. "Marcus's twin, Colton."

"You fought Marcus that one night about him, didn't you? The night you beat Kevin up."

"Kevin thought we were fighting about him. He had nothing to do with it, but he walked in and said the wrong shit. My patience was already gone, so he got the hit I really wanted to land on my brother."

"On Marcus?"

"Yeah." He grimaced. "I'd never hit Colton."

He softened his tone and a far-off look came over his face. I knew he was thinking about his brother, but I was on a mission. I wanted more information. Caden wasn't the sharing type. He'd stop talking, think everything through in his head, and forget we were having a conversation. He'd leave me hanging and start talking about something else, or just go back to watching the game.

I scooted to the edge of my seat and leaned forward. "Why not?"

"Why wouldn't I hit my other brother?"

I nodded. "Does he go to school somewhere else?"

"No." His tone wasn't just soft now, it was filled with regret. "He's at home. He doesn't go to school. Joining our dad's fraternity was his dream. He was supposed to do it. Our dad would've been happy. Colton would've been happy, and so would Marcus and I. I wouldn't have had to join then."

"Wait, when did you join?"

"Last year."

"When you were a sophomore?"

He nodded. He wasn't looking at me any more. I wasn't even sure he was really in the room.

I needed to leave this alone. He had given me the clues— looking away, his jaw clenching, pain like I'd never heard from him sounding loud and clear. My instincts were telling me to shut up, but I couldn't. I had this burning need to know more about Caden. I needed to get in there, past his walls, and I wanted to understand him.

I wanted to help him.

Caden was hurting, and I wanted to take that away.

"What happened?"

"He was hit."

I pushed still. "By who?"

Caden turned his gaze to me now, and I felt branded by the pain I saw. His eyes were stricken. "Does it matter?"

"No." My breath caught and held in my chest. I wanted to go to him, but I also wanted to slink away. I was stirring up his pain, but I had to know. "What happened, Caden?"

"Why do you have to know?"

"Because it's hurting you."

"What?"

I made a decision, though I had no idea what the ramifications were going to be. I stood, my legs going numb and my stomach clenching, and I moved to his side. He leaned back, his head falling to the couch, and he watched me.

The need to ease some of his hurt outweighed the fear of what would happen next. Swallowing tightly, I stepped over to straddle him and sat down.

"What are you doing?"

He asked that softly, still holding his beer. I took it from his hands and put it on the stand next to the couch. Then I just sat there. He had to do the rest. I'd already made the first move.

I glanced down at his hands, feeling like an idiot. "What happened to your brother?"

"Why are you pushing this?"

I looked back up to find confusion warring with need in his eyes. He wasn't pushing me away, so I sank further into his lap.

"You haven't told anyone else about this." It wasn't really a question, but I saw the confirmation in his eyes. My chest tightened, thinking about whatever secret he held. "Please tell me."

"No." He shifted forward, and I braced myself, expecting him to push me away. He didn't. His hands grasped the backs of my legs and lifted me so I was more fully on his lap.

I could feel him between my legs, and my breasts almost pressed against his chest. I waited. I wanted to see what else he'd say

"But not because I don't want you to know," he added. "Because it's not my secret to tell. It's Colton's."

I nodded, my stomach doing somersaults now. "That makes sense. I can respect that."

And there we were. His hands cupped my ass, and the pain in his gaze became something darker, something I felt too, something that began to turn off all rational thought.

"What are we doing here?" he questioned, his voice like a caress in itself.

I leaned forward, my gaze lingering on his lips. "I didn't really think it through."

"And now?"

"Still not thinking it through."

"You're okay with that?"

In that moment, the truth exploded in me. I wanted him. I wanted this—but it was more. I *needed* this.

I didn't answer.

I closed the distance between us.

CHAPTER TWENTY

My lips found Caden's, and they were everything.

I melted into him, my hands moving over his chest and arms. I felt like I was drowning as we kissed. He answered. His mouth opened under mine, taking over, and a tremor went through me. I sank further down on him, almost grinding, and he pulled me more tightly against him, tighter than I could've gotten us. Then before I knew what was happening, he stood.

I gasped, wrapping my arms around his neck. I started to pull away, but he murmured, "No," and kept on kissing me. It was dizzying. My body was burning up, my need for him building.

By the time he dropped me onto his bed, I could do nothing but clasp his shoulders. I dragged him down with me. I couldn't get enough of him. I couldn't get enough of this.

"Summer."

His hand came to my arm, and I paused, my mouth still on his. He pulled his head back to look at me. His eyes darkened again, and I saw the primal lust on his face. I felt it in me. It spread all over, like a drug. I was intoxicated, and adrenaline pumped through me, making me need more and more.

I slid a hand up under his shirt, savoring the feel of him. His muscles rolled and shifted under my touch, and I dipped down, lingering at his jeans. My thumb rested over the button. If I flicked that open, this was going to go farther than I'd anticipated.

I pulled away and looked up, holding his gaze.

We were both breathing heavy.

He waited, letting me make the decision.

I wanted to. My legs wound more tightly around his back, and I shifted against him. He closed his eyes at the contact. When they reopened they were dilated, like he was drugged right along with me.

My heart pounded in my chest. The ache was almost combustible. I'd never felt this before. I'd lost my virginity to the 4-H guy, but that'd been painful and awkward. I hadn't enjoyed sex with him, and then the only other time had been with Kevin. That'd been a little more pleasurable, but it was nothing compared to this. Just the kissing with Caden was already more than what I'd felt having sex before.

My hands let go of his jeans, and fear slammed into me.

I wasn't ready for this.

This could break me. I didn't know if I could come back.

Caden responded to me immediately. The only thing I'd done was move my hand away, but his touch changed. It had been demanding and hot before, but he switched it to soft and comforting.

Shifting to lie beside me, he rested his forehead to my shoulder and let go of a deep breath. "Holy shit, woman."

I let out an awkward and relieved laugh, hitching up on the last note. "You said it."

His hand smoothed over my stomach, and he slipped it under my shirt, rubbing in comforting circles there.

I closed my eyes, letting out a silent sigh. My entire body was relaxing, feeling exhausted like it had run a marathon just now.

"You okay?"

I opened my eyes to find him watching me. I nodded. "I'm okay."

Then the side of his mouth lifted. "Good, and just so you know, any time you want to do that again, I'm down."

I felt the corner of my mouth twitching, mirroring his. "Down?"

A stark promise suddenly appeared in his eyes, and his hand dipped low, pausing just beneath my jeans. "You know what I mean. I'll be hard and ready to go in all the right spots."

Oh hell. I needed to breathe. The room got a whole lot hotter, and I sat up, actually fanning myself. "Stop talking. You're making me come just listening to you."

He bent down, kissing my shoulder before sitting up with me.

I closed my eyes. The quick peck of his lips on my skin sent a thrill through me, reenergizing my already boiling blood. He shifted to sit on the edge of the bed, bending forward so his elbows rested on his knees, his back to me. I looked at him and knew my emotions were shining through. If he'd glanced back at me, he would've seen everything I felt.

We could get physical. We already had with cuddling and holding hands. As long as I was okay with it, Caden would be too. But if he saw my feelings, I could lose him then. I was sure of it. He dated girls who you were more than me. Who was I to compete against them?

"You okay?" he asked.

I couldn't lose him.

He looked back, and I slammed my eyes shut. When I opened them again, everything was gone. I'd tucked it all away, and I smirked back at him. "Other than wondering what the female term for a quick tug is, I'm golden."

Lust moved back into his eyes, and he glanced down at my jeans. "I could help take care of that."

I shifted on the bed. "You're the reason it's there." Alarms were going off. This was the entire reason I'd pulled away. Caden was okay with it. I wasn't.

I coughed, clearing my throat, and scooted to sit next to him. The side of my leg pressed into his, and I felt him watching me. I patted his hand. "I'm good. Really."

"Yeah?"

"Yeah."

He opened his hand underneath mine. "We're still friends?"

My heart twisted, and I slid my fingers alongside his. "Still friends."

"Good." He pressed a kiss to my forehead. "Because I really need a drink now. Come on. We're going out."

"Where are we going?" I followed him out the room on unsteady legs.

He grabbed his wallet and keys, tossing the latter in the air and catching them. "Diego's." He winked at me before heading out.

I couldn't move, not at first. Good God. That wink had gone right between my legs, and I had to catch my breath. This guy had way too much power over my body.

Well…not just my body.

"Welcome, *mis compadres*."

Diego welcomed us with open arms as we walked into his bar. He beamed, wearing jeans and a leather vest with nothing underneath. Right before he would've caught Caden in a hug, he moved and wrapped his arms around me instead.

He winked at Caden. "You used the front door this time too. I'm touched." He tightened his hold on me. "And you brought my new best friend. We are close friends now."

Caden frowned, but I saw his lip twitch. He was trying not to grin. "Just don't get too close."

"Oh?" Diego pulled back and made an exaggerated point of looking from me to Caden and back again. "It's not like that now?" His eyebrow went up, along with his sly grin.

I flushed. "It's not." But it was. Thirty minutes ago, in fact.

Diego stepped away. His hand curved around my back. "Come on." He motioned for Caden to go away. "You get a table. I'm taking my new best friend to the bar. We're going to get shots."

"She's underage."

"Then the shots are not for her." He winked at me.

Caden rolled his eyes and glanced at me. "I'll grab a table outside."

I nodded. I needed the night breeze to cool off.

Diego patted one of the stools. "Hop up." He went around the side of the bar, waving off one of the bartenders. "I got this one."

He pulled out some bottles and placed them on the bar. "Okay. This." He lifted the tequila bottle. "I am pouring for Caden. It looks like he needs some further encouragement, if you know what I mean."

He winked at me, starting to mix. I didn't know what he meant, and I was afraid to ask. Diego seemed in a mischievous mood. I feared what would come next.

"So." He cleared his throat, finishing one of the drinks. "Tell me, *querida*, what is the latest development between you and my long-time friend outside?"

"Um…"

He paused, his gaze intent. "You don't know, or you don't wish to tell me?"

"Both." I smiled.

His eyebrows dipped together. "You are a good girl. You're the only girl he's brought here. That means something. Don't tell me it doesn't."

"It means…" I had to stall. "That Caden and I are friends."

He huffed at that, rolling his eyes sharply before beginning to mix a second drink. "That's bullshit. Don't insult me. I can tell when something's up, and a blind man could've seen the chemistry between you two."

My eyes widened. "Oh."

"So tell me, what's going on?"

I felt cornered by Diego's hawk-like gaze. He hadn't missed a thing, but I really didn't know what was going on. I opened my mouth, having no idea what was about to come out, when someone bumped into me from the side.

"Bartender! Can we get a bunnch of shos?" a girl slurred. "Me an my friends?" She hiccupped, then noticed me.

Her arm felt hot and as she turned, I could see that her eyes were glazed over. Her lips were swollen, and I recognized her as the girl Caden had talked with in my dorm. I stiffened, looking for the guy she'd been with, but didn't see him. Instead there was a table of girls behind her, all of whom looked just like her. They were pretty, hair and makeup done perfectly. Judging from the shrieking, they were just as drunk too.

"Hey." She stuck her bottom lip out, staring right at me. "I know you."

Diego saw my reaction and turned on the charm as a distraction. His smile became smoother. Suddenly a thick accent came out. "*Quieres tiros, mi chinga?*"

She stared at him, repeating what he'd said. Then she smiled. "Shots. Can we get some?"

"Of course!"

She relaxed at his warm tone.

"How many?"

"Oh. Um…" She glanced back to her table, her finger lifting to count her friends. "Two, three, five shots. We need five of them."

"Any kind?"

"Sex on the beach. Or blow job."

I glanced through the back glass door, but I couldn't see Caden. If I couldn't see him, she couldn't either.

As if sensing my discomfort, Diego placed three glasses in front of me. Two were already poured. "For your table," he told me. He quickly poured something out of a pitcher into the third glass. "For me," he explained. He tapped the second glass. "For you." And he winked before moving farther down the bar and lining up five shot glasses. The girl was forced to move with him.

After picking up the three glasses, I nodded my thanks. He gave me a second wink before filling the last of the shot glasses. "Ta da! There you are," he announced to the spellbound girl.

I slipped past the table of her friends. Once outside, I saw half the veranda was empty and instantly relaxed. I only hoped those girls wouldn't come out.

"You okay?" Caden eyed me.

I slid his drink to him, putting Diego's in front of the empty chair. "You have friends inside."

"I do?"

"That girl from my dorm, the one you were talking to while I changed for flamingo night."

He frowned. "Who?"

He didn't remember. I pressed my lips together to keep from smiling. "I don't know. There was a guy too."

"Oh, yeah." Understanding dawned. "Jeremy something. He's friends with Marcus, not me."

"You were talking to them."

He shrugged, glancing at the door. "They said hello. I needed to pass the time. Figured polite conversation wouldn't hurt. Diego's not coming?"

"He had to fill some drinks first."

"Wait." He stilled, his eyes darting to mine. "They aren't coming out here, are they?"

The last knot in my stomach unraveled. I shook my head, unable to hide my grin now. "I hope not."

He grinned back. "It's awkward enough with Diego, much less some chicks Marcus knows. Word would get out that we were hanging out here."

My grin fell flat.

People knew we were friends already. Caden had been in my dorm, for goodness sakes, but the way he said that—it was like he didn't want anyone to know we were hanging out here together. Like I was a secret.

I tried to tell myself that was Kevin baggage, nothing to do with Caden, but the knot in my stomach tightened back up.

"You okay?"

"Huh?"

"You got quiet all the sudden. That's not normal for you."

I forced a smile. "I'm good. Just…maybe tired is all."

"You sure?"

He cared about me. I tried to remind myself of that. "I'm good."

"My friends!"

Diego made his entrance, his arms stretched out once again. Everyone on the veranda looked up, saw it was Diego, and went back to their conversations. A few offered greetings as he made his way to our table, but once he dropped into his seat, it was like the last time we had been here. There was no awkwardness after that.

Diego filled the air with stories, and if he was quiet for a moment, Caden would start a new one. Diego would quickly join in, taking over. I laughed the entire time.

A couple hours passed before trouble started. I felt it coming more than anything else.

I didn't hear the girls approach. The veranda had filled while we were out there. But Diego's gaze trailed past my shoulders, and his smile vanished. His eyes lost their warmth, and a beat later, I heard that same drunken voice, but this time she wasn't slurring.

The air cooled dramatically, and it wasn't the temperature.

"Caden! What are you doing here?" she asked.

Caden didn't turn hostile, but his smile vanished. "I'm here with friends."

She waited, standing there.

He didn't say anything more.

Then her eyes fell on me and lit up. A fake warmth oozed from her. "Oh my gosh, you're Kevin Matthews' stepsister, aren't you? I thought I recognized you." She dragged an empty chair from two tables over to ours, plopping down. She scooted up right next to me, pressing her arm against Caden. "I live in your dorm."

She paused again, looking around the table. When she saw Diego, her head cocked to the side, like she didn't recognize him. "You're the bartender, aren't you?"

Caden started laughing.

Diego cleared his throat. "Yes. I'm the help."

"Oh." Her head bobbed up and down, the smile still plastered on her face.

She looked back to Caden with a calculating gleam in her eyes, then switched it to me.

Something was going to happen. Something shitty.

"Is it true what everyone is saying? You didn't really come to school thinking you'd be with your stepbrother? I thought that was hilarious when I heard it. I mean, that's kinda sick too, isn't it? He's not your blood, but still. His parent is fucking your parent. That's gotta be up there on the ick factor."

Yes. She went there.

She waited for a response from me, but it came from Caden.

"Fuck you."

He said it low, quiet, but the words sent a chill down my back.

Her eyes widened. "Excuse me?"

"You came over to our table to insult my friend?" He didn't move. Not a bit, and that made his words even colder. "Get the fuck away from this table."

Her mouth opened.

He cut her off. "I don't care who your friends are. If you don't walk away from this table in five seconds, I will make my opinion known about you. I can't guarantee you'll still have friends after that."

Diego's eyebrows lifted. He muttered under his breath, "Damn."

Caden ignored him. "I don't like being an asshole, but when it comes to certain friends, I'll be the worst asshole I can be."

He'd laid it out for her, but she didn't move.

Diego got up and put his hands on her shoulders. "You should go. Caden doesn't make threats lightly. When he does, he follows through. Don't test him."

He herded her away from our table.

I was stunned. No one had ever done something like that for me. I wanted to thank Caden, say something to show him my appreciation, but I could only gape at him.

He laughed softly. "Do not cry."

Two tears formed at the corners of my eyes. I wiped them away and blinked rapidly. "Who's crying here? Not me. That's for sissies."

"You're not a sissy."

"Well, we both know you're not. Holy crap, Caden. No one's ever stuck up for me like that before." I felt choked up again. "Thank you."

He shrugged. "It's no problem, but maybe we should get going? I don't want to deal with a crazy chick."

My lip twitched. "No doubt. They're like serial killers. They bounce back."

"Yeah. Just like serial killers."

Our eyes caught and held as we smiled at each other, feeling all sorts of feelings—emotions that maybe we shouldn't have been feeling. Or at least I was.

Caden's eyes darkened. His look was like a sensual caress, moving over me, sending tingles and sensations in its wake, and getting me all sorts of excited. Images of us in his bed flashed in my mind. How I sat down, straddling him. How his hands grasped the back of my legs. How he held me tight, then pulled me on top of him. How he carried me to his bed, our lips touching, kissing, exploring. My hand resting on his stomach, the way his paused on my jeans, his thumb at the ready, just waiting for my permission.

I wondered why the hell we'd stopped in the first place.

"You scared that girl out of her skin." Diego plopped back down in his chair, setting a beer on the table. "I should know. I had to give her three shots on the house."

I coughed, feeling yanked out of my sensual cocoon. It'd been so nice and warm in there.

"You should've let her try," Caden remarked, recovering more quickly than me.

Diego harrumphed. "And let you have a second go at that girl? No, thank you. You might not like having them here, but I welcome almost all patrons. And girls who look like that and drink like that? Bring on all their friends." He began to raise his arms, like he was going to make an announcement, but he stopped. He looked between us. "Am I missing something?"

"No." Caden sat forward and patted his friend on the arm. "We're going to head out. I think we've done enough damage for the night."

Following his cue, I stood.

Diego remained sitting, a befuddled look on his face. "Something happened. What was it? What'd I miss?" Then a gleam appeared. "Wait. Are you guys—"

"Going home." Caden touched my arm, gently guiding me in front of him. "I'm dropping her off at her dorm, and I'm going to my place." His hands came down on my shoulders, and I almost jumped out of my skin. He was touching me, holding me in front of him. He guided me away from the table and out the back way like before.

We were leaving. That was all. I tried to tell myself that, but as Caden said goodbye to Diego and maneuvered us through the remaining tables, I could only concentrate on the feel of his hands.

His thumbs slipped over my collar and began to rub against the skin there. And he was right behind me. I could feel his heat. I could almost feel him. If I paused, I knew I could lean back against him and he would hold me a moment. When we got to the fence, I did just that. I closed my eyes, leaning against him. His hands dropped to my waist. Soon he would hoist me in the air, lifting me over the fence. It'd come any second…but it didn't. He stood like that too.

His fingers tightened around my waist. I held my breath. He'd break our contact any second now.

He let out a soft sigh, warming the back of my neck, and I was airborne as he lifted me up and over.

My legs were shaky as he leaped across, landing in front of me. He moved so seamlessly. He didn't stand there and gape at me, like I had with him. His eyes didn't even meet mine, and I frowned at that for a beat, but then his hand grabbed mine and we were walking to his vehicle.

I didn't say anything when we got inside the Land Rover.

He didn't reach for me, or grab my hand, so I kept it on my leg, palm turned up. He could grab it any time he wanted.

He didn't. A part of me ached at the emptiness, as if the weight of his hand on mine had become natural, like my own skin. I bit my lip, not sure how I felt about that. Well, I knew how I felt. I didn't know how I *should* feel.

When he stopped at my dorm, I murmured, "You really did bring me back here."

He frowned. "Did you want to go back to my place?"

I didn't reply. I couldn't. I wanted him, and I knew what would've happened if we'd gone there instead. I would've kissed him, or he would've kissed me. I would've let him do a whole bunch of other stuff that he would be fine with and I couldn't handle.

I swallowed over a lump in my throat. "No. This is okay. I'm... I'm kinda tired anyway." *Liar. You're wide awake.*

He nodded. "Talk tomorrow?"

My heart slammed against my chest. "About what?"

"About anything. Do we need reasons to talk to each other now?"

"No." I laughed. "I'm being weird again. Okay."

We were friends. That's right. Friends.

"Okay," I said. "I'll talk to you tomorrow."

"'Night, Summer."

I walked away, but I couldn't shake a nagging feeling.

I wasn't sure I knew how to be just friends anymore.

CHAPTER TWENTY-ONE

Family Weekend started off like a zombie apocalypse.

At least it did in my mind. The morning was normal, like any other Friday morning. I woke up, went to class, and got coffee and a bagel before going to Intro to Physiology.

Marcus didn't glare at me. Thank goodness. I never knew what I was going to get with him now. We were making progress. He now mostly ignored me, which was fine. I ignored him back. Afterwards, I brought Shayla with me to lunch with Avery and her friends. Claudia even smiled at me.

If that had happened a week ago, I would've considered it a clear sign of the apocalypse, but I had other issues on my mind now. Caden, mainly, but also, Sheila and my dad called early this morning. They were coming, and so were a lot of others, it soon became apparent. I went to the library with Shayla for a study session, and when we left, parents were everywhere.

People were hugging. Moms cried as dads stood awkwardly to the side. Dads cried. Others shrieked their reunions. Soon I was back in my dorm room, ready for my own hugging/crying/shrieking parents to arrive.

Someone knocked on my door, and I plastered on a welcoming smile as I opened it.

It was Kevin.

My smile faded. "What are you doing here?"

He gave me a crooked grin, raking his hand through his hair. "Mom called and said to meet here." He walked in, his hands in his pockets, and glanced around. "This is nice. You didn't end up with a roommate this year, huh?"

I eyed the door. To close or not? Gah! I would've been all for that a few weeks ago. Close the door, be in my room with Kevin, hope someone would make a move... That seemed so far away, and not far at all. That damn hole inside me started to burn again. I left the door open and sat at my desk. Kevin continued looking around the place like he was the health inspector.

"Do you know what your mom has planned tonight?" I asked.

He flashed me that rakish smile again.

I scowled.

He sat on my bed and sank backward to lean against the wall, his legs sprawled over my entire bed.

Well, just make yourself at home.

"You know my mom. She'll have something elaborate. I'm guessing dinner tonight and then private box tickets for the football game tomorrow."

"Oh, that's right."

"What's right?"

"I forgot we had a football team."

"Family Weekend usually coincides with Homecoming. The football game is a big deal."

"Huh." Now I remembered Caden talking about the game. "That makes sense. There were a lot of extra people on campus today."

"They do a lot of reunions this weekend too. It's kinda a big free-for-all, but there are parent and family activities planned." He leaned forward. "You know about the big brunch before the game tomorrow, right?"

"Uh..."

"Your resident advisor should've told you about it."

Avery and I had other things to talk about. "It's all good. I'll look it up. I'm sure there's information online. I can print out an itinerary."

"You have to reserve tickets ahead of time."

"Oh." I glanced down. "Maybe we shouldn't mention the brunch to Sheila."

"What brunch?" she called from the doorway.

Too late.

She and my dad had appeared, grocery and Target bags in their arms and on the floor by their feet.

Family Weekend had officially begun.

I welcomed them with open arms, and after the barrage of hugs, Sheila beamed at us. My dad started bringing in the bags, and she said, "Okay, we have a dinner reservation in thirty minutes, but we wanted to come here first and drop everything off."

Kevin peeked in one of the bags. "Any of this for me?"

She swatted his hand. "Maybe."

"Maybe?"

"Are you going to tell me where you're living?"

He froze. "What do you mean?"

"I know you're not in the frat house. I called there one morning for you."

"Oh."

Shit.

He didn't say it, but I heard it.

Sheila wasn't amused. She crossed her arms over her chest. "So where have you been?"

"Uh..."

"That's what I thought." She rested an arm around my shoulders and pulled me in for a side-hug. "At least with this one, I always know she's safe and not living with some boyfriend she's not talked to me about."

Kevin fought a smile.

I coughed and stepped forward, disengaging myself from Sheila. "Traffic can be a bitch. We don't want to be late for that reservation, do we?"

The reservation was at a trendy restaurant. All the waiters wore pink, as did the hostess who seated us. She also wore a hard-on for Kevin, flirting and smiling coyly at him. When she had to return to her stand, her hand trailed over his shoulder. He glanced back, giving her a secretive smile, which wasn't that secretive at all. I saw it. She returned it, and when he looked back to the table, his eyes went straight to mine.

"Are you serious?" I asked.

"What?" He picked up his menu.

Sheila glanced between the two of us. "What's going on?"

I ignored her. "Is it the five-month mark?"

"What are you talking about?"

"You know." I shrugged. "Aren't you a little early? You still have two more months, don't you? Maybe my counting is off. When did you move in with Maggie again?"

Sheila sighed. "That's what I was worried about."

Kevin glared at me. He spoke around gritted teeth. "Can you shut up, please? This isn't the time."

"When is?"

He leaned forward and hissed, "What's gotten into you?" His eyes narrowed. "Or maybe I should ask *who's* gotten into you?"

I picked up my menu. "Oh, right. I forgot how you always go to the sexual innuendos because I happen to be friends with another guy. Friends, Kevin. F-R-I-E-N-D-S. I'm spelling it out because I know it's unfamiliar. It's a type of relationship where you don't screw the other person. Those do exist, you know."

"Stop it."

"Or maybe you really don't. Do you ever hang out with a girl and not plan to get in her pants at some point?"

"I did with you."

I sucked in my breath.

"We both know how that turned out."

The fuckhead. I could feel the silence around the table like a two-ton weight. My dad was here. Kevin's mom was here—the woman who had taken me in and loved me.

That asshole. I jerked forward, ready to deliver a retort when my dad interrupted.

"I think that's enough from you two."

"Yes." Sheila nodded. "What has gotten into you? You never talked to each like this at the house."

"Because we never talked."

I kept my mouth shut, but Sheila seemed taken aback by Kevin's statement.

"What do you mean?"

"Summer and me. We didn't talk."

"Because of you," I added. Yeah, the intention to shut up had been a good one…

He regarded me, sitting back in his chair. I felt like we were squaring off. I was going with it. My blood grew more heated by the second.

"Are you kidding me?"

"Do I look like I'm joking?" I asked.

His jaw clenched. "You always look like you're half joking or half going crazy, so yeah. You kinda do."

"Kevin Jamison Matthews!" Sheila's fist came down on the table. "You apologize now to your stepsister."

He didn't. He narrowed his eyes and turned to address his mother head-on. "That's the thing, you never gave me a choice as to whether I wanted a stepsister. I'm assuming she never got a choice about a stepbrother either—or even a stepmother." He turned to my dad, who'd been sitting stoically. "And no offense, sir, but I never wanted a new dad. I have enough issues with my current one."

"Get up from this table and walk away." It was a softly spoken command from Sheila, and it sent shivers down my back.

I didn't say a word. My dad still hadn't. We waited to see what Kevin would do, because this had become an exchange between mother and son.

Kevin waited five more seconds, holding his mother's gaze, before pulling his cloth napkin from his lap. He laid it on his plate. Shoving back his chair, Kevin didn't say another word or look at us as he stood and left.

I'd been holding my breath since Sheila's command. I slowly released it now, blinking back a few surprising tears.

She let out a shaky laugh. "That's been brewing for a while, and I apologize wholehearted—"

"Stop, Sheila." My father cleared his throat, folding his hands on the table. "He's right."

"Excuse me? Did you just say—"

He interrupted again. "They're both right, and what were we thinking? We just got married, Sheila. We didn't give them warning, or time to get accustomed to the new setup. They met a week before we moved in, and he's right about that first year. They barely talked. Everyone barely talked. The only two who did were you and me."

He turned to me. "I should've known. You were quiet that year, but you've always been quiet. I thought you were just missing your mother. I didn't think— No, I didn't want to think. I just decided you got along, so I didn't think about unresolved issues. I'm sorry, honey."

I blinked back more tears. That hole was ripping open inside me. My mom... A wave of longing crashed over me. I could hear her voice. I was right there, holding her hand in the hospital. I felt her fingers brush back my hair as she said softly, *"You won't just have a great life, Summer. You'll soar. I know you'll be better than your father or I ever were."*

My heart started going, too fast.

I couldn't—it was pressing into my throat. I felt like I was being choked from the inside.

"Are you okay, honey?" Sheila's hand came down on mine, warming me.

I nodded, brushing the tears away. "I'm fine. I, uh—" I looked at my dad. "I miss Mom, that's all."

Sheila grew quiet.

Tears welled in my dad's eyes, and my throat closed up at the sight. I turned away.

I didn't want to cry. I felt my mom every day, but I couldn't let myself think about her. If I did? Niagara Falls. Clearing my throat, I dried my eyes and shook my head. That hole—it needed to close.

"Before we hold a candlelight vigil right here and now, can we deal with the Kevin thing?"

"That's what I am? A thing to deal with?"

Kevin had returned. He paused before pulling his chair out.

I waved to his face. "Oh good. Your scowl came back too."

"Summer!"

This time the reprimand came from my dad. "What is with you?"

"Okay." Sheila spread her hands in the air. "This is enough. It's obvious our family has some concerns to air, and I think we should have our first official family meeting tonight. We have a suite. We can talk about this at the hotel, but can we enjoy the meal first?"

Kevin still hadn't sat back down.

She pointed to his chair. "Can you sit? Can you be civil for the next hour?"

Picking up his cloth napkin, he tucked it back on his lap and looked at me, a frosty chill in his eyes.

That would've scared the crap out of me three months ago. But now, I just smiled at him and pulled my napkin from my lap. I held it in the air between our chairs before I dropped it, letting it fall to the floor, and I lifted my chin, my smile reinforced.

If he wanted to fight, game on. I had no problems sparring with him, though my stomach did all sorts of gymnastics.

He snorted. "Really?"

"What? It slipped."

He shook his head, leaning back in his seat. "Is this what you'd imagined for family dinner, Mom?"

Sheila frowned at us. "Not exactly." She picked up her menu and gave both of us a meaningful look. "How about we order? Okay?"

We did exactly that. After ordering, all of us made a point to be polite as we talked and ate for the next hour.

My dad's job was going well. He was getting promoted to the level below the company's CEO. Sheila's last shift had been hard. They lost the patient. Kevin talked a little bit about Maggie, relaying that her father ran the hotel where Sheila and my dad were staying. Everyone was surprised by that, but no one asked any more about Maggie. Then all eyes turned my way. It was my turn to 'fess up to something.

I could've said my classes were going well. I'd gotten high scores on all my tests so far. Mid-terms were in two weeks. There was the flamingo flocking to mention, or the fact that I was becoming good friends with my resident advisor, the same Avery they'd met. But considering my audience, I decided to go another route. We'd finished eating, but perhaps we wouldn't be getting dessert

"A guy I'm friends with punched Kevin," I announced. "Twice."

Sheila's head shot forward. "What?!"

I heard my dad suck in a quiet breath.

"Are you fucking kidding me?" Kevin growled.

CHAPTER TWENTY-TWO

"Honey, someone hit you?" Sheila asked Kevin.

"Summer." I could hear my father summoning me from across the table.

"Yes, Mom. But I'm fine."

"Summer."

"Why were you hit?" Sheila paused for a moment. "Did you hit him back?"

"Summer. Look at me."

"I'm fine, Mom. I really am. He didn't hit me the second time."

"Who is this guy?"

"A second time? There were two separate occasions?"

"Summer, you *will* answer me."

"Mom, I am fine. I swear. Both times were my fault, anyway."

"Are you dating this guy?"

"Your fault? What'd you do?"

"Look at me."

"I didn't do anything. Well, I might've said some things I shouldn't have."

My father fell silent, seeming to give up, but I felt his gaze on the top of my head. I twisted my hands together in my lap.

"You were being a jackass, you mean?" Sheila sat against the back of her chair with a thud. "Why am I not surprised to hear this?"

Kevin snorted.

I looked at my stepmom. "What do you mean?"

"What, honey?" She looked over at me.

"You're not surprised Kevin was a jackass. Why do you say that? You say that like it's a normal thing." I looked at him. "Is that normal?"

His eyes closed to slits, and his hand formed a fist on the table. But then his shoulders lifted on a deep intake of air, and he forced his hands flat on the table.

"There were problems before you and your father moved in, yes."

"Kevin!"

He ignored his mom. "When you moved in, those problems got pushed to the back burner."

"No, they didn't," Sheila countered. "I had no idea how you felt."

He looked to her now. "You did too. I screamed at you the night you told me they were moving in."

She drew in a hissing breath. She'd twisted her cloth napkin into a knot, her knuckles white. "There was no screaming—"

"There was, Mom!" He pounded the table. "I was screaming at you. I yelled like a spoiled four year old throwing a fit. I'm admitting it. Why won't you?"

She turned away. "Because it's not true."

Kevin shook his head. "This is ridiculous. You can't even admit to reality." He regarded my father and me. "I didn't want you guys to move in. I didn't want my mom to remarry. I didn't want a new sister. I'm sorry. It's nothing against you two, but she'd *just* divorced my dad six months earlier, and I knew that if two new people moved into the house, everything else would be shifted to the back. And that's exactly what happened. Everything was all about her new husband, making everything great with her new marriage, and when she felt that was stable enough, she moved on to the new daughter."

Those words punched me in the chest.

He softened his tone. "I'm sorry. I really am. I ignored both of you that year. I ignored everything that year. I didn't want to deal with what she'd done to me, pushing me off like I was a burden to her."

He focused on his mom again. "I wasn't a burden to you. Your failed marriage was, and you took it out on me. When your marriage to him fails, don't take it out on Summer. She already lost one mother; she shouldn't lose a second one."

"Kevin! I would never—" She started out harsh, but her voice trembled by the fourth word.

He cut her off with a brisk motion of his head. "You would."

Placing his hands on the table, he looked right at my dad. "You seem like a great dad. Things have been distant between us, but don't let her hurt your daughter the way she hurt her son."

He stood. "And with that, I have to leave. I'm sorry, Mom. No family meeting for me tonight. What I have to say is between you and me—and your ex-husband who is *still* my father, just so you haven't forgotten. He's still my dad."

Sheila blinked, trying to hold back tears as her son walked away behind her. She didn't get up and go after him. She didn't even watch him go. She sat straight ahead, tears rolling down her face, staring at something beyond us.

My stepmother had never looked as lost as she did then.

I didn't know what to say, so I said nothing. I sat there, and after a few more beats of silence, my dad murmured, "Summer, let's give you a ride back. Sheila and I need to go to the hotel. It seems we have some things to discuss."

I got up. "No. That's okay. I can call a friend. You guys talk."

"Are you sure?" His hand covered mine. He squeezed. "Your mother, your stepmother, and I love you very much. I never want you to feel like a burden."

Sheila couldn't stop the tears now. At my dad's words, they rolled freely.

"I know, Dad." I felt my own tears building. I covered his hand with my free one and squeezed. "I've never felt that way."

"Good." His voice had grown hoarse, and he seemed to be struggling as he smiled. He squeezed my hand once more. "Good."

"I'm, uh, going to go. I'll get a ride."

I gave both a reassuring smile, but it didn't matter. Sheila looked broken. It was the first time I'd seen my stepmother anything other than bubbling and happy. It tore at me, but when I stepped outside and saw Kevin, I knew he was broken as well.

He was waiting on the curb, his hands in his pockets, his shoulders slumped forward. He stared at the ground, and I could see the little boy inside of him, the one who'd been hurt by his mother.

I took in a breath.

He glanced over and grimaced. "She never wanted to talk about him, and I finally snapped today."

I lifted a shoulder. "You're still a cheating jackass, and you were a jerk inside, but I was the bitch first this time."

"You're not a bitch."

"I was today."

He smiled. "Maybe you should be more often."

"What do you mean?"

"You liked fighting in there, didn't you?"

I shrugged. "It wasn't for a good reason. I don't really know why I was doing it."

He laughed, but it sounded sad. "I do. You got sick of the shit that they won't talk about. Your mom died, and she's barely talked about. My parents divorced, and my mom acts like my dad doesn't exist. I took my anger out on you instead of focusing on her from the start. I really am sorry, Summer."

My heart felt tugged all over the place. "I like your mom."

A second laugh came from him, this one a bit more lighthearted. "I do too, but she hasn't wanted to deal with divorcing my dad, and she has to. It's hurting me. She can't sweep it under the rug. I let her get away with it, and that's on me. Talking to her didn't work. Screaming didn't work. So I tried ignoring her back. I ignored the whole situation." He snorted again. "We both know where that ended up—you and me in bed because I finally noticed you that night, and I wasn't ready."

I looked up to find him staring at me. There was a look in his eye I wasn't sure I wanted to see. My mouth dried up.

"I wasn't prepared for you when I saw you, when I *finally* saw you," he said softly. His Adam's apple bobbed up and down. "Did you mean it? What you said in there about Banks—or do you really like him?"

I...wasn't prepared for that question. I kicked at the ground, unsure what to say.

"Or were you trying to get a rise out of me?"

The corner of my mouth lifted. He could take that as the answer.

He let out a sigh. "I lost my chance with you, didn't I?"

This was what I'd wanted, for so damned long. Here it was—right in front of me. Looking back at me. Those words... My chest swelled tight. I could only swallow a lump in my throat.

"You're saying this to me now?" I didn't want to hear it, but I didn't know why. It wasn't about any feelings for him. It was something else...

"I know. Bad timing, right?"

I couldn't. I just couldn't. "Take it back."

"What?"

"Take it back. What you just said, take it back. Say you didn't mean it." My lungs burned. "Say you're just doing what you do. You're playing with me. You're testing to see if I still have feelings. That you don't mean it, and you're actually being cruel. Really, truly cruel right now."

"I'm not—"

"Say it!"

A car pulled up in front of us. Music blared out the windows, and Maggie's voice came from inside, "Kevin?"

He continued to look at me.

I couldn't look away.

"Hey!"

Then he murmured, "I can't lie anymore. I can't take it back."

I heard a whooshing sound as all the air left my lungs.

Kevin walked around the car and got in on the passenger side. He never looked at Maggie. His eyes held mine the entire time, and even as she pulled away, he watched me as he left.

I felt a void in my center that was the size of an ocean. I think it had been there the whole time.

CHAPTER TWENTY-THREE

I could've called Avery. I should've, but I didn't. Caden said he'd been driving home anyway so he pulled up in front of me ten minutes later.

"Yeah. I'm rethinking this now," I told him.

His eyebrows lifted. "This?" He pointed between us. "Us?"

"Calling you."

He motioned me to get in. "Come on. Let's head back."

Once I got inside and he pulled away, I couldn't stop myself from asking, "Are *you* rethinking us?"

"Our friendship?"

"Of course." I tucked my hands behind me. "What else is there to rethink?"

He studied me a moment before pulling ahead at an intersection. He didn't respond, not the entire time it took to get to his place. We went inside, and he looked at his bedroom. His head turned back toward me, and I saw the teasing grin.

"I'm not sure what you mean by rethinking us, but I was hoping for another round. You game?"

Yep. I definitely called the wrong person. "I think Kevin has feelings for me."

"Fuck." He turned and headed for the bedroom. "Now I get your drift."

"Should I stay?"

He motioned for me to follow. "Sure. Pretend I'm your girlfriend. Call me Carrie tonight."

"Are you serious?"

"No."

"Oh."

He sighed as I sat across from him. "So the stepbrother reared back up, huh?"

There were knots galore in my stomach, but I had to talk to him. Avery was a friend, but Caden was…more. I didn't know what more, but I wanted to be here, with him, having him listen to me.

I nodded and spilled everything. I was talking about Kevin, but he wasn't what I really wanted to talk about. The other thing scared me. I didn't know if I could talk about it. My hands twisted together on my lap, and I had formed a new yoga pose by the time I was done.

"What do you think?" I asked.

"You called me."

"Yeah."

"You told me this stuff."

I wasn't sure if these were questions, but I nodded again, just going with it. "I sure did."

"And you know I'm not a bullshitter."

"It's part of your intrigue." I waved a hand at him. "It completes the whole intimidation factor. Also makes girls wet their pants for you."

That didn't even faze him. He didn't blink. "So I'm going to give you my honest opinion."

"Oh." Now I could see where this was leading. "Okay. Yeah. Give it to me straight."

"What the fuck are you doing?"

"What?"

He got up for a beer, placing one in front of me as well when he returned. "That's why you came to me. You know you're being an idiot, so stop being an idiot."

"How am I being an idiot?"

"Why are you talking to me about your asshole stepbrother? You might've had feelings for him before, but I know you. Those are long gone, so what's really going on here?"

My lip twitched.

"What?"

"That used to be my name for you. Asshole." I sighed, taking a sip of my beer. "Those were the good old times."

"Kevin's a better fit for the name."

"It's a term of endearment now for me."

He scowled. "Really? You want to waste your time talking about him? Fine. I'll indulge you." He rolled his eyes. "I bet you $500 he has a new girl by next month."

"That's a week away."

"My bet still stands. And that girl won't be you. He's moving out."

I frowned. "From Maggie's?"

He shrugged. "I'm assuming. He wants a house meeting. He's going to ask to come back."

"Are you sure? I mean, are you sure that's what he's going to say?"

"He has to give the reason for a meeting, and since he was never officially kicked out, we have to let the meeting happen."

He was leaving Maggie... No, he was leaving Maggie's home. Why did I not want him to do that?

I twisted my fingers together. "Are you going to let him come back?"

"Me? Fuck no. The guys? Probably. We're big on second chances here. A lot of the guys get arrested for stupid shit."

"If he moves out, that means they're breaking up."

"Exactly." His eyes hardened. "Don't tell me I'm wrong and you're hoping to be the next girl. You just looked like a starving squirrel who saw its first nut."

I scowled. "What? No, I'm not."

He sighed in disgust. "He's not going to marry you."

"I don't want marriage. I don't want anything. I'm over him."

"Well, something's going on with you." He groaned. "Don't date him. He's a six-month guy. He dates a girl—"

"I know."

My hands were wrapped so tightly around each other, a paperclip couldn't have gotten in between them. He was right. God, he was right. "I don't have feelings for Kevin."

My chest burned. I felt that void opening even more.

"Right." His tone softened. "That's why you look like you're going to cry."

"I'm crying for the squirrel."

"Summer."

"It must've been so hungry."

I closed my eyes and shook my head. Enough with the nonsense. A different feeling descended on us, and I had to be honest too. My throat felt raw.

"I don't have feelings for Kevin, but..." I didn't know what to say. I didn't even know what was going on myself. I just felt that ache inside of me. It was so deep, all the way to my core.

I couldn't feel that. I'd talk about Kevin. Somehow he helped cover that up.

"He was the popular guy. I was a nobody. Every girl wanted him, but he was going to be *my* stepbrother. I thought it was meant to be. Fate put us together. I was so sure of it. I mean, what else could it have been, right?"

I laughed, then cringed, hearing how hollow it sounded. "I waited. I just kept waiting. He had one girlfriend, then another, and he was with a third when he went to college. It was like he couldn't stand to be alone. They always had to be with him at the house, but my graduation night..."

I'd stood there in my graduation robe. My hat was on, the tassel hanging in front of me. When I saw him sneak in through the back door, my heart had squeezed. I'd just known. He was there for me. It meant something.

"He came alone. That meant he didn't have a girlfriend. And that night... We were in the hallway." I winced, remembering it clearly now. "I was the one standing there stupidly. I kept staring at him, and he stared back." His bedroom had been behind me. "But he was just waiting to go to his room. That's all he was doing." My bedroom was up the stairs behind him. "I was drunk, and I just kept staring." Then he'd touched me on the shoulder. "I thought he was making a move." His hand had grazed my shoulder, but I closed the distance. I'd felt something else that night, a pain I didn't comprehend. I couldn't comprehend. "I kissed him. I made the first move. He just—" helped cover up that emptiness in me.

"Took advantage of you."

"No. He'd been drinking. We were both drinking."

"You were drunk."

"So was he—"

"Matthews doesn't drink to get drunk."

"What?"

Caden shook his head, hard-pressed rage barely blanketed in his eyes. "He drinks one or two. That's it. I've never seen him drunk, or heard about him being drunk."

"Ever?" My mouth felt dry.

"Ever." His jaw clenched. "He holds a drink all night long because it helps loosen girls up. If they think he's drinking..."

"...then they'll drink."

He'd had a beer all night at Clarissa's graduation party. "I thought he had a new beer every time I saw him." My hand had brushed against it when he'd put it on the counter before we left. "The bottle was warm."

"He knows what he's doing with girls, Summer." Caden leaned forward, his elbows on his knees. "Did he say he had feelings for you?"

"I wasn't prepared for you when I saw you."

My hands were sweating. It didn't matter. He wasn't the reason for this conversation anyway. That ache in me…

"You know he's a bad guy. You know he's a serial dater. You know he doesn't date longer than six months. You know all this. If he was so serious, why did he leave with someone else?"

I nodded with each statement. "I know all these things. You're right."

"Don't fall for him."

The truth bloomed in my chest. It was the way he'd said those words: *fall for him.* He wasn't Kevin. He was about as far from Kevin as it was possible to get—the anti-stepbrother. Kevin was a flashy light. He was the bobber on a hook, distracting the fish so they'd get caught.

Caden was so much more. He was the real deal. Suddenly that ache in me took on a different form of pain. It throbbed, and I felt a slice of panic.

I couldn't look away from Caden.

Kevin had already hurt me, or I'd thought he had. But that hadn't been real. It was empty. A game I had played with myself. This with Caden. This was real. What happened with this could shatter me.

A wall fell away as if I were seeing Caden for the first time.

It was Caden.

It was Caden…

"Oh, no."

Caden frowned. That gorgeous face of his—shadowed at times, mysterious, elusive, but so beautiful and so addicting. Even his frown didn't stop me from wanting to kiss him.

His head inched back. "You okay?"

"What?"

I was in love with Caden.

The realization was a bomb exploding inside of me. I knew there were feelings, but this… I wasn't prepared for this. I couldn't take a risk like this.

I loved Caden.

"What is it?" he asked again. "You're starting to worry me, and that's saying a lot. I've gotten used to your quirkiness."

I fumbled out, "I just remembered Avery called earlier. I should check in with her. Make sure she's okay with, you know, Marcus and all. He's not being that nice to her."

I was up and backing away.

"Summer." Caden followed me to the door.

"I'm good. She texted me, but I wanted to talk to you. I didn't really think." I backed into the door. I reached for the doorknob. "I'm going to go find her."

"I'm pretty sure they're at the Homecoming bonfire tonight."

"See? Exactly. She's with him. I really need to find her now."

"Summer," he said again.

I opened the door and hurried out, yelling over my shoulder, "I'll call you later."

I didn't hear his response. I was running. It was wrong, but I was acting on pure instinct. If he hurt me, I'd never come back from that.

CHAPTER TWENTY-FOUR

"You're coming Friday?"

"What?"

I was on the phone with Clarissa, and it took me the next second to realize what she was talking about. The road trip.

"Oh! Yes. The road trip in two weekends. Yes. Friday we're coming." Wait. Now the wheels were turning, and I remembered Caden saying something about Thursday. "No. We're coming Thursday." Or was it Saturday?

"Thursday? Okay. We can do that."

I chewed my bottom lip. "It could be Saturday."

I couldn't remember. I'd have to call Caden and ask, and that would be awkward. I'd been avoiding him since Friday night, since I realized my feelings for him. I got out of there before he realized, or I hoped I had.

Caden was a great friend, and I knew he had fun with me, but he didn't have feelings for me. I didn't think… Caden wasn't going to date me. He dated girls who were out of my league. He might kiss me, hold me, have sex with me—yes to all those—but date me and have real feelings for me?

It wasn't going to happen, and I wasn't about to make Caden into another Kevin. I wouldn't let my daydreams and fantasies go off to Fairy Neverland this time. Nope. I wasn't going to get carried away.

I already missed him.

Saturday and Sunday had been bleak. I'd spent Saturday afternoon with my dad and Sheila, but they'd headed home in the early evening. Apparently whatever they'd needed to work through on Friday wasn't fully resolved.

After they left, I'd watched movies with some girls on my floor, and I studied all day in the library on Sunday with Shayla. I'd ordered a pizza with Avery that night. Pre-the big fucked-up emotions unveiling, I would've hung out both nights with Caden. I sighed just thinking about it.

He would've been going to a party. He would've asked me to go. I would've said no, and we would've hung out at his place instead. Sunday night might've been spent the same way. Nothing special, but everything that made me feel seen and important and like I belonged, because Caden was my people. He was mine.

I *really* missed him.

"Okay, what the hell is going on with you?"

"What?"

I could hear the scowl on Clarissa's face through the phone. "We've been talking for an hour, and it's like pulling teeth to get details from you. And you're sighing like a damned train signaling it's coming to a crossing. What the hell is going on? Don't lie to me. We've been best friends since fifth grade. I will sic May on you if I don't think you're being straight with me."

I shuddered. "Not May. Never May."

"Well, then start spilling, Stoltz. This is bullshit. Tell me what's going on."

"I can't." I squeezed my eyes closed.

"It's a guy."

"How'd you know?"

"I'm not even dignifying that with an answer."

"Right." I grimaced. "Best friend."

She harrumphed. "Since fifth grade."

"Yeah."

"So who is it? And please don't say it's Kevin."

"How'd you know?"

"It is Kevin?!"

"What?" *Oh!* "No, but how'd you know about Kevin?"

"You mean how'd I know you used to like him?"

"Yeah."

She sighed this time. "Summer, every girl in school liked him. Trust me. You weren't alone."

"You too?"

"I'm human."

"And May?"

"Her too. She slept with him. Did you know that?"

"Shut up." I kicked against the desk, pushing my chair back on its hind legs again. "When?"

"Our senior year. He came back for a visit."

"Where was I?" *Wait.* "Didn't he have a girlfriend then?"

"He always had a girlfriend."

I groaned, smacking my hand to my forehead. "I really feel dumb now. Please tell me you didn't sleep with him."

"I didn't." She got quiet. "Wait, did you?"

I switched to chewing the inside of my cheek. This was so fucked up.

"When?" she demanded.

My cheeks were flaming red. "Graduation night."

"Summer! You told me you were going to kiss him, but I didn't think it would happen."

"I did? When?"

"At the party, but you were drunk. We were all drunk."

"Matthews doesn't get drunk."

"Was Kevin?" I asked.

"Was he what? Drunk?"

"Yeah." My word came out raspy.

"I don't know. He'd been drinking, but now that you ask, I can't remember if he was drunk or not. I don't think he was." She paused. "Does that matter?"

Yes. So much yes.

"He took advantage of you."

I couldn't get Caden out of my head. I murmured into the phone, "Not anymore."

"Oh, Sum."

There was the best friend doing the best friend thing. She heard the hurt in my voice. "Did he hurt you? Is he coming that weekend? I'll rip off his balls."

I laughed. "I've missed you so much. You know that?"

"I've missed you too. We've all been so busy, but we need to talk twice a month."

"Agreed." My chest felt lighter. I could breathe easier. "Or once a week."

"Yes. Daily emails."

"Group chats."

"Hangout chats."

"Yes!"

"No more of this not keeping in touch. It's bullshit."

"Agreed." I wanted to thrust my fist in the air. I was getting inspired. "Friends make the world go round."

"Damn straight." She cursed. "My roommate just got back. I have to go. You'll like her when you come."

"Okay." I was back to chewing my bottom lip. "Oh hey, before you go, the guys have rented some house for us, I think. But it might be full. If I needed to, could I stay with you guys in your dorm room?"

"Are you serious?"

"Yeah, but only if there's room—"

"We were hoping to crash at the house. It's a big deal here that Alpha Mu is opening up their second house for you guys. It's given us major cred."

I cursed. "Really?" I couldn't hold back my disappointment. "I mean, yay! That's awesome."

"Kevin's in that fraternity. Is he coming? *Is* he the guy? You never answered me."

"What guy?"

"Don't play dumb."

"I'm not." I was.

"I know there's a guy thing going on. I just haven't figured out if it's Kevin or not. Is it him?"

"No. That ship sailed, then kinda returned to dock. He's in a different marina now."

"I'm sorry."

She meant it. "I'm fine with it."

"But I'm assuming *the guy* is coming?"

"Can I plead the fifth?"

"Oh, Sum. I'm sorry."

Pesky tears. I kept blinking. I did not want them to fall.

"Asswipe, let's go," I heard in the background on her end. Clarissa said something back, but it was muffled.

"Look, I have to go," she said, coming back on. "We have something happening, and my usually amazing roommate is being bossy right now."

"I heard that," a voice piped up again.

Clarissa pulled away from the phone. "I meant for you to hear that. I'm comforting one of my best friends here."

There was another exchange, but it was muffled again, and then she came back on the phone. "I'll talk to you later? I know there are people from your end coordinating with the Alpha Mu chapter here, but keep us in the loop too, will you? Let us know what day you're coming: Thursday, Friday, Saturday, or even Sunday. I don't care when. I just want to know, and you can sleep here every single night if you want to."

A wave of gratitude came over me. "Thank you, Clarissa."

"Did you want me to call back later tonight? We could talk about the guy."

"No. I don't even want to talk about the guy."

"So there is a guy! I got that out of you at least."

My cheeks were hurting, stretched tight from my stupid grin. "Love you, Clarissa."

We'd just hung up when I heard, "You okay?"

I hadn't heard my door opening, but there stood Avery with a concerned frown on her face. She gestured to my phone. "I couldn't help but overhear some of that. What's going on?"

I felt raw and exposed, and I was done feeling that way. "Stupid boy stuff."

She came in, shutting the door behind her, and crossed to sit on my bed. "Kevin?"

I started to shake my head, but stopped. "I'm not trying to shut you out, but I just don't want to talk about it."

"No, that's cool, but..." She looked down to her lap.

"What?" I turned completely around in my desk chair, gripping the back of it.

"He broke up with Maggie."

Caden had called it. Kevin had laid out the breadcrumbs for me to follow.

"Really?"

"He moved out, and he's at the fraternity again."

"You've talked to Maggie?"

She nodded, watching me carefully. "She said he had feelings for a different girl."

Oh. My. God.

It was happening.

The evidence was in front of me, all of it.

Kevin really did have feelings for me. He'd ended things first with Maggie. As if he was going to magically appear, I glanced at my door. I could almost feel him on the other side of it. I frowned.

"She actually asked me to ask *you* for a favor," Avery continued.

"Who?"

"Maggie."

"Maggie what?"

"Maggie asked me to ask you a favor."

My mind was spinning. "Huh?"

Avery cocked her head to the side. "You okay?"

"Yeah. Why?"

"You seem a little more out of it than normal."

I gave her a rueful grin. "Caden said something like that to me on Friday. I must need to rein in my weirdness."

She was still giving me a weird look. "Maybe a little. You're having a hard time following this conversation."

I nodded, and then refocused. "Okay. What's the favor?"

"She wants you to find out who the girl is."

"Say what?"

"Kevin always has another girl on standby. If he ended things with Maggie, there's got to be a new girl already. He didn't even make it six months this time. Can you go ask him who it is?"

Cue the awkwardness. It was me, I was pretty sure, but I needed to make sure, or I needed to make sure he knew I wasn't an option. The real reason I was going? I wanted to see Caden. A weekend was too long.

"I'll go."

"You will?" Avery's eyes went wide.

I grinned. "I mean, yeah, I'll go and ask him. I don't think he'll tell me."

She snorted. "You won't have to ask. She'll probably be in his room already."

"Yeah. Maybe." Then I asked, "So we're pro-Maggie now? I mean, you're pro-Maggie again?"

Her hands had been on her knees, but she pulled them back at my question. She lifted a shoulder. "I don't know what I am, but she's bawling in my room, and I couldn't kick her out."

I reached forward, laying my hand over hers. "You're a real friend. You know that, right?"

"Or I'm a stupid friend." She lifted up gloomy eyes. "She's going to go after Marcus again. I can feel it."

"But that won't matter, because he's with you, right?" When she said nothing, I added, "I can see him wanting her to want him, but just so he can enjoy it when he rejects her." I sat back, my hand leaving hers. "I don't think you need to worry."

I hoped I was right.

CHAPTER TWENTY-FIVE

I stood outside the basement door and flashbacks from my first night at North River—the first time I ever came to Kevin's fraternity house—washed over me. I wasn't sure why. Maybe the uncertainty? Because I didn't know what I would find on the other side of that door? Either way, the nerves I felt that night hit me again.

I smoothed my hands down my pants. There was no need for them to be sweaty. I just needed to get this over. "My love life sucks," I muttered under my breath.

"It does if you're heading down there."

I recognized that voice. Of course. I had the best luck in the world. But then again—I looked at Marcus. "Why are you here?"

He smirked, but his eyes weren't amused. "I'm here to see Caden. I thought I'd walk through the house, and I saw you." His face went blank. "I want to state a few facts for you."

He wanted to fight.

Okay. I turned fully to face him and put my hands in my pockets. I needed to get comfortable to hear this, and then it would be my turn. I had a few thoughts to share as well.

"Fine," I told him. "You have the floor." I raised my finger. "For now."

The corner of his mouth lifted. "You are a smartass."

"Your brother hasn't told you that?"

"He did. I didn't believe him. I just thought you were kind of crazy. I've been thinking he's lost his nuts since taking up with you, but I don't know. I like the spine. You should show it more often."

I snorted. "As opposed to the times I haven't? You mean all those times we've hung out since bowling? All those times you just glared at me in class? I've missed my chance to stand up and roar?"

"You don't have to be sarcastic."

"Oh contraire. Your statement just now called for it. Literally."

He rolled his eyes. "Avery's been a little nervous around you. I thought she was nuts too."

I showed him my teeth. "Razor sharp." Wait. Why was Avery nervous around me?

He grunted. My little quips and one-liners weren't working on him. He'd looked at me with disdain when he first spoke, and that disdain was still there.

He motioned to the closed basement door. "Why are you going down there?"

"Because I heard Kevin and Maggie broke up. I was going to comfort him."

"You're lying."

"What? You're here to comfort him too?"

His lip twitched. "Okay, you're a little funny. I'll give you that."

I deadpanned, "My life is complete."

His smile vanished again. "You're here for the same reason I am."

"Didn't think you and Kevin were that close. I must've missed the bonding time while he was screwing your girlfriend, who you're *not* going to start dating again. Right?" I scowled. "Because that'd be a really shitty thing to do to Avery."

Now I had his full attention. He studied me, reassessing. "You're here because of Avery?"

"Who do you think Maggie went to for comfort?" I shook my head, making a *tsk*ing sound. "Not me. That's for sure."

"Maggie went to Avery?" He laughed, raking his hand over his head. "What a piece of work."

Had Maggie called him too, sending him to Kevin's to discover the new girl?

"It's a little weird to have an ex-girlfriend call you when the boyfriend she left you for breaks up with her, right? That's weird." Unless... "Unless she called because she wants to get back with you."

A light flared in his eyes. It highlighted his guilt before he masked it.

I shifted on my feet, crossing my arms over my chest. "Huh."

"Huh?" His lip curled in a sneer. "What does that mean?"

I gestured to the door with my head. "I could change his mind."

His nostrils flared. "You're lying."

I was. "I know how to manipulate Kevin." I totally didn't. "I could make him want to go back to Maggie." I stepped toward him. "What do you think of that?"

I searched his eyes intently. If he wanted Maggie, there'd be a reaction—I saw it. A brief glimmer of irritation flared before he caught himself again.

I stepped back. "I see."

"You don't see anything."

I pointed at his face. "No, I did. I saw the guilt in your eyes. You're here to make sure Kevin really is over with Maggie. Aren't you?" My nose wrinkled. "You're an asshole." I shook my head. "Is *every* guy an asshole?"

"I'm not here to make sure he's done with Maggie."

"Then what are you doing here?"

"I didn't even know they broke up. I was fucking with you."

"What?" I stiffened.

He gestured to the door. "I saw you from the sidewalk. You usually go around the house to see my brother, but you didn't this time. You went in through the front door, so I thought maybe you were doing something else. Like I said before, you're changing my brother, and I don't like that. I wanted to know what you were doing."

"Were you following me?" My mouth hung open.

"No!" He looked disgusted. "I was telling the truth. I really am here to see Caden. I was getting out of my car when you walked past me on the sidewalk. That's it."

Okay. That made more sense, but— "You're protecting Caden?" Bombshell number one. "From *me*?" Bombshell number two.

"Don't fuck with him, okay?"

"What are you talking about?"

"You know what I'm talking about."

I honestly didn't. "Huh?"

He jerked his head to the door. "Go see your bitch brother, but don't go from his bed to my brother's. Got it?"

"Caden told you?"

He didn't answer. He just shook his head, shoved his hands in his pockets, and glared one last time before heading down the hallway that led out the back door.

I gulped. Everything was swimming inside of me. *Did Caden like me? Is that what Marcus was implying?* But I was the one who had feelings for Caden. He was going to hurt me, not the other way around.

I lifted my hand to open the basement door, but let it fall back to my side. I had to know what Marcus meant. Before I could turn, going to find Caden, the basement door swung open.

It hit me in the forehead as I stepped back.

"Ouch!" My hand pressed to my head.

"Oh, hey!" Kevin squeezed through the door. "You were coming to see me?"

Worst. Timing. Ever.

I scowled. "Who is it?"

"What?"

I didn't have time for this. "The new girl. Who is it? Is it me?"

He had a bright smile on his face, but the more questions I asked, the more it dimmed.

His Adam's apple bobbed up and down. "What are you talking about?"

"You never break up with one girl unless you have another one in mind. You dumped Maggie, so who's the new girl? I just want to know."

"Um..."

I rolled my eyes. "For the record, I don't want it to be me."

"You don't?" He looked pained, the lines around his mouth growing tight. "Well, it's not you."

"It's not?"

"No." He still looked pained.

"So who is it?"

He lifted a shoulder. "No one."

"No one?" I motioned to my mouth. "This, right here. You don't see it, but it's on the floor."

"Come on." He glanced to the ceiling for a brief second. "I'm not that bad."

"You *are* that bad. You're the six-monther, remember? #Sixmonthguy."

"Don't start doing hashtags."

"#Sorry."

He let out a breath, sliding his hands in his back pockets. "Look. Truce, okay? There really is no girl. Ever since you said something about my pattern, it's been bugging me. It's not healthy, you know? To always have a girl with me? So I figure I should try to do something about it."

"Like what?"

"Like—" He motioned between the two of us. "—what we're doing here. We're just talking. Nothing else. No flirting. No sexual innuendos, no signals being sent about hooking up later."

"You do that sort of stuff?"

"Don't you?"

I couldn't even figure out my signals to myself. "No. You do all that in a regular conversation?"

"More or less."

I had things to learn. "Wow." So much to learn.

He grinned, seeming to relax. "It feels good. Refreshing."

"What is?"

"A conversation that's just about what we're talking about."

I felt a headache starting. "Okay. I can't wrap my head around the kind of conversations you usually have, so let's let it go."

"Okay. Good." His grin went up a notch, and his hands came to rest on my shoulders. He squeezed. "This is what being normal is like. Huh."

I tensed and looked at his hands. "Not in the slightest."

"What?"

I bounced my shoulders up. "Those."

"My hands?" He let go and backed away, his palms spread out toward me. "That wasn't a normal thing to do, was it?"

"Nope. That's totally normal to do," I paused. "If I were your *girlfriend*."

"Right." He backed away another step and slid his hands back into his pockets. "I might have some things to learn."

"Don't think about sex when you're talking to a girl."

"Well, don't get ahead of yourself." He grinned ruefully at me. "No guy can do that."

"Then I've got nothing for you."

"That's okay. I'll figure it out."

And now cue the uncomfortable silence. Everything in me wanted to go see Caden. Marcus was there, talking to him. He could be saying things about me, about how I was leading him on, how I was hanging out with Kevin. I couldn't defend myself. But instead of bursting in and protecting my relationship with Caden, I was stuck trying to teach my stepbrother how to be a normal, nice guy.

This conversation blew.

"Am I bothering you?"

"What?"

Kevin motioned to my face. "You did like eight eye-rolls in a row there. Is it Caden?"

My eyebrows shot right up. "Caden?"

"You do like him, don't you?"

I couldn't even think about lying because I already felt the heat inching up my neck, and my cheeks warmed. I looked down at the ground.

"It's okay, you know."

It wasn't. He could say something. He could turn Caden against me, or worse, tell him what I was convinced Marcus was already saying. He could tell Caden I was obsessed with him. Or how delusional I could be.

Oh, God. Kevin knew my crazy better than anyone. I was already in the pre-stalker phase. I was beginning to recognize my phases.

Step one: realize you're in love.

Step two: deny you're in love.

Step three: start staking out his hangouts.

Step four: obsess every minute about him.

Step five: I gulped. I didn't want to name it because I was pretty sure I was there. I didn't want to know how far away I was from sneaking into Caden's bed wearing lingerie. A restraining order came after that.

"Hey." Kevin put his hands on my shoulders again.

I tensed.

He shook his head. "I know. I know, but I'm not being flirty here. I'm being a friend, or trying to be. It's okay if you have feelings for Caden. I know a lot of girls do. Half the girls I've hooked up with were just using me to get to him."

"Really?"

"Really."

I nudged his hands off my shoulders.

He backed away, his hands in the air. "Listen, I'm glad you're here. I was coming to find you."

"I knew it!"

He lowered his hands to his side. "Not for that." He sounded hurt.

I shrugged. He'd get over it.

"I was thinking we could start fresh, try to be the way my mom wanted us to be in the first place."

"What are you talking about?"

"We should be more like family, you know? So I was thinking you could help me learn how to be a nice guy, and in the process, we could maybe become actual stepsiblings. What do you say?"

My eyebrows locked forward. "What's the catch?" There always seemed to be one with him.

"No catch. I promise." He offered up a grin, one that seemed genuine. "I mean it. I want to change, and since you're the closest thing I have to a sister, I thought you'd be the perfect one to help." He held his hand out. "Deal?"

I glanced at his hand, then back to his eyes, and I caught his small smile. Then an all-business look took over, and he nodded as if to reassure me. This could go all sorts of wrong, but I found myself reaching out. My hand slid against his palm, and I sucked in my breath. Maybe I hadn't thought this through…

Then he said, "Deal."

And it was too late.

CHAPTER TWENTY-SIX

I never found out if Marcus said anything to Caden. I was a chicken shit. I made that deal with Kevin and as soon as I did, a part of me felt like I was betraying Caden. The next day already, Kevin started coming over. I would've loved this new development a few months ago, but it was weird now.

He showed up in the mornings. We had breakfast together. He would point out the girls he "would do," which was almost all of them. I made him tell me what lines he would use to pick the girl up, then I dissected each statement and explained how it could be rephrased or redelivered so the sexual innuendo wasn't there. Most of Kevin's lines weren't sexually suggestive, but they were when coupled with the boyish grin he always seemed to have on his face.

After breakfast, we'd depart for classes and resume our "lessons" in the evenings.

Avery and her friends weren't ecstatic to find the enemy in home territory, but once I told Avery there was no new girl and explained the new Kevin, they slowly warmed up to the idea. Avery began coming around after the first night. The rest took a few more days and Claudia joined the next week, a few days before the big road trip. Except Shell. She wasn't allowed because she began flirting with Kevin within five minutes of being around him. She was banned from any event that involved my stepbrother.

"Kevin, are you going this weekend?" one of the girls asked from the couch.

Kevin and I hadn't discussed the road trip.

As I looked down at my lap, I could feel his gaze on me as he answered, "Uh, I'm not sure."

Avery asked, "You're back in the frat house, right?"

"Yeah."

I could hear caution in his voice.

"Then you should go. Why wouldn't you?"

"Is that your personal approval?" He sounded like he was joking. "You guys used to hate me. Now you'd be okay hanging out with me over an entire weekend?"

"Well..." Avery coughed, clearing her throat. "I mean, you're trying to change. Who are we to judge that? You know?"

"Thank you for that, but I really don't think it's up to me whether I go or not."

I felt all the attention on me then, and I looked up. Yep. Four pairs of eyes were looking right at me. Avery. Claudia. Two of their friends. The only one not looking was Kevin, and I knew he was trying to be nice. A twinge of guilt flared up.

"You should come," I said.

He shifted, turning to look at me. "You sure?"

The girls didn't know about my feelings for Caden, but Kevin did. My neck was stiff as I nodded. "Yeah. I think you should come."

"Well, fuck. This weekend just got a lot more interesting," Claudia said, shifting back in the desk chair. "Marcus, Caden, and now Matthews. Dude, if you smart off to either of the brothers, I'm not wading in for your defense. I'm clarifying that off the bat."

Kevin's dimples formed, but his lips didn't move as he held back a grin. "Thanks for the warning."

"The more you know, Kev. The more you know."

Avery's eyebrows furrowed together, and she kept glancing at me. Then the girl who'd brought up the weekend plans in the first place said, "He's not with Maggie anymore, so why would it even be a problem?"

I winced. There was no reason. I had feelings for Caden. Kevin was my stepbrother. Yes, there were lingering issues between Marcus and Kevin, but—oh, hell. I was lying to myself. I'd been avoiding Caden for two weeks, and it was only partly because of my feelings for him. The other part of it was Kevin. I knew Caden wouldn't have been happy about my spending time with him, even though it was about strengthening my family relationship with Kevin.

"Um…" Kevin's voice was soft. "You're right. It wouldn't matter anymore, unless Maggie's going too."

Claudia snorted. "No way. She's not invited. The only person who still talks to her in here is Avery."

"Hey," Avery said. "She's friends with *all* my high school friends. There's history there. It's really hard for me to walk away from—"

"We know." Claudia cut her off. "I'm not giving you shit. I hope you'll be as forgiving with me if I ever mess up like that."

Avery frowned. "Thanks, Claudia. I appreciate that."

Claudia snapped her fingers and pointed at Avery. "That's what friends are for."

Kevin smirked. "Forgiveness."

Claudia shrugged, sending him a sly smile. "Appreciation."

"AH! No. Right there."

Claudia's head snapped around to the other girl on the couch. She'd been quiet almost the entire time, so I kept forgetting her name, but pointed at Claudia now. "You were flirting with him. Stop flirting."

"I was not."

Avery looked at everyone. "What? I missed it."

"She was totally flirting. I saw that little smile you sent him. All seductive-like."

"I wasn't." Claudia said to Kevin, "I wasn't flirting. Tell her."

Kevin didn't say anything, looking to me instead.

Well, crappers. I knew where this was going. Claudia scared me. He raised an eyebrow. "Were you watching?"

Claudia turned to me, waiting too.

I groaned, covering my face with my hands. "Don't put me in the middle of this."

"I wasn't flirting!"

Kevin snorted. "Right."

"I wasn't."

The quiet friend threw her hands in the air. "Even the guy is admitting to it. 'Fess up, Claudia. It's okay if you admit it."

"That's all bullshit." Claudia's shoulders stiffened. "Kevin, you know I didn't mean anything by that."

He leaned back and spread his legs out. "Uh, pretty sure that same smile was why we hooked up in the first place."

Everyone went still after that, and I heard Avery mutter under her breath, "Oh, no."

"Wait." Their first friend snapped to attention as she looked from Kevin to Claudia and back again. "You two hooked up?"

Kevin shot Claudia a look. "That wasn't known?"

"Nope." She made a grumbling sound in her throat. "Thanks for that."

"Oops." He sent me an apologetic look. "Did you know?"

"I—" was so fucking busted. I felt Avery's attention at the same time Claudia looked at me. I had one second to cover my ass, and Avery's. I feigned surprise and shook my head. "I shouldn't be surprised, but I had no idea."

Avery muttered next to me, "Seriously?"

Claudia snorted. "Don't ever do theatre, Summer. You suck at it." She gave Avery a scorching look before heading to the door. "Thanks for sharing that private information, which I told you not to tell anyone."

Avery jumped to her feet. "You didn't like her in the beginning. I thought it would help smooth the way."

"It did." Claudia yanked my door open. "It smoothed the way for me to not hang out with you again." She left, letting the door slam shut behind her.

Kevin smiled, looking relaxed and cheerful. "I just had an epiphany."

"What?" the second friend asked.

"This is why I like girls so much. You guys are way more entertaining than guys."

"What do you mean?"

He shrugged. "Guys are all about sports, sex, or beer. Girls are about everything else. That kind of dramatic exit would never happen with guys. If it did, there'd be a beat down involved, but nothing like this. No wonder I date so much. I gravitate more toward girls in general. I'm a straight guy, with this face." He gestured to himself. "No wonder I have girlfriends all the time."

He stood, smoothing out his jeans and shirt. "Thank you, Summer. I'd been thinking I was messed up, but I'm not. I just like girls, a lot."

"So are you coming this weekend?" The question came from Avery.

"Nah." Kevin glanced at me. "I think it'd just cause problems for this one." He bent and collected his bag, putting his notebooks and textbooks back into it. "You take off tomorrow, don't you?"

I nodded.

He threw his bag over his shoulder. "Let's catch up when you come back. I want to hear how it went."

Avery groaned, collapsing on the bed. "Claudia is going to be so pissed at me."

The first friend laughed. "She already is."

Avery gave her a dark look. "I mean for a long time. She's going to be pissed for a loooong time. What am I going to do?"

"She'll get over it. Claudia's just mad because now we all know she should've been honest with us in the first place."

The second friend chimed in. "Yeah. Shell had no idea about Claudia's past with Kevin. She should've been upfront about it, unless it happened afterward. If that happened..." She fell silent as her eyes widened. "Shit."

The first friend shared a look with her. "Claudia broke the girl code."

"Now, we don't know—" Avery paled. "She didn't know Shell that well when it happened."

The first friend frowned in fierce disapproval. "Shit's going to hit the fan when Shell finds out. You don't have to worry about Claudia. She's going to be clamoring for your support in no time. She's got some damn explaining to do."

The two left, leaving Avery behind, and a tear fell down her cheek. "They're wrong. Claudia will just leave the group. What do I do, Summer?"

I shook my head. I could pat her arm, give her a hug, utter some soothing words, but I was supposed to be traveling with Caden tomorrow. I'd been avoiding him for too long. I was in a doghouse of my own.

"I have no idea."

It was after midnight when someone knocked softly on my door.

I was still up, doing last-minute packing, and I opened the door to find a girl I didn't know. She wore an oversized North River University sweatshirt over black leggings, her hair in a messy bun with a pencil stuck through the middle of it.

"Hi." She held up a hand. "You don't know me, but I work the front desk, and a guy is downstairs asking to talk to you."

"Oh." I frowned. "Do you know who it is?"

She shrugged. "No clue. I asked him, but I already forgot. I'm studying. Finals and all. Do you want me to tell him to take a hike?"

"Uh." It could be Caden. "No. I'll come down."

She started back, but said over her shoulder, "Guys can be in the downstairs lobby all the time, but he can't come up here."

"I know."

"I'm just letting you know because I don't want to have to report you and deal with all that paperwork. I have a final in two days. I'll be pissed if you take away from my studying."

"Well, okay then." After grabbing my room key and phone, I shut the door behind me and headed down after her. "Note to self, the midnight desk clerk is kind of a bitch."

When I got down there and saw her back behind the desk, she had her head buried in a psychopharmacology book. I changed my mind. Just the name of her class stressed me out.

No guy waited next to the desk, and I checked the other front lobby across from her desk. No one was there either, so I went downstairs.

Someone was studying a world map, but I didn't see anyone else around the downstairs lobby that could be Caden. "Hello?"

I hadn't checked the computer room. He could've been in there… But then the map guy turned around, and I recognized Diego.

I stopped short. "Hey." Ice plunged into my veins.

The normally loud, happy, and vivacious Diego was not the guy in front of me. He had bags under his eyes and no spark in them either.

He rubbed his hands together. "Hey. Uh, I wasn't sure if this was appropriate or not."

"It's fine." I frowned. "What's up?"

It was Caden. My heart raced. I knew it was Caden.

My voice dropped an octave. "Is he okay?"

"I think so, but I didn't know who else to call." He kept glancing away.

"It's okay. Just tell me what it is."

Please be okay. Please be okay.

"Caden was at the bar tonight when he got a call—"

"From who?"

He shook his head. "He didn't say, but I know it's about his brother."

Marcus?

"Colton. He's in the hospital."

Oh. My frown deepened. Oh! "He's at the hospital?"

"I know there's another brother, but I don't know his phone number. You're the only person Caden's brought to the bar, and I remembered that one girl said she was in the same dorm as you. She kept talking about you that night after you guys left, so the name was burned in my memory." He grimaced, laughing softly. "I had the worst hangover the next morning with that girl's voice on repeat—"

I'd stopped listening. I grabbed his arm, stopping him in mid-sentence. "Thank you, Diego."

His hesitation slid away. His eyes warmed, and his hand covered mine. "I knew it was the right thing to come here. I told the girl your name. I didn't know your last name, but she finally said she'd go see if you were even still awake. It took me ten minutes of arguing with her. I came down here because I didn't want to risk getting thrown out."

I nodded. "Yeah."

My insides clenched. Caden was hurting.

I started for the stairs. "I need to go."

And when I got outside, I remembered I didn't have a car.

Diego had followed me out. "I can give you a ride."

I didn't feel relief, thankful, or even grateful. I should've felt all of those things, said something to indicate how much I appreciated that, but nothing else mattered in that moment. Caden mattered. That was it.

All my usual niceties left me. Even my weird quirks disappeared, and I only uttered, "Yes, please."

I just had to get to him.

CHAPTER TWENTY-SEVEN

I was an idiot.

After circling around all over the hospital and finding nothing, I was given directions to a second waiting lounge. That's where Caden was, and once I saw him standing in the hallway, with his head down and his phone pressed against his ear, I knew how utterly and completely stupid I had been. He'd called a few times during the week, and I'd always made up an excuse. I was a dumbass. It'd been almost a week since I last saw him—a week too long. An invisible weight pressed down on my chest, and I had to stop to swallow a lump in my throat.

I went to him.

His back was turned to me, and he nodded his head as he spoke. "Yeah. I know. Yeah. Okay." He paused. "If Marcus could come, that'd be good. He's going to be moved there tomorrow morning." Then he turned. He saw me, and he went still. "Uh, yeah. A seventy-two-hour hold… Mom, I gotta go. I'll call you back."

My hand ached from wanting to touch him.

He hung up, and his eyebrows lifted in surprise. "What are you doing here?"

"Diego came to my dorm. He said you got a call about your brother, that you were here."

He cocked his head to look behind me.

"He's not with me. He just gave me a ride here."

"Oh." His Adam's apple moved up and down as he swallowed, then a hardness came over him. "You should go." He started past me.

I caught his arm. "Wait."

"Summer, now's not the time for your weird mind fucks. I've got serious shit to deal with here. My brother—" He lifted a hand to point behind me, but stopped. "My brother..."

"What?"

Please tell me. Please let me in, even though you have no reason to.

He looked down at my hand. So did I, and holding a breath, I moved it to his chest.

I asked, a tiny whisper even to my ears, "What happened to your brother? I'm here for you. I just want to be here for you."

"Where've you been the last two weeks?"

"I—" Crap on a stick. I shook my head. "I'm here for you tonight."

"Just tonight?"

That lump jumped back up in my throat. I had to swallow over it again. "And this weekend. For the trip." *And forever, if you want that.*

He leaned back against the wall, folding his arms over his chest. His face was just as gorgeous as the last time I'd seen him, but it was exhausted, like Diego's had been. No, that wasn't true. Caden looked like he might be the definition of exhaustion. But over all of that, a hard mask came over his face. His jaw clenched, and I knew this was the no-bullshitting Caden.

"Just tonight and this weekend?" he asked.

I let out a small breath and glanced down to the floor. My hands twisted around the end of my shirt. "No, not just for then." I looked back. "I can't tell you why I've been avoiding you."

"So you *have* been avoiding me."

I paused. "Was that a trick question?"

He rolled his eyes, shifting so he rested against the wall. I moved so my side was against it too, and we stood even closer now. "Just tell me what's going on with you."

"I can't. That's the problem."

"Why not?"

"Because if I did, that'd lead to a whole other conversation, and to be honest, I'm almost shitting my pants even thinking about that conversation. So yeah. I'm here, but I don't want to talk about why I haven't been here, and I just want to be here for you. That whole last sentence doesn't make sense, but I don't care. Can we truce it for the night?"

"No."

My shoulders slumped. "Why not?"

"Because I don't like it. Why the disappearing act? I won't let you stay until you tell me. Is it because you have feelings for me?"

"WHAT?!" My eyes snapped open.

"Because if you *think* you have feelings for me, you're wrong."

"I am?"

He shook his head, a slight smirk there, and hooked a finger into a loop on my waistband. He pulled me closer, lowering his head. "There's lust between us. I'm going to give that to you, and knowing how screwed up you are about your stepbrother, I can understand if you got it twisted. You don't have feelings for me."

"I don't?"

He was wrong. But he was making it okay to be around him, and I was going with it. I needed to be here. I couldn't have stayed away any longer anyway.

I was so weak.

"No." He pulled me the rest of the way until there was no distance between us.

I felt him. I felt the thump of his heart. I felt the heat of his body, and I especially felt how he wanted me. I was salivating.

He lowered his head until his breath warmed my lips. "But here's my warning for you: I need you tonight. Don't run." He pulled his head back, his eyes searching mine. "Please don't run."

He delivered a bomb to me and stepped back as it detonated. I felt wrecked, but I could only nod, because in that moment, I would've given him anything. I was his for the night. I was maybe his for more than the night, and if he wanted to call it a lie, I didn't care.

I whispered, "I won't."

His hand cupped the side of my face, his thumb resting on my cheek, and I felt the tension leave his body. Everything relaxed, and his forehead came down to mine. "Thank you."

I cupped the side of his face, too, but I bit down on my lip. I kept the words from spilling out, the ones that wanted to be released so badly.

He was wrong. My feelings weren't just misplaced emotions. They were a lot more than that.

"Mr. Banks?"

A nurse came down the hallway in blue scrubs.

Caden stiffened, readying himself, and turned around. "Yeah? Is he okay?"

She nodded, a tight smile on her face. "He's awake and asking for you." Her eyes moved to me. "Family only for now. Doctor's orders."

"Yeah. I know. That's fine." He reached behind him and grabbed my hand. He held on tight. "Thank you."

"No problem." She started to leave, but paused a few steps away. "Would you and your guest like some coffee? I was going to take a quick break myself. I can bring some back."

"That'd be great. Thank you again."

She nodded, and a sad and weathered smile filtered across her face. "I can bring you coffee all night, if you'd like. That'll never be a problem."

I had a flashback to when my mom was in the hospital. Another nurse had said the same thing, *"I'll be here with you all night."* She'd offered blankets, a pillow, coffee, water, snacks. She'd come in every hour to check on us. And I knew she looked through the door more often than that, just to make sure my mother was still breathing.

I felt tears threatening, so I concentrated on Caden and touched his hand. He caught mine and held on tight, only releasing it when he stepped inside his brother's room. As the door opened, I looked down. It wasn't fair for me to see his brother the way he was, not the first time I met him. Every time Caden went to his brother's room, I looked away until the door closed.

That's how we spent the next two hours.

Caden would go in, stay for a bit, and I would wait in the hallway. After the second time she noticed me, the nurse brought me a chair, then a blanket, and I had my perch there. Caden wouldn't stay inside long. He'd do ten or fifteen minutes, then come out when his brother fell back asleep. He'd always grab my hand when he returned, and that made it all worth it. Whatever this was, whatever was going on with us, it would all be worth it.

After the third hour, Caden leaned against the wall beside my chair. The bags under his eyes were drooping further and further. "Maybe you should head back for the night?"

"What are you going to do?"

He glanced in the window, through a crack in the blinds. "I have no idea. I hoped Marcus would come tonight."

Caden hadn't told me what happened. It was on the edge of my tongue to ask, but even before Diego dropped me off at the hospital, I knew it had something to do with Colton's secret. I ached seeing the pain on Caden's face, and I ached even more not understanding what had put it there.

I squeezed his hand. "I'll do whatever you want me to do."

He glanced down with a faint grin. "They're going to kick you out of here once morning shift shows up."

"I know. I can wait in the lobby."

"You sure?"

The same nurse we'd been seeing all night now came toward us with another woman beside her, wearing a long white coat.

"You're Colton's brother?" she called. "I'm Dr. Holbreck. I'm the physician on call today, and Dr. Reinier briefed me with everything going on." She held her hand out, and as Caden shook it, she turned to me. "Are you Colton's girlfriend?"

"She's with me."

Her eyes fell to our joined hands. "Okay, well, I'm going to step in and check on your brother. I'd like some alone time with him, and then I'll pull you in to go over everything once more." She paused, her eyes scanning the hallway. "Is there any other family with you?"

"My dad's in Beijing, and my mom couldn't leave the house."

"There's another brother, isn't there?"

Caden's jaw clenched. "He's not here. It's just me."

The doctor didn't move, but the lines around her mouth softened in sympathy. "And your girlfriend."

"Yeah." Caden's hand jerked in reaction, but he only tightened his hold before stepping back so the doctor and nurse could enter the room. After they passed his hands found my shoulders, and he closed his eyes, letting out a deep breath when the door closed behind them.

My hands came to rest on top of his. "You okay?"

"No." His eyes opened, haunted. "But I will be. Thank you for being here with me."

"But…" I knew it was coming. "Is this when you send me away?"

He started to answer. His mouth opened, then closed, and his eyebrows pinched together. "You know, no. I'm going to talk to the doctor for a little bit. I'll have to sign some paperwork, and then I'll be able to leave."

The real questions were burning my tongue. Where was his mother? Was his dad coming back? Where was Marcus? Had this happened before? Had Caden done this alone before? And the worst—how many times?

I held on to his hands tightly, on top of my shoulders. "I can wait in the front lobby. Would that be easier for you?"

His shoulders relaxed. "Yeah. I think so."

"Okay." I moved forward, closing my eyes, and stepped into his arms. I rested my head against his chest, and after a second, his arms closed around me. His cheek rested on top of my head, and we remained there, leaning against the wall, until the door opened again.

The nurse said, quietly, "We're ready for you, Caden."

He didn't move. Not at first. He held on to me a moment longer, then took a breath to ready himself before he pulled away. I stayed in the hallway for a beat, standing there as the door closed. Whatever was happening inside that room made my heart ache.

I brushed a tear away as I found the front lobby. I had intended to go right for the coffee stand, but I stopped when I saw Marcus sitting in the farthest corner of the room. He was hunched forward, his elbows resting on his knees, and his head in his hands.

I couldn't tell if he was sleeping or crying, or just sitting there.

A seed of anger lit inside of me. He was here? When he could've been with his other brother, with Caden? Caden wouldn't have had to feel alone the entire night. But as soon as those thoughts flashed in my mind, a second wave of sadness washed them away.

I had no right to judge.

My family had its own problems, and I remembered the morning when my mom had passed away. I'd sat like he did, in the farthest seat in the lounge. I was there, but I'd wanted to hide, and I didn't want anyone to tell me it would be okay. It wouldn't be okay. It was never going to be okay, and all I'd wanted to do was sit there and pretend my mother was sitting next to me.

I filled two cups of coffee and put one on the windowsill beside him.

He looked up as I sat down in the seat across from him, my own coffee in hand.

I managed a small smile and lifted the cup in greeting. "Morning."

Then I looked away. No judgment. No questions. No unwelcomed opinions would come from me. Just silence and companionship.

And coffee.

"You were here all night?" He sounded guarded as he asked that question.

I nodded. "Diego told me, and I came here after that."

"Diego?"

He didn't know him. My heart ached even more. "He's a friend of Caden's."

"Oh." Marcus picked up the coffee and leaned back in his chair. "Thank you." He glanced out the window and murmured, almost as an afterthought, "Caden has a lot of friends I don't know."

"I'm sure you do too."

"No." He shook his head. "Caden knows all my friends. Caden knows more about my life than I do."

And there was the elephant in the room. If Colton was Marcus' twin, why was it Caden in that room?

Marcus cursed silently. "This is fucked up. Let me guess, it's just Caden back there?"

"You don't know?"

"Caden called and left a message. That was it. But since you're still here, I'm betting my mom's not back there. I know my dad's sure as hell not back there. Am I right?" His anger grew as he kept talking. "It's fucking bullshit. This is all fucking bullshit."

There was an air in the hospital. It didn't extend to other patients or visitors, but I'd felt it with Caden, with the nurse, the doctor, and I saw it hanging over Marcus now. It enveloped him like a blanket he didn't want, and I realized what it was. Finally.

A secret.

There was a feeling that whatever had happened with Colton, it was wrong. Like it was shameful. They couldn't properly grieve whatever had happened because it shouldn't have happened.

I didn't like the feeling.

I felt suffocated and paralyzed all in the same moment, and if I was feeling that way, I wept for the ones who had really been hurt by whatever *this* was.

I heard myself ask, wincing as I did, "What happened to your brother?"

No. I closed my eyes. I shouldn't ask. It was Colton's secret to tell, but I wanted to know. I felt I could help better if I knew. I'd know the right things to say. I think…

"You don't know?"

"I haven't asked. I was trying to be considerate."

"Oh." He paused, pain evident on his face, and then he shrugged. "Caden will never tell you because he's big on that. If it happened to him, he wouldn't want anyone to know, but Colton won't care if I tell you. He was never secretive like that. Hell, he'd probably love you. Did you meet him? Was he awake?"

"I didn't meet him. I stayed in the hallway when Caden went in."

"For fuck's sake." Marcus rolled his eyes. "That's ridiculous. Colton would've made some lame joke about dressing better if he'd known he was going to meet you, or something stupid like that. And he would've laughed, thinking he was so funny. He would've wanted to meet you. Caden should've taken you in."

"The nurse said it was family only. She was watching."

"Oh." He jerked up a shoulder. "Whatever. I still think it's bullshit. Caden could've at least told you."

And yet, he wasn't telling me either.

He doesn't want to. The reason he wasn't telling me was probably the same reason he hadn't ventured past the front lobby.

I ignored his gruff exterior and said, "Caden was going to talk to the doctor, then fill out some paperwork. He thought he'd be able to leave after that. I came out here to wait for him."

Marcus had gone back to looking out the window, but now he regarded me again. I saw fear buried deep in his eyes, past the annoyance and anger.

I spoke to that emotion when I added, "You should go now, if you want to go. I won't say anything."

"What?" he sputtered, the annoyed and angry Marcus flaring up before he quieted himself. The scared Marcus then hung his head. "Thank you, Summer."

I nodded.

He stood, and I reached for his hand, giving it a small squeeze before letting go. He paused. I didn't look up, but I felt his surprise at that small gesture, and a second later, he left without a word.

Twenty minutes later, Caden came over and touched my shoulder. "You ready?"

I stood, trying to look bright and bushy-tailed for him, but as his own grin slipped, I knew my act wasn't convincing.

"Sorry," I murmured. "I've been told recently that I'll never win an Oscar."

"I don't care." He rested an arm around my shoulders, pulling me against his side. "Thank you for coming, and staying."

My throat tightened, and I nodded again. "Of course."

I expected us to leave, but when he didn't move, I glanced up.

He was looking at the coffee cup on the windowsill. Marcus had left it behind. I tensed, not wanting to lie, but then Caden cleared his throat.

"Mind if we go back to my place and sleep 'till we leave this afternoon?"

My hand lifted to link with his. I held tight. I could miss a couple classes. I'd get the lecture notes later. "That sounds amazing."

He never mentioned the coffee cup, but I knew he knew.

And for that reason, my heart ached even more.

CHAPTER TWENTY-EIGHT

"Colton tried to kill himself."

Caden and I were in his bed. The dawn was just sneaking through the bedroom window. It trickled through the crack in his curtains, and we'd just gotten to his place. I'd thought Caden would fall asleep right away, but I knew now I wasn't alone in laying here, staring at the ceiling.

His words struck me deep, where only memories of my mom resided.

"Caden." I looked at him, my head rolling over on the pillow. He was staring up, like I had been, and I had no other words. I reached for his hand, linking our fingers together. "I'm sorry." My voice was a whisper.

"He was in a fight two years ago. A stupid fucking fight," he said. His fingers curled around mine. "Colton was on the Ivy League track. Not me. Not Marcus. It was Colton who wanted to be in this fraternity. He wanted to follow in our dad's footsteps. He was planning on one day taking over the company, but he was leaving track practice one night, and that ended everything. And it was so fucking stupid. It was one of his friends. Can you believe that? One of his own goddamn fucking friends. They thought it'd be funny to try out these new helmets. They told Colton to put one on, and they whacked him with a bat. Twice."

His hand gripped mine so hard. Our fingers were both white.

I didn't say a word.

"The helmets were defective. They weren't properly lined, so he wasn't protected. He suffered a brain injury, and he's never been the same since."

"He tried to kill himself because of his head injury?"

Caden nodded. "One in three people with a traumatic brain injury has suicidal ideation. Do you know what that means?"

"They think about suicide?"

"Yeah. One in three. I don't know the stats about those who actually attempt suicide, but it's fucking huge. It's bigger than it should be."

My free hand covered our joined ones. I'd hold onto him with everything I had.

"This is Colton's third attempt. *Attempt*. Like he's fucking going for gold or something. That's the terminology. That's what they say, and you know the term they use for people who kill themselves?"

I didn't answer. This was about him. I just wanted to help him.

"They call it *successful*. Some doctor was spitting out facts to us and rambled on about successful and unsuccessful attempts. Like we should give them a pin or a medal. 'Good job, you killed yourself. Oh, you didn't? You were unsuccessful? Too bad. Better luck next time.'" He stopped, drawing in a ragged breath. "I wanted to rip the doctor's throat out when he said that. *Successful*. Like all those fucking stats after Colton's first attempt were going to comfort us or something."

My heart pounded, pressing against my chest cavity like it wanted to go to him. I wanted to take his pain from him. But I couldn't do any of those things.

"I'm so sorry, Caden."

He let out a ragged breath, this one sounding like it was ripped from his guts. "Yeah. I don't want to talk about it any more. I tend to go apeshit when I do."

With reason.

I hated this. I hated hearing a story so miserable, so pain-filled, and with no happy ending. There should always be a happy ending.

"I'm so sorry, Caden."

That was all I could say.

"Yeah." He paused. "It hurts, that's all."

We laid there.

In silence.

Holding hands.

Maybe I moved. Maybe he did. I don't know who started it, but it didn't matter because then we were kissing. His mouth was on mine. I was underneath him. I wanted to be more than underneath. I wanted to be with all of him. And his hand was under my shirt, trailing a blazing path up as he lifted it free. His hands were on my breasts. His mouth was there. He was kissing, licking, tasting. He was loving me.

My legs wound around him, pulling him down to me, as far as he could go.

I could feel him.

He ground against me, and dear God, I wanted that. I wanted everything. I wanted all of him. I was starving.

This wasn't like the first time we'd kissed.

This wasn't the hot and sudden combustion I'd felt then. This was more. This was so beyond more. This was a need we had for each other.

Maybe it was about comfort. Maybe it was one small way to make something good out of a fucked-up situation. Maybe it was because he was hurting, and therefore I was too, and together we could ease that pain.

Or maybe it was because I was in love.

Whatever it was, my brain had stopped working the moment he'd told me he was hurting. My heart took over, and it raced as I slid my hands up his chest. He was strong. He was beautiful. And as he dipped down, his mouth finding mine once again, he was mine.

"Caden," I whispered. I wound my arms around his shoulders and raked them down his back as he arched above me.

His hand went to my jeans, and he paused, waiting for my permission.

I nodded.

"Are you sure?"

"God, yes." I pushed his jeans off as he tugged mine all the way to the floor.

We had to get up in a few hours, finish packing, and travel with a bunch of people I didn't want along. They'd be in the way when it was only Caden I wanted to be with. As he reached for a condom, I knew this was what I wanted for the weekend.

Him. Me.

Then he was inside of me, and I closed my eyes, not feeling my heart hurting. It was filled, and as he went back to kissing me, I moved my hips and matched him. I moved with him, savoring the feel of his body above mine, because I didn't know the next time this would happen, and that was okay.

I had him for the morning. I would do for him what I could.

CHAPTER TWENTY-NINE

"You look different."

I leaned against Caden's Land Rover, waiting as everyone packed their vehicles for the road trip. I'd agreed to ride with Caden, and only Caden, but Avery had ventured over to wait with me.

I didn't feel like talking. The emotional upheaval from going to the hospital, being there for Caden, and then being *with* Caden had rendered me incommunicado. I couldn't think, much less form a sentence, and I'd been worried Avery would want to talk about Claudia. She hadn't, thank goodness. The only thing she'd said was that Claudia wasn't coming anymore. A big thank goodness on that one too. The less drama, the better.

"I'm tired," I told her. "That's it."

"You sure?" She sat on the curb and tilted her head back to look at me. I could hear her suspicion.

I shrugged, keeping my face neutral and everything else about me relaxed. I couldn't break. There'd be no beads of sweat on my forehead. No, ma'am. "Yeah. I was up late packing."

"You skipped lunch to finish packing."

I'd forgotten my earlier lie. "Yeah. I mean, I did as much as I could last night, but I was up late."

"How late?"

"I don't know."

"I was up late too."

Oh, dear God. When did Avery turn into a private dick?

"I don't know. Late. Like, four in the morning." Keep it as close to the truth as possible. I learned that from watching *Veronica Mars*. "How late were you up?"

"Not that late."

Finally. She said that begrudgingly, and I was going to take it and run with it. I cocked my head to the side. "Oh yeah. It might've been later than that." And now I was going to add another truth to further distract her. "I'm nervous about seeing Clarissa too."

"You are?"

I glanced down and saw the concern in her eyes. Sinking down next to her, my knees folded, and I hugged them against my chest. "It's been a while. Plus, she's going to meet everyone too. That's nerve wracking."

"Your other friend is coming too, isn't she?"

"I think so. She's flying in tonight." Or was it Saturday morning? Then I remembered I was supposed to let Clarissa know when we were rolling in. "I'll be right back."

I was hurrying away, my phone in hand, when Caden called my name.

I turned around. "Yeah?"

"Come on. We're heading out." He was heading toward the Land Rover.

"I gotta call—"

"Call on the way."

Well, okay then. I started back, and Marcus cut across my path, heading for his truck. Our eyes caught and held. He slowed, but not enough to come to a complete stop.

As we passed each other, he said, "Thanks."

I nodded. "No problem."

"Huh?"

Avery stood next to me, also going toward the cars.

I would've freaked, because my smoothing skills are nonexistent, but Marcus rolled his eyes and pointed to his truck. "You riding with me or what?"

"I didn't know if you wanted me to."

"Yeah." He said it like she should've known from the beginning.

She perked up and rushed away, calling over her shoulder, "Let me grab my bag quick. Be right there."

The weird exchange between Marcus and me was effectively forgotten.

He turned around to walk backwards. "Don't take this the wrong way, but you'd suck if you were ever interrogated."

I bobbed my head up and down. "Yep. Probably why my high school years were boring. No one wanted me to be an accomplice for anything."

He grunted, chuckling before rotating around and heading to his truck.

"What was that about?" Caden asked as I climbed in.

Shitters. "Hmm?"

"Don't even try to lie to me."

I shut the door and grimaced. From the pot to the fire. "If you think hard enough, you'll be able to figure it out."

"Why don't you tell me?"

"Because I don't want to be a narc. I made a promise."

"To keep a secret from me?"

"To not rat out your brother."

"From me?" His eyes darkened.

"Please, Caden. Just think about it so I don't have to feel like a crappy promise-keeper."

The beginning of the caravan started to pull out of the parking lot, and Caden put the Land Rover in drive, falling in line. He cast me a look from the side of his eye. "I don't like idea of you having a secret with my brother."

"That's why I'm telling you to *think* about it."

And after a second of silence, he said, "He was at the hospital, wasn't he?"

I didn't say anything.

"The coffee cup on the windowsill. That was his."

"I can neither confirm nor deny."

He swore. "Okay, okay. You're not a rat. Congratulations, but don't keep a secret from me again."

I stared at him, momentarily shocked. He'd said that with an underlying vehemence that made my stomach twist.

"Yeah," I said. "No problem."

"Promise." He cut his eyes to mine. "It's important to me."

My mouth fell dry. "I promise."

He nodded, his shoulders relaxing. "It just occurred to me—what are you like when you travel?"

I beamed at him, turning on his radio. "Eighties music, baby. Don't tell me you didn't light the fire."

He groaned. "This is going to be one long ride."

But he was smiling, and that made me smile too.

CHAPTER THIRTY

I fell asleep.

Blame it on my sex life, which is what I told Caden when he woke me. He'd rolled his eyes in response, but I saw the small grin. We hadn't talked about what happened between us. We'd fallen asleep afterward, and then it had been a mad rush since we woke up. He'd driven me back to finish packing while he did the same.

I'd paused right before getting out of his Land Rover to go into the dorm. I wasn't sure what to do. Kiss him? Casual wave? Wink with a sexy suggestion for later? I'd had no clue, so I didn't do anything. Caden had reached over, but he'd only rubbed my arm.

So. Okay. That was more than he'd done before, less than what we'd done two hours earlier, but okay. And that was it. We hadn't talked about it since, and I was now sitting in his Land Rover at Dubrois College, watching as the guys took everything inside a house.

Correction.

I watched as Caden took things inside. There were others around, but I couldn't take my eyes off him.

I bit my lip as he threw two overstuffed bags over his shoulder. His shirt lifted two inches, and I saw the stomach I had reveled in touching earlier. I saw his tattoos too, all the delicious ones that continued past where those jeans began. He shifted, and his jeans slipped down enough to reveal the beginning of the V. I didn't know the technical term, and I didn't care. He was breathtaking, and he'd been mine.

A warm sensation flooded me.

I couldn't hold back a smile, and I sat there, enjoying the moment.

I slept with Caden. I was going to sleep with him again that night—or I assumed.

I frowned. Maybe I wasn't. Maybe he had other plans. But no, he'd been upset before when he found out I tried to stay in Clarissa's room.

Now I wasn't certain.

"Hey!"

I screamed, jerking away from the door.

It was Clarissa. Same dyed-blond hair with dark roots showing. Same perfect white teeth. Same cute little friend I'd been missing.

"Agh!" I threw open the door and lunged for her. "I missed you so much!"

She laughed, hugging me back. "Oh my gosh. This is hot, isn't it?!" She twisted around, watching all the guys moving back and forth. Some had clothes and bedding, but they were mainly taking booze and food, the two most important essentials for the weekend.

Seeing the excitement in Clarissa's eyes, I realized how accustomed I'd become to being around the fraternity. It was normal for me. I'd forgotten the awed feeling I experienced when I first became friends with Caden.

"Yeah."

"Asswipe." She punched me in the arm. "You were supposed to tell me when you were coming in. We found out from some of the guys. They came up to us in our 10:30 this morning. I felt like an idiot, not knowing when my own best friend was showing up."

"I fell asleep on the way here."

She shook her head, rolling her eyes. "I'll forgive you if you get us a prime room to stay in."

"Uh…"

I didn't know what to say. I didn't have any pull, and it felt weird asking Caden to do that, but Marcus was heading toward us.

When he reached for the back door of Caden's Land Rover, he saw me looking at him. "What?"

"You owe me."

An instant scowl appeared. "I distracted Avery before. We're even."

"No way. That's on you. You still owe me."

Clarissa looked back and forth between us, her eyes wide. I could only imagine what she was thinking. Marcus was big and muscular, and rough around the edges. He was kind of a dick, too. He was exactly her fantasy, and I knew she'd be squealing for him as soon as he walked away.

"Come on, Summer. I'm going to carry your bags in. That's payment right there."

I folded my arms over my chest. "My friends want to stay in the house. They'll need a room."

"That's the favor?" He looked skeptical, scanning Clarissa up and down. "You're the best friend?"

"She's the reason we came in the first place."

"Fucking hell. Ask Caden."

"I'm asking you."

He tilted his head to the side. "Why aren't you asking Caden?"

Because it felt weird. I mirrored his movement, tilting my head to the side as well. "Because you're the one who owes me."

"You're serious?"

"As a bumblebee."

He cursed, opening the back door with more oomph than he needed. "You're so fucking weird. You're cool one second, then off the wall the next." He grabbed for my bag, and Caden's.

"Are you going to do it?" I pressed.

"I'll figure something out, yeah." He nodded stiffly at Clarissa. "Nice to meet you."

"You too," she said breathlessly. As he left, she moved to watch him go, bumping into me. "Summer. Please tell me that's not *the* guy."

"It's not."

Marcus was on the sidewalk and moving up the front steps when Avery ran over to him, said something, and darted in front of him. He shifted his hold on the bags to free one hand, smacking her on the butt as she disappeared into the house.

I added, dryly, "But he is for her."

"Do we hate her?"

I could tell Clarissa wanted to hate her. "She's my friend."

"Oh."

"Sorry."

She took in a deep breath, her smile reinforced, and linked elbows with me. "Then let's get in there and meet a different guy. It's prime picking for us, or me. Me. It's prime picking for me."

We went inside, and I introduced her to the guys I knew. When Avery came over, I knew I didn't have to worry about any hating. Clarissa melted as soon as Avery hugged her, saying how much she felt she knew her already through me. The rest of Avery's friends came over too, inviting Clarissa to stay in one of the rooms they'd already sequestered before the guys could claim them.

"Not that all of us are even going to be using these rooms." Avery laughed as Clarissa staked her claim on one of the beds. It was a double for her roommate too, and Avery asked, "When's she coming over?"

"As soon as her last class ends. I kept my Friday afternoons free on purpose, and I came over when I heard the Alpha Mu visitors had arrived."

"Heard?" Avery questioned.

"The Alpha Mu frat is a big deal here. They throw the best parties, so when word spread that another chapter was coming in, yeah—word got around. The party tonight is going to be insane."

A flicker of worry sparked in me. Maybe I should check to see if our bedroom had a lock on it.

"Where are you staying, Summer?"

The question came from Clarissa, but I could feel Avery's keen interest too. I shrugged, feeling itchy all over, all the sudden. "I don't know. I'll figure it out."

"Are you planning on asking for directions and my dorm key later tonight?"

"What?" Avery asked.

"Yeah." Clarissa pointed to me. "This one here called me a couple weeks ago and asked if she could stay at our room if it got too crowded here. I told her she was nuts. Everyone is hoping to get in this party. Why wouldn't you stay? You know?"

Avery laughed, but it sounded a bit forced. "Oh yeah. I know."

I relaxed. We were laughing. It was all good. They were getting along, and then Avery stopped. "Are you staying with Caden tonight?"

We weren't laughing anymore.

The itching doubled, and I tried scratching my ear against my shoulder. "Uh. What?"

"Caden. You rode with him. You said he got upset before. Are you sleeping with him?"

"You mean is that just the place I'm going to crash?"

Her eyes held mine, and when I glanced away, I felt a *gotcha* vibe coming from her.

"You know what I mean," she said.

"Yes. I might crash there, but I don't know. We haven't talked.'

"Who's Caden? The guy outside said his name too."

"You should go ask him."

"Is he *the guy*?" Clarissa leaned closer, whispering.

"The guy?" Avery's attention snapped back to my high school friend. "What do you mean?"

"There's a guy—"

I clamped a hand on Clarissa's arm. "My friend. That's what she means. I told her about my weird friendship with Caden. She thinks it's more than that."

Avery frowned. "It's not a weird friendship." Her tone softened. "You're not weird, Summer. You just think you are."

Now I frowned. What did she mean by that?

"There's Paige!" Clarissa burst out, waving. "Paige, over here."

A girl with short hair, stunning green eyes, and a slim figure darted around a group and came into the room. She was wearing a black sarong-like skirt with a cropped green top. It hung loosely from her breasts, lightly falling over her stomach, and she'd topped it with a tiny black leather jacket. She was punk, edgy, and beautiful, and I was instantly jealous.

Avery skimmed her up and down, and I caught a slight curling of her top lip. I wasn't the only one.

Then Clarissa did the introductions, and as much as I hated it, Paige was nice. I liked her. She had a sweet southern drawl, which was a magnet for the guys. Suddenly Marcus came over to welcome our friends. His buddies were with, and more of Caden's fraternity brothers materialized. They all wanted to "make sure we were okay."

Avery snorted at that excuse, and after the fifth guy wanted to be the polite welcome wagon for Paige, she muttered under her breath, "What are we? Chopped liver?"

Marcus put an arm around her shoulders. "No, you're just spoken for."

That did the trick. Her cheeks grew pink, and she softened all over again.

"What about you, Summer?"

The question came from Paige, but I was having a deja vu moment. "What?"

"Do you have a boyfriend? Clarissa said there was a guy coming."

Avery held back a smile, as did Clarissa.

Marcus grimaced. "Don't say it. I don't want to know any details about you and my brother."

"So there *is* a guy." Clarissa gave me a sly look, pursing her lips together. "Something more than a friendship?"

I was uncomfortable. "Um. You know. We're friends." I began edging backward.

Marcus snorted, and everyone looked at him. "What? You guys don't know?"

Panic sliced through me, and I gritted my teeth. "You don't know anything either." My voice hitched to a higher note. "Because there's nothing to know. We're friends. That's it."

Marcus gave me a confused look. "I know, but I was just going to say you're good friends. That's it."

I swallowed over a knot at the base of my throat.

He shook his head, lifting his arm from Avery's shoulders. "And you're back to being weird. Avery, come get a drink with me." He didn't give her a chance to decide. His finger looped in her waistband and tugged her behind him.

I yearned to follow them, but turned back to the group that had gathered.

It wasn't just Clarissa and her roommate now. There were other guys lingering, and one them shifted on his feet, scratching behind his ear.

"There are a few of us who'd like to know if you're, you know..." He raised his eyebrows.

My mouth opened. I had no idea what that meant. "Huh?"

Paige covered her mouth, her shoulders shaking. Clarissa hit me in the arm again. She leaned close and said into my ear, "He wants to know if you're available."

Oh.

…

OH!

My head jerked back. "What? No." Shit. "I mean, I don't know." I shook my head. I had to go. I didn't want to talk about this any more. "Where's Caden? I need to find my bag."

The guy answered, but I wasn't listening. I said a hurried, "I'll be back," and pushed my way through a crowd.

The kitchen was full, and so was the living room. The amount of people hanging around had already doubled. I guess what Clarissa said was true—this was the party to be at.

But as I kept searching the house, and failed to find Caden, I started to get aggravated.

I walked through the top floors and all the bedrooms, then burst through the last door and slammed it shut behind me. I didn't care whose room it was.

Then I heard from the other side of the room: "You lost?"

CHAPTER THIRTY-ONE

A sick shiver wound down my spine. "Excuse me?"

The bathroom door opened, and a familiar shoe appeared first. It was Caden.

I slumped to the floor in relief. I thought I was in a bedroom with a stranger, and who knew what that stranger would do. I stopped rambling. I was annoying myself.

"Sorry. I thought you were someone else. You found our room." He stopped, staring at me, a towel in his hands. "Are you upset?"

Yes. I hugged my knees tighter. "No."

"Bullshit." He bent down, grabbed my hand, and pulled me to standing. He led me to the bed and sat next to me. "Something happened?"

"Nothing."

"Tell me."

"No, really. Nothing happened."

"I told you no lies with me."

I sighed. Goddamn. He got me with that one, but the longer I sat there—feeling him next to me, hearing his concern—the more I forgot what upset me in the first place.

Melting against his side, I murmured, "Am I staying with you tonight?"

He rubbed my back. "I figured you would. That was the plan ahead of time."

I nodded, my neck muscles so tight. I wanted to ask about us, about earlier this morning, but fear weighed my tongue down. I was a coward.

"What's going on right now?" He leaned away a tiny bit. "Are you feeling weird about this morning?"

Finally! My hands flew up. "Are you?"

"No."

My hands came back down. "You aren't?"

"Why would I?"

"Because..." *Yeah, why?* I mocked myself. "Because sex is a big deal. Sex between friends is an even bigger deal."

"I see."

I glanced at him, biting my lip. The mask was back on—the one he wore when he didn't want me to read him. I never cared when he had it on if the situation involved someone else, but this was me. This was us. I didn't want a damned mask between us.

I asked, hoarsely, "You do?"

What did that mean?

"You regret this morning?" he asked.

My insides screamed no, but my pride kept me from spilling. An anchor dropped to my stomach, and I could only feel it sinking farther and farther. I needed to make sure. One more time. "Do you?"

"*No.*"

"Are you sure?"

He frowned at me, with hooded eyes. "If I was going to regret sleeping with you, I wouldn't have done it. I'm not one of those guys that does dumb shit in the moment. For fuck's sake, my brother's life is a shell of what it should be because of one of those dumb moments."

Tears prickled at the corner of my eyes. I covered them, trying to hide the wetness, but I knew it was useless.

Caden saw everything.

Caden saw me.

So I closed my eyes instead, as if that would do anything.

"Hey." He took my hands, gently. "What is this about? Tell me."

His thumb went to the side of my mouth and moved down, following my lip. I realized I was frowning. I tried to laugh, but it was useless. It came out sounding like half a gurgle and half a hiccup.

Then I whispered, because it was driving me crazy, "What are we?"

"What do you mean?"

"You and me. What are we? What was this morning?"

"You want to label it?"

I held my tongue, wondering if I could go without knowing. I couldn't. I nodded. "I guess. Is that a problem? I'll go nuts not knowing. I just have to know about the expectations."

"Expectations?" His eyebrows shot up.

"Yeah. Like, if I sleep here, are you going to sleep somewhere else, with someone…else?"

"No. What? No." He shook his head. "Is that what this is all about? You think I'm going to be with some other girl tonight?"

"Well, when you put it like that, yes." I jerked my head up and down. "Clarissa's friend is gorgeous. She's got all the guys eating out of her hand."

I looked at him, wondering with a sinking heart if he'd be one of those guys. Because I couldn't take it, not at all, not even a little bit.

"Hey." He gentled his tone. "I thought you knew by now that I'm not that type of guy. Good God, I'm not Kevin. I don't drink, party, and get laid. I used to. For an entire fucking year, and almost all four years of high school, that's all I did. Then I got a phone call that my brother was in the hospital and his future was gone."

He squeezed my hand. "No one gets it. He looks the same. He sounds the same, but he's not. He's dead inside. That's what brain injuries do to you. They strip a person of what makes them them, and leave them feeling pain in ways no one can understand. Colton will never get the future he wanted. He was on student council, track captain, football captain, basketball, he was on the newspaper—

that kid wanted to run for president one day. He had everything planned."

He sighed and looked down. "Then there's me and Marcus. I partied, did sports, got laid. That's all. I didn't want to be in some fraternity. I didn't want any of this. And Marcus? He's almost worse. He's been racing cars since sophomore year. Still does. He and his friends, that's where they go on the weekends." He was losing steam. He closed his eyes, taking a deep breath. "You don't know the half of it, Summer. Not even half, so no. If you think I'm the guy who's making stupid decisions for the rest of my life, think again. I gotta live life for him now."

"Caden." My chest had ripped in half. His hand plunged inside, and he'd taken hold of my heart. He had it in his hand.

I touched his arm, no longer thinking. I half sat up as he turned to me. Maybe it was second-nature now. Maybe he'd read my mind, or maybe this was just what we were supposed to do, but he caught me as I moved toward him and guided me on to his lap, straddling him.

I just wanted to take his hurt away.

I knelt over him, not quite sitting down. Trailing a hand over his chest, I pushed him down on the bed. As I looked down at him, his hands went to my legs. His thumbs began to rub back and forth. My body was warming up.

His eyes darkened, but he didn't do anything. He watched me with those hooded and pain-lidded eyes. I touched the side of his face tenderly, and I held him in the palm of my hand.

He closed his eyes and leaned into my hand. That gave me breath, and then I leaned down and found him.

It was later when I remembered he hadn't given me a label for us, but Caden had fallen asleep holding me to his chest. The music started downstairs, but I closed my eyes.

Everything could wait.

CHAPTER THIRTY-TWO

"JELLO SHOTS ARE FUN AND EASY! DO YOU WANT TO FEEL SO BREEZY? PUT ONE DOWN AND HAVE SOME FUN!"

The yelling seemed to come from right outside our door, and I jerked upright, woken from deep sleep.

"Fuck." My heart pounded.

Caden sat up next to me, skimming a hand down my back. "You okay?"

"JELLO SHOTS ARE FUN AND DREAMY! LOOKING OUT FOR SOMEONE EASY? SHARE A SHOT AND BECOME A FELON!"

My eyes rounded at the second chant. "Are they fucking kidding?!"

Caden was off the bed in a flash. He padded across the room in sweats that hung deliciously low on his hips. I was horrified at the chant, but still able to appreciate the vision. His back was contoured perfectly. All muscles. All ridges. One glorious masterpiece.

I'd almost forgotten the chant when Caden ripped open the door, blocking me from them, and yelled, "SHUT THE FUCK UP! This is not that kind of fraternity!"

"Who made you boss—"

Caden was out the door in a second, and I scrambled, knowing my barrier was gone. I rolled to my feet, the sheet wrapped around me, and glimpsed Caden shoving a guy against the wall, his hand on his throat.

I grabbed my shirt and pants, slipping into the bathroom. Before the door closed behind me, I glanced over my shoulder.

Marcus was standing there, his back to me. He'd taken his brother's position, and I almost sagged in relief. Dressing quickly, I stepped back out into the room just as someone explained, "Getting your ass beat like that is what makes him boss."

"We don't do things like that here," a guy grumbled. "This is our turf. We don't beat people up."

"No, you're right," the first voice retorted. "You're the ones who get beat up."

I edged closer to the door and touched Marcus's back to let him know I was there. He sucked in a breath, then relaxed when he saw it was me. I peeked under his arm to see what was going on.

A group of guys stood in the hallway. There were too many to count, but Caden was in the middle, looking down at the floor.

It didn't take a genius to figure out the wiseass chanter was on the floor.

I leaned closer, trying to get a better view.

Marcus shifted, closing off the small window I'd gotten.

"Hey," I whispered.

"Don't. They know a girl's in here. Don't let them see it's you."

"You're doing me a solid, huh?"

"I'm doing my brother a solid." Marcus smirked. "He's the one who gave you a solid."

I rolled my eyes. "Fuck you." Then grimaced. "And don't even say it."

He chuckled. "You make it so easy, Stoltz. By the way, your friend is hot. Her friend too."

I scowled. "You're with Avery."

"I know. I'm just warning you that your friends are going to get laid tonight." His gaze moved to the bed. "Before five minutes ago, I would've picked you as the type who'd cockblock your friends because of the impurity of it."

"What kind of girl do you think I am?" I rethought that one. "Don't answer that. I don't want to know."

Caden's voice sounded again, rising over the grumbling, "I don't know who started that damned chant, but it's all done now. One recording. That's all you need, and both our chapters could get shut down."

"It's not like we're actually doing it—"

"I DON'T CARE!" Caden roared back. "My father is a legacy, just like most of yours. My brother would give anything to be an Alpha Mu. I won't let a dumbass chant ruin all that. You're better than that, so act better. Now get the fuck away from my room."

"Caden."

"What?"

"Who's the chick in there?"

A couple guys snickered, adding, "Yeah. We want to know so we don't make a move on your territory."

"Fuck off."

A few more chuckled, and I heard them moving aside. Marcus stepped back into me, purposefully herding me farther into the room. Caden appeared. I could see him above his brother, and his eyes found mine. A hand slapped him on the shoulder. "That's why you're going to be president next year. Good job, Caden."

As soon as he was clear of the door, Marcus shut it and leaned against it, folding his arms over his chest. His looked from Caden to me, his smirk deepening. "This is new and exciting."

"Fuck off too," Caden said.

Marcus laughed. "I'm hoping. You already got yours tonight. I still need to get mine. I should feel blessed. It's like the Fraternity God has bestowed his wisdom to me."

Caden flexed his hand. "I just got warmed up. My hand's not even hurting."

I thought Marcus had been joking, but their exchange had gone sour real quick. I stepped between them, clearing my throat. "Okay, I don't know what's going on, but go to your separate corners." I pointed at Marcus. "Go find Avery. Treat her right. Have fun tonight."

His nostrils flared, and I braced myself for a second round. I was ready, but he didn't say anything. I didn't think I was the only one surprised, though I didn't look at Caden.

Marcus jerked around, flinging open the door and stalking out. "Right. Fine."

The hallway was empty this time.

I shut the door and looked back. "What was that about?"

"Colton," Caden grunted, going to his bag. He changed his pants, pulling on jeans and then a shirt. He tugged it on, shoving his head through the hole before grabbing socks and shoes. The last thing he picked up was a baseball cap.

I'd never seen him wear one before. When he tugged it down, it covered his eyes, leaving only that strong jaw, perfectly kissable lips, and cheekbones that had me salivating. It also gave him an angry look, and I stifled an internal sigh. That just made him even hotter.

"So…"

His jaw clenched and his gaze skirted away. "Look, this has nothing to do with you, but I'm in the mood to drink tonight. Heavily."

"I see."

"I'm fucked-up right now. I want to be with you tonight, but I shouldn't be around you right now. I don't want to snap at you. You don't deserve that."

"So it's not me, then?" I clutched the ends of my shirt in a tight fist. "I didn't do anything wrong?"

A savage curse slipped from him. "No. No way. You've been the one good thing about tonight, last night, this morning—all of it. I'm just in the mood to fight, and I need to change my tune real quick. I'm afraid I'll say the wrong thing to you. That's all."

"Okay."

"Okay?"

"Okay." I nodded. "I'll see you down there."

His shoulders relaxed, and he crossed the room to kiss me on the forehead. "Thank you." His hand grazed mine as he left. "Find me in an hour. I'll be in a better mood by then."

"Sure. Yeah. Be right there," I said to myself as the door closed.

I stared at our emptied bed. The sheets were still messed up.

CADEN

Summer thought I was going to drink. Good. She didn't need to know where I was really going.

As I got to the main floor, I moved through the crowd. These were my guys. I didn't run the house. I wasn't their president. That job was reserved for a senior. But I was their unofficial leader, and everyone knew it.

It wasn't something I wanted. I hadn't chosen this. Colton had, and just thinking about that made my fire burn hotter.

I saw Marcus, and I zeroed in.

He was talking to Avery and two other girls. I didn't recognize them, and I didn't care to. I was closing in. Fifteen feet. Twelve. Ten. Marcus looked up, a beer in his hand and a wary look in his eyes. He saw my baseball cap, and his eyes widened. He knew what the hat meant. It was my way of hiding. I wore it when I wanted to fight, when I wanted to be the bad guy lurking inside of me, and he started looking around me.

He wanted Summer to be here.

Too bad.

He knew she calmed me. She quieted me. She made the anger go away, most of the time. But not this time. And I closed the distance. Eight. Six. Four.

"Hey." He held his hands up, along with his beer. "Truce, okay? I'm sorry about what I said up there."

I shook my head. "Not a chance."

I took the beer and thrust it at Avery. She took it, and I clamped onto my brother's shoulder and shoved him in front of me.

"Where are we going? What are you doing?"

I didn't say a word. He fucking knew what we were doing.

"Caden?" Avery called. "Marcus!"

I stopped. "Tell her to stay."

The blood drained from his face. "Why? What are we doing?"

"Marcus!" Avery yelled again.

"Tell her."

"Where's Summer?"

"She's in the room. I asked her to give me an hour."

He studied me. "Why?"

"Why do you think?"

"This is about Colton?"

"Hey!" Avery's last shout was a lot closer. Those two girls were right with her.

"Tell her to back off unless you want her to hear all about how much of a weak-ass brother you've been," I warned him. My hand tightened on his shoulder. "Does she even know you're a twin?"

He shoved my arm off. His eyes flashed. "Shut the fuck up."

"Hey, you guys!" Avery was too close, for her good and his. "Caden, where's Summer?"

Marcus continued to stare, studying me. I meant business. I was prepared to haul him outside, not giving a shit who followed us. I had nothing to hide, not like he did.

"I gotta talk to Caden," he finally growled. "Give us a minute."

"You sure?" She came up next to us. Those two girls stuck with her like glue, both wide-eyed. "Where's Summer, Caden?"

I held my brother's gaze as I answered, "She's coming down. She was in the bedroom."

Marcus coughed, nodding to me. "We'll be back in a bit. Don't, uh, don't follow us." He started forward, and I rotated on my heels, moving to the back door and then outside. There were people in the yard, so I led the way, going until I found a private area by a clump of trees.

I waited.

This time, I knew my brother was coming.

CHAPTER THIRTY-THREE

CADEN

"What are we doing, Caden?"

"You were at the hospital."

My brother paused, a harsh chuckle leaving him. "She told, huh? I shouldn't be surprised. I mean she was in your be—"

"Finish that sentence, and that's the last thing you'll remember from tonight." My hand flexed, and his gaze fell to it.

"Yeah. So what?" He bit out. "I was there."

"You were there, Marcus! There. Right there. You could've gone to see him. He would've wanted you there. I'm tired of you coming, but not being there. There's a big fucking difference."

He flared up now. His eyes were wild. "Are you kidding me? Do you know what it's like to look at him like that?"

"YES! Because I was there."

"Back off this, Caden. I get it. You're the older brother, but this is between me and Colton. It's different."

"How?" I wanted to shove him. It was wrong to do that. It was wrong to hit too, but I'd already hit one person tonight. "How's it different? Because it's you?"

"Stop."

"Because it could've been you in that bed instead? In that hospital gown?"

"I said stop it." A vein popped out from the side of his neck. "Stop, Caden."

I stepped closer. "Those were your friends that day, Marcus."

"Caden!" His voice rose an octave.

"Your friends." My voice lowered. "Your face. The helmet was for you. They wanted to hit you, not Colton."

"Shut up."

"You got in a fight with them the day before. I heard all about it."

"SHUT UP!" He shoved me.

I didn't move. I was right there, right in his face. "Is that why you don't go see him? Because they did that to hurt you?"

"They were his friends too."

"No." I shook my head. "They hung out with him, but they were *your* friends. Your pals. You raced with them every weekend. Your fight. It should've been you. That's what you think, isn't it? They hurt him to hurt you."

He couldn't talk. His chest heaved up and down. His shoulders were tight. He was close to breaking. I *wanted* to break him.

"Why were you at the hospital? Why didn't you go to the room? Why, Marcus?"

"Because it should've been me!" he spat out.

I broke him.

"You're right. Is that what you want to hear?! Yes! It should've been me. They wanted to hurt me, so they picked on him because—"

"Because?" I grabbed his shirt, forming two fists. "Because why? Say it."

"Because he was weak." He pushed me back, a hard, fast hit to my chest. "They chose him because he would do what they wanted. He put on that damn helmet. They knew it was defective. I was the one who told them that. *Me!* I told them about the helmet in the first place."

His eyes shimmered with unshed tears. They pooled on his bottom lashes, but they didn't fall. Not yet.

"It was my fault, Caden," he choked out. "The whole thing was my fault. You got the truth. Is that what you wanted?"

"I wanted to know why you refuse to be there for your brother, when it's obvious you want to be."

"Well, there you go. Now you know. What are you going to do now?"

"Nothing."

"What?" He laughed, weakly. "You're not going to do a goddamn thing? After all of that?"

"There's nothing to do except tell you you're a moron."

The tears fell then.

"What?" he asked.

"You didn't give him the helmet. You didn't tell Colton to put it on. You didn't pick up the bat. You didn't do any of those things." I moved close, lowering my voice. "You didn't swing. It wasn't you."

"Stop it, Caden."

He started to turn away. I caught him and hauled him back. I wouldn't let him, not when he needed to hear this. "It's not your fault. It's those assholes. It's their fault. They chose to do it. They chose to hurt him. You didn't choose that. Fucking hell, Marcus. I had no idea you thought all that."

"Why wouldn't I?!"

"Your face. That's what I thought was the problem. That every time you look at him, you see yourself. You think it could've been you." I paused. "That's what I see. I see me. I see another life I could've had. I'm the one who fights. You race. I party and fight. Colton was the one who shone. He was the star, not you or me."

"I know." His mouth pressed closed. "I know."

"Stop skirting around him, okay? Go see your brother. At home, at the hospital, wherever."

He held my gaze again. "Okay. I will."

"I just need help with it. That's why I snapped tonight. I knew you were at the hospital. Summer never said a word."

"How'd you know?"

"You left your coffee."

"Shit." He straightened. "I didn't even think of that."

I clasped him on the shoulder, this time in solidarity, not intimidation. I shook him gently. "I just need help. That's all."

He nodded. He clasped a hand on my shoulder. "I will."

We watched each other steadily. It was just us. Our mom was in denial, waiting for the day her son would "get over it," and our father had been on business trips almost the entire time. He'd rather be away than see his son the way he was now.

Broken.

SUMMER

After getting a drink, I waded through the house, but I couldn't find my crew. No Avery, no Clarissa, and no Paige—I guessed I'd include her too. I told myself I wasn't looking for Caden, but I knew I was. I couldn't find him either. He wasn't in any corner of the house, basement, living room, garage even. I had no clue, so I circled back to the backyard and finally heard my name called.

"Yo, Sum Sum! Over here."

Clarissa waved me over to a picnic table set up in a far corner. An entire group had gathered there. Clarissa blinked a few times, flashing her dimples, before throwing her arms around my neck.

"Where'veyoubeen?" Her voice was muffled, tickling my neck.

I patted her on the back. "I was upstairs. Where have you been?"

"We've been here." She beamed, stepping back, but still holding my hands. "I'm so happy you came this weekend. I've missed you. I miss May too. Oh! She called. She got sick, and something else happened, but I wasn't understanding it. Anyway, she's not coming, and I miss her. I missed you too."

"I've missed you too." I did, but my happiness was warring with worry about Caden at the moment. I glanced around the table again.

Avery sat with her friends at one end. Paige stood at the other, a guy next to her.

She waved. "We were looking for you."

"Yes!" Clarissa grasped the tops of my arms, surging onto her tiptoes. "We saw Caden. Is it Caden? Is he the guy?" She leaned close, giving me a good whiff of beer breath. "Please tell me he's the guy, because holy moly, he's gorgeous. And he is one unhappy camper with your friend's boyfriend right now."

"Who?"

"Your friend." She pointed at Avery.

"Her boyfriend?" My mind was moving slowly, but caught up. Caden was mad at Marcus, but... "Are they drinking somewhere together?"

"They didn't look like they were going to drink together." Clarissa giggled again, sticking her hands up, balled in fists. "They more looked like they were going to throw a couple of these." She jabbed at the air with one hand, tucked it against her chest, and jabbed with the other. "If you know what I mean."

"Okay." I pushed her arms down. "Never do that again, but yes, I know what you mean."

He told me he wanted to drink.

He lied to me.

I needed to find them. No matter how angry Caden was, I knew he didn't want to hurt his brother.

"Where'd they go?"

The girls all shook their heads, shrugging.

I zeroed in on a few of the guys. "Where?"

"It's a guy thing."

I stomped my foot and instantly regretted it. That hurt, but I did it again. "Where?!"

"Just tell her. She's Caden's girl."

I wasn't sure who said that, but I scanned the table again. "Thank you." And he was right. I *was* Caden's girl.

Right? It had to be true now, after two times together. *Shut up, Summer.* I lectured myself. *Now's not the time to start obsessing and worrying about it.*

The guy on the end pointed behind a second house. "They headed over there. They haven't come back yet."

I was off.

"You wad us to come wid oou?" Clarissa yelled, slurring her words.

"No!" I waved her away, but then Avery got up and hurried after me. "Ave—"

"I'm coming. It's my boyfriend too."

I stopped and shot her a grin. "Boyfriend, huh?"

She grinned back, elbowing me. "Caden's girl, huh?"

"I would laugh and say something ridiculous at this moment if I wasn't worried about them."

She sighed. "Me too. Let's go."

I was ready for anything. Blood. Shouting. Punches. I was even prepared to find Marcus unconscious on the ground, but I hadn't planned for what they were doing when we found them.

They were laughing.

I shook my head. "I have no words."

"Me neither."

Marcus looked over first, and his face warmed. "You guys finally thought about checking on us, huh?" He walked over, opening his arms, and hugged Avery to his chest. "My girl. Being all concerned." He looked down, flicking her ear. He wasn't smiling, but it was obvious how much he adored her.

"You told me to stay. What was I supposed to do?"

"Nothing." He pressed a kiss to her forehead. "You did exactly what you were supposed to do."

"Ignore you?"

"Get backup." He turned to me. "I thought you narced on me. You didn't. Thank you."

I kinda had, but I looked at Caden. He gave me a tight smile back. His eyes weren't smiling, not like his brother's. "Who do you think I am? Some kind of crappy promise-keeper."

Caden's smile eased, but just a bit.

Marcus snorted. "Never that. Ever." He winked at me, rocking Avery back and forth. "Right?"

I stepped closer to Caden, but he didn't touch me, and I didn't touch him. I leaned toward him, though. I couldn't help myself.

Avery noticed and clapped Marcus on the chest with both hands. "You and me, let's go back to the party."

"Why? I'm liking it here."

"Because..." She couldn't think of anything. "Just because. Come on." She tugged him with her, raising her eyebrows at me. "I'll keep an eye out for your friend."

"Thank you."

Caden watched them go, then looked down to me. "Why do I feel like I'm the one in trouble now?"

"Because you kind of are." I touched his chest. "What's wrong?"

"I'm good. Marcus and I were just catching up."

I dug a finger into his chest. "You said no lies. You lied to me."

He opened his mouth, but nothing came out.

"Fuck," he finally managed. "You're right. I'm sorry."

"So make it up to me by telling me what's wrong."

That was when the tension left him. The lines around his eyes eased, the rigid corners of his mouth softened. He reached for me, and his hands fell to my hips, pulling me to him. He anchored me there, right where it felt perfect.

He sighed and lowered his forehead to rest on mine. "Thank you."

"For what?"

"For making me let it go."

I didn't know how I'd done that, but okay. I'd take it. I pressed both my hands against his chest, and I could feel his heart there. I knew I was part of the reason it sped up a little bit.

My own heart skipped a beat. I murmured, "You need to tell me what's wrong."

"I know." His hand tightened on my waist. "I'll tell you later, but it was about Colton."

I glanced at one of his hands. They had moved back to my sides. "Those don't look bruised or, well, more bruised." One was a little red. I touched it, knowing that had come from the chanting guy in the hallway.

"You inspire me," I told him.

"I do? What?" He leaned back to see my face.

I turned up to him. "You do the right thing."

"I *try* to do the right thing." He winced. "I had a whole lot of years where I didn't. If you'd met me two years ago, even a year ago, we wouldn't have been friends. I was a dick."

"Maybe." Maybe not. I had a feeling he still would've been hot. "Thank you."

"For what?"

"For organizing this whole trip."

He laughed. "Now I know you're just making shit up. I didn't organize this. The guys did."

"They did?"

"They did."

"I'm thanking you."

He traced some of my hair and tucked the strands behind my ear. His hand lingered there, resting on my neck. He rubbed my cheek. "You should hang out with your friend while you're here."

"I will. I wanted to make sure you were good."

"I'm good." His eyes darkened, and we were no longer in this feel-good moment. The air spiked, and my body instantly heated. "I'll be better tonight, later tonight."

I laughed. "And on that note, I suppose we should head back?"

"No." He hugged me against him. "Not quite yet."

So we didn't.

CHAPTER THIRTY-FOUR

The weekend was beyond words.

There were no other words for it. Clarissa couldn't get over the me+Caden thing. That's what she kept calling it. The thing.

I knew part of that was because I refused to give her a label, mainly because Caden and I never got back to that conversation. I didn't want to stick a title on us he wouldn't agree with, so Clarissa made it "the thing."

She kept it up right until the moment we got back in the Land Rover and drove away, and I was okay with it, I'd decided. It was loose, elusive, mysterious. It couldn't be pinned down. Free.

Did I mention loose? Like, it could run away? That's what being free meant too. Free to go away. Free not to stick around. Free to be not committed—and I was working myself up again.

Caden wasn't that type of guy. He hadn't been all weekend. He'd been tentative, kind, considerate, tender, amazing, wonderful, and the kind of guy a girl like me didn't end up with. Cue my paranoia. I felt a ride coming soon.

The phone interrupted my emotional roller coaster ride through my dorm room. I picked it up, sighing from relief. "Hello?"

A male voice replied, "I can pick up my little brother."

"What? Caden?"

Oh, man. He sounded so wonderful. Warm. Strong. Steady. Not crazy like me.

"Yeah. I was calling to tell you the doctor released Colton."

"Oh." I dropped the phone this time. Shit. Fuck. I grabbed for it, sitting down on my chair. "Sorry. Are you going to get him?"

"I was wondering if you wanted to come?"

And my brains were scrambled once again. "Are you serious?"

"Apparently Marcus called Colton yesterday, and you were a big topic between them. Colt's insisting you come. He doesn't care about the circumstances."

"I…" had no idea what to say. "Is that—I mean—he's okay to be around someone who's not family?"

"He doesn't care, honestly. Once he found out you'd been at the hospital the entire night, his mind was made up. He said you're a girl he has to meet, said you had meat."

"Meet? Like meet and greet?"

"No. Meat like beef or chicken."

"Oh." I chuckled, thinking about that. "He sounds kind of funny."

"He is. He still has that." He paused for a beat. "Do you want to come with then? It's last minute, but I'm going right now."

"Yes!" I didn't need to think about it. "Of course."

"Good, because I'm outside your room."

"What?"

I looked over, and at the same time, the door opened. Caden stood there, tucking his phone back into his pocket. He gave me a smile that had my heart skipping a beat and my stomach flip-flopping.

I hoped that'd never go away.

I put on a big smile, maybe with a little extra oomph because I saw the dark shadows in his eyes, and I went over to him. "Hey."

And like it was the most natural thing in the world, he lifted his arm and I stepped into his embrace. My head went to his chest, my cheek against his heart, and his arms closed over me, holding me to him.

The most natural thing in the world, like breathing.

"Thank you," he said.

I looked up. "I'm honored to be asked."

He was tense, but he tried to smile back. It faltered. "Colton is…" He stopped.

I shook my head. "You don't have to say anything. You love him. That says it all."

He cracked a grin. "That's really cheesy."

"I don't care." I didn't. It was the truth.

I didn't know anything about head injuries, but I'd done some research over the weekend. I snuck it in when there were moments of quiet, which had been few and far between. Some of the testaments I read on the internet broke my heart, and I ached, thinking that Caden's brother was going through something similar.

I was nervous too.

The feeling didn't go away. Half an hour later, I was sitting in the parking lot, waiting in the Land Rover as Caden went inside to get Colton. I tapped my foot on the floor. I tugged on my shirt. I pulled on some loose threads, and if I kept going, my shirt would probably unravel from the bottom up.

I'd been there ten minutes when another truck wheeled into the spot next to me. I looked over to find Marcus. He was alone, and he held a hand up in a hello, but he was just as tense as Caden—more than Caden. His face was a little green.

When he got out, I rolled my window down. "You look like you're going to throw up."

He grimaced, pressing a hand to his stomach. "I don't know if it's from this, or if I actually am sick. I think Avery got sick from the weekend. She was puking this morning when I left."

"Avery, huh? At your place?"

He rolled his eyes. "Don't even start."

"But you see, I have to. I have to start. Avery's my friend. I'm hanging out with your brother. You and I are classmates. I think we can develop our friendship to the stage where I give you shit. We should even start sitting next to each other in class."

"Don't press your luck."

I kept going, "It's a natural progression. Don't fight it, Marcus. It's like evolution. Don't fight evolution. You'll never win. Mother nature is a bitch. She's always going to win."

"What the fuck are you talking about?"

"How I get to give you shit. It's an amazing experience in life, like giving birth. It's painful for one person, but breathtaking for another. I'm the baby here. I get to feel air for the first time on my skin. Let me breathe, Marcus. Let me put my baby lungs to work and scream."

"I swear you're making me even sicker."

"If you gotta puke, don't suppress. It's a natural body process."

He eyed me a moment. "Did you rhyme that on purpose?"

"Maybe. Or I might be crazy?" I winked. "Or just a classy lady?"

"Stop. I'm really going to puke now." He groaned, pressing his arm against his forehead. "I was going to tease you back about Caden, but forget it. I don't think I have the energy to deal with your rhyming."

"I've been told I'm amazing like that."

"Who told you that?"

"Who *hasn't* is the real question."

"You're not making sense."

"I do that too. That's very true." I wondered if I should find him a bag, in case he actually was going to upchuck.

"You just made me excited for when Caden and Colton finally show up. I thought I was nervous about seeing them, but no. It's you. My nerves can't handle you."

I had another joke ready and was about to let it fly when I looked across the parking lot. The words died in my throat.

Caden and a guy that had Marcus' face and Marcus' height—close to six feet—walked toward us. Colton's brown hair was lighter and longer than Marcus', the ends framing his face in a wispish manner. As they approached I could also see that their eyes were a little different. Colton's had slight hints of amber in them, like Caden's. Marcus' mirrored his hair color, a dark mocha.

My nerves came back in an instant. My hands shook, s
smoothed them down my pants.

Marcus straightened and looked over his shoulder. He took a step toward them.

Taking a deep breath, I got out of the Land Rover. I had no words. For once.

"Hey, man." Marcus held a hand out.

His lookalike looked at that, lifted the corner of his mouth in a crooked grin, and grabbed Marcus' hand. He jerked him forward. "What the fuck is that? You hug a brother. You don't shake hands." He wrapped his arms around Marcus. After a second, Marcus lifted his arms and hugged him back.

When they stepped back, Colton kept a hand on Marcus' shoulder. "It's good to see you."

"You too."

Marcus bobbed his head up and down, grabbing a fistful of Colton's shirt. He rested his hand on his shoulder and tugged him back in for a second hug.

Caden stayed back, watching the exchange. His eyes found mine, and I saw the same strain from before, but some of it had lifted. After his brothers separated a second time, he held up a closed fist. "What are you doing here, man?"

Marcus met it with his own fist. "Stepping up."

Colton grinned from ear to ear. "About damned time. Now that Caden's settling down, I'm going to need you to take me out. I need a girlfriend too."

Caden laughed. "I think Avery's got some friends. Right, Marcus?"

"Avery?" Colton looked between his brothers. "Who's Avery? Is she the girl from before?"

Marcus stiffened. "That was Maggie."

"Avery was before her."

"And she's back again? Damn. I really do need to hang out with you more." Then Colton turned to me and held his hand out. "You gotta be Summer."

I couldn't do anything.

I saw the pain, the sadness, and the storm in his eyes. I could see into him. He wasn't just Marcus' lookalike. He was Caden too. He had Caden's eyes. He was so much like Caden, it took my breath away. Then I saw an undercurrent of strength, a determination to keep going, and more. I couldn't put my finger on everything, but suddenly, and so completely, I was awed.

My voice came out a hoarse squeak. "Hi."

His hand reached for mine, and a warm smile spread over his face. "I'm Colton."

Colton was amazing.

He laughed. He teased. He interrogated me with a wink and wiggling eyebrows. He gave Marcus shit—extra points for that one—and he worshiped Caden. And he was who he was.

We stopped at an outdoor restaurant, and when he sat down, his shirt rode up, exposing more than a normal share of scars. He reached for his sleeve, like he was going to pull it back down, but saw my gaze.

He let it go and instead laid his arm out over the table and turned it over so I could see it better. He pointed to a scar that ran the entire length of his arm. "This is the one people think is the SA."

"SA?"

"Suicide attempt."

He said it casually, and a shiver wound down my spine, but I shoved that away. If he could handle it, I'd be damned if I'd be the one who squirmed.

"It wasn't that?"

"Nah." He pulled his sleeve down now and propped his elbows

on the table. Then he nodded toward the line. "You guys go order. Summer and I can talk like good little boys and girls."

Caden stood, squeezing my hand once under the table, and headed off without a word. Marcus remained behind, his hesitation obvious.

"Go, douch—" Colton started.

I cut in, "I'm going to start rhyming, Marcus."

He groaned, but nodded. Rapping his knuckles on the table, he stood and pointed at me. "Don't start. I'm going to be dreaming that shit."

I winked at him as he went around the table. "You calling me a nightmare?"

I heard his laugh before he was past two more tables and out of earshot.

Colton gazed at his twin with his head tilted to the side. A soft smile accompanied his soft words, "He likes you."

"I'm a rhyming genie. I can work some magic."

"No." He shook his head, his eyes still thoughtful and eerily somber. "Marcus respects you. I can tell. That's impressive. I've never seen it before."

I scoffed. "Oh, come on. I'm sure he respects lots of things."

"No—"

"Hooters. Porn. Wet T-shirt contests."

Colton laughed.

"Christmas presents. Shoes. Jock itch. A future dog he might have. Morning sex." I waved at him. "I could keep going all day."

"I see it."

"See what?"

"Why they both like you so much."

He'd been through hell, and was still there, trying to get back, yet he was focused on me, on his brothers.

I felt a pang in my chest. "He respects you too, you know."

"No, he doesn't."

"He doe—"

"He fears me." Colton's eyes were clear and focused. He meant what he said, and he was okay with it. There was no sorrow, just a concise analysis. "I make him nervous because it could've been him. That makes him feel guilty for not becoming what Caden has become. It's easier to deny something than accept it."

I…any words I might've formed died in my throat. I had nothing. I glanced down at my lap before looking at him once again. My eyes had a traitorous mist over the top of them.

"Marcus isn't that bad," I said.

"You're right. He's not. Caden was worse."

"What do you mean?"

His smile faded. "Nothing. I think that's for Caden to say. And look at me, I'm talking shit about my brothers when they were nice enough to pick me up, take me to get some food, and introduce me to a pretty girl." He tried to bolster his smile so it was less haunting. He failed. "You'll have to forgive me. I've just met you, but my smooth social skills aren't what they once were. I tend to rush things now. My therapist keeps telling me to slow shit down."

"You don't have to slow anything down with me."

"Still." He pointed to my face. "I can tell I'm scaring you. That wasn't my intent. I'm sorry for that."

"You didn't."

"It's okay."

"You didn't." I leaned forward and whispered since Caden and Marcus were coming back with our food. "If you haven't noticed, I'm not the smooth social skiller you were either."

"Smooth social skiller." He bent his head toward the table, his shoulders jerking in silent laughter. "You're right. We can't all be smooth criminals, you know."

I shook my head, dead serious. "Fuck no."

Caden and Marcus were sitting down.

I added, "But it's something to aspire to."

Colton barked out an abrupt laugh. "Yes. Yes, it is, I guess." His laughter continued until he had tears in his eyes, but they were the good tears. The healing kind. The kind you wanted to see because they brought relief. They brought out the side that was good, like the sun appearing for the first time in months.

Caden and Marcus went still, and I knew what they were thinking.

I wasn't the sun.

I was just a reprieve in the darkness.

Colton grasped my hand across the table and squeezed it. "Thank you." He seemed a little choked up, but moved right on to his food.

An hour later, we were going to take Colton home, but Marcus volunteered.

"You sure?" Caden asked, a slight frown on his face.

"Yeah." Marcus stood and flicked a hand toward his twin. "Come on. I owe you a heart-to-heart anyway." His jaw firmed. "And I owe mom a piece of my mind too."

A sheen of tears appeared over Colton's eyes, but he blinked them back and cleared his throat. "No, it's good." He stood next to Marcus, clapping a hand on his shoulder. "I think it's time too."

Caden didn't seem convinced, and to be honest, neither was I. Since meeting Colton, even in this short amount of time, I'd grown protective of him. Maybe I'd inherited some of Caden's feelings concerning his brother, or maybe I'd caught Marcus' hesitation. Either way, I found myself holding my breath, hoping everything would be okay between the twins. I didn't want Marcus to do more damage than was already done.

Staring at the two side by side, the similarities were glaring. So were the differences.

Marcus had personality just standing there. While despite his jokes and teasing, Colton looked like a shell of a person. If his pain was an ocean, his facade was the whitecaps on top. They were there if there was enough force to conjure them, and they distracted from what was underneath, but I saw through them.

Colton's eyes dropped to mine, and the good-natured smile on his face dimmed into his real emotion: fear. He was scared just like I was, and like I guessed Caden was too.

"Okay. I see the judgment." Marcus cursed, stuffing his hands in his pockets and shifting back on his heels. "Chill the fuck out. I've been around, but I've not waded into the foray, if you can call it like that. I'm doing it now. So I'm going to take Colton home. I'm going to grovel and probably cry trying to make it up to the guy who shared the womb with me." He closed his eyes, and his shoulders lifted as he took a short breath. He coughed again. "You guys know what I mean."

"And Mom?" Caden asked.

"Mom's been worse than me," Marcus said.

Colton looked at the ground, shifting away so his back was to the conversation. He began picking at imaginary lint.

Marcus gentled his tone. "I was never in denial. I knew it was bad, I was just—"

"Scared."

Marcus looked over, but Colton hadn't looked back as he cut in.

"Yeah. I was scared," Marcus said. "But Mom's in denial. It's time we talked to her."

"I should be there for that," Caden said.

"Why?"

Colton started laughing, bitter and dry.

Marcus repeated his question to Caden. "Why do you have to be there?"

"We need to do it together. She won't listen otherwise."

"She won't listen anyway." Colton turned back now, shaking his head. "You guys have no idea. Caden, you've been there the most, but you don't know what Mom's like when you leave. She pretends to be supportive in front of you. She knows. But then she tells me 'to get over it.' She asks when I'm going to college. She asks why I don't have a job, and why I'm not exercising anymore." He added, hoarsely, "I spend more time with the dog than anyone else. Gus is more supportive than anyone."

I had no words. Marcus was the same, half turning away. The only one who responded was Caden.

"That's why Marcus and I will do it together," he said. "You shouldn't be there at all. Your fight is to keep going. Our fight is to stand up for you."

Colton looked away.

Marcus's head hung low.

Caden looked to the sky.

The emotions were high, and the air was thick. These three loved each other. It was glaringly obvious, but they were limited in how they expressed it. They needed a girl—someone who'd say what needed to be said, explain what needed to be done. Their mom should've been that person, but it sounded like she'd abandoned them in a way.

I decided. "Colton, you can hang out with me that day." I was going to be their girl.

All three looked at me, with varied expressions of relief.

"And how could you have a dog and not tell me?!"

They broke into chuckles.

Caden raised an eyebrow. "I wasn't aware you liked dogs, and besides—"

"It's mine," Colton added. He slid his hands into his pockets, mirroring the way Marcus was standing, and faced me squarely. "You can come see Gus anytime you want." His eyes skirted to Caden. "If that's okay with you?"

Caden nodded his head. "She can go whenever she wants." His voice sounded raw.

Colton jerked his head up abruptly, giving a shaky smile. He tapped his brother's arm. "We should go. I'm kinda keen on hearing you grovel."

Marcus groaned, clapping him on the shoulder. "You're going to put me through the wringer, aren't you?"

"Shovel and rake. Get ready to dig deep."

Marcus nodded to us. "We'll see you guys later."

"Don't say anything to Mom, not without me there."

"Yeah, yeah."

With that, Colton and Marcus headed over to Marcus' truck. They were gone not long after that, and I let out a soft sigh, my heart breaking. I didn't understand Colton's injury, but I understood pain, and he had more than anyone should carry. I knew that much.

Caden cursed under his breath, then folded me into his side.

I broke for someone who couldn't break.

CHAPTER THIRTY-FIVE

I was sprawled over Caden's chest two weeks later, replete after a climax that I'd felt all the way through my tippy toes. I never would've considered myself a nympho, but the last couple weeks I'd entered the realm of that possibility. Okay, maybe not. Nymphomaniacs were doing it a few times a day. I wasn't that bad—or Caden and I weren't that bad—but who cares. Logistics. I felt I'd entered a new chapter in my life, one where sex was an active component.

A stupid smile stretched over my face.

I was completely naked. Normally I'd be self-conscious. Not anymore. I'd begun to adopt Caden's whole I-don't-give-a-fuck attitude, and it was amazing. I'd had my first incident a few days ago when Maggie cornered me in the mail room on campus.

She was all, "You want Kevin for yourself."

And I was like, "Fuck no. I have someone else."

But I didn't elaborate, because there'd been no actual conversation that made Caden and me official. I'd brought it up once, but the conversation never happened again. I was scared to hear what Caden would say, so mum had been the word since then.

Maggie had spouted out a bunch of other accusations, but I'd tuned her out, not sure where this was coming from.

Kevin and I still hung out, but it wasn't as much. Okay, it was hardly anything. I'd seen him twice, but he hadn't asked for more lessons, and I was preoccupied. The brother/sister bonding could happen some other day. He was usually with some other guys, and he seemed happy. Maybe not having Maggie in his life was part of that.

"Your breakup to Kevin had nothing to do with me," I'd told her. "Yell at him."

She'd huffed, sucking in a breath, but before she could blast me again, I held my hand out. "I don't give a fuck. Get away before you piss me off."

She smirked. "What are you going to do?"

"I'll tell Claudia you vowed to sleep with all her future boyfriends."

That worked. She fell silent, and I'd slipped away. Exit to the right.

I hadn't seen her since, but I kept a watchful eye out every time I went to my dorm and while I was on campus. She was a slippery bastard. She could attack at any moment, like a hyena with rabies.

I asked Avery about their friendship, but she said they were done. She and Claudia were still on the fritz as well. I was happy about the first one. Avery deserved better, and that helped lower the chances of Maggie lingering for a dorm-floor ambush, but I wasn't sure about the latter.

Claudia shouldn't have been so pissed. Based on the Girl Code Rules of Etiquette, she messed up. But Claudia was also scary. Still. It would be better if she were on our side and not against us. If Maggie kept pushing me, though; I might have to follow through on my threat, but only with Avery's permission. No one was a better weapon than Claudia.

"Hey." Caden smoothed a hand up my back, returning me to the present. "What are you thinking about? You just tensed up."

I groaned, kissing his chest softly, before I rolled over to lay by his side. "Stupid girl stuff."

"The Maggie thing?" he asked as I gathered the sheet to cover me, tucking it under my arms,

I nodded. "Guys are easy. You either punch each other, threaten each other, or just stop hanging out. That's it. Girl warfare is way harder to tackle."

He grinned as he traced my arm and hooked a finger over the sheet, right where it covered my girls. "That's not true all the time. Guys can be catty too."

"Really?"

He nodded, his eyes darkening. He rolled to his side and moved to kiss under my ear. "Oh yeah. Especially the House. There's a whole bunch of gossip. Cliques, exiling—all that sort of stuff."

His breath tickled me and sent my heart racing once again. I stretched away from him, exposing my neck so he could kiss it. His hand moved to my hip and rested there. I knew what was coming next. He'd guide me to my back, continue to torture me with kisses and caresses that should be illegal, and then when I was begging for him, he'd finally slide inside.

My eyes closed. Pleasure and lust mingled together, intertwining and sending my body afloat. His mouth slipped down to my throat, then to my breast.

Hot damn. Caden was a sex weapon. No guy should be this good in bed. It was too dangerous.

"Dangerous, huh?" He lifted his head.

I paused. "I was talking out loud, wasn't I?"

He laughed, bending down to rest his lips over mine. "You do that quite often."

"I do?"

"I rather like the play by play of how awesome I am." His mouth brushed mine, sending my heart into somersaults.

"That's so embarrassing."

"It's a real ego-booster. I liked being compared to a hot Italian stallion."

"Stop." It was so cringe-worthy. "I can't take any more."

He laughed, his lips pressing mine again before he whispered, "But my absolute favorite was when you said I was the Santa Claus Magic Mike, and I could bring my presents down your chimney all year round."

I couldn't even laugh. "I did not say that."

"You did." He lifted his head. "That kept me going for the rest of the night."

I pushed him off, rolling to my side and covering my face with my hands. "I'm appalled!"

"You shouldn't be. Hey." He pulled me back and moved my hands away.

I kept my eyes closed.

"Look at me."

"No." I peeked through one, opening it a tiny slit. "You can't say anything to make me feel better. There's nothing that can take away my humiliation."

"I like it."

I cocked an eyebrow up. "You're bullshitting me."

"I'm not. I'm really not." He tried to stifle his laughter, but his mouth was still twitching. "I have never enjoyed sex as much as I do with you."

"That doesn't make me feel better. You've never laughed during sex like you do with me, that's what you really mean." I tried to cover my face again.

He tugged my hands down and kept hold of them. "No." He pressed my hands to the bed above my head, and as I moved to my back, he rose above me. His eyes darkened once more, and all the humor left his face. Stark hunger spiked there instead.

"I've never enjoyed sex as much as I do with you. Your humor is part of it, but it's you too. Being with you is different." His gaze lingered on my lips before flicking to my eyes. "You're different."

The last remnants of my mortification melted away, replaced by all sorts of gooey warmness. The butterflies zipped around in my stomach, along with other lustful sensations, and I wondered why we were still talking.

I slid my foot up the back of his leg, raising it until my leg wound around his thigh. I watched; his eyes were pure black now, no hints of amber anymore, and I shifted to wrap my other leg around him. Then I lifted up, feeling him right between my legs, right where I wanted him to slide inside. He was hard and ready to go.

Caden had admitted once that he was always hard when I was around.

"I'm ready to go as soon as you enter a room," he said. I thought he'd been joking, but feeling him ready so soon after our last time, maybe not.

I wound my arms around his neck, cupping the back of his head. "How about you show me how different I really am?"

He bent down, and I felt him grin against my lips. "Fuck yes."

And his lips were hard on mine.

My phone was ringing.

I lifted my head, once again sprawled on top of Caden. I didn't remember at what point our positions had reversed, but I was fine with it. I could wake up on top of Caden for the rest of my life, and I didn't think I'd get tired of it.

"Your phone," Caden prompted me, touching my hip.

I groaned and slid over him and onto the floor. My phone was in my bag, which was at the bottom of a pile of clothes. As I sorted through them and fumbled with my bag's zipper, Caden sat up. "You could just get up. You didn't have to fall to the floor."

"Nah." I shrugged, grabbing my phone. "This was more fun."

I heard him chuckling as I answered. "What's up?"

My stepmom's voice filled my ear as Caden got up and headed into the bathroom.

"Hey, sweetheart."

I checked out Caden's ass. It was tight and round and moved seamlessly under his back, sculpted like a freaking Greek god. I held back a groan. I'd never get tired of seeing his backside.

"Honey?" Sheila asked. "You there?"

I coughed, clearing my thoughts. "I am." And because Caden had left the door open, I moved so my back rested against the bed. Tugging the sheet down and draping it over me, I asked, "What's going on?"

"I need a favor."

"Oh?" I frowned.

The shower turned on in the bathroom, and images of me joining him flooded my mind.

"I just got off the phone with Kevin. I was hoping you could check in on him, make sure he's okay."

Mention of my stepbrother pulled me out of my shower stupor. "What?"

"We had a bad fight. It's about his father, but he seemed more upset than normal. Could you go 'round to the fraternity house? See if he's okay or not? He said you guys have been hanging out more."

"He did?"

"He said you and your friends were helping him with something. I'm so happy, by the way. I know the two of you hadn't bonded, but I hoped things would be different when you went to the same college. Thank you, Summer. It means so much to me."

I held back a sigh. I loved Sheila. She'd been great to me, but something about this phone call grated on my nerves.

"I'll go see him in a few."

"Again, thank you so much, Summer. I also wanted to apologize for the last weekend we were there. Your father and I just had to square a few things away. We should've had some of that conversation much earlier, but it's all good now. I wanted to let you know that. Your father and I are quite good now."

I was struck by that. A month ago, I might've been concerned. I might've wondered how everything really was between them, or how Kevin was doing with whatever was going on with his father. But I wasn't. Not anymore.

I straightened up, the back of my head pressing into the mattress. *What did that mean? Was that a bad thing? Was I becoming selfish?*

I should be worried about them…right?

"Okay, honey. I'm going to let you go. Thank you again for checking on Kevin, and please give me a call tomorrow. Let me know if everything's all right."

"Yeah."

"Talk to you later. I'll give your father your love."

"Oh, yeah. Okay. Thanks for that."

I hadn't even considered sending that message, and as she hung up, my insides were swimming.

I was staring at the phone in my lap when Caden came back from the bathroom, a towel wrapped around his hips.

"You okay?" He gestured to the phone. "Who was that?"

"My stepmom. I have to check on Kevin. She said he might be upset about something."

Caden rolled his eyes and turned toward his closet. "God forbid Matthews is mad about something." He pulled on briefs and jeans, turning back. "Why is that your problem?"

I tried not to let his chest distract me. "I guess it's a sibling thing? Would you check on Marcus if he were upset?"

"Marcus is my real brother, and he isn't a scumbag trying to get in my pants."

Touché. "You know what I mean."

He tilted his head and lifted a shoulder. "Guess it depends on who was asking me, and how pissed he seemed. Marcus wouldn't want me to check on him. We don't have that kind of relationship."

"Colton?"

"Colton's different. Colton doesn't ask for anything, so I'd go in a second with him."

"Are you saying I shouldn't check on him?"

"I'm saying…" He sat on the bed right next to me. I rested my head back, gazing up at him, and his eyes softened as he looked down at me. His hand brushed my hair from my forehead. "It's your family. You can do whatever you'd like, but I don't trust the asshole."

I grinned up at him. "You think he'd make a move?"

"In a heartbeat."

My grin fell away. "Are you serious?"

"He broke up with Maggie to be with you."

"No, he didn't. He's trying to change. He's trying not to be like that any more."

I sat up and turned around to face him. I tucked the sheet more firmly under my arms to cover me. The rest pooled in my lap, the sides falling to the floor to cover my legs.

"He wants you." Caden watched me steadily. "Trust me. Guys know." He leveled me with a hard look. "Are you sure you don't still have feelings for him?"

That stopped me. "I thought you didn't think I *had* feelings for him? You said that before."

"Yeah, but that was before *I* fell in love with you." He stood up, grabbing his shirt. Then he walked out, pulling it on.

I sat there, my mouth on the floor. It wasn't until the door closed that words came out. "Wait. What?!"

CHAPTER THIRTY-SIX

Caden loved me, and I had to go check on my stupid stepbrother. Those two thoughts repeated through my mind. I could only sit there, my mouth on the floor.

Oh my God. Caden actually loved me. I never thought... How could...

"There's nothing plain about you. Don't let some dickhead like your stepbrother make you think that."

The idea that Caden could love me had never entered my realm of possibilities. I wasn't just floored, I was actually still on the floor. But I had to find him. Kevin could wait.

I went outside, but I couldn't find him. Anywhere. He wasn't in the backyard, in the house. He wasn't on the lawn, and I couldn't see his Land Rover either. He left.

I couldn't believe it. I stood there in the doorway of his shed, deciding what to do, then my phone buzzed a text.

Let me know after you talk to him. Thank you again, Summer! XOXO

I sighed. It was from Sheila.

I needed to deal with this. The irony wasn't lost on me as I went down the steps to the basement. Unlike the first time I went to this basement, I wanted to find a girl with him.

"Come in," he called.

Kevin was alone and at his desk when I entered. No such luck.

"Oh, hey. What are you doing here?" He got up and cleared a spot on his bed for me. It was covered with his clothes. "It's my night to do laundry. Don't worry. Those are all clean."

I perched on the end and folded my hands on my lap. Caden's words were still in my head. I felt them inside of me, and I couldn't focus for a moment.

"So, huh." Kevin cleared his throat, sitting back down at his desk. He faced me, an arm resting on the desk and his legs out. "What's up?"

"Your mom called me."

"Oh." His eyebrows furrowed, and he turned slightly away, tucking one leg under the desk. "You're supposed to check on me?"

"Pretty much."

He laughed, quietly. "Sorry. This is probably the last place you want to be."

I glanced down at the floor, but lifted my head again. "What do you mean?"

"I know about you and Caden."

My heart stopped. He did? He couldn't know what Caden just said to me...could he? There had to be more to that. My head inclined forward. "Yeah?"

"So..." His head moved forward, matching my movement. "I get it. I'll tell my mom you checked on me, and everything is great. Don't worry about it. I doubt Caden would want you in here."

"He doesn't."

His eyes widened again. "You told him?"

"Why wouldn't I?"

"You guys are more serious than I thought."

Now my eyebrows pinched together. "How is that your business?"

"It's a big step when you have to run everything by the other person." He grunted. "I usually get out then, but it takes me six months to get there. It's been two weeks for you guys."

"What are you talking about?"

"Being accountable to another person. That's a big step, Summer."

"I was with him when your mom called." I cursed. That was none of his business either. Why was I explaining any of this to him?

"Oh." The ends of his mouth dipped down in thought. "It's still a big deal. So there is a you-and-Caden thing." His head perked up like he'd caught me in a lie.

My blood was starting to boil. "That's none of your business."

"Fine." He pulled his other leg under the desk too. "Then my fight with my mom is none of your business either."

"She's the one who asked me to check on you."

"Oh yeah." His voice softened, and he cursed. "Sorry. I'm being an asshole."

I had a retort on the tip of my tongue, but no. I was being a good stepsister here. I swallowed it down and tried to smile. That was the whole point of this. Brother and sister. Family.

"So, are you okay?"

He let out a small breath, his hands moving to slide into his pockets. He leaned back in his chair and stretched his legs out so he looked nice and comfortable. "Who knows? I want a relationship with my dad, and my mom's claiming he doesn't want to see me."

"You don't believe her?" My hand itched to text Caden. *"That was before I fell in love with you."* My heart picked up its pace.

"I don't know. Maybe. He's a selfish prick too." He flashed me a grin. "I get that from him, but what father wouldn't want to see his kid?"

"What started the fight?" Why was I standing here? Caden was more pressing.

"I emailed him and then told her what I did. She flipped out."

I forced something out that sounded interested. "Really?"

Caden had blown up my world. I had to concentrate on what Kevin was saying.

"I don't know what all happened with them." He sighed. "I think she's afraid he'll tell me, and I'll get mad at her. Families hide the biggest shit. I think my family is somewhat normal. You're the one not normal."

"Huh?"

He snorted, his grin upping a notch. "You had a family that loved each other. Your parents were happy, weren't they?"

My parents? My mom... I felt a knife of pain burrowing inside of me, making its place again. I thought it was gone. I hadn't felt it in weeks. It *had* been gone. Why was it back? I glanced down to my chest, as if I could see it.

"Yeah." There'd been fights, just not that many.

"If your mom was still alive, your parents would still be together, probably."

"Yeah." I echoed. "Probably."

My mom...

The hole suddenly doubled in size.

"If your mom was still alive."

"Sorry." He grimaced, shaking his head. "You get sad whenever your mom is mentioned."

I gripped the ends of my shirt. "I see." My voice was hoarse. A boulder sat on the top of my throat, blocking my airway.

That fucking hole. I began itching there, right next to my heart.

"Aw, shit." He moved around in his seat again to face me. Leaning forward, his elbows rested on his knees. "I'm sorry. I shouldn't have said anything."

"Then why did you?"

He clapped his hands together, and the side of his mouth crinkled in. His eyes found me—those chocolate brown ones I always used to wish would look at me the way they were right now.

"My mom and dad hated each other most my life. I knew they were going to get a divorce, and I wanted it. The fighting would stop then, you know? But if I had my ultimate dream, they would've been like your parents. Love, happiness, normal amount of fights. That type of bullshit. I wish I had it."

"I'm sorry?"

Kevin laughed, straightening in his chair. "Don't worry about it. This is a Matthews thing. It's not your problem. My mom shouldn't have involved you." He grew thoughtful, and the side of his mouth lifted. His right dimple showed, blinking at me. "Plus, you were probably busy with Caden, right?"

Was he kidding, or was that genuine? I wasn't following at all. He ripped that hole back open. I frowned, remembering when the gnawing pain had first appeared. It had been before him. Before I met Sheila. Even before my mom died.

My mom. That hole *was* my mom.

Kevin stared, not saying a word. I felt like he was deciding what to say, and right then, the air shifted. An intimate vibe filled the room. It made my insides clench, and my stomach started to churn.

I was in pain.

I felt like my organs were being crumpled into tiny pieces. Someone's hand was in there yanking them out and crushing them before dropping them on the floor.

He murmured, almost too softly for me to hear, "What if I told you I was jealous of Caden? Would that be a problem?"

I didn't respond, but his words were *in* me, and they were bouncing around. They mingled with Caden's parting words. *"That was before I fell in love with you."*

I wasn't hearing Kevin anymore. I could only hear Caden's voice, and feel that hole. I felt my mom. She was everywhere. She was nowhere. She was inside me, beside me. She was being buried. The alarm that sounded when her heart flatlined was deafening.

My mom was gone, and I'd never dealt with it.

I'd pushed it off for so long. I'd pushed her off, and now she was back. That hole was gaping wide, oozing, and she was overwhelming me. I couldn't see. Tears began to fall, and I stepped backward. "I'm going to leave."

"No." Kevin got to his feet. His arm shot out, like he was going to grab me, but his hand just hung there. "Don't go. I'm sorry if I pushed. I shouldn't have."

I edged backward. "I don't like this."

"Don't go. Please, Summer."

I shook my head, pulling my shirtsleeves over my hands. I clenched them tightly, straining my shirt over my shoulders and chest. "Stop it," I shook my head, seeing her next to me. In front of me. Her eyes were too knowing, but too damning at the same time. "Don't look at me like that."

"Summer."

I kept edging away until I was at the door. Kevin reached for me. His mouth moved, but it wasn't him I heard. It was my mom.

I shook my head even harder, like I could banish her away with the motion. I couldn't… I couldn't deal with this. I choked on a sob, feeling my knees bend. I was going to fall, and then it would be over. She'd be in me again. I'd never be able to not feel her again.

"No," I whispered.

"Summer." I turned to see it there again—that same look in her eyes. They were Kevin's, but it was her. She was looking at me through him.

I shook my head. "Stop it."

"Summer."

He was touching me. No. She was touching me.

I was having a breakdown. A small part of my mind was telling me this. I had put off grieving her, and now she wouldn't have it. She wouldn't let me go, not anymore. Then I was falling.

Arms caught me. Tears wet my cheeks, and suddenly I felt a soft touch on my cheek. Someone brushed my hair back from my face. I looked up. It was my mother. She'd caught me, and she was crooning to me. Everything was going to be all right.

Everything was going to be all right.

CADEN

I tried to tell myself I needed something from Phillip, and that was why I was in the basement. It wasn't because his room was next to Matthews', or because Summer was in there at the moment. None of those things. I really did just need the stapler.

I hated this.

This girl, she got inside of me. She wound me up, and I hated it.

I hated how I felt for her, and missed her, and wanted her with me no matter where we were. I hated everything about it because of how fucking exposed she made me feel.

As I came downstairs, I heard the crying first. He'd hurt her. I was going to rip him apart, but I stopped in the doorway. I couldn't unsee what lay before me. Kevin cradled her, and she grasped onto him like he was her lifejacket.

He kept brushing her hair back, rocking her, and saying it was going to be all right. Over and over. All I could do was stand there. Pure horror and hatred filled me at the same time—horror that she was hurting, and hatred that he got to be the one to comfort her.

I started forward. "Let me take her."

He tightened his arms around her. "I told her how I felt about her. Why do you think she's crying?" He looked at me like he pitied me. "I missed my chance before. I won't let her go now."

"She's not crying because you professed your love, dumbass. Why is she crying?" I touched her arm. "Summer."

But she clasped him harder, burrowing her head against his chest.

Kevin gave me that smug smile, brushing a hand over her hair once again. "See? I told you. I'm the one she wants."

"You're lying." I reached for her again, but it was the same result. Her cries grew louder, and she pressed into Kevin, almost shuddering.

"If I am, you'll find out later." He jerked his head toward the door. "Go. She's going to stay with me tonight."

My hands itched to hit him. I couldn't. It'd hurt Summer, and that was the last thing I wanted, but I couldn't keep them from flexing into fists beside me.

His eyes fell to them, and a dry laugh slipped out. "You know what's funny? I didn't even want this, not until later. I had it locked down in high school. No guy asked her out because why would they? I was living with her. I could take her away from them any time I wanted." He shrugged. "It wasn't a problem, and I thought it'd be the same here. I could fool around. She could have her fun. But she's always my end game. At least, I had her in the back of my mind."

Something was way, way off here. Why was he talking like she couldn't hear him? What had he done to her? "You were stringing her along this entire time."

"Until you." His words chilled. "Until she fucking fell in love with you, But not anymore." He lifted her, cradling her in his lap. Her hands reached for his shirt and twisted there, holding on. "I got her now. I'm not letting her go."

"There's a special place in Hell for you."

Summer continued crying, and I was afraid to upset her more. "Once she stops crying, I'm going to find out the real reason for this."

None of this made sense to me. Choosing to be with Kevin and dissolving into tears wasn't something Summer would do. I sat back and pulled my phone out.

"What are you doing?"

Oh yeah. Kevin suddenly seemed all too alarmed.

"I'm calling in her friends."

Once Avery was on her way, I sat back and waited. There was no way I would leave Summer with Kevin, not in this state.

I'd been wrong to question her before. I did trust her. I just didn't trust him.

It was an hour later when everything came to light. Avery arrived, along with a few other friends, and they took Summer into the bathroom.

Thirty minutes after that, Avery came out. "She's not making sense, but I think this is all about her mom."

"Her what?"

"Her mom."

"That doesn't make sense. She never talks about her mom."

"I think that's the point. Something happened, and she snapped." She glanced over her shoulder to where Kevin was sitting, two of our fraternity brothers keeping guard. I wasn't sure if their purpose was to keep him there or to keep me from pummeling him.

Avery called over to him. "She wasn't holding on to you. She thought you were her mom."

"What'd you say to her?" I was across the room in a second. Brushing past the guys, I grabbed Kevin by the shirt and hauled him up.

"Nothing!" His Adam's apple bobbed up and down. He looked toward the door, like he could bolt for it. "I swear. I just told her I had feelings for her. That's all..." Then he slumped in my hands. "Oh."

"Oh?!"

"Oh?" Avery was right there with me. Her hand found her hip. "Oh what, Kevin? What did you say?"

"Nothing." He jerked up a shoulder, or tried to. I was still holding him. "I did mention her mom, but it wasn't in a bad way." He held his hands up, pleading. "Really. I didn't mean to upset her. I just thought she was having a hard time because she didn't want to hurt your feelings."

"My feelings?" I growled.

"You know, because I told her how I felt. I didn't know she was crying about her mom. I thought it was about being with me, like she'd made a mistake or something. I was trying to tell her everything would be all right."

I wanted to do so much more than bodily harm, but I forced my hands to let go. He dropped to his feet, and I stepped back. I was going to rip this guy if I didn't get out of here. Turning, I said to Avery, "Take care of her."

"Where are you going?"

"Anywhere away from that guy."

I ended up at my parents' house, and Colton sat next to me. He handed me a beer, keeping a water for himself. Marcus came in and sat down. I hadn't called him, but I assumed Avery had. Colton got up and came back with a second beer for his other brother.

Marcus leaned forward. "What do you want us to do to him?"

CHAPTER THIRTY-SEVEN

SUMMER

Caden...

A voice whispered his name in the back of my mind. Bits and pieces came back to me. Caden said he loved me, and I remembered going to see Kevin after that. Then the big fucking hole that I'd covered over since my mom's passing ripped open last night, and there was no closing it again. I broke down. There was no other way to say it.

Summer Stoltz had taken a cruise to Insanity Sea, and now I was docked back on land. And I felt the shit. I was the shit. Shithead Summer—that was my new name. I groaned, catching my head in my hands. "Oh, no."

"What?"

"He was here, wasn't he?"

Avery was here with me. Shell. And I think Claudia, but I couldn't bring myself to look. I still wasn't a fan of the bitchy pit bull who never apologized for her wrongdoings. I sat on the floor of a bathroom. I guessed it was Kevin's because of the towels with an embroidered K on them.

I scrambled up from the floor. "I have to go."

"Wait. Where are you going?"

"He told me he loved me, and then I broke down. I have to make it right."

I was out the door when I heard Avery ask behind me, "Kevin did?"

"He's not here."

The shed was empty, so I went looking for Caden in the house. I followed a guy to the kitchen and out to the backyard.

"What do you mean he's not here?"

He dumped the bag of ice he'd been carrying into a cooler and shrugged. "I mean he's not here. He took off for a bit."

"Where'd he go?"

"Carl," another guy yelled, sticking his head out the door. "Fill that up and just stay there. We've got the drinks coming. I need you to man the bar. Got it?"

"Got it."

The guy at the door stared at me before he slipped back inside. I frowned. What had that been about? It didn't matter. I needed to make everything better, explain my feelings. That's what mattered.

I folded my arms over my chest. "We were talking."

He frowned, glancing at me. He had to stay put to man the bar, so that meant I had him cornered.

I wasn't above tapping my foot like a five year old. "Spill it." Caden was their unofficial leader. They always knew where he was.

"Look, you should go talk to Phillip. He had front row seats for what went down."

"So something *did* go down." Victory flared up in me. "What happened?"

He narrowed his eyes. "You been to your stepbrother's room yet?"

"No. Why would I?"

"So you don't know he got kicked out?"

"I was in the bathroom for an hour."

"Shit went down in that hour."

I gazed around with new perspective. Carl was only manning one cooler. There were four others around the yard, along with a new bonfire pit and two tables getting set up for beer pong. A sick feeling began to develop deep in my gut, and I didn't like it.

I asked, feeling faint, "Is Kevin here?"

"Nope."

Caden wasn't here.

Kevin wasn't here.

A buzzing started in my head. "You said Phillip was there? When whatever happened?"

"Yep."

I cleared my throat, my hands becoming sweaty. "Where's Phillip?"

"He's the one who just told me to stay here."

"Lovely," I murmured to myself. That guy didn't like me. I had a feeling he wasn't going to be too forthcoming.

Still, I headed back inside and asked the first guy I saw. "Where's Phillip?"

"Downstairs."

Oh, crap.

My knees grew weak, and my hands trembled as I made my way down the same stairs I'd been up not long ago.

I moved forward, the hallway suddenly looming. One room had a closed door, but the other two stood open. I couldn't look away from my stepbrother's room.

It was completely bare. Even the sheets had been stripped off the mattress. Two guys were moving around in there, one picking up garbage and the other vacuuming. They finished as I watched, then grabbed all the cleaning supplies and packed them away. They moved past me on their way out, and I gulped. Within moments they came back with new bedding and made Kevin's old bed.

Avery, Claudia, and Shell came to stand in the bathroom doorway. One of the guys reached behind them and grabbed Kevin's towels.

"What's going on?" Avery asked me.

I had no idea. I shook my head.

"We're done, Phillip," the cleaning guys called.

"Good. Did you put condoms in there?"

One cursed. "I will now." And he was off.

I was in shock. My knees knocked against each other as I turned to find myself face to face with the screen door guy.

I saw the hostility and rasped out, "What'd you say to Caden?"

He snorted, motioning behind me. "You can go, D. Thanks for getting that room done so quick."

"Hey." Claudia took off after him. I heard her asking as they went up the stairs, "What is going on?"

D nodded and nearly sprinted upstairs. I stepped forward, standing in Phillip's doorway. He couldn't shut the door in my face that way, and I reached out, bracing myself so I'd be ready if he tried.

"What happened?"

"Your stepbrother's a piece of shit."

"I'm aware," I repeated. "What happened?"

I needed to know where Caden was. Badly. It was becoming imperative now.

"Caden called a house ultimatum."

"Ultimatum? What does that mean?"

"Him or your stepbrother." He snorted. "Take a big guess who we picked. Your stepbro's out. We sent him packing as soon as the vote went through."

"What?"

Avery pointed to the bathroom. "We were just in there. How did all this happen so quickly?"

Phillip shrugged. "Your boy decided. Called it in, and the house rallied real quick. That's all I can say."

"Where is Caden? I know you know."

"You haven't called him?"

I looked at my phone. There was a text from Kevin. **Call me! Got kicked out because of your boyfriend!** A second one from Sheila.

Did you talk to Kevin yet? Then nothing. It was blank. No calls. The empty screen was like a knife plunged into my chest.

Caden had left me, like my mom did.

No. I pushed that fear away, stomping it down.

"Can I use your phone?" I didn't know what was going on between Caden and me. He might not answer my call, but he would answer a call from one of his fraternity brothers.

"Why?"

"My phone's not working."

He snorted. "Since now?"

"Yes." I dropped it and stomped a foot on it. *Fine, you fucker.* I held my hand out. "Let me make one call."

He swore, but handed me his phone. "Fine, but I'm going to cover my own ass if he doesn't want to hear from you."

My hand closed around the phone like it was a life raft. "Deal."

I dialed Caden. His voice came on the line. "What's up?"

"Caden," I started.

Phillip yelled over my shoulder, "I'm sorry. She took my phone. I'm trying to get it back now." He reached for it, but I swatted his hand away. I shot him a dark look, and he held up both of his hands.

For good measure, I left. If I kept moving, the world wouldn't crash down on me.

I went up the stairs and into the hallway. "Hey. It's me. I didn't know if you would answer my call." I made one more turn, went down the hallway where I'd first met Caden, and out the side door.

"What are you doing on Phillip's phone?"

"Ah. Fuck." A large truck blocked my way. More guys were unloading it, taking kegs to the backyard.

"I think your house is having a party tonight."

"That's why you're calling?"

"No." The guys began taking the kegs past me to the backyard. I cupped my hand around the phone, lowering my voice. "I had to call. I broke down. I don't know why—well, I think I do, but I know you saw that."

"I saw you in another guy's arms. Yes."

I had to stop. Everything had to stop. This was it.

Closing my eyes, I took a breath. I heard the door open behind me. I didn't know who was there. I didn't look. Whether it was Phillip coming for his phone or Avery, or even Claudia, I held up a hand, hoping they'd stop. I needed this time, right now.

"I am in love with you."

There it was. It was out there. I couldn't take it back. I kept going, "Kevin said stupid stuff, but that's Kevin. He's stupid, and for some reason I broke down." I paused. He wasn't saying anything. "I think maybe I should do this in person—"

I considered that. Him standing in front of me, waiting, completely shut down as I poured out my heart. No. Now was good. I was going for now.

"Kevin came into my life when my mom left. It happened so fast. She was gone, we were burying her, and then *boom*. I had a new family. And that family came with a stepbrother who was my high school crush. He was everyone's high school crush. I don't understand it. I can't really explain it, but I had an aching hole in me, and I used stupid daydreams and fantasies to cover it up." Still no response. "Have you ever done that? Used alcohol or cupcakes to fill in something you don't want to feel? That's what I did, but on an extreme level. I couldn't handle losing my mom. What daughter can? Especially when she's fifteen. My mom was gone, and then Kevin was there, and I let it all get out of hand. You have to know that whatever you saw in his bedroom earlier, my feelings for Kevin never had anything to do with him. It was all my mom."

The ache was still there. I felt it sizzling, burnishing my skin as I talked about it, but it wasn't as bad. Some of it had lessened. There was still more to come. I knew that. I wasn't looking forward to it, but Caden could help me.

He just had to be in front of me. He had to be with me.

I bent down, crouching on the balls of my feet, and I wrapped my arms around my knees. My eyes closed, and I whispered into the phone. "I clung to something that wasn't real. But you, you're real. You make me feel loved. You make me feel whole. You put me back together."

I paused. I had to. My lungs needed air, and after filling them up, I opened my mouth to start again.

"It's been you since you asked if something was wrong with me." I smiled now, in the midst of all of it. "It's been you since I hit you by accident in the hall at the frat house." I hugged my legs even tighter, burrowing my forehead into my knees. "I love you, Caden. It's been you this whole time. If anyone's the fairy tale, it's you."

I had nothing more. My chest hurt. My lungs hurt. Everything hurt because I'd poured out all I had to him.

There was silence, complete and agonizing silence.

Finally I heard from the phone, "Fairy tales end, Summer."

Wait—that voice was too close, too loud. I looked up, and he was there. He was gorgeous. His hair was messy, like he'd raked a hand through it, and it made me love him even more. His eyes were fixed right on me, cloudy with emotion.

He was hurting. But why?

I stood, dropped the phone, and went to him. "Caden—"

He shook his head. "Stop."

I stopped a few feet from him. I wanted to go to him. My body wavered forward, leaning, but I held it back.

"Fairy tales aren't real."

My voice broke as I said, "But you are. You're real life. You're real."

I couldn't lose him.

I moved forward a step. I held my hands to my chest, wrapping them together. "Did anything I said make sense?"

He tried to smile, but it faltered.

I didn't know if that was a good sign or not.

"I know grief, Summer. Colton's brain injury didn't break just him. It broke my whole family. I know what it's like to grieve and to want to put it off. The difference between you and me? I didn't hide from it. I felt it. I experienced it, and you still haven't."

I frowned. "What are you saying?"

"I think you need time to mourn your mom."

"Caden." I reached out for him.

His gaze went to my hand, and for a moment, I thought he was going to take it. He didn't. He let it hang there.

"Without me," he said softly.

"What?" Pain sliced through me. "What does that mean?"

He shrugged and put his hands into his pockets. "I want to hold you, and kiss you, and tell you everything is going to be okay. I can't believe Kevin did that to you. It killed me to see you in his arms, but I get it. I understand what happened now, and I believe you." He paused, lowering his head a moment. "But I need to ask you a question."

"Okay." I was suddenly nervous. My hands grew sweaty. "What is it?"

"Promise you'll answer honestly."

"Promise." My mouth was dry.

"When we were together, did you feel your grief for you mom?"

"I…" The answer was no. I felt none of the pain. I only felt loved. How was that a bad thing, though?

"You promised, Summer."

I had to answer. "I was only happy when I was with you."

He closed his eyes and stepped back. "Right there. See, I can't be with you. You need time, Summer. You have to feel what you lost, and you have to mourn her. You used Kevin to cover that up, and I can't be the next Band-Aid you use. I won't do that to us. If you can't mourn her when you're with me, you have to do it without me."

He shook his head and began walking backwards, away from me.

"I'm sorry, Summer. I can't be with you now."

CHAPTER THIRTY-EIGHT

Two and a half months later.

I hated February. It was fucking love month.

"Hey."

Avery didn't knock, but she hadn't been knocking since she'd found me in bed, feeling like my insides had been yanked out and dumped in a pile on the floor. That was back in November. I stopped answering the door, and she started letting herself in. We were in a symbiotic relationship.

I looked up from my laptop and watched as she grabbed a bag of chips, then plopped down on one of the beanbags. Those were also new, courtesy of Sheila, who felt bad because I'd been dumped. Kevin had told her, because everyone had told him. It was all over campus.

I'd been dumped.

Caden gave me the boot, but no one knew he did it *for* me. He was giving me time to process the loss of my mom, and I was. There'd been a couple more moments where I felt like I was breaking down, but I knew he was right. It hurt him too. Avery said he called and asked how I was doing every day. I just wished he would call me instead.

To say my step had lost its bounce would be an understatement.

I wasn't even crawling.

Most days I stayed in my room. That's how I coped for the first two weeks. Then a phone call from my father reminded me I was in college. Classes were a requirement, apparently. So then my routine became dorm room, class, dorm room, class.

Marcus was in my health class this semester. So was Shayla, my old physiology study partner. We had both been sitting there one day when he walked in.

My lungs had ceased working for a moment. He'd looked so much like Caden in that moment, and I worried he'd leave. He'd stopped, stared at me, and then sat in the empty chair next to me.

I could've cried. I was so happy.

He'd patted my leg. "My brother thinks he's doing the right thing. He's an idiot."

Okay. I did start crying.

Marcus pulled his hand away. "Don't make this weird, okay? I don't even like it when Avery cries."

I brushed my tears away quickly, and that night Caden had called.

He'd seemed so quiet. "Marcus told me he's in your class."

"He is."

"He said you've lost weight."

Marcus said the same about him. "Are you okay?"

Caden laughed lightly. "I'm supposed to be the one asking you that."

I wasn't okay. I didn't want to say it, though. I wasn't ready. I sighed, sinking down on my bed. "I'm trying to let her go, but it's hard."

He'd been quiet a moment. "Could you do it if we were together?"

I'd heard the yearning in his voice. I felt it too, but I had to be honest. We'd promised no lies. "I would be distracted by you."

Another beat of silence. Then, "Let me know when you're ready. I'll be here."

I nodded. I knew he couldn't see that, but I couldn't talk. My emotions were choking me, and when he hung up, I'd just curled on my side and hugged the pillow to me.

It wasn't Caden I'd been holding, not like I'd been dreaming. It was my mom, and in that moment she was there. She'd been holding me right back.

I wanted him back, but it was time I took care of myself first.

"What are we doing for supper tonight?" Avery asked, turning around in my desk chair and separating me from my memories.

I grunted and tossed a package of ramen over my shoulder.

She groaned. "Not again. Please. You need real food, Summer."

"Noodles are real food. They're a relative to real pasta, which came from Italy and we know how kick-ass Italian food is. Boom. They're gourmet badassness."

She tossed them to the corner. "They're not, and I'm pulling my friendship card."

No way. She couldn't.

I rotated around in my chair to stare at her. "Not the friendship card."

"Totally the friendship card."

I pretended to gasp and shudder. Okay, I really did shudder. I'd never admit it, but the ramen wasn't doing it for me either.

She pulled out a plastic card from her purse and waved it in the air. "This states that when a friend needs an intervention, I can step in. You are long past an intervention."

"I do everything necessary to sustain my physical and biological needs. Case in point." I pointed to my water and the fridge. "Liquids. Solids. I go to the bathroom. I sleep. I also uphold higher-function necessities, like class. I go to class… Now," I added after a moment. "I go now. I had a short hiatus, but that doesn't count. I go now. That counts."

Avery wrinkled her nose and scratched behind her ear. "Okay. We've been back from break for two weeks, and I'm calling it. We're going to eat."

I opened my mouth, ready with an empty promise to order Chinese food, when she added, "But we don't have to go on campus, not that he even eats there." She softened her voice. "I was thinking we could go to a restaurant or something."

"What is this you speak of? A dwelling where they serve many varieties of solids?"

Her lip twitched in a grin. "Yeah, that. You and me, we're going to dress up, and we're going to dine like queens."

"Can I wear a tiara?"

"Without a doubt." She winked at me as she got up and went to the door. "Thirty minutes, then we're leaving."

"Avery?"

"Yeah?"

"Is that really a friendship card?"

She laughed, brandishing the card in the air. "You're damned straight. It's a credit card, the best friend a card could be."

"We should actually make a friendship card."

"A friend card." Her smile deepened. "I like it. Let's do it." She pointed at me. "Thirty minutes. You can get dressed in two, so I know you can manage."

I managed. But when we got there, the restaurant was bustling, with people spilling out to the patio in front. I wasn't even going to pretend we could get in right away. I plopped down on one of the benches.

Avery paused, but I waved her on. "This was your idea. I'm not dealing with that crowd in there."

She snorted, rolling her eyes. "Nice to see your spunk is coming back."

I leaned back on the bench. My spunk was always there. It was a part of me. No way would my spunk leave me. I noticed an older lady looking at me. I glanced down. Oh. My legs weren't crossed. Feeling some of that spunk, I spread them even wider. Take that, old judgmental prude.

She wrinkled her nose and lifted it in the air. Literally.

I was tempted to scratch my balls.

"Summer?" Colton was sitting on the bench next to me.

"Hey." I sat up. "What are you doing here?"

Was Caden here too? I started to look—

"He's not here." He made a sad attempt at a smile. His eyes were dead, and he looked like he'd lost weight. "Sorry."

"No." I shook my head. What should I say here? I gestured to the empty spot next to him. "Can I, uh, can I scoot over there?"

He patted the space next to him. "Have at it. I'm hiding from my folks."

"Your parents are here?" I sat.

He nodded, slumping back the way I'd been earlier. "Our dad came home last night from Beijing, and I believe divorce papers showed up this morning. They had a hellava row last night."

I winced. "I'm sorry, Colton."

He lifted a shoulder. "This will get blamed on me, I'm sure." He gave me a crooked side-grin. "Turns out brain injuries are hard to live with." He paused. "Or even just be around. People don't like when they're lives are upended by something they can't see."

Caden had said something similar once before. I remembered his anger and sadness, and seeing the utter defeat in his brother, I covered his hand with mine. "I'm sorry, Colton."

He patted my hand. "I'm not that torn up about it. It is what it is."

I didn't believe him. "Does Caden know you guys are here?"

He shook his head. "He and Marcus don't even know Pops came home last night. I know Caden's always there, but he doesn't need to deal with everything. If I told him, he'd come here and rip into our parents, telling them to suck it up and act like adults. Marcus would just, he'd probably hide with me. We tend to leave the heavy lifting to Caden. It's not always fair to him."

I knew Caden wouldn't want Colton to deal with this. And he'd be pissed if he found out I knew and didn't tell him. I sighed. "I have to call him, Colton."

He looked at me, ready to protest.

I stood, clutching my phone, and backed away. "I'm sorry. I have to. If you want to escape, my friend and I will take you."

Avery came up at that moment, overhearing the last of what I said. She looked at Colton, her eyebrows pinched together. "What's going on?"

"It's your choice," I said to Colton. "We can be your getaway car." I gave him two thumbs up. "Two hot chicks. How about it?"

"Thanks, Summer, but I'll stick around. If there's going to be fireworks, I should be here for them."

"Okay." I waved my phone in the air. "I'll be back."

"But..." Avery watched me slip farther away, confusion evident on her face. "What's going on?" She looked back at Colton, stepping closer as I moved out of earshot and eyesight, wading around a large group waiting to be seated.

Cue the nerves.

My hand shook as I dialed Caden's number. He'd called that one night, but since then we hadn't talked. My heart was trying to leap out of my chest.

"Summer?"

My shoulders sagged in relief. I clutched the phone even tighter. "Hey."

"Hey. Are you okay?"

I cleared my throat. "Avery and I are at Carabera's and Colton's here. I thought you should know."

"Colton?" His voice was suddenly alert. "What's going on?"

"Your parents are here. He said they're getting a divorce."

"And they're hashing it out at a restaurant?" He cursed. "I'm on my way. Thank you for calling."

"You should know that I offered to be Colton's getaway if he wanted to leave," I said quickly before he hung up.

Caden was silent a moment. "Did he take you up on that?"

"No. He wants to be here to watch the fireworks."

He grunted. "Damn straight there's going to be fireworks. Thank you, Summer. Are you going to stick around? I mean, can you?" His voice dropped low. "I think I'm done waiting. I don't think I can hold off any longer."

I almost squeaked. My hand was so sweaty now. The phone almost slipped. "Uh…" My heart was pounding. "Yeah. I'll be here."

"Thank you." His voice softened.

God. To hear that tenderness from him… I remembered the last time we were together. How he'd held me, touched me, gently kissed me. I gulped. I wanted that again, so much.

"I care about him too," I whispered.

"I know." Then he hung up, and I couldn't move for a moment. Caden was coming.

Here.

Where I was.

Where his family was.

And he'd asked me to stay too. He was done waiting.

"That's Marcus' brother?" Avery appeared next to me, pointing back toward Colton.

I nodded. I couldn't talk at that moment.

"Holy crap. Marcus told me he was a twin, but I've never met him. You have?" I could hear the envy in her voice. "He looks just like Marcus, only thinner."

I nodded. But he wasn't just like Marcus. There were differences, ones she couldn't see on the outside. I'd forgotten about that problem.

Avery didn't know about Colton's brain injury.

I had to do damage control. "Uh, maybe you should go."

"What? Why?"

"Um…because Caden is coming, and I think this is a family thing now."

"Caden's coming?" Her eyebrows arched. She grasped my arm. "Do you want to leave before he gets here?"

"He asked me to stay."

"Oh." She let go and moved back a step. "So you're just trying to get rid of me?"

Why hadn't I thought of a great lie? I would suck being a spy.

"No, no. It's not that. I'm not going to be a part of the family thing either. I'm just staying here because Caden asked me to."

"I can stay with you then." She looked me up and down. "You look like you're going to pass out."

I wavered on my feet, but no. I shook my head. "I'll be fine."

"You really don't look good."

I wanted to growl. How dare she point out the truth? "I'll be fine. Caden asked me to stay."

She had to understand how important that was, how I'd been waiting so long to hear words like that from him. He was done waiting.

"I'm not going anywhere," I told her.

I'd take root on one of those benches if need be.

She sighed. "Okay. Are you sure I should leave?"

I nodded. "Caden will give me a ride home."

She grinned. "You thought that through, huh?"

"I'm not a complete nincompoop."

"Score one for using the word *nincompoop* in a conversation."

"Thanks. It's the largest word I've used in a while."

She laughed, raking a hand through her hair. "Okay. I'll leave you to it, but promise me you'll tell Caden you're not feeling the best. And maybe try to eat something. That's why we came here, remember?"

"Oh fooey. I'll be good."

Her concerned eyes skimmed over me again. "Maybe I should mention it to Colton."

"No." I grabbed her before she could go. "He has enough to deal with. He doesn't need to worry about me too."

"Okay..."

It was obvious she didn't mean it. I gently pushed her toward her car. "I'll be fine. I promise. I really will get some food in me. They offer bread to the people waiting. I'll just grab some of that."

"Okay, okay. I'm going." But she kept glancing back as she made her way to the car. I was sure Marcus would be calling in the next five minutes.

And when my phone lit up before I had even moved around two large groups, I congratulated myself on being psychic.

I sighed, answering as I made my way back to Colton. I rounded a third group. The waiting list seemed to have doubled in the last ten minutes. "Summer Stoltz's Fan Club Line. How may we help you?"

"Cut the bullshit, you're not funny."

"*Au contraire, mis compadre.* I'm a walking laughing stick."

He groaned. "I don't have time for this. Av just called me and said Colton's at some restaurant with you."

"He is, and I already called Caden. You can get the deets from him."

"He won't answer my call. Is Colton okay?"

"Did you try calling your twin?"

I sat next to Colton as I asked that question, and he looked over, hearing it.

He checked his phone, and shook his head.

"Forget it. Call him if you want answers." I hung up, hearing a roar from Marcus.

Two seconds later, Colton's phone was blowing up. He pressed the ignore button, looking pleased with himself. "He'll have to come here to find out what's going on."

"Did he and Caden have a talk with your mom about accepting your brain injury?"

He nodded, frowning. "Yeah. It didn't go well."

"So she's still denying?"

"Yeah. So's our dad."

I scratched behind my ear. "I have to ask, why are they talking in a restaurant if they're actually getting a divorce?"

"They booked a private room here, and they can only talk about stuff out in public. People just end up leaving the room at home or throwing and breaking things. Mom and Dad both have horrible tempers."

"Gotcha."

"Colton."

Caden was here.

Holy mother of my ovaries. My mouth was already watering. He looked delectable in low-riding jeans, a white shirt, and his leather jacket over the top. He'd lost weight. I hadn't been the only one. Marcus had told me, but seeing it was another thing. He had on a cap. It didn't hide his features like a baseball cap did, but it gave him a serious no-nonsense vibe. I almost asked him if it was a serial killer stocking cap, if he could pull it down and do some damage, but I bit the words back. He didn't look to be in the joking mood.

It was also my nervous rambling habit talking—or trying to.

A whole host of nerves blasted me as he stepped closer, his eyes lingering on me before moving to Colton.

"You should've called me," he told his brother.

"Why? They're going to get a divorce anyway."

"You don't need to be here for that."

Colton stood and placed a hand on his brother's shoulder. "Hate to break it to you, Caden, but you can't protect me from everything. Mom and Dad might be pains in my ass sometimes, but they're still my parents. They're stupid when it comes to my disability, but they still love me." He added, "In their way."

"They're in the private room here?"

Colton nodded.

Caden looked at me. "You'll stay?"

I'd stay forever. "Yeah."

"Okay." He turned to Colton. "You want to come in for this or stay out here?"

"I'll stay out here." He gestured back to his seat beside me.

"Marcus is coming, too. He won't know what to do without a greeting chorus."

One corner of Caden's mouth lifted, but the half-grin didn't reach his eyes. He looked serious, and a tingle went through me— he looked dangerous too. I pitied his parents.

"I'll be back," he said.

Once he was gone, I turned to Colton. "And down to two."

He laughed, leaning back in his seat. "He's really only going in there to yell at them for being selfish. That's all he's doing. He can't stop the divorce. I don't even think anyone wants to stop the divorce. It's been coming since I got hit."

I covered his hand with mine. There were no words.

He patted my fingers. "I'd turn my hand around, but I don't think Caden would like that. Speaking of, what's the issue with you guys? He said you needed time, but it doesn't seem like you're the one who wanted time away."

I pulled my hand back and clasped my fingers together, pressing them down in my lap. "That was part of the problem. I wasn't dealing with something."

"Have you now?"

Had I? I thought about my mom every morning when I woke up. I could smell her perfume. I felt her fingers when she'd tucked my hair behind my ears. I could hear her whispering, "I love you, my little Summer." I'd heard, felt, smelled, and thought about my mom nearly constantly over the last two months. Every time that hole hurt, but it was getting smaller and I didn't always feel like I had to shove it down anymore.

"Yes." I hadn't realized it myself until then, but the answer was yes. I hadn't lost my mom. She was still with me. She wasn't ever going to leave me.

"Good. Not that I don't love having him around, but he's been at the house almost every night. You know it's bad when he's choosing to spend that much time with me and not staying at the fraternity, or with you, who he really wants to see."

"You make it sound like he doesn't want to hang out with his brother. I know that's not true."

He patted my hand again before pulling away. "I'm not throwing my brother under the bus, but no one wants to spend time with a brain-injured person. Trust me. You've seen me on some good days. For a while I can put up a good front. Wait one more hour and you'll see the real Colton. I'm not a picnic anymore."

My throat swelled. "Don't talk like that."

"It's true." He tried to smile. He failed. "We're like walking zombies that don't want to eat people. It wears on a normal person. Caden will never admit it, but I know it's hard on him to see me like this."

I didn't know what to say, so I rested my head on his shoulder. It felt right, being there on that bench with him. We were both waiting for someone we loved to come.

"Summer?"

Kevin stood a few feet away, holding a girl's hand. He frowned at me, and my gaze lifted over his shoulder. Caden was coming back. I could see him weaving through the crowd, his eyes on me. A group of waiting customers moved aside for him, and he was here. His eyes found mine. It was time. I started to stand, and then the patio and crowds of people started swimming around. Stars began blinking at me, and everything went dark.

I fainted.

CHAPTER THIRTY-NINE

I heard beeping when I woke, then saw the hospital gown. There were tubes going into my arm, and an ID bracelet around my wrist. The next things I noticed were in this order: the putrid smell of anxiety and sickness, that my body ached everywhere, and that there was a hand holding on to mine.

I looked up and could hear heaven's doors opening, along with a choir singing alleluia. Caden sat next to me, his eyes closed, and his head resting on my bedrail.

I almost didn't want to move. He looked too beautiful to wake. I just wanted to sit and enjoy, but holy fuck my throat was killing me.

"Agh!" I croaked out, suddenly feeling nauseous.

Caden lifted his head, his eyes opening. Oh yes. So dark and chocolatey and yummy. It helped with some of the nausea. Some. Not all. My stomach still rumbled, and I pressed a hand to it.

"What happened?" Wait. I remembered. "I passed out?"

"Yeah." He stared at me intently, before leaning forward and brushing my hair from my forehead. His touch was so tender. "You haven't been eating. You haven't been drinking enough fluids. You haven't been sleeping enough, and according to Kevin, you're barely going to classes." His lips formed a thin, disapproving line. "What were you thinking? I had no idea you were this bad. You're not taking care of yourself."

I beamed at him. More of my nausea was going away. "I've missed you too."

He softened, sitting back and shaking his head. "I about lost it when you fainted at the restaurant. Colton caught you enough that you landed on the bench. Then you almost rolled and hit the floor."

"But you caught me?"

"Your stepbrother caught you." He laughed. "Never thought I'd be grateful to that ass, but I am. You almost hit your head."

"I thought fainting was all graceful and feminine."

"It's not. It's stupid and dangerous." He leaned close again, gripping my hand tightly. "Especially when it could've been avoided." He breathed out, the lines around his mouth relaxing. "Fuck, Summer. You could've been seriously hurt. Why haven't you been taking care of yourself?"

It was my turn to swear. "Are you fucking kidding?"

"Because of me?" He looked pained. "I didn't mean to do this to you. I didn't...it killed me to be away from you. I thought I was doing the right thing. I really did."

"You were." I squeezed his hand. "I needed time, and I didn't waste it. I'm with my mom every day. I can feel her, and I know I won't shove those feelings back down. I don't want to. I love her so much, and I miss her so much. It was unbearable before. I found a way to cope, by ignoring it, but not anymore. I need to remember now. I don't feel whole if I don't, so I'm good. I really am." I smiled. "And just to be clear here, you do want to continue having sex with me?"

He barked out a laugh, tracing a hand over my forehead again. He cupped the side of my face. "I want more than that. I want it all. You. Your laugh." He pressed a kiss to the side of my mouth. "Your random idiocy that I find hilarious." A kiss to the other side. "Your kindness." He moved down to my throat. "Your strength." The other side of my throat.

I was buzzing here. Totally buzzing.

His hand slid down, lingering on my chest between my breasts.

I tugged the nightgown down. I needed to do what I could to help him cop a feel.

He leaned over and pressed a kiss where his hand was.

My blood was more than buzzing. It was almost boiling.

"Your love, even when it's not deserved," he added, He lifted his head, his eyes finding mine. "I want you." His eyes grew serious as he hovered above me. "I love you, completely and whole-heartedly. You're the best thing that's ever happened to me."

"I am?"

He didn't answer. His next kiss landed on my lips, and I sunk into it. My hands cupped his face, and even if he wanted to pull back, I wasn't having it. This was my moment. This was my man. I wasn't letting him go any time soon. I kept kissing him, and kissing him, and kissing him.

My heart pumped so fast; all the blood was rushing around. All sorts of tingles, sensations, and melting feelings coursed through my body. Even my toes curled.

And I still kissed him.

I never wanted to stop.

CHAPTER FORTY

I was packing when Kevin knocked on my dorm room. "Hey."

To give him credit, he looked scared. His eyes kept skirting around the room, only able to look at me for a second. I straightened from my bed. My suitcase was open, and I set down the tank top I was folding, putting it on top of the other shirts for my spring break trip.

"Hey," I said back.

He still hesitated to come in, his hand coming to rest on the doorframe. He gestured inside. "Uh, can I come in? I mean, I don't want to bother you."

This was the talk. We hadn't had one since the disastrous conversation before he got kicked out of the fraternity. I was surprised at how easy it had been to avoid him, especially considering we'd both been home for holiday break, and he'd come to the hospital after I fainted.

There it had been a quick "How are you? Good? Good. I'll leave you alone, then." And he'd run off. I knew he had a new girlfriend. I'd seen her with him at the restaurant. I was glad he wasn't waiting for me—if he'd ever been actually serious about that—but it was bittersweet too. Avery told me the girl was nice, really nice, and I knew my stepbrother would fuck it up. I had no doubt.

I waved to the couch. "Have a seat. It's time we had this talk, right?"

He took two steps, but paused and glanced at me. "Yeah. I suppose so."

I sat at the desk, putting us at opposite corners of the room. I folded my hands over the back of the chair. "You told Caden what happened when I fainted at the restaurant." I'd never thanked him for that.

He kicked out his legs, then rested his elbows on his knees instead. "You fainted, and he looked ready to punch me. I was preserving my life." He cracked a grin. "I think he blamed me for you passing out. Had to make sure he knew the real reason: him."

"It wasn't just him." It had been me. Mom. "You know, I'm stuck right now. I have to thank you for telling him, but you're a piece of work. You know?"

"I'm sorry for my part in fucking with you and Caden."

I lifted an eyebrow.

"And for fucking with you in general," he amended. "I knew you liked me in high school, and I liked that." He extended a hand toward me. "You're gorgeous, and you have no clue. You're funny. Witty. Feisty. And you're just a good person. Girls like you don't come along every day. I'm lucky enough to have found Kiara. She's one of those girls, but I don't think I'll find another."

"Then don't fuck with her."

"I'm not planning on it."

"I mean it, Kevin. Don't cheat on her."

"I won't. I promise. The whole lesson thing we did? It didn't last long, but it actually helped."

"Were you really trying to change then? Or was it a con?"

He gave me a rueful look, laughing lightly. He held his hands up. "It was both. It started out as an act. I was planning on getting with you, but then you showed up at my room to find out if I'd left Maggie for you. I did, but it was obvious you weren't into me, so I ran with it."

I groaned. "Kevin."

He scratched his head. "I just wanted to spend time with you. I figured I could get you under my spell again."

"Caden told me some of what you said to him while I was out of it, having my breakdown." This one hurt. "Is it true? Did no one ask me out in high school because of you? They all thought you'd steal me away from them?"

"You had boyfriends."

"Yeah." I snorted. "Three very lame boyfriends. They don't count. They weren't real relationships."

"I'm sorry for that too. And yes, every guy knew not to mess with you because I could snatch you up. I kinda let that be known."

I wanted to chuck a shoe at him. I looked around, maybe I could throw something else, something that wouldn't do as much damage. I wanted to do damage, though. I wanted to do a whole lot of damage.

I said instead, "You're a piece of shit."

"I know." He held his hands up again in surrender. "Some of the stuff I said to you, I wasn't actually lying. I wasn't ready for a girl like you. And I didn't know how to handle it. I'm a selfish piece of work. I'm sleazy. I'm a manipulating manwhore. But I swear, you helped me want to change. You wouldn't talk to me at home over the holiday, and this is the first time I've worked up the courage to approach you. I know I messed up." He pressed a hand to his chest. "I lost my shot with you. That affected me. It's because of you that I'm even with Kiara. If I'd met her back in November or December, I never would've looked twice at her. She's a good girl. I can't be with good girls. I ruin them."

I wanted to growl. "I already warned you not to hurt her."

"I'm not going to. If anything happened to her..." His smile softened. "Caden could've lost you. I saw the look on his face when you fainted. That guy really loves you."

I frowned. "I was dehydrated. That was it. They gave me fluids for half a day and I was fine."

"I'm not talking physically. He almost lost *you*. Caden's lucky to have you."

"Oh." Well, that made me feel good. "Thank you."

"Sooo, are you going to keep hating me at family stuff? We have summer coming up soon. Things will be awkward if we're both home and you want to kill me."

"I never wanted to kill you. More like maim, rip out your guts, castrate you." I lifted a shoulder. "You couldn't hurt if you were buried. But if your guts had been pulled out and then put back in with some really bad stitching? Yeah. That would've been perfect."

"Yeah." He echoed, a hard glint in his eyes. "That's what I meant."

"Just so we're on the same page."

"And you have absolutely no feelings for me?"

I didn't think twice. I grabbed the shoe next to my suitcase and threw it at him.

He ducked, and it hit the wall behind him. "Okay, okay." He stood, his hands covering his face. "I'll get out of here." He paused at the door, turning back. "It's been three years, but I'm excited to actually have a sister now. For real. No bullshit."

I scowled. "Let's just try casual acquaintance first. I still don't fully trust you."

"And you shouldn't, but you will. I'll prove myself to you. I can be someone you can think of as family." He waved as he disappeared down the hall.

The jury was still out, but after this talk, my need to rip out his guts might've lessened. Just a small amount. I had to stop and appreciate this moment, because right here, it hit me how thankful I was. I came to college to be with my stepbrother, but I fell in love with the anti-stepbrother instead. Kevin was an ideal, a Band-Aid over a wound, but not Caden. He was the good, the bad, and the stuff in between. He'd make me feel all of it. He was everything.

He was *my* everything.

Avery appeared in my doorway a second later. She jerked a thumb over her shoulder. "Was that Kevin?"

"He wanted to apologize for being a slimeball."

"He's going to need more than one apology for that."

"Yeah." I tossed a pair of sandals on the bed. "How many pairs of shoes did you pack?"

She picked up the sandals and placed them in the suitcase, sitting on my bed. "Uh, I packed…twelve different outfits and four pairs of sandals. I'll probably end up buying clothes and shoes there. You can never have enough, especially when we're going to Key West. I can't wait for tomorrow. It'll be amazing."

Marcus, Avery, Colton, Caden, and I were going on spring break together. There were rumors that Diego might fly down to join us. Caden wasn't sure about that, he tended to be selfish. He liked to keep Diego for himself, but since I took Colt to Diego's bar one time, there'd been no turning back. Marcus and Avery came the next time, and I was pretty certain that Marcus developed a guy crush on the bar's owner. Diego wasn't having it, though. Diego had a new bromance going, and it was with Colton. He declared it the weekend before. I wasn't sure who was more miffed, Caden or Marcus. Then again, Colton looked a bit wary himself.

All in all, I was hoping Diego would come.

"I know it's kinda sad that their parents are getting a divorce, but yay for their dad relocating down south and having a house for us," she said. "That's a major perk."

"For us, since we're the girlfriends."

She shared a smile with me. "Oh yeah. And I know I've not said it yet, but thank you for passing out in February. Ever since then, Marcus has been the most attentive and loving boyfriend ever. Apparently you scared the shit out of him. He said he never wanted me to do that." She glanced down to her hands. "He said Caden could've lost you, and he never wanted to lose me."

I laughed. "I'm glad. You guys made it official the next week too." I stood back, gazing down at my suitcase. "I'm done. I think my bag is over the weight limit."

She picked up one of the bikinis. "Caden will tear this off of you in two seconds."

"Here's hoping."

And the next night, after we flew to Key West and spent the evening dancing and drinking, he did just that.

THE END

www.tijansbooks.com

For more information about brain injuries,
go to http://www.biausa.org/ or call 1-800-444-6443

For information on suicide, go to https://afsp.org/about-suicide/
or call the National Suicide Prevention Lifeline
if you are in crisis at 1-800-273-TALK (8255)

ACKNOWLEDGEMENTS

Always, always, always a huge HUGE thank you to the readers, and the ladies in the fan group. You guys make me smile daily! It helps so so so much, especially when I'm tired and need an extra burst of motivation. And on that note, I have to thank the admins, especially the ladies who post daily to keep the group running. I notice and I'm beyond thankful. Thank you to Debra Anastasia and Cami, both of you cheered me on so many times while I was writing this book. And The Rock Stars of Romance, for helping me with cover reveal, release blitz, excerpt reveal, and blog tour! You guys are amazing for all that you do.

Agh! There's so many others. My editor was amazing, especially being adaptable with me and my craziness. Lol! And to Kara and Chris, and Elaine!

I had so much fun writing this book. Summer was a different character for me, and there were so many times when I was like, "No one is going to like this book." But I kept writing because I hoped someone would enjoy her craziness as much as me! So for anyone who did, THANK YOU!

I've got some fun announcements coming in September, so stay tuned! Make sure to follow me on Facebook, or join the fan group to keep up on the latest with me.

www.facebook.com/tijansbooks

https://www.facebook.com/groups/TijansFanPage/

CPSIA information can be obtained at www.ICGtesting.com
Printed in the USA
BVOW06s1505021016

463935BV00023B/326/P